D0027614

KRINARD

Dark of the Moon

HQN™

ISBN-13: 978-0-373-77258-2
ISBN-10: 0-373-77258-0

DARK OF THE MOON

In loving memory of my dear friend, loyal companion and soul mate. I will never forget you.

Brownie 1993–2007

Acknowledgment:

Special thanks to Jakob Whitfield for his generous help with 1920s aircraft, and to Sun Ray Verstraete for providing Spanish words and phrases.

"Seeking to forget makes exile all the longer;
the secret of redemption lies in remembrance."
—Richard von Weizsaecker

Dark of
the Moon

PROLOGUE

HIS HANDS WERE stained with blood.

Dorian ran blindly through the woods, the inside of his head roaring with emptiness. Branches tore at his clothing and scraped at his skin. Bloody scratches streaked his flesh, closing before he could run another hundred paces. He felt no pain. He felt nothing except the disintegration of his mind.

Raoul was dead.

The gun had become part of Dorian's hand, metal seared into his palm like a brand.

Raoul was dead, and there was no undoing it.

He didn't know how far he traveled before he came to himself again. He stopped at the edge of a small human town, somnolent in the warm summer sun. People stared as he walked down the main street, a man bundled up in ragged clothing and mud-stained shoes. One good Samaritan, a middle-aged man with deep laugh lines around his eyes and work-roughened hands, called to Dorian as he passed by.

"Are you all right, mister?" he asked. "Need some help?"

Dorian turned to look at the human, hardly comprehending the offer. No one had ever asked such a question of him before. But when he met the man's gaze, the human flinched, backed away and quickly left Dorian to himself.

So it had always been. They were always afraid.

With that grim knowledge, Dorian's sense returned. He found a twenty-dollar bill in his wallet and walked to the town's tiny bus terminal. No one on the bus would meet his eyes. He sat quietly in his seat until the bus arrived in Manhattan. He got off and began to walk again, letting his feet carry him where they chose.

He could not go home. There was no home with Raoul dead and the clan in shambles.

How he came to the East River, he never did remember. The waterfront was raucous with human activity, heavy with the smells of oil and sweat and stagnant water. Dorian drifted alongside the river, looking down at the greasy black surface.

It was hard to kill a vampire. It was even harder for a vampire to kill himself. But Dorian had never lacked will.

He stood on the edge of the pier, the toes of his shoes hanging over the edge. One more step was all it would take.

"I wouldn't do that if I was you."

The old man came up behind Dorian, favoring a gimpy leg and squinting through a nest of wrinkles. He was lean as an old hound, dressed in a motley collection of rags.

And he wasn't afraid.

"It can't be as bad as all that," the man said, offering a smile that was missing several teeth. "Never is." He shoved his hands in his torn pockets. "Everyone's down on their luck now and then. That's why folks like us got to stick together."

Dorian stared at the man. The man stared back.

"Name's Walter. Walter Brenner." He thrust out his hand. Dorian hesitated. No human had ever done that before, either.

"I ain't got no diseases, if that's what you're scared of," Brenner said. "But I do have a little food, if you're hungry. And a place to sleep, at least for tonight. Then you can decide what's best to do. Things always look better in the morning."

Slowly Dorian took the gnarled and knotted hand. "Dorian," he said. "Dorian Black."

"Well, Dorian Black, you'd better come along with me. That's a good lad. Ol' Walter will take care of you."

Dorian went. There was nothing else to do.

He was free, but his life was over.

CHAPTER ONE

October 1926, New York City

THE BLACK SUCKING water closed over her head. She flailed blindly, her arms and legs as heavy and inert as logs. Red light flashed violently behind her eyes; she couldn't think, couldn't do anything but cling to the instinct that kept her from opening her mouth and swallowing the vile brew that swirled around her.

Is this what it's like to die?

The thought came and went in a moment of lucidity that vanished before she could grasp it. She sank, her muscles no longer obeying the weak commands of her brain. A fish, goggle-eyed, paused to examine her in astonishment and then disappeared into the sable depths. Her lungs began to burn.

Breathe. Breathe. Breathe...

A stream of bubbles spilled from her lips. All at once she remembered. She looked up at the distant, pale blur of reflected moonlight shining on the river's surface. It was a million miles away.

Swim. Swim, damn you.

But the air was gone, salvation beyond her reach. She stretched her arms, clutching at a substance that literally slipped through her fingers. An inky curtain fell over her eyes. She made one great effort, propelling her aching body a few feet closer to heaven.

Something gripped her hand, seizing her like the jaws of a killer shark. Her cry emptied her lungs. The last thing she saw was a face…a face that might have belonged to an angel or the most enchanting devil hell ever imagined.

"BREATHE!"

The voice was both harsh and beautiful, like music from another world. It came from very far away, a place out of space and time, and yet it pulled her from the seductive darkness with all the tenderness of a mob enforcer working over some poor schmuck in an alley.

Rough hands turned her over and pummeled her back. A rush of liquid surged into her throat and pushed out of her mouth. She coughed violently, jagged sparks zigzagging through her brain.

"Breathe!"

She gasped. Blessed air flooded her chest. The hands that had shaken and bullied her softened on her arms and lifted her against a warm, firm surface. She heard a heartbeat, slow and steady, felt ridges of muscle under a once-fine broadcloth shirt, smelled a slightly pungent but not unpleasant scent, as if the one who held her had been living in the same clothes for a week.

Still dazed, shivering from a chill dawn wind against her wet skin, she let herself be held. It was absurd to feel so safe in the arms of a total stranger, even one who had saved her life. Crazy to feel as if she could stay there forever.

She pushed at her rescuer, muscles still not entirely under her control. He released her and steadied her as she struggled into a sitting position on the weathered wood of the pier.

For the first time she got a good look at his face. It was the devil-angel she'd seen in the river, distorted then by brackish water and her own clouded vision. Now that she could see him more clearly, she still couldn't decide if he belonged in Heaven or that other place.

His features were those of a young man in his prime, handsome in the truest sense of the word. Bright moonlight picked out planes and angles joined in perfect symmetry. His skin was smooth, free of stubble, though everything else about his appearance suggested that he hadn't seen a razor in several days. His cheekbones were high, his chin firm and a little square, his hair dark and badly in need of a good cut, his brows straight above deeply shadowed eyes.

It was the eyes that captured her attention. Gwen couldn't make out their color, but that hardly mattered. They simply didn't belong in the face of a good Samaritan who had probably risked his life to save a stranger, a man in his midtwenties with at least forty good years ahead of him. They were as dangerous as a storm about to break, as grim as the bloodstained steel of a Thompson's machine gun. If they'd ever seen a smile, it was in some distant past she could scarcely imagine.

Most women—yes, even most men—would have cringed from that remorseless gaze. Not Gwen Murphy. She continued her scrutiny, taking in the frayed cuffs of his shirt, the jacket that had seen better days, the patched trousers and scuffed shoes. This was a fellow down on his luck; there were still people like him in New York, though business was booming and almost everyone seemed to be sharing in the general prosperity.

Everyone except the unlucky few: men crippled in the Great War, widows struggling to raise fatherless children, immigrants who hadn't yet found their way in a strange country, drunks who couldn't keep money in their pockets.

Her savior looked perfectly healthy and whole. He didn't appear to be drunk. He could be a foreigner who didn't speak enough English to find a decent job.

There was only one way to find out.

"You saved my life," she said, her voice emerging as a croak. "Thanks."

The man cocked his head, his gaze still locked on hers.

She cleared her throat and tugged her drenched glove from her shaking right hand. "I'm Gwen Murphy," she said, offering the hand.

He glanced down, studying her trembling fingers as if he suspected she had some nasty and highly contagious disease. She was about to withdraw her hand when he seized it in the same bulldog grip that had snatched her from a watery grave.

"Dorian," he said, filling the air with that strange music. "Dorian Black."

Gwen almost laughed. She recognized the edge of hysteria that lurked beneath her enforced calm and swallowed the laughter. Once she started, she might have a hard time stopping. And Mr. Black didn't look as though he would appreciate the reaction.

"Mr. Black," she said, returning his grip as firmly as she could. "I don't know how you happened to show up right when I needed you, but I'm grateful."

He dropped her hand and curled his fingers against his thigh. "It was no trouble," he said, each word clearly enunciated, as if English were a second language painstakingly acquired. "Do you require a doctor?"

She suppressed a shiver. "I'm all right. Just a little cold. And waterlogged."

Still no smile cracked his sculpted face, but his brows drew down in an expression that might have been concern. He shrugged out of his jacket and draped it over her shoulders. The coat wasn't entirely clean, but Gwen was grateful for both the warmth and the gesture.

"Thanks," she said.

He lifted one shoulder in a shrug that betrayed a whole world of discomfort. "How did it happen?" he asked.

The question took Gwen a little by surprise. Black was so taciturn that prying an interview out of him would be worse than pulling teeth. Maybe he wasn't really interested, but she had to give him points for trying.

"I'm a reporter for the *Sentinel*," she said. "I was on the docks investigating a lead when I was jumped by some hooligans who thought I'd be an easy mark." She suffered an annoying surge of embarrassment and probed at the growing bump on the back of her head. "I wasn't that easy. When I fought back, one of them hit me over the head and dumped me in the river."

Black's eyes narrowed. He looked up the pier to the board-walk, as if he might still find the young men who'd done the deed. Even if they'd hung around to make sure their victim had well and truly drowned, they would be lost to sight; the nearest street lamp was a hundred yards away, and there were plenty of places to hide. It was close enough to dawn that longshoremen and sailors on leave were starting to turn up at the docks. If it weren't for the relative isolation of this particular pier, the rough-necks never could have gotten away with their attack in the first place.

"Do you usually come to Hell's Kitchen in the middle of the night?" Black asked, turning back to her with subtle menace.

Gwen sat up straighter, squaring her shoulders beneath the oversized jacket. "Certain activities are less conspicuous in the dark," she said. "I didn't want to be seen."

"*Someone* saw you."

"But not one of the someones I was trying to avoid."

"And who would they be, Miss Murphy?"

Sudden nausea gripped Gwen's stomach. "That's confidential," she said. Her ankles wobbled as she struggled to stand. "I think I'd…better call a taxi."

Black jumped to his feet with an athlete's grace and caught her arm as she tottered and nearly fell. "You're in no condition to walk alone, Miss Murphy. I will escort you to the nearest telephone."

"Really, I'll be fine."

Without answering, he pulled her closer to the dry heat of his body and led her a few halting steps. The nausea increased, creeping up into her throat. It had to be a combination of things: the filthy water she'd ingested, the head injury, the shock of nearly dying. She should be able to overcome it. She was Eamon Murphy's daughter, for God's sake….

Black stopped. "You won't make it," he said bluntly.

"Yes, I will. I just need a little more time."

Her savior looked pointedly toward the east, where the sun was rising over Queens. "No time," he muttered, and then raised his voice. "You will come with me."

Gwen passed her hand over her face, fighting a nasty headache. "Come with you where?"

"To a place where you can rest."

Her skin prickled with warning. "I'm grateful. I really am, Mr. Black. I'd certainly—" Bile pushed into her throat. "I'd like to return the favor, but I have to get back. If you'll just…"

A flood of sickness overwhelmed her. She jerked away from Black, emptying her stomach. The humiliation was excruciating. She wasn't some damned cub reporter who couldn't deal with a little adversity.

A steadying hand touched her elbow. She pushed it away.

"I'm fine," she said.

"You're coming with me, Miss Murphy."

She shook her head, and suddenly she was seeing stars. Her lungs seemed filled with concrete. She couldn't catch her breath. It was the darkness all over again, dragging her down like the treacherous river currents.

The water closed over her head, and this time there was no reaching the surface.

VOICES WOKE HER. The first thing Gwen noticed was that she was lying on something reasonably soft. She listened for a moment before opening her eyes, recognizing the newly familiar intonation of the enigmatic stranger who called himself Dorian Black. The other voice was older and less steady, slurred with drink and amiably loquacious. The conversation was too soft to be intelligible, and when Gwen opened her eyes she saw only her dark-haired savior, crouching in the light of an old-fashioned gas lamp.

His eyes were gray. They'd seemed colorless in the night, yet she'd thought of steel. She'd guessed correctly. That granite stare gave no quarter and asked for none.

Gwen tried to sit up. Black pushed her back down, his hand spread on her chest with no apparent regard for her anatomy. The feel of his palm on her breasts, her flesh and his separated by only the thin georgette of her blouse, startled her into stillness.

Apparently he'd judged that she would be more comfortable without her jacket or his, but at least he hadn't relieved her of anything else but her shoes. Her skirt, hose and blouse were nearly dry, hinting at the length of time she'd been under Black's care.

She hated the very idea that she'd been so helpless.

"Where am I?" she demanded.

He held her gaze with unnerving steadiness. "In a safe place."

Some answer, Gwen thought, turning her head to examine the space around her. To the left was a solid, windowless wooden wall. To the right Black loomed over her, blocking her view. She couldn't have seen much beyond the reach of the lamp in any case, but she sensed an open area partitioned off by the stacked crates that created a sort of room just large enough to accommodate her makeshift bed, a stool with one wobbly leg, and a smaller crate spread with a few items, including a mug, a basin and sundry objects she couldn't quite make out. Hanging from nails hammered into the stacked crates were a pair of stained and threadbare shirts, a patched jacket, and a folded set of frayed trousers. It was evident that Black had made a home for himself in a place most people would consign to spiders and rats.

She'd seen men living under worse conditions, but not often.

"Are we still on the docks?" she asked.

He nodded, apparently considering a verbal reply unnecessary. Gwen pushed herself halfway up on her elbows.

"I guess I fainted," she said, swallowing her pride.

"You fell unconscious," Black said.

"You aren't responsible for me just because you saved my life."

He arched a brow at her sharp tone, and for a fleeting moment she thought she saw a sort of smile on his lips. "Having saved your life," he said, "I would not like to see my efforts go to waste."

"It must be daylight by now. Someone else would have found me."

He shifted his weight, letting his long, elegant hands fall between his spread knees. "You do not strike me as the sort of woman who would want to be discovered sprawled on the boardwalk in a pool of her own vomit."

His bluntness took her aback, but she couldn't fault him for it. She preferred straight talk herself…a characteristic that often flabbergasted her male associates at the *Sentinel*.

"Well," she said, "when you put it that way…" She licked her lips. "You wouldn't happen to have some water, would you?"

He turned away, lifted a cracked pitcher from the table crate and poured a measure of water into the mug. Gwen took it hesitantly, gave a surreptitious sniff and put her lips to the rim. The water was surprisingly fresh.

"Thanks," she said, handing the mug back to him. She opened her mouth to begin another argument about why he should let her go, but the words died in her throat. She found herself staring at him instead…staring like a girl suddenly confronted in the flesh with her favorite matinee idol. It was the most ridiculous thing in the world. And she couldn't help herself.

"Who are you?" she said. "I mean, what is this place, and what are you doing here?"

He regarded her for a moment, as if he were considering whether or not it was worth his while to answer. At last he settled back against the crates behind him, stretching his legs across the space between them.

"I've told you my name," he said. "I and a few others live in this abandoned warehouse. We trouble no one."

She wondered why he'd included that last statement. Did he suspect that she'd detected something dangerous in his eyes?

"Most people wouldn't live this way by choice," she said.

His eyes took on a bleakness that hinted of some past tragedy, which came as no surprise to Gwen. "I don't see what business that is of yours," he said.

Pride. Even men without homes had it, sometimes more than those who had everything. Gwen knew she should just shut up and leave well enough alone. After all, once she walked out of this place, she would probably never see Dorian Black again.

But she'd spent a lot of time on the streets talking to people who didn't know what it was like to make a fortune on Wall Street or drive the latest model sedan…who didn't even know where their next meal was coming from. Telling the stories of the forgotten men and women of New York had been her personal crusade. Until Dad had died, and left her with his own private obsession.

There was something about Dorian Black that just wouldn't let her leave it alone, something that told her he wasn't the average unemployed guy with a chip on his shoulder. She would almost have guessed he'd come from a criminal background.

But your typical petty criminal didn't usually let himself sink into dire poverty. He was either in jail or setting up another job, selecting another mark, planning a new scam. He was by no means the kind who would save someone from drowning. And guys involved with the mobs didn't generally find themselves on the street. They were either working for a gang or, if for some reason they lost their usefulness, they were disposed of. It was just too dangerous for any mob boss to let one of his former subordinates run loose.

So what in hell was he?

She girded her loins and shaped her voice to a careful neutrality. "You've fallen on hard times," she said.

He shrugged.

"You haven't been able to find a job," she persisted.

Something large rustled among the crates, and Gwen thought she glimpsed a long, naked tail. She shuddered. Black ignored the noise and leaned his head back against the crates.

"Why should you think I want employment?" he asked.

Deliberately testing him, she sat up. "You're young and healthy," she said. "Obviously intelligent. Educated."

"So?"

That voice could have stopped a train in its tracks. Gwen held his gaze. "Let's just say that I'd like to know a little more about the kind of man who'd rescue a total stranger."

"You doubt the natural gallantry of the stronger sex?"

She stifled a snort. "I'm not a romantic, Mr. Black."

"Neither am I."

"Nevertheless, I'd really like to hear how you came to be living here. Are you alone in the city?"

His face was expressionless. "Would you perhaps be planning to write a special-interest story for your paper, Miss Murphy? An essay on the plight of unemployed men who live on the docks?"

Weary cynicism laced his words. She almost felt guilty. "If I did write such a piece, Mr. Black, I wouldn't use your name. But that isn't my intention." She scooted around to lean with her back against the wall, drawing her knees up and pulling her coat over them to preserve her modesty. "Were you in the War, Mr. Black?"

"No."

If there was one thing Gwen was good at, it was telling when someone was lying. She saw the true answer in Black's eyes even before he opened his mouth to speak. They clouded over, losing their sharpness. As if he were remembering. As if he feared that another word might send him tumbling back in time to a world he had never quite left.

She swallowed, dodging memories of her own. Black had saved her life, but she didn't think he would want her hanging around dredging up memories of the past, and there was another subject she wanted to cover before he tossed her out on her ear.

"You must know just about everything that goes on around here," she said.

He frowned at her sudden change of subject. "Perhaps."

"Are you familiar with the recent murders?"

Abruptly he rose. His movements were jerky, lacking all their earlier grace. "Is that why you're here, Miss Murphy? To investigate the murders?"

Gwen was certain then that he not only knew about the bizarre deaths, but that he had some personal interest in them. Perhaps he'd seen something. Perhaps he'd witnessed the attacks, or had an idea who'd committed the crimes. Maybe—

Whoa, girl, Gwen thought. Even if her instincts were generally correct, this wasn't the time to let them run away with her.

"According to the coroner," she said cautiously, "the bodies must have been lying on the boardwalk for several hours before the police were called in."

Black turned his head from side to side as if he were seeking an escape route. "You should leave well enough alone, Miss Murphy," he said.

"I can't. You were right, Mr. Black. It's my job to investigate how such a terrible thing happened and who might have done it."

"They put a woman in charge of such a task?"

"You'd be surprised how good we are at finding angles men don't even consider."

"Such as visiting the docks alone and unarmed?"

"The prospective witness I was supposed to meet didn't show up." She studied his face intently. "You don't happen to know a man who goes by the name of Flat-Nose Jones, do you?"

"No."

Lying again, though he did it very well indeed. "I figure he either lost his nerve or met with an accident before he could tell his story, whatever it was."

"Perhaps he should have been more discreet."

"I can't blame anyone who keeps his mouth shut under these circumstances. The bodies were obviously left as some kind of message. By someone with a very bad grudge."

"You would seem to have your suspects already, Miss Murphy."

"I have a few ideas. Whoever killed those men was obviously deranged."

Black said nothing. He paced across the small space, fists clenched. "Are you certain the roughnecks who assaulted you were not attempting to silence your inquiry?"

"Those kids? They were amateurs. They might dump a troublesome mark in the river, but they wouldn't think to drain all the blood out of one of their victims. The corpses were completely…"

Her words trailed off as Black came to a sudden halt. His face flushed and then went pale. His pupils shrank to pinpoints, though the makeshift room remained as dark as ever. His fingers opened and closed, opened and closed, in a sharp, disturbing rhythm.

"Mr. Black?"

His breathing became labored. "No," he muttered between clenched teeth. "I wasn't…"

Gwen began to rise. "Dorian, are you all—"

He swung on her, teeth bared. Cruelty and rage replaced pain and bewilderment. The tendons stood out in his neck, his pulse throbbing visibly at the base of his throat. Muscle bulged beneath his shirt. His fingers arced like claws.

There was nothing human in his face. Nothing that regarded her as anything but an enemy.

Or prey.

CHAPTER TWO

GWEN PUSHED UPWARD against the wall, letting her coat puddle at her feet. Maybe it would have been better to remain still, but she intended to be prepared if he attacked. Even if she didn't stand a chance against him.

"Mr. Black," she said. "Dorian. It's me, Gwen."

His lips curled, and she saw that his incisors were ever so slightly pointed. Like a wolf, she thought. Or a stalking tiger just before it tore out the throat of a hapless deer in some Far Eastern jungle.

For an instant she considered the possibility that she'd been looking for the killers in all the wrong places. Maybe the murders weren't the work of a group of lunatics. Maybe one man—a man sufficiently strong and clever and crazy—was responsible for the bloodbath.

But then she remembered the gentle arms around her, the face so full of remembered pain, and she knew her suspicions were worse than insane.

Dorian Black had been crippled by a terrible experience. He was troubled and sick, but he was no murderer.

"You don't want to hurt me, Dorian," she said, touching the cross at her throat. "You're a good man. I want to help you."

A sound came out of his throat, fury and despair intermingled. He whirled about and slammed his hands against the crates, toppling them like a child's blocks. When he turned back, his face was slack, like that of a man sinking into sleep.

"Go," he said hoarsely. "Get out of here."

"I'm not leaving you like this."

Slowly he raised his head. He might as well have been blind. "Please."

That pride again. Pride and dread and horror. Here was a man who had suffered, who had lost control, who hated himself for his weakness. Gwen had seen it all before. Barry had sacrificed everything to the War. He'd come home so badly shell-shocked that marriage had been out of the question. Even his family couldn't take care of him. He'd been at the asylum for two years before he shot himself.

Men who seemed to have no visible wounds from the War were sometimes the most damaged of all. Barry used to scream at the slightest glimpse of blood.

You thought you were safe here, Mr. Black, Gwen thought. *Away from people, hovering on the edge of life. But you couldn't escape, could you?*

"It's all right," she said aloud. "I'm not afraid."

"You should be."

"You wouldn't do me any harm, Dorian. I'm sure of that."

He passed his hand across his face, pushing his dark hair into disorder. "Naive," he said. "Naive, foolish…"

"Not as naive as you think. You need a doctor, Dorian. Someone to talk to."

"No doctor can help me."

How could she hope to convince him, when all the best doctors in New York hadn't been able to cure Barry?

"All right," she said. "I can't force you." *But I sure as hell can wear you down, Dorian Black. Because I owe you. I pay my debts. And if you can help me find the murderers…*

She shook off the unworthy thought and flung her coat over her shoulders. "I'll go now," she said. "But if I can do anything for you, anything at all…" She suddenly remembered that her cards were gone, along with her pocketbook, doubtless stolen by the young hooligans. She didn't even have a nickel for a telephone call.

Well, at least she was alive and fully capable of walking now that the sickness had passed. She could ankle it to the nearest police station and call from there.

She looked at Dorian, struck by a powerful urge to stroke the wayward hair out of his face. He wouldn't welcome such familiarity. Maybe he was even regretting pulling her out of the river.

"Listen," she said. "I'd like to come back sometime. Maybe I can't completely repay what you've done for me—"

"I don't want your charity."

"Couldn't you at least accept a haircut? I'm a mean one with the shears."

His eyes were still clouded, dull with exhaustion and that strange paralysis she'd so often seen in Barry before his death. He didn't meet her gaze.

"Don't come back," he said.

Gwen puffed out her cheeks. *Sometimes it doesn't do any good to argue,* Dad had told her more than once. *Learn to let it go, Gwen. Learn to be patient. Sometimes patience is what a reporter needs most.*

And patience was a virtue she still hadn't quite mastered. But she was willing to give it the old college try. For Dorian's sake.

"Okay," she said. "How do I get out of this place?"

"I'll show you."

The voice belonged to the other man she'd heard speaking when she'd woken up. He came out of the shadows, an old gentleman with clothing every bit as worn as Dorian's. His face was seamed with deep wrinkles, his nose had been broken in several places, and his eyes were filled with that sort of peculiar sweet-tempered innocence that blessed a certain type of inebriate.

"Name's Walter," he said, tipping a moth-eaten fedora. "Walter Brenner. We don't have too many ladies visit us. Wouldn't want you to think we're lacking in manners."

"How do you do, Walter," Gwen said, offering her hand. "I'm Gwen Murphy."

"So I heard." His palm was dry and papery. "Had a bit of a dip in the river, did you?"

"A regular soaking." She walked with him out of the warehouse. "I'm lucky Mr. Black happened to be there."

He ducked his head conspiratorially. "Dorian ain't always like that, you know, so short-tempered and all. It's just this mood… comes on him regular, every few weeks, like. Best to leave him alone until it passes."

"I understand. Have you known Dorian long?"

"'Bout as long as he's been on the waterfront. Three months, I figure."

"Do you know anything about his past?"

"He's been through something awful, Miss Gwen. Don't know what it is. He won't talk."

"He's never mentioned the War?"

"Nope. Could be that's it, but I worry about him. He don't go out, except at night. Holes up here during the day like one of our rats. And he hardly eats. He brings stuff for me, but he don't touch nothin' but crumbs."

Gwen remembered the bleakness of Dorian's "room." There hadn't been a sign of food, not even the crumbs Walter spoke of.

"You're his friend," she said. "You want to help him, don't you?"

"Sure. He took care of me when I was sick. My heart, you know. Gives out sometimes. Don't know what I'd do without Dory."

Gwen decided to risk a more troubling question. "Did you see the bodies, Walter?"

The old man shuddered. "Heard about them. But *he* saw. Made it worse, next time he had one of his nasty spells." He touched Gwen's arm tentatively. "He ain't bad. You see that. I never seen him take such an interest in another human being until he brought you here."

Interest. Under normal circumstances, Gwen never would have interpreted Dorian's behavior as anything but grudging tolerance. But she had only begun to glimpse what might be in Dorian's soul. And she knew she had to keep digging until she discovered exactly what made him tick…and why he had aroused her curiosity in a way no one had done since Barry died.

"You'll come back, won't you?" Walter said, as he led Gwen out into the sunlight. "Do him good. I know it would."

Gwen met the old man's gaze. "Even if I didn't have other reasons for coming back to the waterfront, I wouldn't abandon him. He saved my life."

"But it's more than that, ain't it?" Walter peered up at her with greater perception than his drawl and easygoing manner suggested. "Dory ain't easy to like, but you like him anyway."

Did she? Gwen looked away, testing her feelings as carefully as she might probe a sore tooth. Mitch and the other reporters thought she was too impulsive and emotional, like all women. But when it came to men…

Like him? Maybe. And if she were completely honest with herself, as she always tried to be, she would admit that she found Dorian Black strangely attractive. His looks had something to do with it, but it went deeper than that.

"You're a crusader," Mitch frequently told her. "That'll be your downfall, Guinevere."

She knew damned well that she couldn't save the world. But she might save one tiny part of it.

"Don't worry, Walter. I promise I'll do what I can."

Apparently satisfied, Walter retreated into the shadows, doubtless to nurse a bottle for the rest of the afternoon. At least Dorian Black didn't seem to drink. Maybe he would have been better off if he did.

With a half shrug, Gwen set off to find the nearest police station.

DORIAN WATCHED HER walk away, careful to remain within the shelter of the warehouse door. She had a long, confident stride; the wool worsted suit, with its boxy jacket and pleated knee-length skirt, was plain and businesslike, but it didn't disguise the curves of her figure or the bounce of her walk.

Gwen Murphy. He'd never heard her name before last night; even when he'd worked for Raoul, he hadn't paid much attention to the newspapers. That hadn't been his department. He'd done his job, dispassionately and efficiently, until the world he knew came crashing down around him.

It was about to fall apart all over again, the way it did every month at the dark of the moon. He'd begun to feel the first effects a few days ago: irritability, confusion, thoughts spinning out of control. And his emotions…they could be trusted least of all. He only had to remember how he'd turned on Gwen like an animal, fully prepared to drain her dry.

He shuddered, thinking of the bodies on the wharf. At least he was reasonably certain that the murders weren't his doing. As far as he could remember, he hadn't killed anyone since Raoul's death.

No, that massacre was almost certainly the work of one of the warring factions that had formed after the clan had disintegrated. Though Dorian had deliberately removed himself from any involvement in *strigoi* affairs, he had no doubt that the level of violence committed by the city's vampires against their own kind had increased in the past three months. Internecine bloodshed was no longer simply a matter of one clan leader keeping his subordinates and human employees in line. It had become a case of two well-matched coalitions vying for control of Raoul's carefully built bootlegging operation and all the power that went with it.

Regardless of the reason for the killings, whoever was responsible for them had either been extraordinarily foolish or dangerously overzealous to have left the corpses drained of blood. Such unusual characteristics set the murders apart from the usual human mob hit—and attracted the attention of inquisitive humans like Miss Gwen Murphy.

Dorian turned away from the light. The fate of New York's *strigoi* was no longer any of his concern. His own life had become a weary succession of nights spent hunting just enough to keep his body functioning, days crouched in his fetid den with nothing but the company of an old man who had no idea who or what he was. Only the instinct for survival, a vampire's deepest and most powerful impulse, had kept him from letting his body fade into oblivion.

But now there was something else. Something he hadn't

expected. Something that had started when he'd seen the girl sinking beneath the river's surface and had made the decision to save a human life.

Gwen Murphy. She should have meant nothing more to him than what humans called a "good deed," an act that made not the slightest dent in the vast weight of guilt accumulated over three quarters of a century.

Dorian rubbed at his face, feeling the raw bones of his cheek and jaw. He still had no clear understanding of what had happened, what unfamiliar impulse had led him to bring her here and watch over her until she could take care of herself. It hadn't been a simple hunger; he hadn't even been thinking of feeding when he'd rescued her. Nor had it been the troubling attraction with which he found himself struggling now.

If Miss Murphy had collapsed into a hysterical heap on the boardwalk after he'd pulled her from the river, he might have dismissed her. Old habits were slow to die, and he had no more need for human companionship than he did for that of his own kind.

But Gwen hadn't collapsed. She'd gamely accepted what had been done to her, and if it hadn't been for her body's very human weakness, she would have gone on as if nothing had happened.

That had made all the difference. Her courage had awakened Dorian's emotions as nothing had done since he'd held a gun in his hand and put an end to an evil few mortals could comprehend. Her refusal to surrender to fear had reminded him of the only other woman who had been capable of touching his heart.

Dorian returned to his corner, carefully restacked the crates and sank down against the wall. Of course he'd realized his mistake as soon as she'd started to ask questions, to behave as if his heedless act had created some sort of bond between them. He had tried to get rid of her even before his vague admiration had begun to give way to a reaction far more insidious: a growing awareness of her piquant beauty, the scent of her skin, the allure of her femininity.

If the sensation had been only the natural hunger for her

blood, he could have assuaged it quickly and sent Miss Murphy away none the wiser, as he had a thousand other humans. But he'd wanted her with a dangerous insanity that became more deadly when he'd recognized how easily he could hurt her, how thin was the line between physical lust and violence.

He didn't want to hurt her. He didn't want the responsibility for what she might feel if she looked beyond her noble determination to help him and discovered that he desired her, even in the most human sense of the word.

Their relationship would never advance so far. There would be no relationship, no feelings, no joining in any sense of the word. If she came back…

"Penny for your thoughts."

Walter ambled into the room and crouched next to Dorian, a half-empty whiskey bottle dangling from his hand. "Don't tell me," he said. "I can guess. She's quite a peach, ain't she?"

Dorian sighed. There wasn't any point in reasoning with Walter. For all his easy nature, he was as irrational as any other human. In fact, he was worse than most. He saw everything through a prism of optimism and goodwill.

"She is an unusual woman," Dorian admitted, resigned to an awkward conversation. "I would like to think that she won't venture here again without a proper escort."

"Ha," Walter snorted. "You don't know women, Dory. Though I never could understand how a man like you could turn out so ignorant of the fair sex." He scratched his shoulder. "You'd better get used to the fact that she's taken a shine to you."

"I doubt that her interest will be of long duration."

"Saving someone's life tends to make a body grateful."

"I made it clear that I don't desire her gratitude."

"You just can't tell someone what to feel, Dory. Did you ever consider she might do you some good?"

"I would hardly wish to save her life only to ruin it."

"Your problem is that you don't have any faith in yourself. Just because you have a problem don't mean it ain't fixable. Maybe all you need's a little encouragement."

"I get plenty of that from you."

"It ain't enough. *She's* the type you'd listen to. She's brave and smart. I'm just an ignorant old man."

And as harmless as a scorpion, Dorian thought. "Perhaps I won't be here when she comes back."

Walter got to his feet. "Oh, you'll be here. You got nowhere else to go." He took a swig from the bottle, offered it to Dorian as he always did, and shrugged when Dorian refused. His walk was a little unsteady as he returned to his own dark corner.

A muffled silence fell in the warehouse. It was empty now except for Dorian and Walter; other men came and went, but most felt uneasy in Dorian's presence even when he was perfectly sane. They moved on after a few weeks, leaving him to his welcome solitude.

Solitude he could only pray Gwen Murphy would never break again.

THE CITY ROOM WAS busy when Gwen arrived, as it was at almost any time of day. Reporters at their desks shouted into telephone receivers or punched at typewriters, pencils tucked behind their ears. Eager copy boys rushed back and forth doing errands and carrying messages for their superiors. Mr. Spellman, red in the face, was gesticulating at an assistant editor behind the glass walls of his office.

It was all comfortingly familiar. No one had noticed her arrival. Mitch wasn't at his desk, but then again, he seldom was. He preferred legwork to the labor of composition. Gwen waved at one of the friendlier reporters and left the city room for the small office to which she and the less privileged employees were relegated.

Lavinia was filing her nails, watching the melée across the hall with a vaguely amused expression on her long face. She caught sight of Gwen and waggled her fingers. Gwen wound her way between the desks to Lavinia's quiet corner and fell into a chair.

"What is it, honey?" Lavinia said, subjecting Gwen to a pointed inspection. "You look like something the cat dragged in."

Gwen laughed. "That's exactly what I feel like."

And that was putting it mildly. She could still taste river water and feel it in her hair, in spite of a quick bath and change of clothes. In the taxi back to the office she'd gotten the shakes, finally realizing how close she'd come to death.

"That bad, huh?" Lavinia said. She offered Gwen a cigarette. "Take this, honey. It'll make you feel better."

"Thanks, Vinnie, but you know I don't smoke."

"Pity." Lavinia lit her own cigarette and took a drag. "Where have you been all day? I was beginning to worry."

"You know I went down to the waterfront—"

"In spite of Spellman's lecture about sticking to your own beat."

"The society pages are your bailiwick, not mine."

"You mean they aren't good enough for you. No, I'm not scolding. It's boring as hell, even for an old lady like me."

Gwen planted her elbow on the desk and leaned her chin in her palm. "No one does it better than you, Vinnie."

"Sure." The older woman stubbed out her cigarette. "So how did it all come out?"

"My contact didn't show."

"Sorry to hear that."

"I might have found another lead, though."

"Do tell."

Gwen's shoulders prickled. She hadn't really stopped thinking about Dorian Black since she'd left the warehouse. "We'll see how it pans out."

"You mean you don't want to talk about it."

"Don't take it personally, Vinnie. It's Hewitt I don't trust."

"You still think you can scoop him?"

"Even if it kills me."

"Or until Spellman kicks you out." Vinnie gave a lopsided smile. "Keep your secrets. I'll find them all out eventually."

"I know you will, Vinnie." She got up. "Listen, I've got some research to do. Let's plan on lunch sometime soon."

"You just let me know, honey."

"See you then." Gwen pushed the chair back in place and

walked across the office to her desk. It was every bit as cluttered as any of the men's, with only a small debris-free space around a framed photo of Eamon Murphy perched on the corner.

Tossing her pocketbook on a precarious stack of papers, Gwen sat on her hard chair and glanced at the headlines of the late edition that had been left on her desk. More on the Ross Kavanagh trial. Gwen shook her head. Dad had always said that Kavanagh was one of the few good cops in Manhattan. He'd been handed a raw deal for sure. There was no doubt in Gwen's mind that he'd been framed for the murder of Councillor Hinckley's mistress, almost certainly because he hadn't agreed to play along with the corrupt administration.

Well, there was nothing she could do about that but pray for Kavanagh's acquittal. She shoved the paper aside, settled deeper into her chair and opened the desk drawer. Inside were Eamon's clippings, articles and notes carefully preserved by her father during his long years at the paper. She glanced around, pulled out a folder and opened it, holding it half-hidden in her lap.

Brown-edged newsprint crackled between Gwen's fingers. The story had been buried in the back pages of the morning edition on June 5, 1924. A man had stumbled into a hospital, badly injured and mumbling about crazy people who drank blood. He'd died not long after. No one had bothered following up on the man's bizarre claims.

The rest of the articles and clippings were in a similar vein. Stories about strange murders attributed to certain notorious gangs. Interviews with witnesses who'd seen or heard things no one in their right mind would believe. Paragraphs gleaned from every newspaper in New York, most of them meaningless to anyone who didn't know their collector's particular interest.

By the end, everyone at the *Sentinel* had known something was wrong with Eamon Murphy. He'd lost his edge. He was distracted, late with his assignments, always shuffling papers he wouldn't let anyone else see. Spellman had called him in for a long talk, but nothing changed. Eamon Murphy was a man obsessed.

"If something happens to me," he'd told Gwen, "don't let an

old man's fixations end your career before it's begun. Find your own stories, Gwennie. You're as good a newsman as I'll ever be. It's what you've always wanted."

He'd been right. She'd dreamed of becoming a reporter ever since her fourteenth birthday, when her father had brought her to the *Sentinel* offices. There hadn't been a single woman reporter there at the time, but that didn't worry Gwen. She'd gone to college, absorbing every available course in writing and journalism. She'd spent hours composing mock stories on her second-hand Remington, and applied for dozens of jobs.

No one had hired her. But Dad wasn't about to let his daughter's dream die. Two weeks after Eamon's death, Spellman had offered Gwen a position as a cub reporter. Sure, her assignments had been the ones every man in the office considered unworthy of his attention, but she'd clung to the memory of her father's encouragement, his unwavering belief in her abilities. She'd continued to study and observe. And when the three bodies had been found on the waterfront, every one of them drained of blood, she'd gone back to his files and read them all over again.

I'm sorry, Dad, but I can't let this go. If it was important to you, it's important to me. And I'm going to find the answers.

"I see you're back from the beauty shop, Miss Murphy."

Randolph Hewitt's booming voice swept over Gwen like a foghorn.

She turned slowly in her chair and smiled sweetly. "Why, Mr. Hewitt. I see you're back from the Dark Ages."

Her chief rival's mocking grin lost a little of its joviality. "Very funny, Murphy." He shifted his bulk forward, hovering over her desk. "What have we here? More of your father's crazy theories?"

Gwen shoved the clippings back in the drawer and slammed it shut. "You can rag me all you want, Hewitt, but leave my dad out of it."

Hewitt held up both hands. "Pull in your claws, missy. I had the utmost respect for your father."

"Sure you did—until you saw a way to stick a knife in his back."

"Such intemperate accusations. I believe you've picked up

some very bad habits, Miss Murphy." He shook his head. "It would seem to be an unfortunate consequence of a woman attempting to compete in a man's world."

Gwen stood up, knocking a stack of papers onto the floor. "I don't consider you competition, Hewitt."

The reporter's belly jiggled with his laughter. "I wouldn't want to shatter your illusions." His round face hardened. "Just remember what Spellman said. Keep your pretty hands off my story."

He sauntered away, clearly satisfied with his part in the exchange. Gwen fumed silently. It didn't do any good to lose her temper; Hewitt only viewed such lack of control as further evidence of a woman's natural weaknesses. If she was going to prove him wrong, she would have to stay cool and use her head.

She picked up her father's photo. *I could really use your advice, Dad.*

His face, darkened by the sun, smiled back at her. *There'll be times you'll want to quit,* he'd said. *It isn't an easy job, even for a man. But you'll do just fine. And someday you'll find a fellow who recognizes all the fine qualities you inherited from your mother. Just don't settle for less, Gwennie.*

Dad had guardedly approved of Mitch, who'd come to work at the *Sentinel* a year before Eamon's death. He hadn't objected when Mitch started pursuing his daughter.

Gwen set down the photograph. It had almost slipped her mind that Mitch was taking her to dinner tomorrow night. She felt more resignation than anticipation at the prospect. She didn't feel any differently than she had months or weeks ago. Mitch was a good friend, but she wasn't ready to marry a man she wasn't sure she loved.

With a sigh, she began work on the inconsequential stories Spellman had assigned to her. She would do her best with them, as she always did. They wouldn't have any excuse to discharge her. And when she could prove her father's story, they would know she was truly worthy to compete in a man's world.

Tomorrow she would go see Dorian Black again. The thought absurdly cheered her. Even if he couldn't help her with the murders, her reporter's instincts told her that his story might be well worth the telling.

And as for those "nasty spells" that apparently afflicted him every few weeks, she would just remember to watch her step.

THE BELT SLAPPED against Sammael's back for the twentieth time. His flesh quivered in protests, but Sammael welcomed the pain. He raised the scourge again and brought it down with all his strength.

Forgive me, he prayed. *Forgive me for my foolishness, my overweening pride. You have set me a test, and I have faltered. Let me earn Your favor once again.*

He counted out another nine beats and let the belt fall, working the knots from his hands. His back was on fire…the holy fire, the promise of redemption that would come only with pain and blood. He got slowly to his feet and moved to the basin in his tiny cell, splashing water on his face. His back he would leave untouched. There would be neither scabs nor scars in the morning.

Tomorrow he would begin all over again.

He shrugged on his shirt, leaving the collar undone, and sat at his desk. The book lay open before him, ready for amending. But as he lifted his pen, someone rapped on the door.

"Come," he said.

The guard who entered was young and strong, as were all the new recruits…unquestioningly loyal to Sammael and the synod. He inclined his head to his master and stood at attention.

"We have a new report on the girl," the younger man said. "She has been seen at the waterfront with one of Raoul's former enforcers."

"Indeed?" Sammael leaned back in his chair. "And which one would that be?"

"Dorian Black, my liege."

"Ah, yes. I know of him. How did he and Miss Murphy come to be acquainted?"

"Our informers told us that he saved her from drowning."

"How did this event occur?"

"She was assaulted. A number of young men were seen fleeing the pier."

Sammael shook his head. "The Lord has said that humans must inherit the earth, no matter how unworthy they may seem to us." He picked up his pen and rolled it between his fingers. "My impression of the enforcer was that he would not become involved with any human."

"He took her to his kennel. She left unharmed."

"He did not Convert her?"

"There was not enough time, and it was still daylight when she left."

"Ah." Sammael waved his hand. "As long as Black remains isolated, he is of no interest to us. But should he see the girl…"

"Understood, my liege."

"What of Miss Murphy's investigation?"

"It appears not to be progressing," the guard said. "We believe she was to meet someone at the waterfront, but the individual failed to appear."

Sammael set down his pen. "She may indeed remain as ineffectual as her father, but perhaps it is time we revisit her apartment. It is always possible that something was missed the first time. And take every precaution. Give her no reason for suspicion."

"As you say, my liege." The guard bowed again and withdrew, closing the door quietly behind him.

Sammael leaned over the book, his head beginning to throb. Miss Murphy was only a minor concern at present, but she and Hewitt would be entirely harmless if not for Sammael's own error in leaving the bodies in a state that would raise so many questions. And it was not his first mistake; he had failed to keep the original book safe, and now it was out of his hands. Aadon was dead, but the book remained lost. Until it was recovered, there was grave danger that Pax's humans and civilians would be led astray.

They must not doubt. They must never doubt.

Fragile paper sighed as Sammael smoothed the pages before him. Over half of Micah's text was already crossed out, replaced

by the words Sammael's visions had given him. A few more
weeks and his work would be complete.

"'And those who have taken the blood of man shall die,'" he
wrote carefully above Micah's blackened lines. "'So it is written.
So it shall be done.'"

CHAPTER THREE

DORIAN FELT HER EVEN before he moved to the door of the warehouse.

Gwen Murphy strode across the boardwalk, late afternoon sunlight striking sparks off her curly red hair. Over one arm she carried a basket overflowing with white linen. Her fair face was set with determination, as if she was preparing herself for a cool reception.

If Dorian had possessed any sense at all, he would have found a way to disappear. But dusk was several hours away, and he was not in the habit of retreating in the face of the enemy.

For she *was* the enemy, and he dared not let himself forget it.

He stepped back into the darkness to wait.

"Mr. Black?" Gwen's heels tapped on the warehouse floor as she made her way toward Dorian's corner. "Are you there?"

"Miss Murphy," he said.

She jumped a little, startled by his sudden appearance. "Mr. Black. Dorian." Her gaze met his, curious and briefly wary. Dorian observed that her lashes were a shade darker than her hair, perfectly framing her green eyes.

The treachery of his thoughts nearly undid him. He looked away from her, counting off all the arguments he had mustered yesterday morning.

They were nearly useless. Today he found himself entranced all over again, struggling against an overwhelming desire to touch her. To stroke her fiery hair. To feel the warmth of her full, expressive lips…

"I've brought a picnic," Gwen said, shattering the spell. "It's a little late for lunch, but—"

"You shouldn't have come."

"Why am I not surprised to hear you say that?" She smiled, the uneasy curve of her mouth betraying what he already realized was uncharacteristic self-consciousness. "Still, I'm here. And I'm not leaving until you eat some of this food."

"I'm not hungry."

"That I don't believe. Walter says you hardly eat enough to keep a bird alive."

"Yet here I am."

She set down the basket and folded her arms across her chest. "Oh, how I adore a man of few words." She held his stare. "You tried to scare me off yesterday, and it didn't work. Nothing's changed."

He hardened his expression, beginning to feel the tightening in his body that warned of the madness to come. "You aren't welcome here, Miss Murphy."

"That's never stopped me." She hesitated, perhaps remembering how he had turned on her the day before, and then squared her shoulders. "You don't want charity. I understand that. But it's not just disinterested kindness on my part. I still have a hunch that you know more about those murders than you let on."

"You're mistaken."

"Maybe. Let's discuss it over a nice bottle of wine." She bent over the basket and withdrew a bottle the color of blood, displaying it for his inspection. "I'm sure we can find a patch of ground outside to lay out our feast."

Dorian withdrew a step, his gaze moving to the open warehouse door. "I prefer to remain here."

She released an explosive breath. "No wonder you're so pale, hiding here in the dark. Sunlight will do you good." She reached for his arm. "Come on."

Her fingers grazed his sleeve. He raised his hand to strike out. The brave expression in her eyes stopped him cold.

It would be so easy to hurt her. So easy to sink his teeth into the soft flesh of her neck, taste the sweetness of her blood.

He staggered, his feet slipping out from underneath him. Gwen seized his arm and held on.

"That's it," she snapped. "If you won't come outside, we'll eat right here." With surprising strength, she turned him about and half dragged him behind the crates that formed the walls of his room. Once he was safely seated on the floor, she went back for the basket. She set it down in front of him and sat beside him.

The smell of fresh bread, pungent cheese and savory meat rose from the basket as Gwen spread the white linen cloth on the floor and laid out the meal. Dorian's stomach churned, rebelling against its enforced deprivation. No vampire could survive long without blood, no matter what other forms of nourishment he might take. But since the blood enabled *strigoi* to digest human food, most ate on a regular basis.

"Walter," he said hoarsely. "He needs this more than I do."

"There's plenty for both of you." She sliced off a generous chunk of the bread, constructed a sandwich out of roast beef and thinly sliced cheese, and thrust it at Dorian. "Eat."

Their fingers touched as he accepted the sandwich. He almost dropped it. Gwen pressed it into his hand. Once again their eyes met, and Dorian saw the sympathy and compassion she tried to conceal.

"It's all right," she said.

There was no more fighting the demands of his body. He took a bite, closing his eyes as the bread melted on his tongue. In seconds the sandwich was gone and Gwen was making another. While he ate, she used a corkscrew to open the wine and filled the two glasses that had been tucked in the bottom of the basket.

"It's not the best," she said, "but I hope you won't find it too disappointing."

Dorian took a glass, careful this time not to touch her, and stared into the dark red liquid. "What makes you think I would know the difference between good wine and poor?"

"You speak like an educated man."

"That hardly proves anything."

She looked at him over the rim of her glass. "Where did you attend school?"

The wine turned sour in his mouth. He swallowed it with difficulty.

"My past isn't worthy of your interest, Miss Murphy."

"Let me be the judge of that." She wrapped up the remaining cheese and meat, tucking it back in the basket. "You attended college. You worked in a position that required both skill and intelligence."

A sense of fatalism washed over Dorian. Gwen Murphy wouldn't give up. He couldn't force her to leave without resorting to violence, and he was already too close to losing all control.

"I didn't attend college," he said, setting down his glass. "I was born in Hell's Kitchen. I went to public school until I was ten. Then I went to work in a factory. There wasn't any time or money for higher education."

Gwen gazed at him, a sandwich halfway to her mouth. "Well," she said at last, "that's definitely one of the longest speeches you've made since we met."

"I trust it assuages your curiosity."

"Not really. It doesn't explain why a kid from Hell's Kitchen uses words like 'assuage' in casual conversation."

Dorian found himself studying the delicate arch of her brows and the curve of her forehead. "It is possible to learn without formal instruction. There are such things as public libraries, Miss Murphy."

"Is that how you did it? You're self-taught?"

He shrugged, carefully looking away from her face. She finished her sandwich, brushed off her skirt and rose. "Are those books I see there?" Without waiting for his answer, she stepped over him and bent to pick up one of the volumes he'd arranged on a plank against the wall.

"Frankenstein," she said, cradling the battered volume. "You enjoy the classics, Mr. Black?"

"Occasionally."

"It's a sad story. Both the creator and the created are ultimately destroyed."

"Is that so surprising, Miss Murphy, when the creator chose to set himself up as a god?"

She smiled at him. "So you're a philosopher as well as an autodidact."

"You seem to share my predilection for long words, Miss Murphy."

"Writing for a newspaper doesn't allow me to use them very often. I used to read the dictionary when I was a kid."

Dorian felt a jolt of surprise, remembering the discarded dictionary, its pages moldy and torn, that he'd found left in a rubbish heap outside his family's tenement. He'd made himself learn at least two new words every day, practicing their pronunciation with care. His father had laughed at him.

Won't do you no good, boy. You'll never amount to anything. Not as long as you live…

Dorian's father had had no idea just how long that would be.

"What else do we have here?" Gwen said, sliding the book back in place and picking up another. "Dante's *Inferno*. You don't go in for light reading, do you?"

"I'm devastated that you disapprove."

"No. It's not that." She tapped the book's spine against her chin. "Do you believe in eternal punishment, Mr. Black?"

"Do you, Miss Murphy?"

She touched the cross hanging from a silver chain around her neck. "I believe in the possibility of redemption."

The tightness Dorian had felt earlier returned, squeezing his heart beneath his ribs. "Some souls cannot be redeemed."

"Are you speaking of yourself?" Her eyes were penetrating, ruthless in their understanding. "What happened, Dorian? Why do you think you deserve to suffer?"

He got to his feet, his mouth almost too dry for speech. "You assume too much."

"I can see that you're punishing yourself by living in this

place, refusing human company, hardly eating. Is caring for Walter the only thing that keeps you alive?"

Dorian closed his eyes. He could feel it coming. Total darkness, a time when most *strigoi* walked freely and celebrated their power.

For him, it was a kind of death. A temporary death that never quite took him but let him survive to despise himself yet another day.

Oh, yes. He believed in hell.

"It can't be as bad as you think," she said.

Suddenly she was beside him, her warmth caressing his cold skin, her breath soft in his ears. "You found your way out of Hell's Kitchen. You made something of yourself, didn't you? But you took a wrong turn somewhere. And now you don't think you can get back again."

It took all his self-discipline to keep from responding to the thrum of the blood in her veins, the fragrance of her body that told him she was ripe for the taking.

"Did it never occur to you," he said softly, "that I am not quite sane?"

"You mean because of what happened yesterday?"

He leaned away from her. "Yes."

"If you'd really wanted to hurt me, you've had plenty of chances to do it." Her implacable voice battered him like a hail of bullets. "Whatever you may have done, whatever you experienced, you want to make it right. But first you have to go back out into the world and face both it and yourself."

The muscles in Dorian's body slackened. Somehow he kept his feet. "Where did you acquire such faith in your fellow man?" he whispered.

"From my dad. He saw a lot of horrible things in his days as a newsman, but he never lost his belief in the essential goodness of humanity."

Humanity. *But I am not human. I can never be again.*

With exaggerated gentleness, he took the book from Gwen's hands. "Do you make a habit of attempting to save every vagrant you meet?"

"I'm not *that* good." She picked up the basket. "Shall we take this to Walter?"

Dorian was greatly relieved by the change of subject. "He wasn't feeling well earlier this afternoon. If you would leave the basket with me…"

"Of course. Is there anything I can do?"

"No. An old man is prone to ailments. He will recover."

The warmth in her eyes increased. "Do *you* make a habit of attempting to save every vagrant you meet? Most people wouldn't bother with a homeless old man."

"Why do you bother with me?"

His question caught her at a rare loss for words. She tugged at the hem of her jacket. "Is it too shocking to say that I like you?"

"You have no reason to like me."

"Do I have to have one?"

"I fear for your judgment, Miss Murphy."

"Let me worry about that." She pushed russet curls away from her forehead. "I'd like to stay, but I have an appointment this evening. I'll be back tomorrow afternoon with some clothes and a few other things you might be able to use."

All the cold-bloodedness that had served Dorian so well in his work for Raoul, all the dispassion he had deliberately fostered within himself, none of it was of any use now. He might as well have returned to his childhood, weeping in a corner because his mother was dead and his father couldn't be bothered to comfort his own children.

He had never felt so unutterably weary.

"I ask you once more to stay away," he said.

"I never give up on something once I've started," she said, "and I still haven't cut your hair. Unless you're afraid you'll lose all your strength, like Samson in the old story?"

He almost smiled. "I'm in no danger of such a fate, Miss Murphy."

"It's about time you called me Gwen, don't you think?" She held out her hand. When he didn't take it, she grabbed his and squeezed it firmly. "Gwen."

The feel of her skin had an instant effect on his body. He grew hard, and it seemed as if all the blood in his veins rushed to his cock.

She released him, taking a step back as she did so. A slight shiver ran through her.

"Good," she said, a little too sharply. "It's a date, then." She turned away, half tripping in her haste. "I'll see you tomorrow."

Dorian let her go. When she had left the warehouse and he could no longer hear the clack of her heels outside, he sat down heavily and dropped his head between his shoulders.

Yesterday his mind had been full of the resolve to ignore his attraction to Gwen Murphy. Of course he'd made the mistake of allowing himself to hope she wouldn't return and force him to take decisive action. But she *had* come, and he had failed miserably at keeping her at a safe distance. He admired—yes, *liked* her—more than ever before.

Far worse, he'd only sunk more deeply into the maelstrom of his own hunger. And the irony of it was that he had never developed a resistance to such weakness, because he had never before suffered the particular illness that caused it.

One of the first things any newly Converted *strigoi* learned was that most vampires were unrepentant sensualists, reborn to the lust for pleasure no matter what they had been in human life. Raoul had certainly been a prime example of the principle, with his love of luxury, his grandiose manner and his extensive harem of protégés, both male and female.

Dorian had been different. When he'd first been Converted, he'd had no choice but to focus on duty, since he'd virtually become Raoul's property. Yet even when he had proved his value and loyalty many times over, earning privileges generally granted only to trusted lieutenants and vassals, he had preferred work to pleasure. His needs were few, his desires nearly nonexistent. That hadn't been altered even when he'd recognized his genuine admiration for Allegra Chase and accepted the consequences.

To say he was no longer the man he had been was a gross

understatement. His new need for physical closeness, for the intimate touch of flesh on flesh, for a woman's body, seemed the least significant change of all. But it was enough. Enough to ruin the very person who had changed that part of him irrevocably.

Perhaps Gwen might have escaped the perils of his interest if she were the type of modern young woman who saw no shame in lying with a man simply because she desired it. The fact that she'd retreated so hastily after she'd taken his hand told him that she'd finally seen him as a man, not merely an object of charity or a lunatic deserving of her pity. And he had no doubt that she was fully capable of surrendering to the instincts that brought male and female together, regardless of species.

If Gwen could simply acknowledge such instincts and give them full control, she might disarm his need with a single act of sex. But Gwen, for all her brash confidence, would never agree to a casual liaison with him or any other male. There was a hidden core of conventionality in her that he could sense as strongly as he sensed the rhythm of her pulse and the beat of her heart. She might be unstinting in her willingness to help those less fortunate, but there was a part of herself that she would always hold back. Especially in matters of romantic intimacy.

Romance and love were concepts as alien to Dorian as the fear of death. And though Gwen might see him as a man, "liking" was a very long way from the ominous human emotion that could bring about her downfall. Even if she allowed herself to feel more for him than she did, more than what mortals called "friendship," she would never be able to understand what he had been, how he had lived, what he'd done. She would never know what had shaped his life, what drove him so near madness, why he couldn't be trusted.

Even *her* courage wasn't enough to face the truth.

Dorian covered his face with his hands. Tomorrow came the madness, and he couldn't be sure that he would recover. Today he was rational enough to separate his lust for Gwen's body from his desire for her blood. But instinct, among *strigoi* as among men, could be more powerful than reason. Physical wanting, unchecked by clan law or the command of a liege, could become the drive to procreate. And there was only one way that vampires could produce more of their own.

Disgusted by his weakness, Dorian coldly considered his options. If he survived tomorrow night's ordeal, he would plan an escape. He knew of a few places in Hell's Kitchen where he and Walter might find temporary shelter until he could think of something better. Places where Gwen wouldn't find him.

Soon enough, she would forget him. And he would remember her as just another human who had passed in and out of his life, as insubstantial as a ghost.

Dorian picked up the basket and went to find Walter.

LORD BYRON'S, it was said, had the best steaks in Manhattan. It had always been a fashionable watering hole for the elite, overpriced and overdecorated, with crystal chandeliers and ornate mirrored walls that echoed an earlier age. Women in Chanel gowns and ropes of pearls, ferried in black limousines, arrived on the arms of men in top hats and tuxedos. A small orchestra played discreet melodies as Wall Street brokers discussed their latest stock purchases and young couples danced cheek to cheek.

To an outside observer, Lord Byron's looked positively staid. But like any club or restaurant worth its salt, it had a private room in the back that catered to those who wanted a little alcohol and excitement with their meals. And like any good reporter, Mitch knew the right password to get in.

He spoke briefly with the maître d' and led Gwen to a table near the band. They were playing a recently popular tune, a little ditty about someone who done somebody wrong, and several couples were on the dance floor kicking up their heels.

Gwen and Mitch had barely sat down when a waiter brought a cooler holding a bottle of wine. He displayed the label to Mitch, who nodded his approval.

"I didn't know you could afford Chateau D'Or," Gwen said, shaking out her napkin with a snap.

Mitch gave her an exasperated look. "Trust you to say something so damnably prosaic at a time like this," he said.

"A time like what?" She sipped at her ice water, casting Mitch a glance of childlike innocence. "Aren't we here to celebrate your latest triumph?"

The blare of trumpets briefly drowned out Mitch's reply, but his handsome face was eloquent.

"...should know me better than that," he said. "*I* haven't forgotten."

Gwen resisted the urge to put off the forthcoming conversation with more banter, but she could see that Mitch wouldn't play along. He'd decided on formality tonight, which was a very bad sign.

"Okay," she said with a faint sigh. "I'm sorry, Mitch. I'll try to be good."

He relaxed a little, allowing the waiter to decant the wine. He held the glass under his nose, breathed in, and then tasted the Merlot with appreciation. After a moment he gave the waiter an approving nod, and the man filled Gwen's glass.

The first thing Gwen thought as she drank was that the wine really didn't taste any better than the cheap stuff she'd shared with Dorian a few hours earlier. She'd enjoyed that impromptu picnic more than she had her last few meals in Manhattan's finest restaurants, enjoyed sparring with a man who was as unpredictable and volatile as a summer storm....

Don't think of him. For God's sake, keep your mind on your—

"Gwen?"

She came back to herself and smiled. "Sorry, Mitch. Woolgathering."

"Still scheming about Hewitt's story?"

"*Hewitt's* story," she said with a snort. "It was my dad's long before it was his."

"Your father, good as he was, had some crazy ideas. Spellman never would have let him pursue them even if he'd—" He broke off and coughed behind his hand.

"Even if he'd lived," Gwen completed. "I know. But the murders mesh too well with his theories, Mitch."

"A secret cult of blood-drinkers?" Mitch said, careful to keep the overt mockery out of his voice. "You know that's hardly likely, Gwen, no matter how much Eamon believed."

"You make it sound ridiculous," she said, bristling, "but I'm not letting it go until I can prove he was wrong—or right."

Mitch rubbed at the faint lines between his brows. "I just wish you'd consider the consequences," he said. "Hewitt could make real trouble for you, Gwen. He's never believed women belong on a newspaper."

"It's not as if it's unknown. There are plenty of feature writers—"

"I thought you wanted to work in the city room, covering the big stories?"

"I won't get there if I don't take a few chances."

Mitch's mouth set in a mulish look that was all too familiar. "There are some things a woman just shouldn't do."

Gwen controlled her urge to shoot up out of her chair and answered with deliberate calm. "Is that really what you think, Mitch?"

"You know I'd support anything you chose to do."

"Within limits."

"Yes." He met her gaze. "I want to take care of you, Gwen. Even if it means protecting you from yourself."

"But that's exactly the trouble. I don't want—"

The waiter reappeared, his face molded into a professionally bland smile. "Are *monsieur* and *madame* ready to order?" he inquired with a bow.

"Two filets mignon, rare," Mitch said, before Gwen had a chance to express a preference. She pressed her lips together and stared down at the table. The band struck up a slow, sensuous jazz melody, and Mitch rose from his chair.

"Shall we dance?" he asked, offering his hand.

The last thing Gwen wanted was a scene. She took his hand and stepped with him onto the dance floor. He pulled her close.

"I've been waiting for this all night," he said, his breath tickling her ear. "We've hardly seen each other the past few weeks."

"That isn't exactly my fault," she said.

His voice took on a real note of apology. "I didn't mean to neglect you. This story is taking all my time and attention. But you haven't exactly been around when I'm free, Gwen."

"Am I supposed to wait until you find it convenient to bestow your attention?"

He pulled back a little, frowning. "You sound peevish, Gwen. It isn't attractive in you."

"I wonder why you put up with me at all."

Suddenly he stopped. He cupped her face in his hands and looked into her eyes.

"I put up with you because you're the brightest and most interesting woman I know, not to mention gorgeous."

Gwen said nothing. Mitch really believed that he would support her in any career she chose—as long as he got to decide how much time and effort she spent at it. As long as *he* got to make the rules.

Mitch began dancing again, his lips against her hair. "Ah, Guinevere," he said. "When are we going to end this game?"

This was it. The conversation she'd been dreading. The one they'd had a dozen times before. Only this time she wasn't sure she could worm her way out.

"You know what I want," he whispered. "We were meant to be together, Gwen. You know it as well as I do."

"Mitch…"

"You're fighting it just because you think you want independence. You don't. No woman really does."

It was all Gwen could do not to jerk out of his arms. "It must have been a dangerous journey," she said with forced lightness.

"I beg your pardon?"

"Your voyage into the darkest recesses of a woman's mind."

He laughed and ran his hands along the russet silk draped over her hip. "It's not as difficult as all that, Gwen. Some men think women are mysterious. I know better. In many ways, they're far simpler than men."

"Thanks," Gwen murmured.

"That's not meant as an insult." He nuzzled her cheek. "Let's put this indecision behind us and set a date."

Tension made a fist in Gwen's chest. "I'd like a little more wine first, if you don't mind."

"By all means, if it'll make you more cooperative." He ushered her back to the table and held the chair out for her. Gwen tried not to gulp her drink and sought desperately for a way to distract Mitch.

You won't be able to do it forever, she told herself. *You're so proud of your honesty. You'll have to be honest with him.*

And what exactly did that mean? She was very fond of Mitch. Most of the time he was reasonable. He was usually an ally at the *Sentinel.* She found him attractive, often witty, generally decent…though he could show a surprisingly ruthless side when he was pursuing a story.

For all that, she was never quite sure she really knew him. Most women would have given their eyeteeth just to have him look at them, but Gwen couldn't escape the feeling that rushing into marriage with Mitch Hogan would be the worst mistake of her life.

If I loved him, I wouldn't have so much doubt. But she'd never quite been able to bring herself to say the words, even in her own heart.

Maybe I can't love anyone. Maybe it's just not in me.

Unwillingly, she found her thoughts flashing back to the warehouse and to a cool, unreadable face that had none of Mitch's charm. Dorian and Mitch couldn't be more different. Mitch was serious now, but he was capable of playfulness when he was in the right mood. Dorian was about as lighthearted as an undertaker.

But something strange had happened when she'd taken Dorian's hand just before she'd left the warehouse. The literary cliché was very apt: a bolt of electricity had shot right through her, and she'd known that Dorian Black was far more dangerous than she'd let herself believe. Oh, not because he would hurt her. What she'd glimpsed behind his eyes had heated her like three gins drunk straight.

And she couldn't seem to forget the feeling of his hand on hers.

"Thinking about that date?" Mitch said.

She smiled, covering her confusion. "I promise I'll consider it."

"Not too long." He reached across the table to take her hand. "I want you, Gwen. In every way."

His hand was warm and firm, but his touch had almost no effect on her. Maybe it would have been enough if she'd felt a spark of desire when he held her. It just wasn't there.

"Let's dance," she said.

They did. Mitch almost crushed her in his embrace, as if he had begun to sense the depth of her doubts. His arms felt like a cage. She pretended not to care.

And did her best not to think of Dorian Black.

SOMETHING WAS WRONG.

Mitch knew Gwen...her walk, her speech, every expression and every mood. She was as easy to read as a headline and an utter failure at deception. He knew by the ever-so-slight stiffness in her body that she was not entirely there with him on the dance floor.

Someone else was present. And he had no idea who that someone could be.

When dinner ended, he was the one to suggest that they both needed a good night's sleep. Gwen didn't argue. She looked positively relieved, and her slender body relaxed as if a great weight had been lifted from her shoulders.

Mitch walked her to the curb, tipped the valet, and drove Gwen home. She hardly spoke. Her mind was on that other presence, and Mitch could barely control his anger. If he challenged her now, she would only retreat with a quip and an even deeper silence. She was more forthright than most women, but she was fully capable of fighting dirty.

Gwen thanked him and gave him a peck on the cheek when he dropped her at her apartment building. He grabbed her and kissed her before she could escape. It took several seconds before her lips softened under his, and even then he could feel her resistance. Most men would hardly have noticed. Mitch had his worst assumptions confirmed.

He watched her cross the sidewalk and slip through the door into the lobby. The seductive sway of her hips was entirely unconscious, but it only aroused his anger the more. Any man could enjoy her figure, poured into that scarlet satin gown like a glass of wine waiting to be sipped. Any man could imagine himself in her bed, savoring that lovely body.

So far no one, not even Mitch, had made it that far. Mitch wasn't about to let another fellow poach on his territory. He'd been more than patient with Gwen's starts and peculiar theories. She needed discipline and guidance from a man who cared about her…a man who wouldn't be moved by her foolish ideas.

Once she was his wife, she wouldn't need to rely on her career for fulfillment.

You don't know what's good for you, Guinevere, he thought. *But I'll teach you. And you'll learn to enjoy the lesson.*

CHAPTER FOUR

BY THREE O'CLOCK in the afternoon, Dorian knew Walter couldn't wait any longer. His body was wracked with fever, and his pulse beat frantically beneath his nearly translucent skin. He would no longer drink the water Dorian offered; his lips were like parchment.

Only a human physician could care for him now.

Dorian threw on his long coat, put on his hat and wrapped a scarf around his neck and lower face, grateful that the cooler weather made the garments less conspicuous. He bundled Walter up in his cleanest blankets and lifted the old man in his arms. Walter was all bone and sinew; he weighed little more than a child.

The nearest hospital was a dozen blocks away. Dorian didn't have enough money for a taxi, but he could move very fast when it became necessary.

Longshoremen and laborers turned to stare as he ran past. He dodged from the path of a cumbersome platform truck, whose driver cursed him roundly. He might never have noticed Gwen if not for the sudden, powerful awareness that sliced through his preoccupation.

"Dorian!"

He slowed, debating whether or not to ignore her. Gwen was carrying bundles stacked up to her chin, her face a pale blur above them. She was a distraction he could ill afford, and the dark of the moon was only hours away. But she had money that could pay for a taxi, and there was no doubt in Dorian's mind that she would want to help Walter as much as he did.

Gwen ran up to him as he came to a stop. "What's wrong?" she demanded, peering into Walter's face. "Is he sick?"

"Yes." Dorian found himself all too inclined to gaze at Gwen like any infatuated human. It was a dangerous lapse under the circumstances. "He needs the services of a doctor. Will you summon a taxi?"

"Of course!" Abandoning her packages, she paced Dorian as he broke into a jog. "What happened?"

"I don't know. He's fragile, like most—" He caught himself. "Old men are prone to sickness, are they not?"

"You did say…something about that." Her breath came in short bursts, but she didn't falter. "Go on. I'll follow."

They ran between offices and warehouses until they reached South Street. No cabs appeared, so they continued west to Cherry. Gwen flagged a taxi down with a whistle of impressive volume. She scooted into the backseat and cradled Walter's head and shoulders as Dorian gently pushed the old man in beside her.

"The hospital, as fast as you can make it," Gwen said. The cabbie complied, peeling away from the curb on screeching tires.

Gwen settled back in the seat, careful to keep from moving Walter more than necessary. She laid her hand on his forehead. "He's burning up," she said. "You should have brought him sooner."

Dorian shuddered, struggling to ignore the allure of Gwen's scent. "I wasn't sure the hospital would take a charity case."

"You could have called me at any time. I would have covered the expenses."

"I wasn't aware that you were wealthy, Miss Murphy."

"Gwen, remember?" Her gaze swept from his hat to his collar. "What's with the coat? I can hardly see your face."

He hesitated, weighed the risk, then carefully unwound the muffler. The sunlight was filtered by the taxi's windows, but he still felt a slight burning on his cheeks, nose and lips.

"My skin," he said, "is somewhat sensitive to sunlight."

"Oh? That must be very inconvenient."

Dorian shrugged. Gwen fell silent, though a slight frown lingered between her brows. She returned her attention to Walter, dabbing the sweat from his forehead with her handkerchief.

It was no more than ten minutes before the cabbie pulled up in front of the hospital. He jumped out and opened the door for Gwen, who waited until Dorian had a good grip on Walter. She rushed ahead of Dorian and held open the doors. In a surprisingly short time Walter was in the care of white-clad nurses, while Gwen consulted with a young man Dorian presumed to be the doctor.

"They have a bed all ready for him," she told Dorian. "I'm going to sit with him. Will you stay?"

The look in her eyes told Dorian that she fully expected him to answer in the affirmative. He didn't dare risk it. Soon he would feel only hunger and black rage, and anyone within reach would be in terrible danger.

"No," he said. "I trust that the doctors will be far more effective than I could ever be."

"He relies on you—"

"I'll return tomorrow." He turned to go.

"Wait." Gwen walked up behind him and placed her hand on his arm. "You don't like doctors, do you?"

He didn't answer, glad to let her believe that such a simple fear was the reason for his departure. "I…thank you for your offer to stay with Walter."

"It's no trouble at all." She tightened her fingers. "I brought you some things, but I dropped them at the wharf. I'll bring more tomorrow."

"It isn't necessary." He swallowed, hearing the thrum of her blood, smelling her ripeness.

"Let's not argue again. Here." She pressed several bills into his hand. "Taxi fare, and get yourself something to eat."

He couldn't risk returning the money and touching her skin. "Very well. Good afternoon, Gwen."

This time she didn't follow. Dorian felt his way to the door. His throat swelled with the need for fresh blood. His head pounded, and his legs would barely carry him to the street.

Only desperation made him call a taxi rather than walk back to the waterfront. The sun was sinking when he reached the warehouse. His breath was harsh in his chest, and his pulse throbbed madly at his temples.

His only hope was to hide himself in the warehouse, to fight the hunger and violence. When the night was over he could seek the nourishment he needed, but not before. Not while there was any risk that he might kill.

The warehouse door was nearly broken off its hinges. He swung it closed, knowing it wouldn't keep him in if he chose to leave. The effect was purely psychological, and he needed every advantage he could find.

The sounds of human activity faded. He turned toward his corner, each step awkward with excess energy. His vision sharpened. His skin felt every stray shift of the air around him.

Half stumbling, he lurched past the crates and into his improvised shelter. An instant afterward, he knew he wasn't alone.

"Hello, Dorian."

Javier stepped away from the wall, the backs of his dark eyes reflecting red. He wore a perfectly tailored black suit, and his handsome face was fixed in an unpleasant smile.

Dorian closed his eyes. He would not find any peace this night.

"Javier," he said, his voice hardly a croak. "How did you find me?"

The enforcer drew a silver case from an inner pocket and tapped out a cigarette. "It took a little doing," he said, "but I never doubted that you'd return to the city."

Dorian felt behind him and sank down onto a low crate. "You've made a mistake."

"Yeah. I'll bet I'm the last man you want to see." Javier pushed the cigarette between his lips. "Did you really think you'd get away with it?"

Dorian's skin began to burn. "You'd better get out of here, Javier."

"Why?" The other man produced a lighter and lit his cigarette. "You think I'm letting you off?" He blew smoke toward

Dorian and took another drag. "You betrayed me. You were sup-posed to shoot Chase. You bungled it. And when I tried to do your job…"

He didn't have to finish the sentence. Dorian remembered every moment of that night three months ago…the night he'd been ordered to assassinate Allegra Chase, the only vampire who'd had the nerve and determination to stand against Raoul's tyrannical rule of the clan. The very same night he'd realized that Raoul's ongoing existence would ultimately destroy the few truly good people he had ever known.

Javier, who had been his partner for two years, had had no compunctions about obeying Raoul and killing Allegra. He'd picked up the rifle when Dorian dropped it and would have put a bullet through Allegra's brain if Dorian hadn't taken him down first. But Dorian had left Javier alive. And Javier had seen him with the gun in his hand seconds after Raoul had fallen.

"After all Raoul did for you," Javier said, blowing another cloud of smoke, "you killed him. Left the clan without a leader." He threw the half-finished cigarette on the floor. "It's because of you that the *strigoi* are at war. And all for a woman."

The fire that licked under Dorian's flesh worked its way up, slowly penetrating his brain. "She—others like her—will be the salvation of our kind."

Javier laughed. "Don't kid me. You went soft, Dorian." He stepped on the discarded cigarette and ground it into powder. "How did it happen? You were good at your work until that bitch Allegra showed up."

Oh, yes. He had been good. Good enough that his mere ap-pearance struck fear into any poor breeder or vampire who fell afoul of Raoul Boucher.

And he'd been loyal. Unquestioningly so. But he had never taken pleasure in violence, not like Javier. His own quiet manner had played well against his partner's viciousness. Threats were usually enough to keep rebellious underlings in line. He and Javier had served Raoul efficiently and well.

Until they'd been sent after Allegra Chase. And Dorian had

learned he still had emotions that could be touched by courage and a commitment to ideals he had left behind half a century before.

"Weak," Javier said. "I saw it from the beginning. You always held back."

Dorian's lungs expanded, sucking in air to feed the transformation that would claim him at any moment. "Get out," he whispered. "Get out if you want to live."

"You think you could kill me?" Javier glanced around the room, his mouth curled in contempt. "You don't have it in you. Look at this place. You've fallen too far, Dorian. You might as well be human." He began to take off his coat. "You know, in a way I owe you. When the clan fell, I had a chance to make a new name with the factions. I'm a full vassal now, one of Kyril's right-hand men. And when Kyril wins this war..." He folded his coat and laid it over a stack of crates. "There's no telling how far I'll go."

The animal crouching inside Dorian's head scratched and clawed, fighting to get out. "So this is...all for revenge," he said.

"You're getting off easy. If anyone else knew you'd shot Raoul, they'd tear you to pieces. I'll be quick, for old times' sake." He flexed his hands. "Stand up."

Dorian rose. His muscles seemed to stretch his skin, expanding and swelling to monstrous size. Javier didn't see. It was all illusion.

Except for the desire to kill.

He lifted his hands, making one last attempt to send Javier away. It was a wasted effort. Javier charged, slamming Dorian into the wall.

Everything that followed was a blur of motion and rage. Dorian's fists worked like pistons. Bones snapped. He heard the grunts and groans of his opponent, felt flesh give way, tearing like paper.

And then he tasted blood. Not the sustaining blood of humans, but the bitter stuff that flowed in *strigoi* veins. The liquid filled his mouth. He spat it out, shoving at the body hanging from his arms.

All movement stopped. The creature who had been Dorian

Black stalked from the room, leaving his enemy behind him. He smashed open the warehouse door and stalked the night, searching. The one he wanted was not here, but a fragment of memory emerged from the distant, rational part of his mind.

He moved from shadow to shadow, avoiding the circles of light cast by the street lamps. Cars glided by, the noise of their engines muffled to his ears. Breeders walked the streets, oblivious, easy victims for his hunger. They instinctively shrank away as he passed by.

Still he continued on, the need growing to a wrenching pain in his belly. A single light of reason flickered in his brain, leading him to the place where he would find *her*.

The building he sought was quiet in the cold hours past midnight. A single ambulance was parked in the hospital drive, and a white-coated doctor leaned against the wall, blowing puffs of cigarette smoke into the frigid air.

Dorian made his way toward the door. A pair of chattering females emerged just as he approached. He turned, hiding his face. He could have snapped their necks with a single blow, but his beast's cunning told him that to do so would expose him too soon.

The space inside the doors was brightly lit, hurting his eyes. He kept his head low. Humans spoke in quiet tones, but to him their voices were like shouts. He hurried past to a desk where another female in a starched uniform sat tapping at a typewriter, her face expressionless, her blood rushing steadily under her skin.

"May I help you?" she asked. He didn't answer. His mouth refused to form the words. He stared into her eyes until she looked away and then strode past the desk into the corridor.

No one stopped him. The doors were all alike, but his steps didn't falter. He knew where she was hiding.

He paused at the end of the corridor. His tongue was swollen with thirst, his eyes like hot coals in his skull. He put his hand on the last door. It swung open soundlessly.

She sat in a chair by the bed, her hands folded in her lap, her chin lolling on her chest. The man in the bed snored softly. Neither one heard him enter the room. He moved to the side of the bed and looked down into the old man's face. That one was unimportant. He turned to stare at the woman. Hunger and desire gave the room a cast of black and red.

He walked around her chair and stood behind her. He would strike so swiftly that she would never wake before he was finished.

But he hesitated, frozen by something inside him that he couldn't name. His hands hovered over her shoulders. He lowered his head, lips drawn back from his teeth.

One swift bite would sedate her. Another would drain her life. Or make her into one like himself…

Voices intruded, conversing just outside the door. He leaped away from the girl. There were too many humans here, too many to kill. With a snarl, he ran for the window and forced it open. He jumped through just as the strange humans opened the door and walked in.

After that he ran. Breeders were everywhere, but the scent of their blood sickened him. He reached the waterfront without having taken a single drop.

He charged into the warehouse and grabbed the nearest crate, tossing it across the building. He smashed the walls of his den to splinters, then tore at the blankets until nothing but shreds remained. Only when he had destroyed everything within his reach did he collapse against the wall. His muscles turned liquid, and he sank into blackness.

When he opened his eyes, faint light was filtering into the warehouse doorway. Dorian dragged his hand across his face, swallowing the foul taste on his tongue.

Then he remembered. The details were blurred, as if seen through a tarnished mirror, but he remembered enough.

He pushed himself up with his hands on the wall, testing the steadiness of his legs. He was always weak afterward. It was the small price he paid for his madness. Others paid much more.

The body lay where he'd left it, the head wrenched sideways at an impossible angle, arms twisted, throat torn. There was surprisingly little blood. Javier's face was still unmarked, still handsome even in death.

Dorian turned his head aside and heaved. Nothing came up. He was empty, on the verge of starvation sickness. He welcomed the cramps in his belly and the fire that smoldered under his skin. It was hardly enough punishment for the things he had done at the dark of the moon, or in all the years before.

He knelt and closed Javier's eyes with a pass of his hand. He would have to remove the body before anyone else discovered it. If he threw it in the river, humans would assume it was another mob hit.

They would not be so far from the truth.

Leaving Javier where he lay, Dorian wandered about the warehouse. Not a crate remained unbroken. Anything that could be moved had been shattered or torn or smashed. There was no sign of Walter's bed or any of the small, precious mementos he'd collected on his visits to the rubbish bins and junkyards.

It wasn't the fight with Javier that had done this. Dorian had run rampant after he'd returned from his fruitless hunt, blinded by rage and lust. He hadn't been content to find the nearest human and drop him in some alley with just enough blood left in his body to keep him alive. This time he had sought very specific prey.

He had come within inches of killing Gwen Murphy.

Shaking with reaction and horror, Dorian went to the warehouse door. He edged his foot into the sunlight. All he need do was remove his clothes and take another few steps and he would begin to burn. Soon his skin would crack and blister, causing excruciating pain. But it would be over in minutes as his body's resources were exhausted, every last particle of his *strigoi* strength and vitality given up to a hopeless fight.

Yes, it would be a quick way to die. Gwen would be safe from him. But even if someone else found his body before she did, she would learn of his death eventually.

Dorian stepped back. Exposure to sunlight was not the only way a vampire could end his own life. He could shoot himself in the head or sever his own spine.

Or he could simply stop feeding.

Knowing he had only a limited time, Dorian put on his over-coat and hat, and left the warehouse in search of something he could use to wrap Javier's body. He found a roll of canvas among a stack of boating supplies. Another warehouse provided a coil of rope and a length of heavy chain, which he hid under his coat.

Javier's body was stiff and brittle. Dorian wrapped it in the canvas, bound the bundle with the rope, and coiled the chain around everything. He couldn't wait for nightfall to discard the body, so he dragged it out the door and scanned the docks to either side. The nearest humans were some distance away, busy loading a large freighter. Dorian carried Javier out to the end of the pier and dropped his body into the river.

It sank beneath the surface, trailing bubbles. As soon as it was out of sight, Dorian returned to the warehouse. He started at one end and began picking up the splintered remains of crates and unidentifiable objects scattered over the floor. He piled them neatly against one wall. When the concrete was bare, he put on his hat and coat again, and left without a backward glance.

DORIAN WAS THERE.

Gwen searched the warehouse in growing panic, bewildered by the heap of broken crates and the utter bareness of the space around her. Everything she saw hinted at some sort of violent struggle, and yet the way the shattered objects had been stacked so neatly against the wall hinted that someone had taken the time to clean up after-ward. There was no sign of the knickknacks Walter had asked her to gather, no clue as to where Dorian might have gone.

Her heart stopped when she found the bloodstain where Dorian's room had been. She crouched to touch the irregular circles, feeling sick. There wasn't enough blood to suggest that someone had been killed, but Gwen didn't doubt that the one who'd lost the blood had suffered a serious injury.

Was it Dorian?

But who would have attacked him? His past concealed a darkness she had yet to penetrate; he might have enemies. Yet this might as easily have been a random assault by hoodlums like the ones who had cornered her on the pier.

If he was hurt, why did he leave? Why didn't he come to me?

Forcing herself into a state of rational calm, Gwen searched the waterfront. A few discreet questions gave her little to go on, though one longshoreman had seen a man in an overcoat skulking about early that morning.

By late afternoon she was sure Dorian was no longer in the area. She caught a taxi back to the hospital and rushed to Walter's room, where the old man was taking a sip from a glass offered by the nurse at his bedside.

"Gwennie!" he said, trying to sit up. He looked past her toward the door. "Where's Dorian?"

"Mr. Brenner," the nurse said reprovingly. "You must lie down."

Walter sank back, a little pale from his exertion. "Still couldn't get him to come?" he asked.

"I can't find him," Gwen said, pulling a chair up beside the bed. "He's not at the warehouse. It looks as if something might have happened there."

"What?" Walter attempted to rise again, only to collapse in exhaustion. "What d'ya mean, something happened?"

Gwen cursed herself for upsetting him. "I don't know," she said carefully. "His things…" *Were destroyed,* she thought. But she couldn't tell the old man that. "His things weren't there."

Walter uttered a mild expletive. "I was always afraid he'd run off someday."

"Why?" Gwen asked.

"It was hard for him to be around people, even me. He thought he was taking care of me, but sometimes…" He cleared his throat. "Sometimes I pretended to be more sick than I really was, just to keep him from…doing something bad."

"Something bad to somebody else?"

"No. I'd never believe that." Walter closed his eyes. "The way he talked, sometimes…I thought he'd do himself a mischief."

Gwen gripped the arms of her chair. "And now he thinks you're in good hands."

The old man opened his eyes again. "I won't impose on you, Miss Murphy. Soon as I'm out of this bed…"

"Don't you worry about that. We'll find some decent place for you to stay until you're well again."

Walter was silent for a long half minute. "I hoped," he said at last, "I hoped you'd make a difference. Give Dorian something else to think about. He took to you, Miss Murphy. Never seen him so interested in another human being."

"Maybe you hoped for too much."

"Maybe. But if he's really gone, it ain't because of you. He—"

The nurse intervened. "Mr. Brenner, it's time for you to rest." She gave Gwen a stern look. "You may return tomorrow, but our patient has had enough excitement for one day."

"Just a few more minutes, please," Gwen said. She leaned forward in her chair. "Walter, I have to find Dorian, especially if there's a chance that he may be in trouble. Do you have any idea where he might have gone?"

The old man shook his head. "Always got the feeling he knew the city like the back of his hand. Could have gone anywhere."

"You must have some notion, even if it's just a guess."

"Well…he used to talk about the place he grew up. Some old tenement in Hell's Kitchen. Made it sound like he'd lived there a hundred years ago."

"Did he say where this tenement was?"

"He mentioned Thirty-fourth Street."

Gwen pinched her lower lip. "It's a place to start."

"Wish I could help. My damned heart…"

"I don't want you to worry." She squeezed his thin arm gently. "I'll find Dorian, even if I have to turn this city upside down."

He met her gaze with a crooked smile. "You know, I think you will."

Gwen patted his arm again and rose. "I'll report as soon as I know anything." She nodded to the nurse and hurried to the door, her mind surging ahead of her feet. No one at the paper was likely to notice that she hadn't returned to her desk; no one except Mitch took her seriously enough to care what she did or where she was. She could start looking for Dorian tonight. And if Mitch asked any questions...

Shrugging off her unease, Gwen took a taxi home and changed into a smart ensemble more appropriate to a night on the town. She applied rouge and lipstick, tied a bandeau around her hair and examined herself in the mirror, feeling self-conscious, as she so often did when she dolled up. The dress had been a gift from Mitch; she only wore it for him, and she felt like some sort of impostor every time. She'd never been glamorous and never would be.

Glamorous or not, tonight she would be entering a world of gangsters and speakeasies. She had to look like one of the regulars if she wanted to travel in that world with even a modicum of safety.

She stepped into a pair of patent pumps, threw on a coat and called another taxi. She had a feeling it was going to be a very long night.

CHAPTER FIVE

THE TENEMENT HAD been gutted, scheduled at the behest of a newly enforced city ordinance to be demolished and replaced by a more modern building. It was, Dorian thought, much like him: the obsolete product of an earlier age, useless and ready to die.

Consciousness came and went like sun and shadow glimpsed through the broken basement window. Sometimes he was entirely lucid, remembering how he had come to be in this place, and why. More often he hovered in a dream world, only half aware of the pain, well beyond hunger or any desire to feed. Even when a herd of laughing children hunted through the ruins looking for abandoned treasures, Dorian felt nothing but indifference.

Until the past came to claim him.

THE BOYS WERE older than he by several years. Their faces were already hardened by abuse and starvation and long hours in the factories; they had no mercy for one weaker than themselves. Especially one who read books and pretended to be better than they were.

"Come on," the leader said. "Show us what you've learned, pretty boy." He lifted his fists. "Aw, look. He's afraid. He's going to start bawling any minute."

The boys laughed, but Joseph knew they weren't going to stop. They would probably let him live; a murder would draw too much attention. That didn't mean they wouldn't beat him to within an inch of his life.

He raised his own fists and waited. When the leader attacked, Joseph punched the way he'd seen the boxers do that time when Da had bought into a bare-knuckle fight and forced him to watch. The gang boss collapsed with a woof of pain.

Fifteen minutes later Joseph lay in an alley, his face a bloody mass of cuts and bruises. He told himself it wasn't so bad. Da had done worse.

But next time they wouldn't have it so easy. Next time he would teach them to leave him alone....

DORIAN OPENED HIS EYES. He could no longer see well enough to make out the details of the room. The rats had crawled over him at first, trying to determine if he was edible. In the end they'd left him alone. Even when he was dead, the scavengers would leave his body untouched.

THE NIGHT WAS BITTERLY cold. Joe and the boys had been waiting for hours, knowing that Schaeffer and his gang would be coming this way after an evening of robbing hapless sailors who'd strayed from the waterfront.

Benny spat a curse and flapped his arms across his chest. "Where the hell are they?" he complained.

Joe gave him a hard look, and he subsided. The other boys shifted knives and billy clubs, working frozen fingers. When their rivals appeared, they were ready.

The fight was vicious. Two boys went down and stayed there. Schaeffer got the worst of it. What remained of his gang ran or limped away as fast as their legs would carry them. By the time the coppers arrived, Joe's boys were long gone.

DORIAN RAISED HIS hand to his face, feeling for the scar Schaeffer's knife had carved into his flesh. It wasn't there. He mourned its loss; it had served him well in the old days, terrifying his enemies and followers alike. No one had challenged him after Schaeffer. No one except Little Mike.

"You're finished."

Little Mike grinned at the pickpockets, muggers and thieves who crowded behind him. Most of them were close to Joe's age, the youngest perhaps sixteen and the eldest in his midtwenties, like Joe himself. They laughed, as much out of fear as appreciation. No one wanted to be on Mike's bad side.

Joe knew he was as good as dead. His own bunch had fought hard to keep their territory; they'd been the last gang to maintain their independence after the Nineteenth Street band started taking over Poverty Lane. Now Joe's boys were scattered or had given their allegiance to Little Mike. Only Joe had refused.

Mike was about to make him an example.

They handcuffed him and hung him against the wall in a boarded-up slaughterhouse, suspending him by hooks and chains. One by one, the Nineteenth Street boys punished Joe, each according to his own vicious nature. Little Mike was last. When he was finished, Joe was close to unconsciousness. His chest was on fire, making it nearly impossible to draw breath. Blood flowed from his mouth and numerous cuts, pooling beneath his feet. His eyes were nearly swollen shut, and several of his teeth were loose. At least one of his arms was broken.

Mike strolled up to him and drew his knife. "I'll kill you quick," he said, "if you call me boss."

Joe spat blood in the gang leader's face. Little Mike roared and raised the knife to slit Joe's belly.

"Stop."

The voice rang with authority, echoing from wall to wall. Mike swung around, knife raised. His followers also turned, but instead of confronting the intruder they melted into the shadows and kept their weapons at their sides.

The man was not tall, nor was he particularly big. He wore a top hat, a handsomely tailored frock coat, a gleaming white shirt and a perfectly tied cravat. His every movement was elegance itself, hinting at wealth and power. His face was handsome and utterly without fear. No man had ever looked more out of place than this one.

"Good evening," he said, planting his gold-headed cane on the stained floor. "I see that you boys have been amusing yourselves."

Little Mike stepped forward. "So?" he said. "What's it to you?"

The stranger regarded Mike as he might a particularly ugly rat. "You've chosen a poor place to conduct your business," he said. "If you wish to continue, you will have to work for me."

"Who the hell are you?"

Dark eyes fixed on Mike's. "My name is Raoul Boucher. I am claiming this territory on behalf of my…associates."

Little Mike burst out laughing. His underlings tittered, but their amusement didn't last. They fell silent as Mike advanced on Boucher, a length of chain in one hand and the knife in the other.

"You've made a big mistake, boyo," he said. "There won't be nothing left of you when we're finished."

Not a hint of apprehension touched Boucher's smooth face. He simply stood, waiting, until Mike charged. Then, with a movement almost too swift for Joe to follow, he thrust out with his cane and caught Mike in the belly. Little Mike stumbled and fell flat on his face.

"One last chance," Boucher said. "Swear allegiance to me."

Mike struggled to his feet and scrambled away, wiping blood from his nose. "Get him!" he shrieked.

No one moved. Frothing with rage, Little Mike lunged at Boucher. This time the stranger caught Mike by the collar, transferred his grip to Mike's neck and twisted his hand. The sound of Mike's neck snapping was grim and final.

Boucher dropped the corpse to the ground. The leaderless Nineteenth Streeters scampered away like rabbits, leaving only a handful behind.

"Well," Boucher said. He looked over the remaining hoodlums with appraising eyes. "You may live, if you do as I say without question. Return to this place in two days' time, at midnight, and my vassals will instruct you."

The gang members glanced at each other, uncertain.

"Go," Boucher said. They ran. Boucher glanced at Joe. He sauntered toward him and stopped a few feet away.

"Will you survive, human?" he asked.

Joe forced his tongue to obey him. "I will," he said thickly, "if you'll cut me down."

Boucher cocked his head. "I believe you will," he said. Still he made no move to help. "You didn't cry out," he said.

"I...don't..."

"You made no sound when they tormented you. You have courage."

Joe felt his body shake and realized that he was laughing. "What...good would it do to scream?"

Boucher studied him for a moment longer and then released the chain that held Joe suspended. Joe fell, striking the ground hard. The pain nearly destroyed him.

Boucher knelt behind him. Joe felt the cuffs spring open, though Boucher had no key.

"Can you stand?" Boucher asked.

Joe crawled to his knees. Whirling blackness tried to suck him under. A strong, narrow hand pulled him up by the ruins of his shirt.

The eyes that stared into his were a deep brown tinged with red. "Will you serve me?" Boucher asked.

A coldness washed over Joe. "How?"

"As my enforcer. You will keep other humans obedient to me."

"Hu-humans?"

Boucher smiled. There was something wrong with his teeth.

"Don't be concerned, boy," he said. "You will no longer be among them."

He leaned forward, tearing open the collar of Joe's shirt. It seemed for a moment that he was kissing the base of Joe's neck, and Joe thrust out his arms in panic. But then he felt a strange sort of peace mingled with incomprehensible pleasure, and his muscles relaxed.

When he woke, there was no pain. He was naked between clean sheets, not a single injury marking his body. The room in which he lay was spartan, holding little more than a bed and a washbasin, but fresh clothing hung in the plain armoire against the wall.

Joe rose from the bed, feeling the strength surge through his body, aware of a ravening hunger such as he had never known. He had just begun to dress when Boucher walked into the room.

In an instant Joe remembered everything. And something strange happened inside him; when he looked at Boucher, he knew he was bound to the other man by means he had no way to explain.

"Good," Boucher said. "You will come with me, and I will instruct you in what you must know." He smiled and touched Joe's face in the way a man might stroke a favored pet. "You shall keep your name for the time being. Someday, when you earn it, you may choose your own."

He turned for the door. Joe closed his eyes, caught in a maelstrom of sensation.

"What am I?"

Boucher paused. "You are more than human, my protégé. And you will live a thousand years."

DORIAN WOKE AGAIN. It was several minutes before he could distinguish the past from the present.

Joseph. Dorian. Neither name had any meaning now. Soon the husk of his body would begin to rot. He would become incapable of movement, and then his brain would start to die.

He let himself sink back into the half world of formless dreams and visions. Sometimes he thought he saw Gwen Murphy, her heart-shaped face framed with soft red curls, green eyes blazing, full lips parted as she prepared to admonish him. "You can't die," she said. "I won't let you."

Strange how clear her voice was. Clear and strong, as if words alone could draw him back from the precipice. But it was for her sake he'd come here. It was easy to let go when he remembered her sleeping in the hospital chair, her lashes brushing her cheek, completely unaware of how close she had come to death.

His cracked lips moved in a smile. Gwen. She had saved him. Saved him by showing him what he had to do. He closed his eyes.

"No!"

He felt something touch his arm and tried to brush it away. Perhaps the rats had grown bold again.

"Dorian!"

Air blew softly in his face. He imagined that he smelled flowers. "Wake up!"

Someone began to shake him. He rolled onto his side, too weak to fight his attacker. It kept after him, claws furrowing his shirt and digging into his skin.

"No," he murmured. "Let me be."

"Never."

The blow stung his face like a hive of angry bees. Instinctively he reached for the thing that had hurt him. His fingers closed on smooth flesh. He twisted, provoking a purely human cry.

He opened his eyes. The face above him was a blur topped with a corona of fire. An avenging angel come to drag him to hell.

"Dorian," she whispered. "Please. It's Gwen. Listen to me."

His senses turned traitor. He couldn't block the fragrance of clean skin and perfume, the sound of a heartbeat he knew as well as his own.

"Gwen." His voice was hardly audible even to his own ears. "Go away."

She leaned closer. His strength failed him. He released her, knowing he had no hope of forcing her to leave. All he could do was beg.

"Please," he said. "There's…nothing you can do."

GWEN HEARD HIM WITH disbelief and horror. The creature below her bore almost no resemblance to the man she'd known: his skin was cracked, each wound seamed with dried blood; his eyes were deeply sunk in his face; his body was strangely attenuated, as if he were slowly disintegrating before her eyes.

He was dying. And he wanted it.

"Dorian," she whispered. "Why?"

He turned his head away, dismissing her question. Dismissing her.

"It's been two weeks," she said, convinced that she had to keep talking, to keep him clinging to life even against his will. "I've been searching everywhere. All Walter could tell me was where you used to live. That wasn't enough. I had to walk through every tenement and speakeasy, talk to people I wouldn't trust as far as I could throw them…and this is my reward."

The sharply outlined muscles beneath his jaw tensed. He was listening. She touched his shoulder with the greatest care, afraid his flesh might crumble under any pressure at all.

"I don't know how you got this way," she said, "but if you think I've wasted my time only to let you die, you've got another thing coming."

A husk of sound emerged from his chest. She thought it might be laughter.

"Too late," he said. "Debt…is repaid."

"The hell it is." Gwen looked around the filthy room, considering how she might drag him into the hallway without hurting him. "Can you get up?"

The breath rattled in his chest. Her eyes flooded, and she felt close to emptying the contents of her stomach…not that she'd had much of an appetite since Dorian had gone missing.

"If you can't move," she said, "I'm sending for an ambulance."

His body heaved. He rolled over, eyes more red than gray. "No…doctors," he said.

"You don't leave me any choice." She moved to get up. He seized her hand, trembling with the effort.

"No good." Thick, dark blood trickled from his mouth. "I'm…no good for anyone."

Oh, God. Tears spilled over her cheeks. "You're good for me," she whispered.

His eyes rolled up beneath his lids, and he fell back. Gwen dropped to her knees and laid her head on his chest. His heartbeat had slowed to an irregular tap, like water dripping from a leaky faucet.

"Whatever you did," she said, "it isn't worth this. Please, Dorian."

She felt his hand on her hair. "Goodbye."

He took one breath, another. His chest ceased to move under her cheek. His heart stopped.

"No!" Gwen sat up and thumped on Dorian's ribs with her fists. Nothing. The tears were falling so thick and fast that she could hardly see him. She shook him, heedless of the raw skin beneath his torn shirt. She shouted until her voice was hoarse and her tongue like a roll of cotton wadding.

Nothing she did made any difference.

Gwen stretched out across his body, gasping with shock and grief. She pressed her cheek to his. She closed her eyes and willed herself to pretend. Pretend that he was still alive, that they were lying side by side in some peaceful place, awakening to shafts of sunlight streaming over the bedcovers.

A tickle of sensation stroked her neck. She shifted, aware of a peculiar prick of pain there at the juncture of her shoulder. It was gone as quickly as it had come, replaced by heat and a feeling of pleasure that spread through her body. Her grief began to slide away from her, dissipating into a mist of peace.

"Gwen."

She sighed and stretched, pleasant lassitude feeding her delusion that Dorian was speaking. If this was a dream, let it continue. Let her pretend she felt his arms cradling her head, his pulse beating strong again, his hands touching her hair.

"I'm here, Gwen."

Slowly the veil of tranquillity fell away from her eyes. She found herself staring at a wall covered in graffiti and unidentifiable stains. The surface beneath her was firm and unyielding.

Dorian's body was gone.

She sat up, acid burning a trail down her throat. Hands grasped her arms from behind. She swung around on her knees, fists clenched.

"Gwen," Dorian said, his eyes clear as bright water. "It's all right."

Her heart stuttered to a halt. "You—oh, my God—"

"Yes." He cupped her cheek in his palm. She stared, unable to comprehend the transformation. His face was still gaunt, his skin deeply lined. But the bloody slashes were gone; his gaze was steady, and his voice, oh, his voice...

"I did not wish to be saved," he said, "but you saved me nevertheless."

All the strength drained out of Gwen's legs. Dorian eased her to the pockmarked floor. He was extraordinarily gentle, more so than he'd ever been with her before. But his gaze was filled with sorrow.

"You were dying," Gwen said, stumbling over the words. "I saw—"

"Yes," he said again. "It is possible for the body to appear bereft of life when it continues to function."

Gwen was in no state to argue. She stiffened her spine, afraid she would throw herself into his arms in a display that would embarrass both of them.

"Tell me," she said. "Tell me why. Why you ran away. Why you let yourself..." The lump in her throat threatened to melt into more treacherous tears. "What was so terrible that you couldn't bear to go on living?"

His hands fell from her shoulders. "You would wish me dead if you knew."

"You idiot." She laughed, half-crazy with relief. "I could never hate you."

"You are not at all sensible, Miss Murphy."

"Oh...Gwen, *Gwen,* for God's sake." She grabbed his hands, stroking her fingers across the veins and tendons that stood out beneath the skin. "Tell me. Get it off your chest before you—"

She realized that he was staring at her lips, a muscle ticking at the corner of his mouth. She pulled away.

"I'm not going to insist," she said, "not after what you've just been through. About that ambulance..."

His sharp glance silenced her on that subject. "All right," she said. "But you've got to see a doctor."

He shook his head, and she knew this was a battle she couldn't win. "In that case, you're coming back to my apartment," she said. "You're going to stay in bed until you're fully recovered."

"That would not be at all wise."

"Sure. I've heard it all before." She got up, tested her legs, and debated how best to get him on his feet. "I'd carry you if I could, but that's obviously not an option."

He laid his hands flat on the floor and pushed. He failed in his first attempt, but when Gwen grabbed him under his arm, he was finally able to stand.

"Slowly," she said. "There's no rush."

Dorian allowed her to steer him toward the door but stopped on the threshold.

"What time is it?"

"Why does that… Oh, of course. Your sensitivity to sunlight." She checked her watch. "It should be just about dark by now."

He didn't move. "Think, Gwen. Consider what you're doing."

"I have." She took a firmer grip on his arm and supported him along the corridor, feeling her way, dodging rats and cockroaches that had emerged with the coming of night. When she stumbled over a pile of abandoned furniture, Dorian took the lead, though his pace was still carefully measured.

The night air, even in a place like Hell's Kitchen, was sweet compared to the close, decaying atmosphere inside the condemned building. There were no taxis in the area, so Gwen half carried Dorian in the direction of Midtown. A few hooligans, seeing a woman and a crippled man, attempted to harass them, but Dorian turned his stare on the boys and they quickly absconded.

After a good half mile, Gwen spotted a taxi and managed to get the cabbie's attention. She settled Dorian beside her in the backseat and braced him against the driver's reckless speed and sudden turns until they were safely in front of her apartment building. She got out and assisted Dorian from the cab.

"You need help, lady?" the cabbie asked, examining Dorian with a frown.

"I can manage, thanks." Gwen felt Dorian lean more heavily on her arm and knew he was at the end of his strength. With a last, determined effort, she hauled him up two flights of stairs to her door. She fumbled with the key, pushed the door open with her foot, and tugged Dorian through the tiny living room and into her bedroom.

Dorian made no protest as she dropped him onto the bed. He was breathing deeply, and his skin was very pale; fresh worry blossomed in her chest.

"You just stay right there and rest," she said. "I'll get something for you to drink, and a little food."

He opened one bloodshot eye. "Water," he said. "No food."

"All right. But you'll have to eat sooner or later." Reluctantly she left him and hurried to the kitchen. Plain water hardly seemed enough. She settled on making him a cup of weak tea instead, and placed a half-dozen soda crackers on the saucer.

When she returned to the bedroom he seemed to be asleep, but his eyes were wide open and she had the uncanny impression that he really wasn't sleeping at all. She set the teacup down and stood over the bed.

"Dorian?"

He didn't respond. Once again Gwen considered calling a doctor, but she decided to wait a while and see how well he did on his own. He'd already made a miraculous recovery.

"I'll have to get you out of those clothes," she said, watching his face. Still nothing. Doing her best not to disturb him, she knelt and began to unbutton his shirt. It was stiff with blood and sweat, but she was finally able to ease it off his shoulders. Dorian didn't stir, even when she lifted his head from the pillow. She threw the shirt into the corner of the room and paused to look for injuries.

Dorian's chest, lightly dusted with dark hair, rose and fell steadily. For a man who had obviously been near starvation, he was in reasonably good shape; his ribs were prominent, but the sleek muscles of his torso were still intact.

Gwen bit her lower lip. There was no doubt that she'd always found him attractive. If she ignored the bruising that marked his upper body, she could only judge him beautiful: perfectly proportioned, strong, undeniably masculine. It would be easy to stand here staring at him for hours.

Retreating into a purely clinical state of mind, she unbuttoned his trousers. Halfway down, she could see he wasn't wearing any drawers. And that was hardly the least of it. His...member was fully erect, straining against the fabric under her fingers.

Torn between curiosity and self-consciousness, Gwen hesitated. She'd never seen a naked man before, though she'd read enough about sex to know that there was nothing unusual in Dorian's "equipment" except perhaps in size. He was quite...impressive.

Watching his face to make sure he was still unaware of her movements, Gwen finished unbuttoning him. His erection almost jumped into her hand. She stepped back, swallowed and tugged the trousers down his legs.

If Mitch could see me now...if he had any notion of the crazy thoughts going through my mind...

Dorian made a low sound and turned his head on the pillows. Gwen froze, but he sank back into unconsciousness immediately.

Gwen retreated to a chair and sat on the edge. He desperately needed a bath. She still didn't know how many of the marks on his body were the result of injuries.

And oh, how she longed to touch him.

You think Dorian is crazy. How about you, Gwennie-girl? What do you think will happen if he wakes up to find you—

She could barely complete the thought. Her face was on fire, and she knew if she looked in the mirror she would see every freckle standing out in sharp relief. She shot up from the chair and rushed into the kitchen, where she found a bottle of whiskey she'd kept in a cupboard for ages. She poured herself a shot and downed it in a single gulp.

There were just some things even the most modern woman

shouldn't take lightly. Losing her virginity was one of them. And yet. And yet…

Gwen set her glass down with a bang and strode into the bathroom, selecting several towels and washcloths from the linen closet. She took a washbowl from underneath the sink, filled it with warm water, and carried it and the towels into the bedroom.

If it hadn't been for the rise and fall of his chest, anyone might well have believed that Dorian was dead. Gwen knew otherwise; already he looked a thousand times better than he had when she'd found him. She set the washbowl on the bedside table and dipped one of the cloths into the water. She took a deep breath and laid the washcloth on Dorian's shoulder. When he didn't react, she stroked the cloth over his skin, working from the base of his neck to the bulge of his biceps.

The cloth came away soiled, but it was clear that Dorian's injuries were not nearly as severe as she'd first feared. She began to wash the lower part of his arm, then moved to his chest. Her fingers strayed, drifting over the curve of his pectoralis. Even at the peak of health, Mitch wasn't this well developed. Of course she'd never seen anything below his waist, but she had the feeling…

Her insides tightened as she moved lower. Dorian's stomach was ridged and firm, though it was mottled with fading bruises. She swirled the washcloth around his navel, fascinated by the sculpted vee of muscle that plunged from hips to groin.

And then there were only two choices. She could make a jump to his legs, or touch him like a lover.

She closed her eyes and stroked the cloth downward. His cock—a vulgar word, but one that could hardly shock an experienced newswoman—had relaxed and was quiescent for perhaps twenty seconds before it began to swell again. Soon it lay flat against his stomach, surprisingly smooth from base to head. She touched it with her fingertip. It was as silky as it looked, yet hard and unyielding. It would do its job beautifully.

Wanton images crowded Gwen's head. With infinite care she closed her fingers around him.

His hand shot out like a striking cobra and seized her wrist.

Half afraid of what she might see, she glanced at his face. If the man on the bed had been Mitch instead of Dorian, she would have expected a healthy dose of shock. He would have every reason to wonder when she'd adopted such a shameless attitude, what a good Catholic girl was doing handling a man's private parts, even if that man wanted to make an honest woman of her.

But Mitch's instincts were all male. He was impatient for their marriage because he wanted to share her bed. Whatever his momentary reservations, he wouldn't be able to conceal the hunger in his eyes.

Dorian could, and did. His teeth clenched, and the tendons in his neck stood out like steel cables. He looked at her as if her touch was as unwelcome as a case of the measles.

"Go," he rasped. "Get out."

Gwen snatched up the bowl and fled the room, feeling more shaky than she had right after he had rescued her from drowning.

Once in the bathroom, she closed the door and leaned over the sink, too dizzy to trust her balance. Her reflection in the mirror looked drawn and haggard, the result of two weeks of balancing her work at the paper with the desperate search for Dorian. Now that she'd found him, she didn't know what do to with him.

She didn't know what to do with herself.

Gwen blew out her breath and splashed water over her face, knowing it would take a lot more than a good dousing to make her forget what she'd seen and felt tonight.

CHAPTER SIX

"You were right, Mr. Hogan," Pete Wilkins said, patting the Leica thirty-five millimeter camera hanging by his side. "Miss Murphy brought some fella back to her apartment. I think he was sick…he didn't walk too well."

Mitch kept his face a blank. Wilkins had been glad enough to help him; the boy had ambitions to be a photographer for the *Sentinel,* and he would have done just about anything to obtain Mitch's good word. But under no circumstances would Mitch allow the kid to see his true feelings, especially when they were caused by a woman.

"Did you get photographs?" he asked.

"Sure." Wilkins hesitated. "I don't know how well they came out, though. The guy had his head down most of the time."

"I see."

"I can go back, Mr. Hogan. The man didn't leave the building. He's probably still there, and—"

"I may need you again, Pete. That's all for now."

"Sure. Anytime." He backed away and walked out of the city room.

Mitch turned and bent over his desk, shuffling papers with numb fingers. He finally had an idea of what had been making Gwen behave so oddly for the past two weeks, working like a demon during the day and vanishing every night. He still couldn't wrap his mind around the fact that she'd been seeing another man; she could have no earthly reason for looking elsewhere when she had a devoted suitor—personable, respectable and comfortably situated—ready to marry her at a moment's notice. And it wasn't like her to sneak around. If she had fallen in love with someone else, she would have told him outright.

Would she? She hasn't given you a straight answer to your proposal. You knew she was hiding something. Why should she tell the truth about this?

He crumpled a blank sheet of paper between his hands. Why had Gwen taken a sick man to her apartment? It certainly didn't seem like a standard assignation. And for all his doubts, Mitch found it impossible to believe that she would casually share a bed with someone she couldn't have known for very long.

It's only recently that she's been so distant. This is something new.

Something new, but surely not serious. And that meant that he still had an excellent chance of nipping the relationship, whatever it might be, in the bud. But he wouldn't confront Gwen. Not yet. He would use Pete a little longer and see what else he could learn.

Everyone has something to hide, Guinevere…even your new friend. And when I find out who he is and what he's afraid of, I'll make sure he disappears from your life. And mine.

DORIAN LISTENED TO THE door close and opened his eyes.

Gwen had believed he was asleep, as he'd pretended to be for most of the previous day and night. They had hardly spoken since he'd caught her touching him, the memory of her bold actions suspended between them like a hangman's noose.

Blushing and self-conscious, Gwen had made him a simple dinner and let him eat it alone. She'd retired to the living room to sleep on the sofa, as if that small distance would protect them both from a serious breach of propriety.

Not that he'd given her any reason to fear that he would return her advances. Quite the contrary. He had deliberately maintained his distance, pretending an indifference he didn't feel while his body raged with need. His senses were stretched thin, attentive to her every movement. The slightest scent of her body made him harden, and all he could think of was taking her in this very bed.

Now she was gone, if only for the day, and the relief was overwhelming. He sat up, propped against the pillows, and flexed his arms. It had taken only twenty-four hours for him to recover, though he was still a little weak. Gwen's blood had worked a miracle.

He swung his legs over the side of the bed, noting the clothing she had laid out for him on the room's single chair: a sand-colored fisherman's sweater, a pair of flannel trousers, stockings and plain brown oxfords. It was the uniform of an ordinary man, no doubt purchased by Gwen at some local shop. Dorian hadn't worn apparel even remotely like it since his youth, not in all the years since he'd started working for Raoul.

Slowly he pulled the sweater over his head and stepped into the trousers. Leaving the oxfords and stockings at the foot of the chair, he went into the living room. A pile of blankets lay heaped on the sofa. Against his will, Dorian walked to the couch and lifted one of the blankets, pressing it to his face. His cock came to instant attention.

He inhaled deeply, rubbing his cheek against the blanket. For months he'd lived rudderless, with no one to command him and no duty to consume his thoughts. Death had seemed better than such emptiness. But then Gwen had come into his life, and suddenly the hollow in his heart was filled.

He had never been as afraid as he was at this moment.

With another ragged breath, Dorian tossed the blanket back on the sofa. A folded piece of paper fell to the carpet. He picked it up and opened it. The lines were written in a strong cursive, as eloquent of Gwen as the scent of her hair.

Good morning, Dorian.
If you're reading this, you're up and about. Don't push yourself. There's more food in the kitchen. Take as much as you like. I'll pick up more on my way back from the office.

　　Something I forgot to mention, and since you may be wondering: Walter is fine. I've set him up in a little boardinghouse where he'll be around other people and the doctor can visit him occasionally. Considering his age, he's in pretty good shape. I'll take you to see him once you're up to it.

Rest. I'll be back by seven.

Gwen's signature was a broad flourish, a confident sweep of the pen that belied her earlier unease. Dorian refolded the note and laid it on the sofa. He'd hardly thought of Walter once he'd committed himself to suicide, convinced that Gwen would see to the old man's welfare. And she had. Even if Dorian feared what she'd done in saving his own life, he owed her greatly for saving Walter's.

His thoughts in turmoil, Dorian wandered about the small apartment. The furniture was modest both in price and design, suitable for a woman who spent little time at home. There were only four rooms, including the bathroom, every one neat and well organized. The one exception was the secretary near the single window in the corner of the living room. It was scattered with manila folders and blotched with ink stains, though there were indications that Gwen had recently attempted to clean it. An antique typewriter took up the center space in front of the battered steno chair.

Also on the desk was a photograph of an older man holding a certificate, which on closer inspection proved to be a Pulitzer Prize in journalism. Dorian picked up the photograph. The man had graying auburn hair and lively eyes that forcefully reminded Dorian of Gwen. The name on the certificate was Eamon Murphy.

Dorian set down the photo and opened one of the folders. In it were several obituaries for Eamon Murphy and a number of newspaper articles written by him; the sheer volume of the stories and their prominence among the front pages suggested that he'd been a senior reporter at the *Sentinel*.

His interest fully aroused, Dorian continued to study the

notes and clippings. At the bottom of the stack he found a torn sheet of newsprint, a page out of the *Sentinel* dated eight months previous. The page number indicated that the Murphy article, circled in red pencil, had held a lowly position at the back of the newspaper. But when Dorian began to read the headline, all the fine hairs at the base of his neck came erect.

Is Blood Cult Responsible for Recent Deaths?

He quickly scanned the columns. Murphy advanced the seemingly bizarre theory that several murders committed in the months before the paper's date, attributed by police to mobs fighting over territory, had actually been perpetrated by a secret cult operating out of Manhattan, a cult that engaged in the unique practice of draining all the blood from the corpses of its victims. The story was no more than a few paragraphs, unaccompanied by pictures. Clearly the *Sentinel*'s editors had not found Murphy's conjecture plausible enough to warrant a more prominent place in the newspaper.

At the bottom of the page was a barely legible scrawl in a feminine hand: *Waterfront murders?*

Dorian dropped the paper. He'd foolishly assumed that Gwen's interest in the triple murders on the docks had been nothing more than that of any reporter doggedly pursuing yet another story about gangland assassinations.

None of the remaining papers shed further light on Murphy's conjecture or Gwen's query. The drawer at the front of the desk was locked. Dorian forced it open and found a folder bulging with lined notepaper and more clippings. The label read Dad's Notes. Dorian laid the folder on the table and spread the clippings on the desktop.

About half of the articles were stories covering homicides that had occurred over the past two years, ranging from presumed mob hits to unsolved murders. Notations written in a masculine hand decorated the browned margins, most unintelligible.

A single torn sheet of white paper, neatly typed, revealed Murphy's thoughts.

They exist. I don't know who they are
yet, but I do know that I'm on the verge
of uncovering something important, something that will expose the killers and
vindicate me.

   It is increasingly clear that this
organization bears no loyalty toward
any of the various gangs in Manhattan,
but has a very specific agenda of its
own. Today a man came to see me, calling himself by the name of Aadon and
claiming that he possessed invaluable
details of several past murders that
would open my eyes to a world hidden from
all but a privileged few. He brought with
him a book, which I have only just begun to read. I now have reason to believe

And there the note ended. In the bottom margin Gwen had
written: *Pages missing. Why? What book? Who is Aadon?*

The last three words were heavily underscored. Dorian
rubbed his chin and stared at the closed, dusty curtains behind
the desk. *Aadon.* He had never heard the name, nor did he have
any idea to which book Eamon had referred. The reporter's
ideas would certainly seem the ravings of a lunatic to most
humans. But it appeared as if he had unwittingly come close to
exposing a truth mankind had only suspected throughout its
history: the existence of the nonhuman races.

Dorian set the typed page aside. Beneath it, clipped to a
sheet of thin cardboard, was a photograph. It showed a young-
ish man with a narrow face and intense eyes, and underneath
someone had written: *Aadon.* On the reverse side of the cardboard was glued yet another clipping, this one about a corpse,
badly burned, dredged from the river on the afternoon of
February 4, 1926. That had been only a few weeks before
Eamon Murphy died.

Murphy's theory should have died with him. But he had a daughter who had kept his notes and clippings, a reporter in her own right. Her father couldn't have known about the most recent murders, but Gwen did. She knew the corpses had been drained of blood, and she had clearly decided that there was some merit in her father's ideas, or at least that she had an obligation to continue his investigation.

And what did she have to build on? Blood cults. Human corpses bled white. A mysterious man who had turned up in the river—perhaps after he'd promised Eamon information that would prove his theories.

It all added up to a very dangerous equation. And Gwen was in the middle of it.

The apartment door rattled. Dorian shoved the papers back into the folder and was just putting them in the drawer when Gwen walked in.

"You're up!" she said, her eyes sparkling with pleasure. "Are you sure you should be—" She saw what he had in his hands and stopped. Her gaze flew accusingly to his.

Dorian backed away from the desk and lifted his hands as if she were holding a Tommy gun pointed at his head. She charged forward, slammed the drawer shut and spun to confront him.

"You broke into my desk," she said, "Why?"

No ready answer came to Dorian's mind. "I was curious about your profession," he said.

Her shoulders relaxed. "If you'd wanted to know," she said, "all you had to do was ask."

"I apologize." He retreated to the sofa and sat down, hoping to allay her distress. "I was unaware that there were aspects of your work you preferred to keep secret."

"A locked drawer usually means—" She took a deep breath and blew it out. "Okay. There's no reason why you shouldn't know, as long as you don't tell anyone at the *Sentinel*."

"About your father's ideas?"

She nodded, swivelled the steno chair to face him and sat down. "I only came back to the apartment because I forgot my notebook," she said, "but a few more minutes won't matter." She pulled her skirt over her knees. "How much did you read?"

"Enough to know that your father's theory of a murderous cult did not meet with the approval of his employers at the *Sentinel*."

"That's right." She slumped in the chair. "It was almost all Dad thought about during the year before he died. Everyone saw how much he'd changed. When he approached the city editor with the cult story…" She knotted her hands in her lap. "They thought he'd gone crazy."

"Had he?"

"No! He…" She sighed. "The odd thing is that he seemed to become very quiet in the last weeks, as if he'd given up. It wasn't like him. He wouldn't talk to me about it. And all these notes…" She made a helpless gesture. "I didn't know anything about them until he was gone."

"He was a gifted reporter, was he not?"

She smiled wistfully. "He was the best there was."

"Then you accept his theories."

"At first all I could think of was proving he was right. But in spite of all the work Dad had done, all this stuff he'd locked away in his files, he'd left too many questions unanswered. Until the cops found the bodies on the waterfront, it didn't seem I had much to work with."

Dorian was careful to keep his expression one of restrained interest. "But the state of those bodies led you to believe that your father might have been correct."

"It's crazy, I know. But I've never heard of regular mobsters who did that kind of thing."

"Indeed." Dorian settled more deeply into the sofa's sprung cushions. "So you've continued to pursue the story on your father's behalf?"

"Strictly on the Q.T. Officially the triple murder case belongs to Randolph Hewitt. He's one of the senior reporters in the city room. He never liked my dad, and he already suspects I'm poaching on his territory."

"You don't think he'll support your father's conclusions?"

"Even reporters are human. Sometimes they see only what they want to see."

Dorian curled his fingers around the arm of the sofa. "Do you have any specific information that would confirm the cult theory?"

"Not so far. But I'm getting close. Remember how I told you that I was supposed to meet a witness on the waterfront the day those hooligans introduced me to the fishes? That lead hasn't panned out, but there was this man, Aadon…" She smoothed an imaginary wrinkle in her skirt. "After I read through Dad's notes and saw the photograph, I realized that the same guy was found in the river not long after he met with Dad." She shook her head. "I hit a dead end with that lead, too, but I'm sure I missed something important. This time I'll push on until I find the truth."

"And what of this book?"

"That's the biggest puzzle of all. There wasn't any sort of unusual book among Dad's things. And he didn't mention it again in his notes. It's as if he wanted to keep it hidden."

Dorian leaned forward, unable to contain his disquiet. "Have you considered what you'll do if you discover that your father was wrong?"

"He wasn't. If I can expose the presence of a genuine murderous cult in Manhattan, I'll not only redeem my father but also prove that I can handle the big stories. They won't be able to shuffle me off to the back pages anymore."

Briefly Dorian closed his eyes. It was every bit as bad as he'd feared. "I advise you in the strongest terms not to continue," he said.

Her silence was as sharp as a knife. "Why?" she asked. "Do you know something I don't, Dorian? Something you've been keeping from me?"

"I know the waterfront. I know the city. I know how far certain elements will go to eliminate their rivals. Gwen…" He raised his hands and let them fall again. "The evil that men do needs no arcane explanation."

Gwen got up, shoving the chair against the desk. "You'll

forgive me if I don't take your advice." She checked her watch. "I have to get back to work. There's some sandwich meat in the icebox and a loaf of bread on the table." She snatched a notebook from the desk, took her father's folder out of the drawer and hurried to the door. Then she was gone, the smell of her lingering just inside the doorway.

Dorian sprang up and paced the length of the room and back. He still wasn't sure how completely Gwen believed the cult story, but she obviously wasn't going to rest until she'd found an answer that satisfied her.

Either Raoul hadn't known of the senior Murphy's quest, or he hadn't considered it a threat. All throughout history, *strigoi*—whenever they organized in families, colonies or clans, as they periodically did—had worked to silence those who might expose their hidden presence in society. Though he had never been involved in such a task, Dorian knew that past clan leaders, and quite possibly Raoul himself, had ordered hits on humans who showed a little too much curiosity.

Most reporters pursuing stories about mob assassinations or related crimes naturally assumed that they were committed by the high-profile human bosses in the city. They never suspected that Raoul's gang was different from any other, and that usually protected them.

If Raoul had known of Gwen's father, his would-be heirs, Kyril and Christof, might possess that same knowledge. They might or might not realize that Gwen and Hewitt had continued Eamon's investigation. And whether or not they found out and took action to hinder Gwen's work depended entirely on how close her persistence took her to the truth of vampire existence.

Dorian slammed his fist against the nearest wall. He never should have gotten involved with a human. He never should have given in to instinct and taken Gwen's blood just to keep himself alive.

But the damage was done. He'd fed from her only once, in the most basic sense—there had been no danger of inadver-

tently Converting her. Yet now that he had tasted her blood—
now that he had allowed her to influence the course of his existence—he couldn't permit her to throw her life away.

So what was to be done? Arguing with her would only make
her suspicious of his motives. He must find a way to keep careful
watch on Gwen's progress and eventually derail her investigation. To do so, he would have to remain close to her. But human
morality would scarcely sanction his continuing to share living
quarters with a young, unmarried woman.

For the rest of the afternoon he read through the notes Gwen
had left and considered his best course of action. He made
several sandwiches and ate them quickly, tasting nothing. He
scarcely noticed when the light from the window faded and the
street lamps began to shine feeble defiance against the night.

Gwen burst into the apartment at a quarter after seven. "Good
news!" she cried, throwing her pocketbook on the sofa. "I've got
you a job."

Her words hardly made sense to him. He stood awkwardly,
hands folded behind his back. "A job?"

She looked at him more carefully. "You haven't been
resting, have you?"

The ease of Gwen's speech suggested she had overcome her
self-consciousness about her behavior of the previous day.
Dorian had received no such benefit from their hours of separation. Her nearness triggered an almost unbearable hunger that
tightened every muscle in readiness for the hunt.

"I am quite well," he said stiffly.

"You do look a lot better. I've never seen anyone recover
so quickly. It's downright spooky." She unbuttoned her coat.
"Did you eat?"

"Yes." He turned from the sight of the blood pulsing beneath
her fair skin. "Was your day pleasant?"

She laughed. "Where did you learn to small talk, Dorian? Oh,
never mind. I'm no good at it, either." She sprawled on the sofa,
kicking off her pumps with a groan of appreciation. "I've been
thinking about how to get you back into the world of the living.

Today I found out that our night janitor is leaving for another job. I told Mrs. Frost—she's the woman in charge of hiring support staff—that I knew of a perfect candidate to replace him. You."

"I don't understand."

"What's to understand? A job will get you off the streets. Unless you think that kind of work is beneath you."

Dorian circled the room, his thoughts fogged with need. "No," he said. "I...why should you trust me with a post at your newspaper?"

"Why shouldn't I?"

"How much do you really know of me, Gwen?"

She sighed and pushed her hand through her hair, all the laughter gone from her eyes. "Okay. Let's have it out here and now. What happened at the warehouse, Dorian? Whose blood did I find?"

So it comes, Dorian thought grimly. *The chance to drive her away once and for all, or to commit myself to saving her from herself.*

But the decision was already made. "The blood was mine," he said. "I had an...altercation with several hooligans."

"The warehouse looked as if an explosion had hit it."

"Yes."

"You obviously survived. Why did you try to kill yourself, Dorian?"

The time had come for a small part of the truth. "I am prone to regular intervals in which I find myself...drawn back to another time and place. During such intervals it is inadvisable for anyone to approach me with less than friendly intent."

"Walter mentioned something about that. He called it a 'mood.'"

"I fear he is too mild in his description."

"How?"

"I am not rational at such times, Gwen. That is why I warned you away when we first met."

"I remember." The look in her eyes told him that she had no trouble recalling how he'd behaved after he'd saved her from the river. "You didn't hurt me, and you never hurt Walter, either."

"But I did injure the men who attacked me."

She went a little pale. "Did you kill them?"

"They are not likely to attempt to harm anyone again in the near future."

"And that's why you tried to commit suicide? Because you dared to defend yourself against a pack of wharf rats?"

Dorian looked away. "Losing oneself…is not a pleasant prospect. I had no desire to risk harming anyone else."

"And that proves you're not as lost as you think you are. Once you have a steady job, we can find a way to help you. There are plenty of other men who suffered from the War in the same way you have."

The War. Once again she assumed that he'd fought in Europe, when he'd never set foot outside the state of New York.

"Are you certain you still wish me for the janitorial position?" he asked.

Gwen caught his gaze. "You can't solve your problems by hiding for the rest of your life. Maybe a little regular work is exactly what you need."

"And if I prove unsuitable?"

"We'll cross that bridge when we come to it. And if one of these moods comes over you, you'll have a place to go. I've gotten you the room next to Walter's at the boardinghouse."

"That was unnecessary."

"You can't stay here, you know. And I won't let you go back to that horrid warehouse."

He inclined his head, conceding defeat. If Gwen was not discouraged by his partial confession, he could not refuse her offer. Though he couldn't stay by her side every moment, he would have access to any research she conducted from the newspaper office. And he would have an excuse to continue their relationship, should she begin to lose her crusading determination to reform him.

An excuse, indeed. An excuse to continue taking her blood. An excuse to go on feeling the strange mingling of frustration and exhilaration he experienced whenever she was within his reach.

"Sit down, will you?" Gwen complained. "I get the heebie-jeebies when you loom over me like that."

Dorian retreated to the far wall. "You were generous to do this on my behalf," he said.

"I told you I wasn't going to give up on you. I meant it." She stretched her arms over her head. "You can move to the boardinghouse tomorrow morning."

"And I will begin to repay you when I receive my first compensation."

"There's no hurry. I know you're good for it." She stretched again and rose, padding toward the kitchen in her stockinged feet. "I'm starved. Do you want some soup?"

Dorian hesitated, dreading the thought of sharing even closer quarters with her.

Tonight, he told himself. *Tonight, while she sleeps.*

He followed her into the kitchen.

"Who is he?"

Mitch stood over Gwen's desk, his face flushed with anger. She'd hardly ever seen him so emotional; he'd always prided himself on being in complete control of his feelings. Only lately had he begun to reveal open frustration and annoyance with her. She didn't like the results.

"I've told you all I know," she said, drawing on the rags of her patience. "I found him on the streets. He reminded me of Barry, so I decided to help him."

"You just 'found him on the streets.'"

"That's right. It was obvious that he was a doughboy who'd suffered since the War. Was helping him so wrong?"

"A doughboy? He can't be much older than you are."

"Some of them served at fifteen and sixteen."

"But you don't know anything about his past."

She shrugged. "If he can't do the job, we'll find out soon enough."

Mitch lowered his head like a bull about to charge. "What else is going on, Gwen?"

"Don't tell me you're jealous of some poor guy who doesn't have a dime to his name?"

He stared at the far wall. "Of course I'm not jealous."

"Then give him a chance. You'll hardly have to see him, anyway."

Fury boiling behind his eyes, Mitch stalked away. Gwen leaned on her elbows and rubbed at her forehead. Dorian had only been at the *Sentinel* for a few days, and Mitch had been brooding the whole time. The first night, when he'd been finishing up a story and Gwen had introduced him to Dorian, there had been a palpable hostility on his part. It was as if he'd guessed that Dorian had spent several nights at her apartment. As if he knew she'd behaved in a way that would have shocked him.

Whatever had been going through his mind, then and now, she had to admit that his instincts weren't entirely wrong. There *was* something else going on. Something that had possessed her from the moment she'd held Dorian's dying body in her arms. Something she had done her best to deny, entirely without success.

She'd felt some measure of relief when Dorian had moved out of her apartment and taken up residence with Walter, but she found herself thinking of him when she should have been concentrating on her assignments. Looking forward to the hour when he showed up for work, quiet and contained, less and less like the disturbed and antagonistic recluse she'd met at the waterfront or the man who'd so recently wanted to end his own life.

But Dorian was still dangerous, for all his willingness to carry out his humble duties. She often worked late; when he came into the office with mop and broom and dustpan, she couldn't stop watching him, the working of muscle under his corduroy trousers, the flex of his arms and shoulders. Sometimes he looked up and met her gaze, and she almost let herself believe she saw hunger in his eyes before he turned away.

That, of course, was wishful thinking. If he'd really wanted her, he'd had plenty of chances to show it. There was no doubt that he'd become a loyal friend, even affectionate in his own way. He cared enough for her to warn her, however misguidedly, about the potential dangers of her work.

But that was the limit of their relationship. Either she just wasn't his type or he'd had a bad experience with a woman before. She would bet dollars to doughnuts that he would never discuss *that* with her.

And anyway, why borrow trouble? Why make things more complicated than they already were, just because her emotions had gotten out of control? He might not be more than a passing fancy that she would outgrow in time.

Handling Mitch was difficult enough, especially since he'd stepped up his efforts to win her. Flowers waited on her desk every morning. He insisted on taking her to lunch, sacrificing his usual single-minded devotion to the pursuit of a story. She didn't have the heart to refuse. Mitch was a good man in most ways. He shouldn't have to suffer just because she'd gotten cold feet.

You'll have to break it off. But if she did it now, Mitch would think it was because of Dorian. He could get Dorian fired. She didn't dare risk igniting a war between the two men in her life.

Don't kid yourself. Dorian isn't in your life. He wants to repay a debt, that's all. You took liberties with him that you didn't have any right to take.

Whereas Dorian hadn't taken any liberties at all.

Gwen rubbed at her neck. The last thing she needed was to lose her job because she couldn't separate work from her personal life. Hewitt would love to see her fail.

Pushing both Dorian and Mitch out of her mind, she returned to her story. She fully intended to leave before Dorian arrived, but when she looked up, bleary-eyed from staring at lines of typewritten text, it was already dark. Mitch had gone, perhaps to prove his complete lack of jealousy.

Gwen threw on her coat, put on her hat and gathered up the library books she'd checked out earlier that day. The starless sky hinted at snow. The subway ride home was uneventful. She walked into her apartment with the same empty feeling she'd experienced every night since Dorian had moved out.

Shaking off her melancholy mood, she turned on the radio, changed into a pair of silk pajamas, and curled up on the sofa with a cheap novel and a cup of cocoa. It was well past midnight when she closed her eyes.

The dream was so real that she was sure she was awake. Dorian was kneeling on the floor beside the sofa, his fingers stroking her cheek. She could feel the heat of his skin, the strength of his arms, the warmth of his breath. He hardly touched her, and yet it was as if his hands were all over her body, cupping her breasts, caressing her stomach, moving lower and lower…

She jerked awake and knew at once that she wasn't alone.

"You are well, Gwen?"

Dorian stood over her, his face made more devilish than angelic in the shadows. Gwen scrambled to the corner of the sofa, her knees drawn up to her chest, her neck prickling with the electricity of his presence. She regained her composure with an effort.

"How did you get in?"

"You left the door unlocked."

"You could have knocked."

"I apologize." His eyes narrowed in a frown. "It would be wise to take more rigorous precautions for your safety."

"It's not as if there are murderers living in this building."

"Nevertheless…" He sat in the desk chair. "I didn't see you at the *Sentinel* this evening."

"Oh. Yes. I was a little tired, so I left early."

"I see." She had the distinct feeling that he didn't believe her. "Are you sure you're well?"

"I'm fine, Dorian. And you?"

"Perfectly adequate."

Laughter caught in her throat. "Such enthusiasm." She straightened her legs, pretending a casualness she didn't feel. "Is the work boring you?"

"Not at all. As you predicted, I find the physical labor advantageous."

"I'm glad." She dared to look into his face. Though he was utterly still, the intensity of his stare penetrated right down to her bones.

"It's late," she said, feigning an exaggerated yawn. "Don't you think you should get some rest?"

"I require very little."

"Well, I need my beauty sleep." She edged off the sofa and turned off the lamp on the table beside it. "Good night, Dorian."

He didn't move. "What is he to you?" he asked.

She never doubted his meaning. Mingled anger and excitment raced through her, washing away all thought of sleep. "Mitch," she said, "is an old and dear friend."

"Is he your lover?"

CHAPTER SEVEN

FOR A MOMENT GWEN couldn't find words to answer. "That's none of your business," she snapped.

He rose, grace and menace perfectly combined. "He is weak. Too weak to stand as your equal."

"You don't know anything about him."

"I've seen enough."

"You mean you've been spying on us? On me?"

"Your conversations at the office have hardly been private."

"They don't concern you."

"But they do." He moved toward her, soft as a panther. "Your suitor has made it so."

"Did he say something to you?" she asked. "Threaten to fire you?"

"Not in so many words." He held her stare. "Your suitor suffers from resentment and jealousy, does he not?"

"Does he have reason to?"

Instantly she regretted her challenge. The sensual dream of Dorian's caresses came back in all its erotic detail.

Did she really *want* to know if Dorian was jealous, too? What would she say if he came out and admitted that he cared for her, not as a friend or a savior, but as a woman?

She braced herself as Dorian came to an abrupt halt. His face had become a perfect blank.

"I wish to spare you the unhappiness of an unfortunate alliance," he said. "That is all."

His answer dropped into the pit of her stomach like an indigestible meal. "Thanks," she said, "but I don't need that kind of help."

"Surely you see that his principal desire is to control you."

"He's a man," she said. "Isn't that what men do?"

"Only those who lack the courage to attain what they want by subtler means."

"As subtle as you are right now?"

"I believe you deserve happiness, Miss Murphy. You will not find it with him."

"And you're an expert on happiness, right?"

She could have sworn he flinched, though he covered it quickly. Tongue-tied with anger and confusion, Gwen fled to her room. She closed the door and collapsed on the bed, wondering how she was ever going to get to sleep. After a few minutes she heard the front door open and close. She crawled under the covers and pulled the sheets over her head.

So he isn't jealous. Isn't that a good thing? Won't it make it easier to remind him that he's not my keeper any more than Mitch is?

With a snort of self-disgust Gwen rolled over and closed her eyes, praying she wouldn't suffer from the curse of more disturbing dreams.

DORIAN TOOK THE LONG way back to the boardinghouse. It was still a week away from the dark of the moon, yet he was restless and angry, dissatisfied with both his feeding and his conversation with Gwen.

He hadn't intended to go to her tonight. He could easily have avoided her once he'd realized that she'd left the office before he'd arrived. There were plenty of other donors from whom he might have taken the necessary blood, men and women who roamed the nighttime streets seeking amusement or less legitimate activities. None would suffer or remember his presence.

With Gwen it was different. He'd had the sense that she was aware of his touch. She'd moaned tonight while he fed, her body moving in ways that had aroused him to a state of considerable discomfort.

If he had been like Javier or Raoul, he would have taken her while she lay oblivious and vulnerable. But he was not like them. He had sacrificed the last shreds of honor that had remained to him after years as Raoul's enforcer, but he would not exploit one under his protection.

Dorian remembered Gwen's face as she asked him if Mitch Hogan had reason to be jealous. The question had startled him, and it had taken him a moment to realize what she was implying.

She'd wanted to know if he resented Mitch because of his own jealousy if he, too, wished to court her. That question had answered two questions of his own, questions that had been tormenting him for days.

He no longer had any doubts that Gwen felt a strong physical attraction to him. He could not attribute it entirely to such mundane factors as his appearance or personality; once a *strigoi* had bitten the same donor more than once, the temporary bond of desire that made the feeding pleasurable for the human could easily carry over into waking life.

Nevertheless, that particular hazard he could continue to deal with. The other was far more problematic. Gwen had finally stepped over the line of friendship and into the realm of infatuation. She had no way of knowing that the more permanent bonds his kind formed with humans would be incomprehensible to someone ignorant of them, one who thought in terms of love and marriage and a traditional human family.

Love was a word that rarely crossed *strigoi* lips, and even then with little sincerity. It was simply another means to draw a desired protégé into the vampire's sphere of influence. Some *strigoi* indulged in a perfunctory courtship, but the tie between a vampire and his protégé, unlike human marriage, could never be broken except by the death of the patron. It could last many human lifetimes. And it could be hell for the man or woman unlucky enough to fall under the spell of a cruel master or mistress.

Gwen would never accept such bondage, even one born of

real affection. If she believed she wanted Dorian's romantic attention, it was only because she didn't understand the consequences. And Dorian had no intention of explaining them to her.

I could tell you I hold you in esteem, that I find your body attractive, that I would gladly enjoy it if such a liaison meant nothing more to you than pleasure and release. But you are not one for such casual encounters, Gwen. With you there must be commitment and complete honesty. You know no other way.

And *he* knew no other way than to be what he was.

His shoes made no sound as he walked into his room. He shed his coat and hat, and went next door to look in on Walter. The old man was snoring, lying on his back with his hands folded across his chest. All lingering signs of his illness had faded.

Dorian returned to his own room, undressed, pulled back the bedcovers and sat motionless in the darkness. The state of quiet waiting was one he'd become accustomed to during his years of service. He'd often spent his spare time reading, but he'd destroyed his few books when he'd left the warehouse and had yet to replace them. He had no interest in the radio Gwen had provided, and the prospect of visiting one of the area's numerous speakeasies held no appeal.

He'd never shared the usual *strigoi* need to be surrounded by others of his own kind. The word "loneliness" hadn't been part of his vocabulary.

Even for vampires, "never" was a dangerous word.

"I thought I heard you come in."

Walter walked into the room, absently scratching at his chest. "You been to see Gwennie?" he asked.

Dorian had long since given up questioning the old man's uncanny ability to guess his thoughts. "Yes," he said.

"How is she?"

"Well."

"That's good. That's real good." Walter glanced longingly around the room, doubtless wishing that a bottle of cheap gin would magically appear. He sat at the foot of the bed. "What's eatin' you, anyways? Ain't the job any good?"

"It's perfectly acceptable."

"Is it this place, then? It ain't fancy, but it sure beats the waterfront."

"I don't disagree."

Walter rubbed at two days' growth of beard. "Well, that just leaves one thing. You like her, Dory, and you still won't admit it. That's why you're wound up like a top. Can't stop thinking about her but won't tell her how you feel."

Dorian looked into Walter's eyes, warning him with a stare generally sufficient to bring most humans to whimpering submission. "We've had this conversation before."

"And I reckon we'll keep having it until you come to your senses." The old man leaned toward Dorian. "She's a grand girl, Dory. And she's strong, or she wouldn't have gone looking for you the way she did. If you let her get away, you're a damned fool."

"I have never denied it."

Walter made a rude noise and got up, groaning as tendons popped and bones creaked. "I'm goin' back to bed. You sleep on what I told you. See if I ain't right." He ambled back into the hall.

Dorian waited ten minutes, dressed again and went outside. Half an hour's brisk walk took him to Greenwich Village and the deceptively plain building that housed Lulu's, one of Manhattan's most popular speakeasies. The doorman studied him for little more than a few seconds before opening the outer door. Dorian passed through the unremarkable storefront to the inner door, where another gatekeeper waved him into the garish, noisy room.

A pretty girl in a very short dress offered to take his coat but quickly retreated when she saw his face. Not everyone in the place responded with such obvious unease, but Lulu's patrons generally knew how to recognize an enforcer. Some of them might even have remembered his name.

Allie Chase wasn't here, of course. She and her werewolf husband had been working to end the war between the *strigoi* factions, thus far without success. Griffin Durant had managed to keep the pack out of the conflict, which was an achievement in itself, but peace was a distant prospect.

Steeling himself against a fresh wave of loneliness, Dorian continued to the bar and laid his hat on the counter. "Whiskey," he said.

The bartender abandoned the drink he was currently preparing and poured Dorian's glass, making no attempt to engage Dorian in conversation. Dorian drank. He watched the humans' heedless celebrations reflected in the mirror behind the bar, listened to their laughter and tried to imagine what it must be like to live every day as if it were your last. Mortality was never far from humans' thoughts, no matter how much they tried to ignore it.

"Another?" the bartender asked him, his voice high-pitched with nervousness. Dorian accepted a second drink, then a third. He continued without stopping until his vision began to waver. It took a great deal to make a vampire drunk. He had never experienced the condition.

"Fella should be dead, the amount he's swallowed," a voice said somewhere at the other end of the bar.

"Bet you a fiver he falls on his ass when he tries to get up."

"You're on."

Dorian swivelled on his stool, planted his feet on the ground and straightened his legs. His balance was slightly affected, but he had no difficulty in focusing on the men who had found him so amusing. He examined the two young gents in the oversized trousers dubbed "Oxford bags," selected one and advanced. Alarm flashed across the fellow's face an instant before Dorian caught him by his silk four-in-hand tie and lifted him several inches off the floor.

"You should never mock those of whom you know nothing," he said gently. "They may express their lack of appreciation in ways you don't expect."

The young man made a strangled sound. His companion started toward Dorian, took a good look at him and stopped in his tracks. Dorian let his prey dangle until the boy's face turned a mottled yellow-red and then released him.

Lulu's had fallen silent. The music and dancing had ceased. People stared, glasses half-raised. Dorian slapped money on the bar—money Gwen had given him—and walked slowly toward the hidden rear door and out into the malodorous alley. The drinking had achieved nothing. It had provided no relief. All the liquor had done was to take the fine edge off the restraint he had tried to practice every day since Raoul's death.

Tonight he'd failed. He'd seen the terror in the young man's eyes as he hung so close to death, terror Dorian had witnessed a thousand times when he'd hunted Raoul's enemies. With a twist of his hand he could have snapped the boy's neck.

Walter had suggested a quaint and naive explanation for Dorian's current mood. *"You like her, Dory, and you still won't admit it. That's why you're wound up like a top. Can't stop thinking about her but won't tell her how you feel."*

But the old man was wrong. The dark of the moon erased the inhibitions that allowed Dorian to function in a human world. But each moonless night only exaggerated what already crouched inside Dorian's soul, if soul he had. His essence remained unchanged. A killer he had been, and a killer he remained.

THE TAP ON THE DOOR was so faint that Sammael almost ignored it. Then he looked up from the invoices spread before him on the desk and sighed.

"Come in."

Vida crept into the room with a timid smile, her soft hair feathered about her face like fine black down. "I'm sorry to disturb you, Sammael," she said.

"You aren't disturbing me, my child," Sammael said, returning her smile. "Is something troubling you?"

She glanced down at her plain, flat-heeled shoes and nodded. "I...I didn't understand part of your talk today."

Sammael gestured for Vida to take a chair across from the desk. "And what part might that be?"

She met his gaze with the eagerness of a new Convert. "Micah was such a wonderful man. He spoke of peace, and freedom from darkness."

"His teachings have enabled Pax to prosper," Sammael said.

"Yes. But today…when you read from the book…" She swallowed, the delicate skin of her pale neck quivering. "Did Micah really say that anyone who doesn't join us is damned?"

Sammael folded his hands atop the desk, letting the girl see nothing of his emotions. "Does it seem a hard lesson to you, my child?" he asked gently.

"Well…" She dropped her gaze. "Yes. It doesn't sound like Micah at all."

Sammael rose and circled the desk. "When Micah died," he said, "he left to me the great burden of continuing his great work. And he told me that his teachings must be passed down with great care, so that they would not be misunderstood." He touched Vida's hair lightly. "That is why only those who have completed each stage of initiation may know all the great truths Micah discovered in his long life of prayer and meditation."

Vida twisted her hands in her lap. "You mean…there are things in the book I…we don't know anything about."

"Exactly so." He nodded approvingly and returned to his desk. "There is reason for this caution. Each step of the path requires great courage, great commitment. And as we grow within Pax, we are prepared to learn all that Micah had to teach us."

The girl was quiet for a dozen heartbeats. "I guess that means I'm not ready."

"Not for Micah's ultimate teachings, no. But you have passed the first test. You are a mediant now, and that is why you were permitted to delve deeper into Micah's thoughts on salvation."

The grandfather clock ticked against the wall behind the desk, counting out the words Vida feared to speak. At last she rose, her hands still clasped before her.

"Thank you, Brother Sammael," she said, not meeting his eyes. "I understand much better now."

"Very good, Vida. I hope you will return anytime you have such questions."

"Yes. Thank you." She slipped out of the room even more quietly than she'd come, and Sammael stared at the closed door through narrowed eyes.

Have I assuaged your doubts, Sister Vida? Is it possible that one such as you could betray me?

The absurdity of such a notion brought him to the edge of laughter. There would be no betrayals. He had taken every precaution against such a possibility. His secrets would remain secret until all were re-Converted. Or dead.

He returned to the invoices. A few minutes later his concentration was interrupted once again.

"Ah, Brother Camarion," Sammael said, setting the papers aside. "Have you news for me?"

"I have, my liege." The guard stood at parade rest, his ordinary clothing concealing his lethal abilities. "We have searched the girl's apartment, as you commanded."

"And?"

"She knows of Aadon, my liege, and has been attempting to investigate his unfortunate death."

"What else does she know?"

Camarion withdrew a folded paper from his shirt pocket and offered it to Sammael.

"We copied a note left by Eamon Murphy," he said. "It contains all the evidence we require."

With a powerful sense of anticipation, Sammael unfolded the paper. He scanned the handwritten lines to the bottom of the page.

Today a man came to see me, calling himself by the name of Aadon and claiming that he possessed invaluable details of several past murders that would open my eyes to a world hidden from all but a privileged few. He brought with him a book, which I have only just begun to read. I now have reason to believe.

"He had it," Sammael whispered. "And the girl… It must be in her possession."

Camarion stiffened to full attention. "The human left her own notes, my liege. They seem to indicate that she had not seen the book."

Sammael pounded the flat of his hand against the desk. "She must know where it is. *She must.*"

"Shall we bring her in?"

Breathing sharply through his teeth, Sammael refolded the paper. "Yes. As soon as it's possible to do so without attracting attention. And she must not be harmed."

"I understand, my liege."

"Go. Make your preparations."

"There is more, my liege." He paused as he met Sammael's gaze. "She is still seeing Dorian Black. He has been staying in her apartment."

Sammael gave Camarion such a dark look that the stoic guard quailed. "She is still human?" Sammael asked sharply.

"Yes, my liege."

Allowing himself a moment of relief, Sammael reconsidered his first reaction. In spite of what he had at first assumed, it was now evident that the connection between Black and Miss Murphy was not merely some brief encounter quickly forgotten. Their initial meeting had been unexpected, but given what Sammael knew of human weaknesses, he found it easy enough to speculate on the reasons Black and the girl had maintained their association.

With regard to purely human relationships, the explanation was simple. It would hardly be a miracle if a young, healthy female like Gwen Murphy developed a strong attraction to the man who had saved her life. Though Sammael had believed, based on the enforcer's observed behavior since Raoul's death, that Black was unlikely to take up with humans, no *strigoi* was entirely predictable in matters of lust and blood. Like most *strigoi*, Black possessed a natural charisma that drew the opposite sex. And since Black had saved the girl from drowning—a peculiar and highly uncharacteristic act in itself—he might have chosen to prolong the relationship for inexplicable reasons of his own.

Ordinarily, under such circumstances, one would expect a free vampire to Convert the object of his "affection." Apparently Black had not. It was impossible to guess what was in his mind, but Sammael knew that the enforcer had never had a protégée of his own. Perhaps he didn't relish the burden of such a bond. Sexual hunger alone might account for his continued interest, though long dalliances with humans based on lust without Conversion were uncommon.

As long as he left Miss Murphy human, Black was simply a manageable complication with regard to the planned operation. And if Sammael's agents should fail—an almost unthinkable possibility, but one he must not overlook—Black might, willingly or no, provide others ways of obtaining Miss Murphy's cooperation.

"Black must know nothing of the operation," Sammael said at last, "and he must not be harmed. Take no unnecessary risks."

Camarion saluted and backed out the door. Sammael abandoned the invoices and left his office, entering the maze of corridors that occupied the rear of the building. He descended the hidden stairs to the great hall and opened the high carved doors.

Today, as every day, the Guard were drilling, each man moving in perfect step with his fellows. Khaki shirts and trousers formed a pale block against the darkness of the hall; the captain shouted a command, and fifty young, earnest faces turned toward Sammael in salute.

Faces of boys who had been human only months ago. Young men taken off the streets, Converted by Sammael and the synod, trained to form a disciplined force honed to kill without mercy or hesitation.

And no one knew of them save the synod and master guides, whose knowledge of the true plan was complete.

Satisfied, Sammael returned to the portion of the building occupied by his civilian followers, the novices and mediants who as yet remained in ignorance. He paused to look in on a novice class, its members gazing raptly at the master guide who taught them of Micah's mercy.

Micah's mercy. Mercy they naively believed applied to all humans and *strigoi*. Those who never proved themselves worthy to progress to mediant would still serve Pax as workers and clerks; they need never look beyond their small, peaceful world. Sammael would use them as he used his agents within the factions, as he would use the Guard, to free humanity from the *strigoi* curse.

And some day they would understand. Someday it would all be told, and Sammael would take his place as one of the great saviors of mankind.

ON DORIAN'S TENTH night working at the *Sentinel,* when the offices were deserted and even Gwen had left the premises, the corpulent reporter named Randolph Hewitt came slinking into the city room with a veiled woman in tow. He cast Dorian a disdainful look, dismissed him with a sniff and led the woman into Mr. Spellman's private office.

Dorian leaned on his broom, gazing at the closed door. He could hear voices, Hewitt's deep rumble and the woman's low, more musical tones. He'd learned enough about the newspaper business to suspect it wasn't the usual practice for reporters to clandestinely bring their sources to the office at night. Yet everything about Hewitt's posture had suggested he was anxious not to let anyone else know of his actions…especially, Dorian suspected, if they pertained to the waterfront murders.

Shifting his grip on the broom, Dorian swept cigarette butts and crumpled paper into a neat pile. By tacit agreement, he and Gwen had avoided each other as much as possible, even when she worked late. But Dorian always had some time to himself, during which he glanced through Gwen's work seeking evidence that she'd made progress on the cult story. From all appearances, she'd found little new information to support her father's theory.

She would certainly be interested to learn if Hewitt's behavior tonight had something to do with the story they were both pursuing. And so would Dorian.

He casually worked his way closer to the office, pausing here and there to empty an ashtray or dustbin. The voices behind the door grew more distinct. It took him several minutes of intense listening before he recognized the woman's voice—and the danger.

He was just beginning to withdraw when the door opened and the woman walked out, followed by Hewitt. She paused in the act of pulling her lace veil over her face, staring at Dorian as if at a ghost.

"If you'll come this way, Miss Romana," Hewitt said nervously.

"Of course," she murmured. Without a second glance at Dorian, she preceded Hewitt from the room. Dorian quickly finished his work, gathered up his supplies and strode down the hall to the janitor's closet.

"Dorian."

He almost didn't stop, but the firm tap of her heels told him that she wouldn't be put off. He turned to face her.

"Dorian," she repeated, pushing the veil away from her face again. "I couldn't believe it when I saw you. What in hell are you doing here?"

Carefully Dorian pushed his cart to the wall and returned her gaze. "How have you been, Romana?"

"Obviously a lot better than you." Her frown drew a faint line between her arched black brows.

"This is hardly the best place for a conversation."

She ignored his warning. "You were the best of the best," she said. "You could have named your price after Raoul died. Kyril would have made you a lieutenant, at the very least, perhaps even a full vassal. And yet here you are—"

"Is Kyril your liege now?"

"Yes. And he'll win. Christof hasn't a chance." She shook her head. "You haven't answered my question. What are you, of all people, doing playing the menial in a newspaper office?"

Dorian knew then that he couldn't distract her any longer. He already suspected why she was there, and if he was right, he had to be very careful indeed. Careful not to mention to Gwen… unless he could get Romana to do it herself.

He shrugged. "You would not believe me if I told you."

"Try me."

"I required funds to keep myself alive."

She laughed, a burst of startled sound. "Keep you alive? When you could be part of things again, with your own people?" She waved a contemptuous hand, indicating the cart with its bucket, mops and brooms. "That's no reason, Dorian. Not one that anyone would believe."

"Then believe this. I am done with serving masters who take pleasure in killing for its own sake."

Her eyes widened. "Are you crazy?" She touched his arm. "Maybe Raoul didn't treat you as well as he should have. It will be different with Kyril. All you have to do—"

"I have no intention of going back."

She stared, comprehension dawning on her face. "Are you actually feeling guilty for serving your master so well?"

"I take no pride in my previous life."

"And that's why you're here? Punishing yourself? Vladimir's balls, Dorian, guilt and regret are for breeders, not for us."

Dorian pulled the cart away from the wall and wrapped his hand around the broom handle. "Why are you here, Romana? Surely it wasn't to find me."

"You've done a good job of hiding yourself, Dorian. I don't think anyone knows you're still alive." She glanced toward the office where she had spoken with Hewitt. "You can bet I wouldn't be here talking to that grotesque pig of a man if there wasn't a very good reason." She showed the edges of her teeth. "Kyril sent me. It seems Hewitt has been conducting some kind of investigation that might lead him a little too close to finding us. I was to pose as an informer and offer information that would draw him off the scent."

"You're referring to the waterfront murders?" Dorian took a step toward her. "What madness prompted Kyril's men to leave bloodless bodies where humans could find them?"

"*We* had nothing to do with it."

"It was clearly the work of *strigoi*."

"Christof's work."

"He never struck me as stupid."

She lifted one shoulder. "It doesn't matter who did it. What matters are the consequences."

"So it's Hewitt Kyril is worried about?"

She studied his face. "Is there someone else involved in the investigation?"

Dorian realized he'd skirted far too close to the truth. "I'm not privy to the reporters' work, and I don't read their articles."

"How did you get the job?"

"I found it listed in the advertising section."

"The great Dorian Black, reduced to reading ads." She studied his face. "You've kept yourself at least somewhat informed. You could be useful to us, even if you stay here."

"No."

She seemed to take his refusal in stride. "All right. But keep my offer in mind. I'm sure Kyril would welcome you at any time." She turned to leave and stopped. "By the way, it might interest you to know that your former partner is missing and presumed dead."

"Javier?"

"He'd been doing very well for Kyril, moving up the ranks. Then he went off on some private errand and just vanished." She snapped her fingers in emphasis. "I never like Javier anyway. Your method was always so much more subtle. And effective."

"I have work to do, Romana."

"And we wouldn't want to keep you from your new profession." Her good humor melted away like candy coating on a bullet. "Just remember, Dorian. The hunt is in your blood. You'll never escape what you are, no matter how much you try to hide." She spun on her high heels and walked away. "You'll come back to us sooner or later. And when you do, be sure you choose the right side."

The sound of her footsteps receded until it was replaced by

welcome silence. The broom handle cracked like a matchstick in Dorian's fist.

She didn't know about Gwen's part in the investigation. Or, if she did, she hadn't thought her worth mentioning. Nor had she shown any signs of being aware that Dorian had formed a relationship with any human at the paper.

For the time being, Gwen was still safe. Even if Kyril eventually learned about her, he was evidently being cautious in his approach, recognizing his vulnerability and undoubtedly less than eager to bring more attention down on the clan with the commitment of additional murders, however traditional.

No, he wouldn't make a deadly move unless every other method failed. And he would consider an established male reporter of far greater concern than a rookie female who wasn't taken seriously by her own peers.

Dorian withdrew a handkerchief from his pocket and blotted at the sweat on his forehead. They had time. Weeks, at the very least, perhaps longer. And a great deal could happen in a few—

"Is it true?"

Gwen's voice shocked him out of the black place in his mind. Her face was flushed, her voice brittle with accusation. And he knew she had overheard what he would have given his life to keep from her.

IT COULDN'T BE.

Even before the question left Gwen's mouth she could not quite believe it, just as she couldn't believe the things the woman named Romana had said. The things Dorian had admitted.

No enforcer was more feared or respected than you, Dorian.

She braced herself, meeting Dorian's gaze without flinching. "Is it true?" she repeated. "Did you work for Raoul Boucher?"

He remained behind the cart as if he feared an attack. Dorian Black, who wasn't afraid of anything.

"How much did you hear?" he asked quietly.

"You were one of Raoul's enforcers," she said, the words sticking in her throat.

The muscles in his jaw bulged and flexed. "Yes."

"You…killed people."

He didn't answer, but the look in his eyes was the same one she'd seen so many times at the warehouse and in her apartment. Pain. Shame hidden beneath a cold mask, behind words of warning she had chosen to disregard.

"Raoul," she said. "One of the worst. A cold-blooded murderer."

"Raoul is dead."

"And that makes a difference?"

"No."

His taciturnity only increased her anger. "Why didn't you tell me? Did you think I'd have turned my back on the man who saved my life?"

"I would not expect you to do otherwise."

"But you—you let me think—" She stopped, sickened by her own dishonesty. *You wouldn't listen. He tried to tell you in his own way, but you wouldn't believe.*

"I don't understand," she said, her thoughts spinning out of control. "How could a man like you…hurt people for money?"

"It was never for—" He closed his eyes. "I have no excuse to offer you, Gwen. None."

She leaned against the wall, too weak with shock to trust her balance. She'd always known there was something terrible in Dorian's past that he refused to share. She'd assumed it was the War. She'd been horribly wrong.

"It can't have been very long," she said, trying to convince herself. "How long did you work for Raoul? Five years? Six?" She raked her fingers through her hair. "When did it start, Dorian? What made you become one of them?"

Dorian seemed about to answer, but thought better of it. Not a flicker of emotion showed on his face.

"I'm trying to understand," she said. "You told that woman that you were done serving masters who killed for the pleasure of it."

"Yes."

"And she offered you a job with one of the bosses fighting for Raoul's territory, but you turned her down."

"Yes."

"I know what mob enforcers are like, what they do. People don't just change overnight without a reason. What changed you?"

He only shook his head. Gwen's heart slammed against her ribs. "You went to live as a hermit on the waterfront. I've always heard that the bootleggers keep close tabs on former employees, if they let anyone leave at all. But that woman didn't seem to know where you'd been. Were you afraid someone would come after you? Someone who didn't want one of Raoul's men running loose and unaccounted for during the middle of a gang war?"

"I had nothing to fear from the factions squabbling over Raoul's leavings."

"Then why? Do you really feel…are you really sorry?"

"I cannot undo the past."

"But that woman was right, wasn't she? You've been punishing yourself. Living on the docks with barely enough to keep you alive. Almost dying…" The image of him lying in that filthy room in Hell's Kitchen nearly overwhelmed her. She couldn't seem to reconcile the memory of Dorian's tormented, dying body with the thought of him gunning down some poor chump who'd run afoul of Raoul's vicious mob.

"You saved my life," she said. "A killer, a man without a conscience, wouldn't have bothered."

She realized at once that she wasn't asking him to explain. She was trying to convince herself. *I can't have been so wrong. Not about him.*

Oh, but she could have. He'd said he didn't know anything about the murders, but he did. He'd even guessed who committed them.

She straightened, half of her longing to go to him, while the other half recoiled. "I think we'd better go into the city room."

Gwen passed him without touching him, not waiting to see

if he followed. The city room was dark; she grabbed the nearest desk chair, turned on the lamp and sat down. Dorian came through the door and paused on the threshold, as if waiting for her permission to enter.

"I'm still not afraid of you," she said, trying to make herself believe it.

"I would not hurt you, Gwen."

She picked out a pencil from the mug on the desk and rubbed it between her fingers. "No. You did everything possible to warn me away, didn't you? You didn't want me to find out what you'd been."

He merely bowed his head, as if he knew she would find her own answers. She remembered his copy of *Dante's Inferno* and the conversation that had followed. *I believe in the possibility of redemption,* she'd told him.

This was her test. A test of her sincerity—or her hypocrisy.

And of her feelings for this man, who had gone so far to protect her from enemies he knew were real.

Her eyes burned with tears she didn't dare let loose. "I believe," she said, her voice catching, "I believe…whatever you may have done, however many sins you've committed…I believe you really want to atone."

He still wouldn't meet her eyes. Shame, guilt, remorse. She could read the emotions in his immobile face, see them in the posture of his body. But she also saw blood…the blood of those three men who had lain, white and still, on the waterfront.

You have to try, she told herself. She faced Dorian and looked into his face. "What if there was a way for you to really make up for your past?" she asked.

His shoulders twitched. "How?" he asked softly.

"By helping me expose the monsters who killed those people at the waterfront."

Her heart sank when he finally raised his head. "I don't know who did it," he said, expressionless.

"But you had a good idea. You knew it had to be one of the factions led by Raoul's former lieutenants."

"You can do nothing about this, Gwen."

"You're wrong, Dorian. We both can." She felt courage begin to seep back into her, channeled through the pencil in her hand, as if the practical requirements of her profession could erase the doubt and the horror. "That woman—Romana—said her boss had sent her to provide false information that would throw Hewitt off the scent. She was afraid he'd expose the truth. But she denied that her faction had anything to do with the murders."

"Yes."

"In that case, why would she be so anxious to impede his investigation? If Kyril's rival were responsible, wouldn't it benefit him if another mob was implicated?"

"So it would seem."

She tossed the pencil down in frustration. "I'm tired of this dissembling, Dorian," she said coldly. "Either you're honest with me or we don't have anything else to talk about."

Dorian leaned his hand on the nearest desk and stared at the scuffed floor. "What do you wish to know?"

"What is *strigoi?*"

He stiffened ever so slightly. "It is a word the warring factions sometimes use to describe themselves."

"But what does it mean?"

"I don't know."

He was lying. Gwen wasn't in any doubt of that.

"All right. What did Romana mean by 'breeders'?"

"The gangs have contempt for those they exploit."

And that's *no explanation,* Gwen thought. "I can see we're not going to get anywhere tonight," she said. "But you can still help me, Dorian. Help me bring the bad guys to justice."

"You won't find this cult your father was seeking."

"Maybe not. Maybe Kyril or Christof or whoever did this is just a gangster trying a new method of intimidation. But I still think law and order is something worth fighting for, especially if it means ending the violence."

"Not at the price of your life."

A sudden chill caught her unaware. "You really think they'd go from planting false leads to killing someone?"

"It has been known to happen in the past."

She got up and shoved the chair back under the desk. "I'm going to take the risk that whoever ordered the hits won't want to give the cops more to go on by murdering a reporter. And my life isn't that important compared to others who might be saved if I'm successful."

He gazed into her eyes, holding her captive with the uncanny power of his stare. "It is important to me."

Oh, God. "If that's true, then help me. Or are you refusing because you want to protect your former colleagues?"

His jaw clenched, and she knew how unjust she'd been in accusing him. But she couldn't let herself soften now. She was dealing with a man who was teetering on the edge of damnation.

"Hewitt won't stop, you know," she said at last. "He may think that he's received new and useful information, but if it's wrong, he'll find out eventually."

"Do you intend to tell him what you overheard?"

Gwen knew very well that she should. But if Hewitt went off on the wrong track, she would have more time to pursue an accurate course without interference.

"Telling him would put him in more danger, wouldn't it?"

"Yes."

"Even though Romana claims her boss has nothing to hide?"

"Even so." He advanced, shedding his diffidence and humility like an unfamiliar garment. "You must forget that you ever saw or heard Romana."

"You know I can't do that."

"You can. Stop this now, Gwen."

"I don't take orders, not even from ex-enforcers."

"You may discover more than you ever wanted to find."

"At least I'll be working for the greater good, not slaughtering people for money."

He jerked back as if she'd reached across the desk and slapped him. "Believe what you wish," he said hoarsely, "but heed my warning. Forget what you heard tonight." He turned for the door. "Good night, Gwen."

"Dorian…"

But he was already walking out the door, and she couldn't bring herself to run after him.

She pulled out the chair again and slumped into it, all the fight gone out of her. She'd said things to Dorian that had come out of shock, hurt and frustration, not factual knowledge. As strange as it seemed, she had actually managed to hurt him. He really did want to protect her from people he knew would stop at nothing to conceal their secrets.

And what if he was right? What if she really did discover more than she expected to find? The murders didn't have to be the work of some hypothetical cult. There were plenty of corrupt politicians in Manhattan, not to mention whole police precincts that had been bought and paid for by racketeers and bootleggers. The faces of the victims had been too damaged for positive identification. Maybe they weren't just simple gang victims at all.

If he was certain of any of that, he would have told me. He would have told me.

Gwen laid her cheek on her folded arms. It would be so easy to let herself become paralyzed by what she'd learned tonight. Easy to just give up and return to her safe and ordinary assignments.

But she'd told Dorian she wouldn't back down, and she'd meant it. Sitting quietly in a corner shivering with fear wasn't something her father would have done, and she wouldn't do it, either.

She gathered her coat, hat and scarf, turned off the lamp and hurried for the door. She walked briskly for several blocks and paused at the foot of the wide stone stairs that led to the heavy oak doors of St. Albert's Church.

The nave was quiet, populated by a few men and women offering prayers for loved ones or asking God's favor in their own lives. Votive candles glowed on a table to the side of the pews, and benevolent saints gazed down from the stained-glass windows.

Gwen crossed herself, pulled her scarf over her hair and found an empty pew. She sat for a while gazing at the cross hanging behind the altar.

Tell me what to do, she pleaded. *I want to trust him. I want to forgive....*

"Miss Murphy," a deep voice said. She straightened and looked into the face of a man in a dark cassock. "Welcome. It's been some time since we've seen you here."

Gwen rose. "I know. I'm sorry, Father."

"No need to apologize." He gestured for her to sit again and joined her on the bench. "What trouble brings you here tonight, Gwen?"

"Is it so obvious?"

Father Sullivan smiled. "An occupational advantage."

Gwen heard the gentle invitation in Father Sullivan's voice and almost poured out the story...not only her doubts and fears, but everything she'd learned about Dorian. Only a reporter's carefully cultivated instinct to protect her sources stopped her.

"I guess..." she began hesitantly, "I guess I need to know something about forgiveness."

"Ah. A very weighty subject." Sullivan stretched with a sigh. "Is it yourself who feels the need to be forgiven?"

Gwen started. "No. I mean..." She swallowed. "I guess we all need that, Father."

"Would you prefer to come to confession?"

"I guess what I really want to do is talk."

"Then talk we shall." He looked into her eyes. "Tell me."

She spoke then, not of Dorian, but of a hypothetical man she knew who had committed possibly horrendous crimes and was unable to believe he could be redeemed.

"And you doubt that atonement is possible?" Sullivan asked.

Words clumped in her throat as if they didn't want to be spoken. "I once told him I believed in redemption," she said. "I thought I believed it."

"What has changed your mind?"

"I keep thinking about the things he's done."

"He has told you what these things are?"

"No."

"Yet you feel qualified to judge him."

She clasped her hands on the back of the pew in front of her. "I...don't know, Father. He's done good things, too. He saved my life. But is that enough?"

"Enough to earn forgiveness?" He covered her hand with his. "You know that God will forgive even the worst sins if the penitent is sincere. Has your friend ever been to confession?"

"To be honest, Father, I don't know if he's ever seen the inside of a church."

"Perhaps it would do him good."

"You're probably right. But I don't think he can be convinced very easily."

Father Sullivan nodded in sympathy. "There is often only so much we can do to help those who suffer most, unless they are willing to help themselves."

Gwen dropped her face into her hands. "How can he do that when even I can't seem to forgive him?"

"Is it your duty to do so?"

"I..." She shook her head. "I told him I'd never turn my back on him."

"You must feel very deeply for this man."

Feel deeply? Yes, she did. She felt...

"Dear God," she said.

"What is it, my child?"

I love him.

"Are you all right?"

Gwen looked up at the priest. "Yes, Father. I'm fine."

As fine as anyone could be under the circumstances...anyone who'd never been in love before. Maybe what the poets called love wasn't the overwhelming ecstasy they claimed it to be. Maybe it was more like a poison, seeping insidiously into your veins until it was too late to take the cure.

The heaviness of exhaustion pressed mercilessly down on Gwen's shoulders. She couldn't think straight, not now. She had to sleep on it, let the shock drain out of her system.

And then you'll have to decide. Decide if you can love a man who is everything you thought you hated.

DORIAN DIDN'T RETURN to work the next night or the night after. He walked the streets, his thoughts twisting and coiling in on themselves, finding no answers. The dark of the moon arrived; he stayed away from the boardinghouse and hid in the shadows, racked by convulsions and tormenting visions of Gwen, her beautiful, honest eyes filled with mingled horror and disbelief.

When it was over, he wandered aimlessly from one end of Manhattan to the other, feeding just enough to keep himself alive. At the end of the week he emerged from his day's shelter, summoned his courage and started for Gwen's apartment.

No one answered his knock. He forced his way in. She wasn't there. He left the building and was halfway to the *Sentinel* offices when the strident cries of the corner newsboy shattered his preoccupation.

"Extra! Extra! Girl reporter found slain in Broadway alley! No witnesses! Presumed to be gangland hit!"

Dorian's feet stopped before he fully understood what he had heard. The world wobbled to a halt. He staggered toward the newsboy and seized him by his dirty collar.

"What girl?" he rasped. "What was her name?"

The boy wriggled free. "Here, mister!" he said, thrusting a paper into Dorian's hands. "Read it for yourself!"

Dorian raised the paper, forcing his eyes to focus. Headlines screamed their fatal decree. Newsprint fluttered from Dorian's nerveless fingers.

Gwen Murphy, girl reporter, was dead.

CHAPTER EIGHT

DORIAN STARED UP at the hotel window, watching the shadows of his enemies moving back and forth behind the drawn curtains.

Kyril crouched in his hotel suite like a venomous spider, manipulating each thread of his ever-expanding web as he worked to consolidate power over the fragmented clan. His evil hadn't moved Dorian to emerge from retirement. Dorian had told Gwen and Romana the truth when he'd said he wanted no part of the war. It was no longer his concern.

Until they'd killed her.

A rational man might protest that he had no proof. He had actually believed that Kyril would hesitate to harm Hewitt, let alone Gwen, of whom Romana seemed to know nothing.

But Kyril was the one who'd sent his agent to lead Hewitt astray. Of the two faction leaders, he was the most violent and unpredictable. Somehow, while Dorian had wallowed in his own pain, Kyril had learned of Gwen's investigation. She had done something to provoke him into a reckless act, asked the wrong questions.

Or Romana had been lying to him, and they had been watching Gwen all along.

Dorian shifted his weight, as if a change of position could ease the pressure in his chest. He had patiently observed the comings and goings of Kyril's enforcers for a week, moving from his position across the street only when daylight compelled his withdrawal. Several times he saw Romana, swathed in furs as she carried out her master's errands, or dripping in diamonds as she and Kyril's favorites went out for a night of hunting and pleasure.

Once Kyril himself ventured from his lair, his sycophants swarming around him like flies on a corpse.

He would not be easy to kill. Dorian knew he himself wouldn't survive the attempt. It didn't matter. He had been prepared to die long before this moment. Now death was his second most powerful desire.

The first was to make Kyril pay.

One last time, Dorian reviewed his observations. He knew precisely when Kyril was most apt to be vulnerable, when the number of bodyguards would be at a minimum. Most of his men returned from their sinister labors just before dawn; there was hardly any movement during the very early hours of the morning. Kyril was obviously confident that none of Christof's followers would dare attempt to penetrate his headquarters.

Chances were good that Kyril thought in terms of an organized attack rather than a lone assassin. *Strigoi* seldom acted as independent individuals; it was the vampire way that each member of a band or clan was intimately connected to his or her fellows by bonds of loyalty and blood. In that respect they were not dissimilar to the werewolves with whom they resentfully shared the city.

Kyril certainly wouldn't be expecting an assault from a former enforcer who had cast off all physical and emotional ties that had bound him to the clan.

Dorian climbed out from among the crates he shared with a motley assortment of bums and hobos. The sun had already set; the street was busy with office girls and businessmen hurrying home from work, while less conventional types rose, like *strigoi,* from their beds to begin another night's carousing. One of the vagrants who lived in the alley staggered past Dorian, a bottle of rotgut cradled in his arms, and collapsed against the wall. A policeman paced out his beat. Giggling flappers in scanty dresses tramped past, their oversized galoshes flapping with every step.

Hours passed. Dorian had no need to consult a watch; he knew when the time had finally come. He checked the two revolvers nestled under his arms and the long, heavy knife sheathed at the small of his back. The drunkards and tramps in the alley behind him grew quiet. Even the cops had disappeared.

Dorian crept from his shelter. Those humans still on the streets—petty criminals, delivery boys, handsome gentlemen and beautiful women returning to their expensive hotel rooms—paid him no attention. He straightened, letting all the tension drain from his muscles. He would cross the street like any ordinary man intent on his own very ordinary business. The *strigoi* guards in the hotel lobby might recognize his face, but not until it was too late.

He stepped from the curb.

"Think again, my friend."

Instantly his hand was on the handle of his gun. The vampire behind him remained still, her breathing light and steady.

"I mean you no harm," she said. "I wish only to save you from a fate you do not deserve."

"Who are you?"

"I'll be happy to explain, but not here."

Dorian backed away from the street, moving past the woman so that he could see her clearly. She wore a plain cape, its hood pulled up over her head. Her face was piquant and beautiful, and strands of golden hair spilled over her forehead.

"Do you work for Kyril?" Dorian demanded.

"Hardly."

"Then Christof sent you."

"No. My people take no sides." She reached for his arm. "Come with me. Everything will be explained."

He gripped the gun more tightly. "I haven't completed my business here."

"The business of death. You are an expert at such work, Dorian Black. But killing is not the answer."

"If you believe that, you should leave."

"Not without you." She closed long, pale fingers around his wrist. "You have a greater purpose than revenge, my friend. One that can bring peace to the city. Isn't that what Miss Murphy would have wanted?"

Dorian's vision dimmed with rage. He twisted his arm free, seized the woman by her shoulder and spun her back into the alley.

"How do you know about Gwen?" he snapped. "How do you know what she would have wanted?"

The woman's face softened with sympathy, an expression as alien to most *strigoi* as sobriety was to the men in the alley. "I know it was a terrible loss," she said. "We have been watching you for some time, hoping to approach you when the time was right. We would never have interfered with your friendship. It was a source of inspiration to all of us."

"Watching me?" He gave her a shake. "Why? Do you know who killed Gwen?"

"No." She held his gaze, unflinching. "Your assumption that Kyril is behind her murder is understandable. No one could blame you for wanting revenge against those responsible. But killing a few *strigoi* will not end the violence that takes so many innocent lives. The change must come from within, from those who are willing to set aside old loyalties and hatreds in the service of a greater good."

Something in the woman's voice, in her quiet sincerity, penetrated Dorian's fury. He released her and dropped his hands. She pushed the hood away from her face.

"You have no reason to trust me," she said. "You have spent your life hunting and being hunted, surviving by regarding every creature not of your blood as an enemy. But that time is at an end, Dorian. We can offer you a new path, one that will make it possible for you to atone for your evil deeds."

He laughed. "At what price?"

"A price far less terrible than the one you have already paid. You will use your skills for the betterment of all *strigoi* and the protection of those on whom they prey."

Dorian glanced across the street. He still had time to finish what he had started. Kyril deserved to die. But the woman's words had reached into a part of him he had thought long dead. The part Gwen had just begun to reawaken.

"Who are you?" he asked.

"We are like you, *strigoi* who have chosen not to align our-selves with either faction. Who prefer peace to war, compassion to cruelty." She smiled, radiant as any creature of the light. "My name is Angela. I ask only that you come with me. Speak to our leaders. If you do not agree with our purpose, we will not hold you." She pulled the hood back over her lustrous hair. "Come, my friend. Come and be saved."

DORIAN WAS HARDLY prepared when Angela took him directly to the waterfront. The building to which she led him was one he had seen many times and dismissed as only one more of the numerous establishments that flourished along the dockside streets: a four-story, late nineteenth-century brick edifice with the bold sign Atlantic Imports hung above the doors. The hour was early enough that there was as yet little activity on the docks, but once Angela ushered him into the marble-floored lobby, Dorian saw at once that business must be prosperous indeed. A bank of elevators stood at one side of the lobby, and a large ebony desk took pride of place in the center.

A uniformed security guard rose from behind the desk with a pleasant greeting for Angela and a nod for Dorian. He passed them through an imposing door at the back of the lobby, which opened into a well-lit corridor.

The main hallway was punctuated by a good dozen doors and branched off into numerous smaller corridors, none of which Angela chose as she continued on to the end of the hall. There a highly polished pair of double ebony doors led into a waiting room furnished with comfortable chairs, potted plants and tables stacked with the latest popular magazines.

A modestly dressed young woman sat behind a desk facing the door. She stood with a smile, showing the tips of her pointed incisors.

"Angela." Her gaze focused on Dorian. "And this must be Mr. Dorian Black."

"Yes." Angela took Dorian's arm and coaxed him farther into

the room. "I was fortunate to find him just at the right time. Dorian, this is Vida."

Dorian inclined his head. "How do you do."

"Very well, thank you." Vida beamed at the room in general. "You'll want to see Sammael right away. Will you follow me?"

Dorian resisted Angela's tug. "Who is Sammael?"

"Our leader." She exchanged glances with Vida. "I assure you, you have nothing to fear."

Having come so far, Dorian saw no benefit in refusing to continue. He followed Angela and Vida through the rear door and into a slightly smaller room furnished with a large marble-topped desk, walls lined with bookshelves and a large free-standing globe. The man at the desk was handsome, his hair going gray at the temples and his posture erect but relaxed. He, too, smiled when he saw Dorian, though his expression was much more reserved.

"Mr. Black, I presume," he said, rising to extend his hand. "I have been looking forward to this meeting."

Dorian regarded the outstretched hand. It wasn't a common form of greeting among *strigoi,* but the gesture seemed harmless enough. He grasped the man's wrist and quickly released it.

"Mr. Sammael, I presume," he said.

"Sammael. We have no surnames here."

That, at least, was not an uncommon custom among *strigoi.* As a rule, members of a clan only used "family" names when dealing with humans unfamiliar with the existence of vampires.

Dorian glanced around the room, noting the window behind the desk and calculating the distance to the door. He subtly positioned himself closer to the exit.

"I don't remember hearing your name mentioned in the clan," he said in a neutral voice.

"You wouldn't have. You see, I only arrived in Manhattan a year ago, and I kept a low profile, as one might say." He nodded to Angela and Vida. "These young ladies were protégées of Raoul's vassals. I doubt you would have met them."

"But we heard your name. Often," Angela said.

"That is why we've asked you to come," Sammael said. "Your

unique skills could be of immense value to our work. The work of peace." He moved around the desk, walking alongside the shelves and running his fingers over the spines of the books displayed there. "Do you know the history of the *strigoi,* Dorian? Our people have shared this world with humans for thousands upon thousands of years. Perhaps once we shared a common ancestor. We shall never know."

"What has this to do with me?"

"We of Pax believe that it is the responsibility of *strigoi* to live in harmony with humanity."

Dorian digested Sammael's incredible statement with surprise and skepticism. *Pax.* The Latin word for peace. He had heard of pacifist organizations before, all founded by humans. The idea that *strigoi* would do such a thing was almost beyond belief.

"Perhaps I can begin to answer your questions by explaining the foundation for our beliefs," Sammael said, as if he'd heard Dorian's thoughts. "Long before the first vampires joined forces to ensure their own survival, *strigoi* recognized that they could not wantonly destroy human lives. If they did so, they would ensure their own extinction." He moved to the globe and spun it gently. "But this position has been one of practicality, not of morality. For too long our leaders, both here and throughout the world, have regarded humanity as cattle to be used and, if necessary, discarded."

Dorian folded his hands behind his back, feeling the knife under his coat. "Humans far outnumber *strigoi.*"

"Yes. But only look at what is happening now in Manhattan. The factions have been waging a vicious war to claim control of the clan and the vampires left leaderless by Raoul's death. Innocent humans have been caught in the cross fire. Thus far the police and politicians have failed to take much note of the increase in violent deaths, but that situation will not hold forever. As long as we *strigoi* fight among ourselves and continue to regard humans as unimportant casualties, our race will be in danger." He rested his fist on the desk. "Our only answer, our only hope of salvation, is to end this war and accept a new way.

The way of humility. The way of compassion. The way of peace."

His voice cracked on the final words. Dorian examined Sammael's face. His eyes shone with sincerity, as frank and guileless as those of the most naive human.

"I know," Sammael continued, "that you are unaccustomed to thinking in terms of peace and compromise. Your entire world was one of violence. But it need not always be so, my friend." He raised an open hand. "You lost one who was important to you…a human who fell prey to *strigoi* savagery."

Suspicion hummed under Dorian's skin. "How do you know about her?"

"We have made it our business to monitor all currently un-affiliated *strigoi* in Manhattan," he said. "There are many more than you might suppose, now that no one master has control. We know where each man or woman resides, and with whom he or she associates. We learned of your friendship with Miss Murphy and naturally took an interest in it, as it so perfectly embodied our goals at Pax."

"Did you know she was in danger?"

"Our knowledge of her was limited to what we observed from a distance. If we had been aware that either of you were targets of the factions, we would have intervened."

Intervened. As if this passionate but possibly insane man could hope to stop a *strigoi* killer with words of peace.

"I see you doubt," Sammael said. "Perhaps you wonder how many *strigoi* could subscribe to such a radical philosophy as ours." He gestured, indicating the room and everything beyond it. "This building houses over one hundred committed individuals who have given up the old ways, some from Manhattan and others who have come to assist us in creating the foundations for a new way."

Dorian had to admit that Sammael's claims were possible. When the clan had fallen apart, not every vampire had joined the factions. Many had been set free by Raoul's death and had chosen not to give up that freedom to serve another master.

Some of those men and women might very well have been attracted to the idea of a different kind of family, one based not on fear but benevolence. If an enforcer could see the need for change, others could, as well.

Sammael obviously commanded great respect among his followers, at least those few Dorian had met. He appeared to present a different model of leadership. But were his disciples willing converts?

"Am I to assume that you control this…organization?"

"*Control* is a violent word, Dorian. I lead, I advise, I attempt to inspire. Work such as ours requires planning and care, so that no lives will be lost. We do not underestimate the skill and stubbornness of those we wish to change." He held Dorian's gaze, and even Dorian could feel his charisma. "Miss Murphy's death need not have been in vain. You can help us make certain of that."

"How?"

Sammael's relaxed facade gave way to a sober intensity. "Both factions are eager to attract experienced enforcers to bolster their armies. We at Pax have begun exploiting this need by recruiting former clan members who have come to believe in our cause. We have been sending our men to infiltrate both factions and gain the trust of their leaders so that we may eventually compel them to meet for negotiation."

"Compel them?" Dorian laughed shortly. "Have you an army to work this miracle?"

"Mere numbers seldom guarantee a victory," Sammael said quietly. "We have conviction on our side. Conviction and the knowledge that what we propose will save not only our people but end the needless killing that makes us no better than animals."

"And once you achieve this truce?"

"We will propose a new form of government for the *strigoi* of this city, one that does not rely on the leadership of the most ruthless. Protégés will be created only with the willing participation of the chosen humans. All will have a voice. In time we shall reveal ourselves to humanity and use our unique strengths to better the world we share with them." He gazed at the far wall as if he saw projected upon it the future he so clearly envisioned. "We can be so much more than we are, Dorian. So much more."

Dorian glanced at Angela and Vida. They were gazing at Sammael as if he were a god descended to earth, their expressions rapt. There was no doubt that they believed everything he had said.

"When did you formulate this philosophy?" he asked.

"We follow the teachings of a *strigoi* who went by the name of Micah. He was a very wise man who came to enlightenment at the end of the last century." Sammael paused. "We, unlike Micah, are not perfect. Convincing others to join us has not always been easy. There have been many false starts, many mistakes. But we have persevered. Our way is the right one. That knowledge gives us the courage we require." He smiled again. "I realize that you must have time to think over what I've told you. You may also have additional questions. I or one of my aides will be glad to answer at length."

He gestured to Vida, who slipped from the room. "I would ask that you remain with us for a day or two, so that you'll have the chance to speak to others in our group. Let them tell you their stories." He noticed Dorian's wary posture. "I see that you're reluctant to place yourself in the hands of strangers. Rest assured that you may choose your own room—we have several vacancies—and retain your weapons."

"And if I wish to leave?"

"You may do so, of course. Though we hope you won't choose to pursue a course of revenge." He resumed his seat behind the desk. "Angela will show you the rooms. When you're ready, she'll give you a tour of our headquarters." He tapped a pencil against the desktop. "I should warn you that *strigoi* are not the only residents. We have a number of humans who've joined us, and who willingly provide sustenance for those who are unable to venture outside."

"Then you haven't given up hunting."

"We prefer to view it as a temporary measure to maintain our bodies until another method can be found. Once humans learn that we mean them no harm, they are often able to overcome their natural fear and distaste for the process."

"They're very brave," Angela said. "We aspire to be just like them."

After urging Dorian to choose one of the unoccupied and plainly furnished bedrooms on the third floor, Angela took him to a spacious common room on the second floor, where a score of vampires and humans spoke quietly among themselves. They looked up with smiles and words of greeting when Angela introduced him. There was no indication that the humans felt in the least uncomfortable. The free humans employed by the former clan as servants, domestics and handymen, as well as collaborators in the racketeering business, had always gone about their business with fear in their eyes.

"There's someone I want you to meet," Angela said. She led Dorian to a gangly young vampire with auburn hair and deceptively innocent blue eyes. "Dorian, this is Nathaniel. He was chief enforcer for the *strigoi* master in Chicago. When Sammael appeared in Chicago to spread the word of peace, Nathaniel left his old life behind and joined us."

Nathaniel grinned and extended his hand. "Welcome, Dorian."

"I'm sure you two will have a lot to talk about," Angela said. "If you need anything, Dorian, just ask. We all work together."

She left the room. Nathaniel gestured for Dorian to sit in the chair opposite his.

"So you just arrived," the young vampire said, stretching out his legs to reveal a length of garish argyle sock. "Must be quite a shock. It was to me the first time I got a good look at what Sammael was planning."

Dorian noted that the other groups scattered around the room had resumed their conversations. None of the men appeared to be armed.

"You can relax," Nathaniel said. "No one packs heat at headquarters." He laced his hands over his lean stomach. "I've heard of you. The name Dorian was a legend even in Chicago. When I was Converted and recruited to Karl's band of enforcers, I aspired to be like you."

"That is unfortunate," Dorian said, looking away.

"It didn't seem that way at the time. I became an expert at what I did, just like you. But like you, I finally realized there is such a thing as good and evil, and I was on the wrong side."

"Sammael convinced you."

"I was already having serious doubts. Fell for a girl who worked at an office down the street from the boss's base of operations. Had a chance to make her my protégée, but when it came right down to it, I just couldn't do it. Had the crazy idea that I wanted to marry her."

A sudden, vivid image of Gwen's face made Dorian catch his breath. "Marry her?"

"I've heard the dogs do it sometimes. Didn't some werewolf marry a vampire right here in New York?"

"Yes."

"So it isn't impossible. Anyway, I knew I had to change completely if I was going to be with her. Only there was no way to do it and still work for Karl. And if you didn't work for Karl..." He shrugged. "That's when I heard Sammael talk about Pax, and I knew I could use my skills for something other than hurting people. I've been holing up here for the past several weeks, waiting to begin my assignment."

"To offer yourself as an enforcer to one of the factions."

"Christof's, in fact." He caught Dorian's gaze. "Some of us have already infiltrated the factions—former enforcers like you and me."

"How many?"

"Our goal is twenty in each faction. But it's quality, not quantity, that counts. We have to be the best so we can get close to the leaders. Close enough so that they trust us implicitly."

"And what of the work you'll have to do for them in order to earn their trust?"

Nathaniel's mobile face hardened. "We do what we have to

do to achieve the greater purpose." He leaned forward. "You could make a big difference to us, Dorian. Either of the factions would kill to have you with them."

Kill. Dorian had been prepared to murder Kyril and as many of the faction leader's supporters as possible before they took him down. Now he was being asked to present himself as an ally to those he despised, to return to the very life he had foresworn.

For the sake of lasting peace. For the sake of the justice Gwen had given her life to seeking.

"I know what you lost," Nathaniel said. "But this isn't about revenge. It's not for any of us personally. If you can't let go of your hate, you'll only harm the cause."

Dorian bowed his head. He could still hear Gwen's voice: *I believe, whatever you may have done, however many sins you've committed, I believe you really want to atone.*

Perhaps she hadn't really believed it. But she'd also asked what he was willing to do to achieve that atonement, and he had left her convinced that he wouldn't help her.

Now he had a second chance. A chance to help create a world where Gwen wouldn't have died. A world where at least one mob would no longer have the power to continue its reign of terror.

Joining Pax wouldn't bring Gwen back from the grave. But if she'd known what the group was trying to achieve, she would gladly have given it her full support. The least Dorian could do was stand in her place.

He rose. "You'll have my decision tomorrow," he said.

"That's all we can ask." Nathaniel stood and offered his hand in the human fashion. This time Dorian didn't hesitate to take it.

"HE HAS AGREED, THEN."

Angela nodded, the gold of her hair catching the lamplight. "He made his decision this afternoon," she said. "I believe he'll be a very valuable addition."

"Of that I've no doubt." Sammael gave Angela his most

charming smile. "You may go. Continue to make Dorian's stay as pleasant as possible. I expect to begin his training very shortly."

"Yes, Sammael." She retreated, and Sammael remained quiet for a moment, considering his great good fortune. No, not fortune... The Lord had seen fit to answer his prayers. He had learned from the incompetence of the soldiers he'd sent out after Gwen Murphy; they had been punished, and other, more capable men had been dispatched to learn if the girl had in fact perished in the failed attempt to abduct her.

To all appearances, she had. But Sammael hadn't been able to dismiss his doubts; his dreams told him that she was still alive. If she lived, she might still know the location of the book. And if her death were a hoax, she would surely be in touch with the man with whom she had spent so many hours.

Dorian Black.

"I DON'T THINK I CAN stand another day in this bed."

Mitch made a sympathetic noise and tucked the sheets a little more firmly around Gwen's waist. "You were badly hurt, Gwen. You can't expect recovery to happen overnight."

"Overnight!" She tried to sit up and winced as almost-healed muscles protested her injudicious movement. "I've been in New Jersey for two months. Two months!"

"You may not remember the night they brought you into the hospital," Mitch said, "but I do. You were covered in blood. You had a hole in your shoulder as big as Antarctica."

"Don't you think that's a bit of an exaggeration?" Deliberately she tested the muscle again. It was stiff and sore, but that was as much due to her lack of exercise as anything else. She'd suspected for several weeks now that Mitch had someone watching her apartment door day and night, and that he would continue to make much of her injuries long after any sign of real pain or weakness was gone.

He's afraid I'll head straight back to New York. And he's right. No hatchet man or arrogant mob boss was going to scare her away from her own turf. Not when she knew she must have been getting very close to the truth.

And she had to find Dorian. They had parted on such bad terms. She hadn't been able to stop worrying about what he might have done if he'd believed the story that she was dead.

Or maybe he was glad to be rid of someone so ready to condemn him.

"I'd like to be alone now, Mitch," she said.

He squeezed her hand. "Of course. You still need plenty of rest." He got up, adjusted a miniature ornament on the small Christmas tree on the table by the door, and left the room.

Gwen turned her head to gaze out the apartment window. The New Jersey sky was leaden and gray, late December at its bleakest. There had been snow last night, lovely and soft as it fell, now undoubtedly crusted over and blackened by soot and exhaust.

She had been recovering here, safely out of the way of her attackers, since Mitch had arranged with the *Sentinel* to publish the announcement of her death. It had been a highly unorthodox move, but even Mr. Spellman had agreed that it was, for the moment, the only way to keep her safe.

Of course, Mitch had been compelled to tell the editor-in-chief that Gwen had been pursuing the triple homicide story in spite of his warnings, and he had found her notes about the two new informants she'd located. The consensus was that Kyril had ordered the hit. So far, Gwen hadn't found any reason to doubt it, though the first of the two informants had been decidedly vague.

Mitch was of the opinion that the meeting had been a setup. He had become more protective than ever, and that protection had quickly turned into imprisonment.

At first his concern had been understandable; she'd been hovering between life and death for several days before they had dared to move her out of Manhattan. But he'd forbidden her to contact anyone in New York. Even after weeks had passed and she had been able to move into an apartment near the hospital, Mitch came to visit at last three times a week.

Gwen leaned back into the pillows. Of course, there really wasn't any legal way that he could keep her confined now that the doctors had given her a clean bill of health.

She had to start thinking seriously about how to get out of here.

But once she did that, what then? The only witness to her near death had vanished before the police arrived. Spellman might let her have her job back, or he might consider her too great a liability. He certainly wouldn't want to be responsible for her actual death if her attackers should realize she'd survived.

But she could continue to pursue her investigation on her own, and she fully intended to do so. After she'd found Dorian. After she'd explained that she hadn't really meant what she'd said about him, that she believed he was sincere in wanting to leave his dark past behind.

God knew she hadn't been able to get him out of her mind from the moment she'd awakened from surgery. Being so near death had a way of clarifying one's thoughts, and she'd been forced to admit that her feelings for Dorian were the real thing.

And so was her physical yearning for him.

Gwen's face grew warm. Sleeping so much had led to many dreams, and Dorian had featured prominently in most of them. His sleek, muscular body, the way he felt when she'd touched him—those images had led to fantasies so vivid that she sometimes woke convinced that he lay beside her, stroking her skin with his long, strong fingers.

She rolled over on her side, trying to ignore the heat and wetness between her thighs. She still didn't now how to make Dorian understand how she felt. And there were no guarantees that he would return her feelings. In fact, the odds seemed very much against it. He'd had plenty of chances to show any interest he might feel and had consistently failed to do so.

Gwen closed her eyes. She'd never allowed herself to be a coward about anything. If she could survive an assassin's bullet, she could survive this, too.

It was time to break it off with Mitch once and for all. He'd been a good friend. She hoped he still would be, after she told him she didn't love him.

When I see him next, she promised herself.

And she was determined that their next meeting would be in Manhattan.

Until then, she had a lot of thinking and planning to do. Gwen Murphy wasn't anybody's prey. And she was going to find the truth, even if it killed her.

CHAPTER NINE

DORIAN SIGNALED TO HIS MEN, listening for the faint scrape of heels in the alley. Christof's enforcers were very good; like Kyril, the faction leader had recruited only the best from among Raoul's former hatchet men. They were hardened professionals, not easily deceived.

But neither was Dorian. There had been a particular animus between him and Pietro, Christof's chief lieutenant, since the last time the two groups had clashed and Dorian had led his band to victory. This fight had been brewing for weeks.

Dorian welcomed it. His madness was still a few days away, but its influence was already beginning to tell on him. It would give him just enough of an edge in the fight, and then—when his duty was done—he would slink away to some isolated place to endure the dark of the moon where no one could see or interfere.

He didn't need the madness to do his work for Kyril or Pax. He had fallen easily into his old ways as an enforcer. As Romana had promised, it had been a simple matter for him to present himself at Kyril's hotel and offer his services. He had admitted that Romana had been right; he couldn't leave the old ways behind.

And of course Kyril had believed him. He had shown little interest in learning about Dorian's activities since Raoul's death; he was as ignorant of Dorian's part in that event as every other *strigoi* in the city. He hadn't mentioned Gwen in any context. If he had suspected a relationship between his new enforcer and the woman he had killed, he had given no indication of it. That had been enough to convince Dorian that he could operate freely without concern that Kyril would ever suspect his motives for joining the faction.

He glanced into the alley, searching for the furtive shapes he knew would be there in moments. His men watched him as a well-trained dog watches its master. Many of them aspired to attain his success; his expertise was such that he'd quickly risen in the ranks from enforcer to lieutenant. Kyril had rewarded him with rank and private apartments in the hotel the faction leader had confiscated for his followers' sole use. He had even offered Dorian the chance to create a protégé of his own…several, if he continued to serve as well as he had over the past two months.

Such rewards did not come without a price. But Dorian had paid it willingly, intent on fulfilling his bargain with Pax and punishing those responsible for Gwen's murder.

Meetings with Pax were necessarily few and brief, but Dorian had learned that considerable progress had been made by the organization's operatives within both factions. He still didn't know the identities of all the agents within Kyril's gang; that information would be given to him only when it was time to act. The denouement of Sammael's plan was no more than a few weeks away.

And so was Dorian's revenge.

"Dorian?"

Melchior's voice was barely a whisper, but Dorian silenced the young enforcer with a lifted hand. Christof's men were almost in the alley, moving slowly and with Tommy guns at the ready. They'd been told by a supposedly reputable source that they would find Dorian Black and one or two of his handpicked cadre in a meeting with human boss Carmine De Luca's lieutenants in a neutral part of town. That neutrality had so far been honored, but Dorian had known that Pietro wouldn't be able to resist the chance to take out his personal nemesis.

That was his mistake. Dorian nodded to Melchior and the men behind him. They took up their positions. Dorian stepped out into the alley from a concealed doorway, pretending to be finishing a conversation with someone within the building.

"Next Thursday, promptly at nine," he said. "Kyril will be waiting."

He heard the unnatural silence behind him and braced for the attack. It came swiftly. A body slammed into him with such force that he would have been thrown to the ground if not for his prior warning. He kept his feet, twisted and caught his attacker's arm in his hands. Bone snapped, and the *strigoi* staggered in pain.

By then the battle was fully joined. There had been no time for the enemy to fire their weapons before Dorian's men poured into the alley; Phineas, Vasily and Melchior were locked in vicious fights with three of Pietro's hatchet men. Two *strigoi*, severely wounded, lay incapacitated on the pavement. As Dorian turned to look for Pietro, a bullet struck Melchoir in the middle of his forehead. He fell, eyes wide with astonishment as the projectile pierced his brain.

Dorian leaped for the gunman. The *strigoi* was a second too slow with his aim. Dorian forced the muzzle of the gun straight up under the enforcer's chin and pulled the trigger. The lifeless body slumped at his feet. Immediately he spun about, looking for new prey.

Pietro stood at the center of the whirlwind, untouched by the storm of bodies raging around him. Dorian started toward him. Pietro backed away, turned and fled for the alley's mouth.

The memory of Melchior's startled face was seared into Dorian's brain. Pietro was responsible. Pietro would pay. But beneath the drumbeat of rage lay the cold, clear note of reason. Pietro wouldn't have run merely out of cowardice. His purpose must be to lure Dorian away from his men. And he would only do that if he had an ambush of his own prepared.

Dorian was beyond caring. His hesitation lasted less than a second. He ran forward, hurling two of Pietro's enforcers aside with a sweep of his arm.

The moment he reached the street he saw how thoroughly he had been trapped. Pietro and another half-dozen enforcers openly waited for him with relaxed and easy confidence, each one heavily armed. Not so much as a rat or stray dog stirred; the humans who lived in the ramshackle tenements that lined the street, long accustomed to sudden violence, remained sequestered behind locked doors.

Pietro smiled, shifting his Tommy gun from one shoulder to the other. "I wasn't sure you'd take the bait," he said. "But you've got quite a reputation these days, Dorian. You've become like an animal, savage and mindless."

Dorian stood very still, hands loose at his sides. "In what way does that make me different from any *strigoi?*"

Pietro's black eyes were hard as obsidian. "You once had a reputation for a certain restraint. What happened?"

"Nothing that would interest you or your master, Pietro."

"But I am curious. Was it Raoul's death that did it? I know a few others who weren't quite right after the bond was severed."

"You obviously came through the experience unscathed."

"I despised Raoul. I served him only because I had no other choice. You always were his creature."

Dorian shivered, seized by a firestorm of memories. Raoul rescuing him in the slaughterhouse. His Conversion. His first successful assignment. His growing disillusionment. The decision that would change his life—and that of every *strigoi* in Manhattan—forever.

"Yes," he said. "I should have died with him."

"I'll gladly grant you your wish." Pietro dropped the muzzle of the gun into his other hand. "I might almost pity you if I believed you'd completely lost your mind to madness. But you know what you're doing." He glanced up the street, noting the sound of an approaching automobile. "It's a shame you couldn't turn your abilities to work for the good of the *strigoi*. Kyril is no better than Raoul. If he's not stopped, he'll see us all destroyed with his senseless violence."

"Will Christof be so much better?"

"A creature like you would hardly know the difference."

"You won't hesitate to kill every one of Kyril's followers to put your liege in power."

Pietro shifted his feet. "There's no other way." He gestured to the big, blunt-featured enforcer standing beside him. "Kill him quickly, and leave his body here as a warning."

The enforcer's face was stony with hatred. He waited until Pietro and his companions bled away into the night, then lifted his gun.

"I'd let you die slow if I could," the enforcer said. "But orders're orders."

He took aim. A taxi turned a corner into the street and pulled up at the curb a block away. A young woman climbed out and paid the cabbie, as yet oblivious to what was happening a few yards from where she was standing.

Gwen.

Dorian's shock lost him the few dwindling seconds left for escape or attack. He dived to the side. The spray of bullets caught him in the chest instead of the brain. He fell to his knees, blinded by pain. The enforcer's footsteps seemed to boom on the pavement. He shoved the muzzle of the gun against Dorian's temple.

"No!"

The scream distracted Christof's hatchet man just long enough. He swung his Tommy gun toward the voice. Dorian gathered his legs beneath him and bowled into the enforcer, who fired wildly into the air. Dorian wrestled the gun from his hands, turned the weapon around and smashed his opponent across the face with the butt. He hit the enforcer again and again until the man lay unconscious, his face a bloody pulp.

"Dorian!"

Gwen ran up to him, her hat lost and her hair in disarray. "My God! You're…you've been—"

Dorian could hardly believe he had not already fallen into the delirium that came before death. Gwen was alive. *Alive.*

She knelt beside him, her hands suspended helplessly in the air above his chest. "You've been shot," she said, controlling her voice with obvious effort. "This time you *have* to see a doctor."

In answer Dorian clambered to his feet, forcing his muscles to support him while blood soaked his coat and shirt and spattered on the pavement under his feet. "You know better," he croaked.

"You'll die," she said. "I won't let that happen."

"I...thought you were dead."

"I know, but—"

"What are you doing here?"

"That isn't important now." She caught him as he swayed, and looked over her shoulder. "Damn! The taxi's gone."

"Afraid," Dorian said. He tried to stand, glanced at his supine enemy and looked toward the alley. Pietro and his men might be gone, or they might be lingering nearby. All sounds of fighting had ceased. Dorian could only hope that his side had been victorious, and that most of his men were still alive. There was nothing more he could do to help them now.

"We must leave immediately," he said.

"You can't possibly walk with those injuries."

"They aren't as bad...as they look." He smiled and touched her cheek with a bloodstained hand. "Courage, Guinevere."

Her eyes swam with tears. "If you can make it...we'll go to my hotel room. I know a little first aid. But if the bullets hit anything vital—"

"All I need is rest." He sucked in a breath. "Where?"

She steered him across the street, supporting his uninjured arm and holding him upright with the strength of desperation. After two blocks of halting progress, she was able to find a taxi, though the cabbie looked askance at Dorian's bloody clothing before succumbing to the considerable bribe Gwen offered. She urged the driver to his fastest speed. They were at Gwen's hotel in fifteen minutes.

"There's another tenner in it if you'll help me get him to my room," she told the cabbie.

Greed won out over prudence. Gwen readjusted Dorian's coat to cover the worst of the bloodstains and, with the driver's help, assisted Dorian in crossing the modest lobby to the elevator. "Drunk," she said to the young couple who paused to stare.

The elevator boy showed little interest in his passengers; he'd doubtless seen plenty of inebriates during his tenure at the hotel. Dorian slumped against the wall, his vision first black and then red, like some traffic signal gone haywire. The elevator door opened at last. Gwen and the cabbie half carried him down the corridor to a room near the end, where Gwen fumbled in her pocketbook for the key. She pushed the door open, herded Dorian to the sofa near the door and paid the cabbie his bribe. The man left with alacrity.

Immediately Gwen ran for the bathroom. She returned with an armload of towels, and knelt before Dorian to remove his coat and shirt. She gasped when she saw the ugly holes in his chest.

He could almost hear her thoughts. *You shouldn't be alive.* If he were human, he assuredly wouldn't be. One bullet had passed so near his heart that it had probably severed a major artery, which was struggling to mend itself before all the blood drained from his body. His lungs were half filled with fluid, and his shoulder hung useless.

"I can't help you," Gwen whispered, her face white as milk. "There must be a doctor somewhere in the neighborhood."

Dorian pulled one of the towels from her hands and wadded it against the worst of the wounds. The initial stream of blood was beginning to slow. Soon it would stop entirely.

"Find all the cloths you can," he said.

She hesitated, sprang up and ripped the coverlet and blanket from the bed. Rumpled white sheets soon lay on a heap on the mattress. Gwen tore them into strips and began to wrap them around Dorian's chest. When she was finished, she used damp towels to wipe away the blood on his face, chest and stomach.

"The bullets will have to come out," she said, "or there'll be a terrible infection."

Dorian closed his eyes and slumped on the sofa. "Most of them passed through me."

"But the wounds need to be properly cleaned and dressed. You may need surgery." She took his face between her hands. "The time for stubbornness is over. I'm calling an ambulance."

He seized her wrist as she turned to go. "It's…unnecessary. Gwen, I will not die." He held on as she fought to break free. Her resistance faltered. She sank down to the carpet at his feet.

"Why do I believe you?" she murmured.

"Wait and see."

"If you get any worse…if I see any evidence that you—"

He put his hand over her mouth, feeling its warmth and softness, exulting in the mere fact of her living presence.

And hungering for her blood.

"Sleep," he said. "When you awaken, you'll have no further cause for concern."

"Right. You're the one who's going to bed, and I'll be watching you every minute."

"I…never doubted it." His eyelids grew too heavy to lift. "You always seem to be saving my life."

"Someone's got to do it." Gwen wrapped her arms around him and lifted him with a groan. He did what he could to help, keenly aware of the touch of her breasts on his bare chest, the brush of her cheek against his. Undaunted by his weakened state, his cock strained inside his trousers.

If Gwen felt his reaction, she gave no sign. Awkwardly she dragged him to the bed and eased him down on top of the hastily spread blanket. He tried to stay conscious for a few minutes longer, his mind spinning with questions. But his body knew better what he must have to live.

He faded into that twilight state that passed for sleep among *strigoi*. When he came to, Gwen was lying beside him, her body curled into his and her face buried in his shoulder. He moved gingerly, reached over to stroke her back. She shifted, flinging her arm over his waist.

His pain was gone. No blood flowed beneath the bandages. He was healed, and Gwen would see that he had done the impossible. She would have a thousand questions, ones he wasn't yet prepared to answer.

Because he'd been granted a miracle, the kind that generally came only to the most devout humans. He had been granted not a second but a third chance. And Gwen was beside him. He would never risk losing her by revealing the truth too soon.

He caressed her cheek lightly, hoping she would sleep on. But she stirred, yawned and opened her eyes.

"Dorian?"

"I'm here, Gwen. I'm well."

She sat up, flung off the coverlet she'd dragged over them sometime during the night and bent above him. Her gaze fixed on his chest, the bandages dark with old blood. She touched him gingerly.

"You're…not in pain?" she whispered.

"No." He sat up. Her face tightened in alarm, but he took her arms before she could try to push him back down.

"Look beneath the bandages," he ordered.

She stared at him as if he were mad, then slowly complied, peeling the upper layers of cloth away with consummate care. The wounds were gone save for faint red puckers in the skin of Dorian's chest, under the right ribs and just above his navel.

"My God." She touched the pink marks and slowly looked up to meet his eyes. "This isn't possible. It just isn't possible."

"Nevertheless," Dorian said, "it is as I told you. I was never in danger of dying."

"But how?"

"There will be time for explanations."

"Who was that guy who tried to kill you? What—"

"Patience." Dorian trapped both her hands so she couldn't escape. "What happened, Gwen? Why did I read that you were dead? Why didn't you tell me it wasn't true?"

She glanced away. "I couldn't. I was shot, Dorian. I almost died, but Mitch got me to the hospital. There was a chance the men that tried to kill me might try again. I was hiding in New Jersey until I recovered enough to leave."

Hot coals smoldered in Dorian's gut. "Who shot you?"

"I don't know. They were dressed in black coats and wore red scarves."

Kyril's colors. The final proof. Dorian clenched his fists until his tendons cracked. "You provoked them," he said. "You continued to follow the story of the murders."

"I never said I'd stop."

Of course she hadn't. And he'd been stupid and cowardly enough to leave her when she'd needed him most.

"What were you doing in this neighborhood?" he asked, keeping his voice level.

"I could ask the same of you." She frowned, and he knew the conversation would be anything but pleasant. "I was supposed to meet another informant…something about a gang fight between Christof's and Kyril's men. It seemed he was right."

He wanted to laugh. "So you walked right into the middle of it."

"You were right in the middle of it, too."

"How long have you been back?"

She averted her eyes. "About a week. I've been trying to find you, Dorian. Not even Walter knew where you were."

"Gwen…"

"I disappeared without even letting you know I was alive. All the time I was in New Jersey I worried about what you'd do, where you'd go."

"*I* was never in any danger."

"No? What do you call being shot three times in the chest?"

A lie would do no good, even if he could bring himself to tell it. "A professional hazard," he said.

Abruptly she jerked away. "You were with them, weren't you?" she whispered. "You're working for the mobs again." She squeezed her eyes shut. "I kept cursing myself for what I said to you that night at the paper. For assuming…" She turned her back on him and went to the window, folding her arms across her chest. "You said you were through with your old life."

Dorian heard the despair in her words and knew he couldn't bear her condemnation a second time. He wanted to speak of Pax and its admirable goal of seeking peace between the factions, peace that would spare many innocent lives.

But he'd sworn not to mention Pax to anyone. And Gwen

wouldn't understand. She would never agree that the end justified the means.

"I joined Kyril to…to ascertain if he had killed you."

"So that you could kill him?"

"Yes."

"No, Dorian." She returned to him and dropped to her knees.
"Not for me."

"I have…other reasons."

"Reasons worth what I saw back on that street?"

"I am not a good man, Gwen. I never was."

"Why can't I convince myself of that?"

He got up, wincing at the residual discomfort of healing
muscle and bone, and drew her to her feet.

"Go," he said. "Leave the city. It doesn't have to be forever.
Sooner or later the factions will eliminate each other or be forced
to accept a truce. They'll forget about you and your investigation."

"But *I* won't. I can't."

"Gwen…" He rested his hands on her tense shoulders. "I've
never begged for anything in my life. I'm begging you. Save
yourself."

Her breath gusted in a long, shuddering sigh. "And if I begged
you to come away with me?"

Silence fell between them, as thick and choking as factory
smoke. He'd given Pax his oath, but if it came to a choice
between the organization and Gwen…

He tipped her head up, compelling her to meet his gaze. "I
care…I care about you. When I thought you were dead…" he
said.

"Please. Please don't say any more."

He didn't. He lowered his head and touched her lips with his.
She stiffened, her mouth half open in surprise. He deepened the
kiss, brushing the inside of her upper lip with the tip of his
tongue. Suddenly she responded, sliding her arms behind his
back, her small body pushing against his. Her pulse beat very fast,
and the scent of her arousal permeated the air like exotic perfume.

Dorian should have stopped it then and there. He should have put on his bloodstained shirt and left the hotel room until his mind was clear.

But Gwen didn't let go. She tucked her forehead into the hollow of his shoulder, exposing the pale, elegant length of her neck beneath red curls. Dorian's mouth flooded with saliva and the chemicals that would numb her to his bite, to everything but the blissful pleasure he would give in exchange for her sweet blood.

He lowered his head and kissed her vulnerable skin. She trembled. He bit gently. She flinched and relaxed as the chemicals did their work, her body softening in his arms.

"Dorian," she sighed.

She was as light as down as he lifted her and carried her to the bed. He lay down beside her, stroked tendrils of hair away from her neck and bit her again. Blood like honeyed wine flowed over his tongue. Though he had taken from her before, it had never been quite like this…this heat that confused his senses and brought him to a full erection in mere seconds.

Though it was common for the human donor to feel ecstasy when a *strigoi* took blood, the sense was not always so strong in the other direction. Dorian had never experienced the euphoria some vampires spoke of, the transcendent emotions that came when a *strigoi* and his donor were in perfect affinity.

Now he began to understand. His own blood seemed to bubble in his veins like fine champagne. He felt an overwhelming need to join with Gwen in every way, body as well as blood. Simple feeding had become a struggle not to release the substance that would transform her from human to one like himself.

He had no right. No right to the blood he took, no right to her body, above all no right to her future.

Dorian released her and rolled away. He lay on his back, staring at the hairline cracks in the ceiling. His hunger had not been appeased, yet he would remain with her until she awoke from her pleasant stupor.

Then he would have to decide how to save her without destroying her.

He had just begun to rise from the bed when Gwen touched him. "Don't go," she said. Her words were slightly slurred, like those of a woman who'd had one drink too many, but her grip on his arm was firm. He turned back, stunned that she should be lucid so quickly. But then he saw her eyes, glazed and dreamy, and the rapt smile on her face.

She hadn't recovered from his bite. Quite the contrary. She was still deep in her dream of ecstasy, and something within her—some boundary, some inhibition—had been breached.

"Dorian," she said, holding out her arms. "I've been waiting so long."

He held himself rigid, knowing he ought to leave before his own discipline broke under the weight of his desire. But her fingers danced over his arm, across his chest, curled around the base of his neck. She had always been so much stronger than she looked. His own body seemed weak as water.

"Make love to me," she murmured. "I want you, Dorian. I want you inside me."

CHAPTER TEN

A TASTE BOTH SWEET and bitter filled Dorian's mouth. Only one in a thousand humans kept some part of their awareness during a feeding. Most of those were simply afraid and struggled against their captors. A rare few responded as Gwen did now, answering hunger with hunger. Willing to give everything they possessed.

Go, his rapidly fading reason demanded. *Go.*

But he rolled toward her, took her face between his hands and kissed her again, seizing her mouth with his own, curling his tongue around hers. She made no resistance as he bore her onto her back and straddled her. She sprawled, her legs parted, her arms stretched above her head. Dorian accepted her invitation. He kissed her lips, her stubborn chin, the trembling skin at the base of her throat. His fingers found the tiny pearl buttons on her blouse and worked them loose one by one. Beneath she wore a bandeau brassiere with narrow, silky straps he could snap with no effort at all.

The sheer fabric did nothing to hide her small, firm breasts. Her nipples were high and hard even before he touched them. She moaned as he sucked a nipple into his mouth, wetting the satin until it became transparent. She clutched at his shoulders and dug her nails into his skin.

He kissed and suckled her other nipple and then broke the straps between his fingers, eager to taste her. He pushed the bandeau below her breasts and cupped them in his hands. He licked circles around her nipple, drawing closer and closer to the center. She arched, pushing herself into his mouth. He took as much of her as he could.

Still it wasn't enough. Her sensible skirt was too long and slim-fitting to push above her thighs. Gwen lifted her hips, urging him to remove the impediment. Dorian unbuttoned the waistband and tugged the skirt down. He tossed it to the floor.

The woman before him was more delectable, more captivating, than even his long-suppressed desire could have imagined. She was completely innocent, almost certainly a virgin, but her eyes were heavy-lidded with seduction, and her lips were parted in excitement. She spread her legs, revealing the garters that held her silk hose in place. There was something indescribably erotic about the look of her nearly naked body still clad in stockings and low-heeled black pumps.

Gwen placed her hands over her gently curved stomach and stroked down to the waist of her satin-and-lace step-ins.

"It snaps," she said.

Never had Dorian felt so much like a boy fumbling in the dark. He found the snaps between Gwen's thighs and pulled them apart. Lace cascaded to caress soft, smooth skin. Her mons were covered with delicate red curls, and beneath them her labia was flushed and swollen, glistening with moisture. He grabbed her hips and pulled her to the edge of the bed, pushing her thighs wider apart.

Her breathing grew labored as he touched the slickness of her vulva and found the nub of her clitoris. He slid his thumb over it, watching her face as she flung back her head and moaned softly. He dipped one finger into the scarlet entrance below. She was tight and firm. No other man had ever been inside her.

"Oh, God," she gasped. "Dorian. I can't…stand…"

He let his hand fall and replaced it with his mouth. His tongue slid over her labia and then stroked between the folds, exploring and tasting every part of her. He circled her cleft, let the juices flow over his tongue, and moved up again to flick lightly over her clitoris. She tensed, arching her back like a cat. He drew her clitoris into his mouth and suckled, gently and then harder. Her head began to thrash on the pillow.

It was almost more than either one of them could bear, and Dorian knew the waiting was nearly over. He was at the very limits of his self-control, barely able to remember that he'd had a reason for leaving Gwen alone. But her blood—her blood and the impending new moon-shredded and scattered his restraint. He rose and tore at the buttons of his trousers, nearly ripping them from the flannel. His cock strained against his drawers. He discarded them and stood between Gwen's thighs, as aching and ready as he had ever been in his long life.

"Now," Gwen begged, her throat hoarse with her own kind of madness. "Do it now."

He wedged his hands under her round, firm bottom. She locked her ankles around his waist. He positioned himself, grazing her labia with the head of his cock. Nothing could stop him now. Nothing could prevent him from plunging inside her, thrusting so deep and hard that she would cry out his name again and again.

But he remained still, paralyzed, for one crucial minute…just long enough for someone to knock at the hotel room door.

"Gwen? Gwen, I know you're in there. Open up!"

Dorian stepped back, disoriented and filled with inchoate rage. Gwen blinked, snapped her thighs together and glanced about the room as if she had just fought her way free of a nightmare.

"Gwen!" The knocking became pounding. "Who's in there with you?"

Gwen felt wildly for her bandeau and step-ins. Finding them in less than pristine condition, she bolted from the bed and raced into the bathroom, emerging a moment later with a towel wrapped around her middle. Her gaze fixed on Dorian in confusion.

"What…why are you…?" Her face turned crimson, and she averted her eyes. "It's Mitch. You have to hide. Please."

Fighting his fury, Dorian yanked the tangled blanket from the bed, threw it over his shoulder and staggered toward the window. It was dark outside; a full day must have passed while his body had recovered and the sun had set again. He pulled the curtains fully closed and leaned against the cool glass behind them.

"Wait a minute, Mitch," Gwen called, her voice shaking. "I'm not decent."

Mitch rumbled an unintelligible reply. For a good five minutes all Dorian heard was the sound of Gwen racing about the room as she gathered up bloody bandages and discarded clothing and began tearing through her suitcase, fabric whispering as she threw on a new set of garments. She snapped the suitcase shut and half ran to the door.

"Gwen!" Mitch said. "What's going on?" A beat of silence. "I heard you talking to someone. Who was it?"

"You must have been imagining things, Mitch. No one knows where I am except you. I'm perfectly safe here."

Mitch's footsteps thudded across the carpet. "Have a bad night?"

"I tossed and turned. Didn't get a wink of sleep."

"Where are the sheets?"

"They were soiled, so I asked a maid to replace them."

"I see." He moved around in an aimless pattern. "Are you sure you have everything you need?"

"Yes. I don't require luxury, Mitch."

"I could get you a much better room."

"I don't want you paying for it. I've enough saved to keep myself in cheap hotel rooms for weeks."

A pause. "Gwen, you're making a mistake."

"We've been through this a hundred times."

"Why won't you let me help you?"

"I rely on your friendship, Mitch. You know—"

"My *friendship*." His voice was laced with bitterness. "I should feel privileged that you grant me that much."

"It was never… I've always…"

"I thought you were that rare breed, Gwen. An honest woman. I guess I was wrong."

There was another long spell of silence, and Dorian imagined them staring at each other, Mitch hostile, Gwen apologetic. Because she'd told him something he didn't want to hear.

"If you don't mind," she finally said, "I really need a shower. I can't afford to be half asleep when I leave the hotel."

"I'll come with you."

"It's better if I keep a low profile."

"Don't expect me to leave you alone, Guinevere. No matter how much you want to be rid of me."

"Okay, Mitch." She had seen the necessity of a temporary surrender. "Just give me a little time."

"I'll expect a call every hour."

The door closed. Dorian pushed the curtains aside, stepped into the room and closed them again.

"He's gone," Gwen said, tugging self-consciously at the hem of her sweater. "I think you…I think you'd better go, too."

"Gwen…"

"I started it, didn't I? I barely remember." She swallowed. "I'm sorry. I just don't understand…how it happened."

"You having nothing to apologize for."

Her skin remained flushed, and she refused to meet his gaze. "I have a lot to think about, and I need to do it alone."

Dorian bowed his head. His blood still seethed with lust, and his control continued to ride on a knife's edge. "I will not be far away," he said.

"Oh, I'm not worried. I have plenty of guardians."

She clearly expected no responses, and Dorian had none to give. Reluctantly he accepted the new shirt, tie and jacket Gwen had purchased for him while he'd been unconscious, and quickly dressed. His mental state was far from stable when he left the room and descended the stairs to the lobby.

You should have stayed. You should have bitten her again, put her into a deeper sleep until you could find a solution.

But if he bit her again, there was no telling what might happen. He couldn't reason with her. Nothing short of flagrant kidnapping would stop her from chasing her story.

That, or putting a permanent end to the threat against her.

The doorman flinched as Dorian strode past him. The man's instinctive fear reminded Dorian of the gnawing hunger that had yet to be assuaged. There was no need to die on an empty stomach.

He located a messenger service, wrote out a brief note, and arranged for it to be delivered to Gwen in twenty-four hours. Then he sought the welcoming shadows of the back alleys and deep canyons of the city, letting his senses lead him where they would.

For a time, for so short a time, he had begun to know what it was like not to be alone. He had grown soft. Now he must put all that behind him for the sake of the one human he had ever cared about.

And as for Pax…they would have to continue their crusade without his help.

MITCH WATCHED THE *Sentinel's* former janitor leave the hotel and fell into step several yards behind. He had known in his gut that Gwen wasn't alone in her room; his reporter's hard-won experience was highly efficient at detecting deceit.

Not that this was anything new. By now he was certain that Gwen had been romantically involved with Black since well before he'd come to work at the *Sentinel,* weeks before she'd finally found the nerve to hand Mitch his Dear John notice.

Stupid girl. She was as ignorant as a child. Mitch worked his hands into fists as he trailed Dorian Black. She didn't seem to have thought anything of the fact that Black had vanished shortly before her "accident." No one at the paper had known where he'd gone or particularly cared.

But Mitch had cared. He'd cared because he'd never trusted Black, who'd come out of nowhere and somehow weaseled his way into Gwen's too-soft heart. Mitch hadn't been able to learn anything substantive about the man's background, his former employment.

A very dangerous ghost. When Gwen had been hurt only a week after Dorian had disappeared, everything in Mitch's gut had told him that it wasn't coincidence. Though he had seen nothing to indicate that Gwen had been in touch with Black while she was in New Jersey, it was obvious that she must have been. And now that she had returned to Manhattan, Black was with her again.

You don't owe her anything, Mitch thought. *She's earned whatever she gets.*

But he still loved her. That was the irony of it. She had to be saved from herself, and there was only one man in the world who could do it. It wasn't enough that Spellman had suspended her from work at the paper. He had to get Gwen into protective custody, even if he needed to do it by force. And he had to get rid of Dorian Black.

No more words. It's now or never.

His thoughts stuttered to a halt, and he found himself at the mouth of an alley, suddenly aware that he had no idea where he was or if Black had slipped away.

He slammed his fist against the nearest brick wall, furious with himself. A schoolboy could have done a better job of tailing Black. And if Black had seen him…

A scraping sound in the alley brought him up short. Probably a bum, he thought, or a stray cat. But something about the sound, and the soft gasp that followed put him on full alert. He switched on his flashlight, felt for the brass knuckles inside his coat pocket and crept into the alley.

A shadow…no, two…stood just out of the path of light cast by a street lamp beyond the mouth of the alley. At first glance the shape looked like nothing so much as two lovers embracing, and Mitch hesitated. But then he saw that the smaller figure hung limp in the larger one's arms, head lolling, body motionless.

He fitted the brass knuckles around his right hand. "What the hell do you think you're doing?" he shouted. "Let her go!"

The larger figure's head lifted. Eyes shimmered like those of an animal caught in bright light, limned with red. Teeth flashed white, and Mitch heard a growl deeper and more threatening than the most vicious mongrel could produce.

There was just barely enough illumination to make out the face.

"Black," Mitch whispered.

Dorian Black bent his head over the woman's neck. Something dark and liquid trickled over her pale skin. Mitch's stomach knotted with horror.

"Let her go," he said.

When Dorian looked up again, his teeth were no longer white. He took the woman by her shoulders and eased her down onto a crate in a corner slightly less filthy than the rest of the alley. He straightened and regarded Mitch with those terrible, glittering eyes.

"You shouldn't have come," he said.

Mitch felt his knees begin to buckle. "You killed her."

"Did I?" Dorian strolled toward Mitch, his gait loose-jointed and menacing in its grace. "Look for yourself."

"You're crazy."

Black stepped aside. "Look."

Curiosity and courage were traits essential in any good reporter, and Mitch had never lacked either one. He edged past Black toward the woman, still clutching the brass knuckles. As soon as he knelt beside the crate he could see that she was still breathing, though she appeared deeply asleep. He touched her neck gingerly, brushing brittle hair aside.

There was no wound. No indication of where she'd been bleeding. She appeared to be perfectly healthy.

And she was smiling.

Mitch swallowed the sour remnants of fear and stood to face Black. "What did you do to her?"

"Nothing that will bring lasting harm."

"You…you *bit* her."

"Very observant, Mr. Hogan."

"What in hell are you?"

"Do you really want to know?" Black showed his teeth again, and Mitch saw something he'd never noticed before. The incisors were pointed and streaked with blood.

"Gwen was right," he said.

"About what, Mr. Hogan?"

"The cult. It exists."

Black cocked his head. "What cult, Mr. Hogan?"

"Men obsessed with blood. You're one of *them*." He expelled his breath harshly. "Those bodies on the waterfront…did you have something to do with them?"

"I have nothing whatsoever to do with them."

You're lying, Mitch thought. He had to be. Too many coincidences, from Gwen finding Black near the murder site to…*this.* But Mitch kept the accusation between his teeth.

"You were drinking her blood."

"An astute observation." Black brushed at the sleeves of his jacket. "But there is no cult in Manhattan. Only those like me."

"You work for Kyril, don't you?"

"Why would you assume that, Mr. Hogan?"

He'd already said too much, but there was no backing out now. "You knew Gwen was getting close. You've been watching her. Kyril tried to have her killed, and you—"

Black laughed. A world of emotion unfurled in that laugh. Contempt. Fury. And an utter disregard for the consequences of their conversation.

"Like most humans," he said, "you see only what you wish to see. Look more closely." He took several steps toward Mitch. "Or are you blind in the dark, like most humans?"

Humans. A word most people seldom had occasion to use. And never the way Black had used it.

Mitch's thoughts raced, sifting through every relevant fact he had gleaned in his career. Men who drank blood. Fairy tales. Fantastic stories. A nineteenth-century novel entitled with the name of a famous fifteenth-century murderer.

"Vampires," he said, incredulity making it difficult to speak. "You claim…you claim to be a *vampire?*"

"We prefer *strigoi.* So many of the common myths are sheer invention."

Myths. Myths based on legends about creatures that hunted by night, dragged their victims into dark alleys and consumed their blood like demons from hell.

Mitch had never once seen Black at the *Sentinel* except after sunset. It had been a condition of his employment that he would only work at night. He was always silent, lethal grace in every step and gesture.

"You're undead?" Mitch asked. "Is that what you're telling me?"

"I have never died."

Mitch began to check off points on his fingers. "You can't tolerate sunlight or holy symbols. You sleep in coffins by day and can be killed by a stake through the heart."

"Ah, yes. How creatively humans have embroidered the truth."

"You wouldn't know the—" Mitch broke off as Black moved closer. He looked into the other man's eyes. There was no doubt that they weren't normal. The pupils were pinpoints in a sea of gray. Redness smoldered behind the irises like a flame.

It was impossible. Utterly irrational. And yet for one stunning moment Mitch believed he was talking with a man who might not be a man at all. A creature whose mere existence proved correct at least a significant part of Eamon Murphy's theories and justified Gwen's pursuit of a seemingly ridiculous story.

The wild speculation boiling in Mitch's brain so distracted him that he didn't notice when Black was only inches away, driving him farther and farther back into the alley.

"You think I had something to do with Gwen's shooting," Black said softly. "I didn't. It is my intention to stop those who would hurt her."

"And *you* don't plan to hurt her? After what you did to that woman?"

"She is quite well."

Mitch had no way of getting past Black to confirm his assertion. "You want Gwen for her blood."

Black hesitated so long that Mitch was sure he'd struck a nerve.

"It is hardly necessary for us to pursue specific donors when there are so many available."

"Donors." Mitch laughed. "Blood donors? Is that what you call them?" He felt his fear rising. "How many…how many of you are there?"

"We have always been among you."

"Where? How do you live?"

"You might not find the answers comforting, Mr. Hogan."

A faint groan blocked Mitch's reply. Black's victim was stirring, her garishly painted face turning this way and that.

"As you see," Black said, "the girl isn't harmed. We will take this conversation elsewhere."

Elsewhere might mean a more public place, which could only be to Mitch's benefit. "What did you have in mind?"

Black smiled. "I can guess your intentions, Mr. Hogan. But I can easily silence you before you are able to escape."

The full impact of Black's statement drove the air from Mitch's lungs. "Are you threatening me?"

"*Strigoi* face many threats. Most of all from humans."

Mitch felt as if he were trapped in a diplomaniac's nightmare. "Then you do survive by killing people who find out about you. Gwen—"

He had barely begun to form the final words when powerful hands closed around his neck. Pressure on his nerves paralyzed him, and he felt his blood whining behind his ears.

"I could kill you," Black whispered, "but I prefer to trust in your good judgment."

The pressure on Mitch's neck increased, and his vision went red. "You…you stay away from her," he gasped. "I won't—"

His vision went from red to black. In a moment he would lose consciousness, and then it would be only a short step to death.

"I care little for what you believe of my motives," Black's voice said from very far away. "But you cannot protect her."

Mitch sagged. "You… I…"

"Hear me, human. You have stumbled upon a secret that could cost you your life. You will return to your paper and say nothing of what you have seen. If you do, you will be considered a madman, like Eamon Murphy."

Even when he was so close to extinction, Mitch was still capable of pride. "They'd…believe *me* if I told them."

"You had best pray they do not." Abruptly Black released Mitch, who sank to his knees, sucking in great lungfuls of air.

"As you noted," Black said, "the evidence does suggest that others of my kind are after those who have guessed at *strigoi* existence. I may be able to stop them. You will only ensure her eventual death."

Mitch rubbed his throat. "I love her."

"Do you? Or do you only wish to make her your chattel?"

Never in his life had Mitch wanted so badly to punch a man in the face. He knew it would be sheer folly. "If you stay away from her," he said, "I won't say anything."

"No bargains, Mr. Hogan. You will hold your tongue, or your life will be measured in days."

Gathering his legs to stand, Mitch knotted his fists until the pain of his nails digging into his palms cleared his mind. "If you think you can keep murdering people and get away with it, you have another thing co—"

But Black was gone. There had been no sound, no movement that Mitch had been able to perceive. Black had vanished. And Mitch was still alive.

Relief kept him weak for another few minutes, and then a very different emotion propelled him to his feet. Rage. Hatred. Black had made a fool and a coward of him. No one did that and got away with it.

He believed. He was convinced that vampires walked the earth. But the same legends that spoke of their existence must also tell of ways to kill them.

Brushing at his trousers, Mitch walked unsteadily to join the young woman.

"Are you all right?" he asked.

She shook her head sharply, and her red wig slipped over her eyes. "What the hell happened?"

Mitch overcame his distaste and offered his arm. "You don't remember?"

She blinked and smiled like an addict still high from the indulgence of her vice. "I remember a guy. Handsome. Gave me a tenner, but what he did after that…" She shrugged.

"You aren't hurt."

She rubbed her neck. "Nah." Her eyes narrowed. "You want a little fun, Jack?"

"No, but I'll be happy to take you wherever you need to go."

"Honey, I've still got a night's work to do. If you ain't interested, I gotta find someone who is." She patted his arm, adjusted her left pump and swayed out of the alley.

Mitch stared after her. Why was she still alive? Why was *he?*

He stepped out of the alley and glanced up and down the street. Maybe there were others like Black lurking just out of sight. But it was getting very close to morning, and odds were that they wouldn't hunt too near each other if they feared exposure.

He set off at a fast pace, the hairs on the back of his neck quivering as he went in search of a taxi to take him back to Gwen's hotel.

MITCH'S EXPRESSION WAS deadly serious. He burst into Gwen's room, stalked the perimeter like a cop casing a crime scene, and finally came to a halt in the center of the room.

"You're alone?" he asked.

Gwen struggled to keep her expression calm. She hadn't expected Mitch back so soon. It had been only about an hour since Dorian had left, and she was still very far from recovered. Her body alternately ached and hummed with energy, leaving her nearly bouncing off the walls.

One glance at Mitch's eyes and she knew she had to pull herself together quickly.

"Really, Mitch," she said as lightly as she could. "You haven't even given me a chance to call."

He ignored her, walked to the window and flipped back the curtains. "He was here with you before, wasn't he?"

"I beg your pardon?"

"Don't lie to me, Gwen. I followed him out of the hotel."

Emotions surged through Gwen so fast that she almost couldn't grasp them; guilt at her deception, regret that Mitch had discovered the truth before she could tell him, anger that he still saw fit to interfere in her life.

Anger won out. "I've had enough of this, Mitch. You have no control over my life. You never did."

He threw his hat on the bed and yanked off his overcoat.

"Maybe you should be asking what kind of control Dorian Black has over you."

"I owe you an explanation, Mitch, but I'm not going to—"

"Did it ever occur to you that *he* might have had something to do with the attack?"

She gathered a furious retort, then stopped. Mitch's wild accusation had stunned her, but she knew she shouldn't be surprised. She'd known it would be only a matter of time before he did enough digging on Dorian to suspect that he had a criminal background. Just because *she* hadn't tried to uncover Dorian's past didn't mean it couldn't be done. His membership in Raoul's gang couldn't have been a close-kept secret, even if his name hadn't exactly been a household word.

Now Mitch had more ammunition than ever. And he wasn't afraid to use it.

"Whatever you think of Dorian," she said carefully, "you don't know him. I do. Don't ruin what we had, Mitch. There's no need for jealousy—"

"Jealousy?" He stalked toward her, jerked to a halt and sputtered a laugh. "Jealous of a thing that isn't even human?"

"What?"

"You heard me." He towered over her, working his fists. "You never noticed that he avoids sunlight like a cockroach in a kitchen?"

"What has that got to do with anything? He told me his skin is sensitive to sunlight. I looked it up. It's a real condition called—"

"Has he drunk your blood?"

The words were so absurd that Gwen had to run them through her head twice before they registered. "I think you'd better sit down," she said, gesturing toward the rickety chair in the corner of the room. "All those weeks of little sleep, the worry…I should have insisted—"

"I saw him. In the alley, with a whore. Do you know what he was doing?"

A hard lump formed in Gwen's throat. "I assume you're going to tell me."

"He had his mouth on her neck, but he wasn't kissing her.

There was blood. It was on his teeth, Gwen. He didn't even try to hide it."

Gwen was suddenly grateful for the sake of her balance that she was in her stockinged feet instead of the high-heeled pumps she'd been planning to wear that day. "You're trying to tell me—"

"He was drinking her blood," Mitch said with an air of triumph. "She wasn't fighting. She didn't even know he was doing it. And he didn't deny it. I stood right there, watching, and he said…"

His voice faded as the odd hissing behind Gwen's eardrums became a roar. She pushed past Mitch to the bed and sat, bracing her weight on her arms.

He's lying, she thought, even though she knew he wasn't. Mitch was many things, but he wasn't a liar.

She lowered her head until her hair brushed the mattress. Dorian had asked all kinds of questions about her investigation, about Dad's belief in the presence of a cult that had an obsession with blood. She'd naturally thought it was simple curiosity, and then concern over her safety.

I know the city, he'd said, long before she'd learned how well he knew it. *I know how far certain elements will go to eliminate their rivals. The evil men do needs no arcane explanation.*

No arcane explanation. Nothing but ordinary, day-to-day gangland violence.

"I don't believe it," she said, forcing herself upright. "Not for a minute."

Mitch's face twisted in a way Gwen had never seen before. "The cult is real. But it isn't what your father thought it was."

"Dorian is a *good* man. He's—"

"Eamon was half-right," Mitch said. "There are creatures in the city who have a very personal interest in the blood of others. But they aren't human, Gwen. And they are far from good."

Strangely enough, the very irrationality of his statement restored her calm. "You know that's not possible," she said.

"They exist, Gwen," he said. "Vampires. Only they call themselves *strigoi.* Black was very careful to point that out."

Gwen stifled a gasp with one hand. *Strigoi.* Dorian had used that word in his conversation with Romana. Just as he'd used the word *human* to describe people different from himself.

She wanted nothing more than to tell Mitch to get out, to go see just how well Spellman would respond to such a bizarre claims. But she didn't. She blew all the air out of her lungs, breathed deeply, and let her reporter's discipline take command.

"Tell me," she said.

Now that she'd agreed to listen, Mitch was perfectly composed, speaking in a matter-of-fact voice that he might have used to dictate an obituary. He recounted everything he'd observed about Dorian's behavior and appearance, down to the red glint in the eyes, the inhuman speed and the tipped incisors. He repeated their conversation: his incredulous questions, Dorian's ominous threats and denial of any involvement in the attack on Gwen.

"But he said there were others like him. He admitted that anyone who got close to exposing their existence was in very real danger of being murdered. He made it clear that he'd kill me if I said anything about what I'd seen."

He paced the room, step by measured step. "He claimed to have had nothing to do with the waterfront killings. Gwen—" He stopped and turned to face her. "He knows what you've been doing. He's known all along."

The muscles in Gwen's stomach contracted painfully. It was too much to take in, even though she'd been trained since childhood to absorb facts and impressions like a sponge. Her mind kept skipping back to the one central issue. The one that eclipsed all the others.

Dorian wasn't human. She didn't accept that just because of what Mitch had told her. Too many other pieces had fallen into place. Dorian's intolerance of sunlight. His remarkable strength and grace. His ability to heal almost overnight from wounds that would have killed any other man.

He hadn't only been concealing a shameful past with the bootleggers. He'd been hiding a secret far more devastating.

To him—or to you?

Gwen counted her breaths. One...two...three...four. If Dorian had worked for Kyril, did that mean that Kyril was a vampire, too? And what about his gang? How was it possible that no one knew?

Because they kill the ones who find out.

The pressure of shock and grief became too much. But she didn't give in. A new strength bubbled up inside her, the kind that almost always came to her just when she needed it most.

"I would have known if he meant to hurt me," she said. "I would have sensed it if he had some ulterior motive."

"Would you? Would you really, Gwen?"

She couldn't give him any logical reason for believing it. Dorian had deceived her so many times that she was losing count. But she had one highly illogical bit of evidence on her side. One that stood firm, even after all the overwhelming challenges to its veracity.

That stubborn, powerful evidence was love. Love for a man whose heart and soul she had only just begun to understand. Love that didn't break even in the strongest winds of adversity.

"Yes," she said. "I know you think he wanted to kill you, Mitch. But he wouldn't. I'd stake my life on it. I *will* stake my life on it."

She expected him to stare, to protest, to shout and berate. He only glanced toward the window, as if he were gauging the night's progress through the half-drawn curtains.

"There's nothing more I can do, is there?" he asked.

"I'm grateful for all you've told me," she said. "But nothing can be resolved until I speak to him myself."

"Resolved?" He gave a tired little laugh. "You'll never get what you want, Gwen. Not from a thing like him."

"I'm willing to try." She extended her hand. "All I ask of you, if you're still prepared to give it, is your continued friendship."

Mitch only stared at the window, seeing nothing. "You'll always have that, Guinevere," he said. "Always."

"Then you have to take care of yourself. Stay away from Dorian. I promise he'll never threaten you again."

Mitch shrugged.

Gwen knew she couldn't stop yet. "Promise me you won't share your discoveries with anyone else."

All the dullness sloughed away from him in an instant. "You can't expect me to sit on this, Gwen."

The story. Always the story came first. "At least keep it to yourself until we have more evidence to work with."

"We?" He snatched up his overcoat and strode to the door. "What are you going to do if you're wrong, Gwen? What on earth are you going to do?"

He opened the door, walked through, then closed it far too gently.

Testing the strength of her legs, Gwen got up, went to the bathroom and splashed cold water on her face. Her skin was so pale that her freckles looked like the spots on a Dalmatian.

Vampires exist. She tasted the phrase, rolling it over and over in her mind. What would Dad have said? Would he have taken Mitch's account as gospel and considered it validation of his ideas? Or would such fantastic tales have reawakened the skepticism he'd abandoned in his later years?

Either way, the things that had happened were too remarkable to dismiss. And though Gwen knew she should have felt trepidation at meeting Dorian again after the incident with Mitch—and after what she'd found herself doing with Dorian in this very hotel room not very long ago—she found that fascinated curiosity was by far her dominant emotion. That, and the need that never left her…the need to get at the truth.

Even if it meant losing the last of her hopeless, lovelorn illusions about Dorian Black.

CHAPTER ELEVEN

THE USUAL CONTINGENT of Kyril's hatchet men stood watch outside the hotel, revolvers tucked under loose-fitting jackets, eyes never ceasing their search for an enemy. They acknowledged Dorian with slight nods, and he walked into the lobby without hesitation.

Kyril's personal guard admitted him to the faction leader's suite, their relaxed attitudes suggesting that their master was in good spirits. Dorian stopped just inside the door and waited to be acknowledged.

"Ah, Dorian." Kyril dismissed the accountant with whom he'd been consulting and beckoned Dorian closer while two of his lieutenants took their positions behind his chair. "I'm pleased to see that you survived the contretemps with Christof's mob." He tapped his long, polished fingernails on the gleaming oak of his desk. "I'm told you accounted for at least three of his best enforcers."

"I'm pleased to have been of service."

"Oh, you have been." Kyril leaned back in his chair. "Tell me, Dorian…how long have you known Miss Gwen Murphy?"

The question was so unexpected that Dorian only just controlled his instinctive reaction. Unexpected because it came now, months after Dorian had joined Kyril, long after the faction boss should have asked it if he had suspected his enforcer's relationship to a certain troublesome human.

"I see the name means something to you," Kyril said mildly.

Dorian recovered. "Yes," he said. "She worked at the newspaper office where I was briefly employed."

"Of course. Then you were aware that her work there involved pursuing questions of interest to us?"

Dorian took a seat opposite the desk and assumed a casual posture. "Romana asked me how much I knew about the reporters' investigations. I told her I was happily ignorant of them, though she informed me about your interest in Hewitt and his developing story about the waterfront murders."

"Ah, Romana. Not the most discreet of my protégés." Kyril crossed one finely clad leg over the other. "We did find Hewitt to be a minor annoyance."

"Then I assume he has ceased to be one?"

Kyril shrugged. "Hewitt is not the topic of conversation. Your connection with Miss Murphy is."

"Was she also a 'minor annoyance'?"

"More, apparently, than we guessed." Kyril steepled his fingers beneath his chin. "How did you meet her, Dorian?"

Dorian swiftly sorted through possible responses. Since Kyril knew that he and Gwen had been acquainted, there was no point in denying it. How he had learned, assuming he hadn't known before, was an important consideration. Of greater concern was what his questions said about his attempt on Gwen's life—and whether or not he knew she was still alive.

He must. Gwen had hardly been discreet, pursuing witnesses while a death sentence hung over her head. Someone had undoubtedly seen her with Dorian after the fight and reported to Kyril.

Dorian relaxed his body further. "There is very little to tell. After Raoul's death, I was living on the waterfront—"

"Ah, yes. You virtually disappeared at a time when your fealty would have been of great value." Kyril leaned forward. "I've wondered why you chose isolation to profitable service. Javier—your former partner, was he not?—mentioned you on several occasions after he came to work for me."

"Indeed?"

"He, too, was of considerable value, though he was too hotheaded for the most subtle work. He vanished several months ago. You never happened to see him during your…retirement?"

"I saw no *strigoi.*"

"But you did see humans." Kyril sat back again. "Continue, Dorian."

"As I said, I encountered her while I was living on the docks. She had come to meet with someone in the vicinity and mistook me for a vagrant in need of her help."

"Which she gave you by securing you a position at the *Sentinel.*"

"I took the job as a means of obtaining a few necessities."

"Which you could more profitably have obtained from me. Or even Christof."

"It was not clear to me then where I should place my loyalties."

"But it is now."

"Yes."

Kyril nodded as if in approval. "Would you say that your dealings with Miss Murphy were inconsequential?"

"I would."

"Then how is it that she happened to arrive at the location of the fight with Christof's enforcers at the very moment you narrowly escaped execution?"

So that was what had prompted this interrogation. Someone *had* seen him and Gwen together after the battle with Christof's men.

Dorian let his lashes drop over his eyes. "At the time I was in no state to question her presence."

"Yet you accepted her aid."

"It would have been unwise to remain on the street."

"Why do I sense that you aren't telling me the whole story, Dorian?" Kyril said, his pleasant expression belying his words. "When Romana first told me of her unexpected meeting with you at the *Sentinel,* she indicated that you seemed curious about what others besides Hewitt I might be watching."

"It was an idle question."

"Idle, Dorian? You?" Kyril chuckled indulgently. "At the time I was more intrigued by the possibility that you might eventually join us than I was curious about any vague connection between you and the human girl." The pleasant mask slipped. "Tell me again why Miss Murphy came to your aid so conveniently."

"She said she received a tip that a fight was about to take place."

"Ah. That's better." Kyril glanced over Dorian's shoulder at the enforcers behind him. "You were aware that Miss Murphy disappeared from Manhattan not long after your conversation with Romana?"

"The newspapers said she had been killed."

"And what did you do when you learned of this tragic event, Dorian?"

"I went on about my business."

"Which included leaving your menial position and joining me."

"Cleaning floors proved to be a remarkably tedious occupation."

"So your offering your services to me had nothing to do with her apparent fate."

Dorian permitted himself a frown. "Our acquaintance was hardly an intimate one. She was not my protégée, Kyril."

"You had no idea that she had survived?"

"No."

"Did you have any suspicions as to who made the attempt?"

"I gave it no thought whatsoever."

"Even though she had come to your aid at the waterfront, no matter how mistaken she might have been in her charitable instincts?"

"She is *human*."

Given most vampires' concept for unConverted humans, that should have been enough. Kyril wasn't satisfied. He suddenly changed the subject.

"During the brief span of your time together, she never suspected your true nature? She never asked you about the existence of nonhumans?"

"Why should she?"

"Something, or someone, prodded her to increase her efforts

to investigate the waterfront murders," Kyril said. "*After* you joined the *Sentinel* staff."

Dorian half rose. "Are you implying that I had something to do with her activities?"

Heavy hands fell on his shoulders, pushing him back into the chair. Kyril showed his teeth. "I would advise you to amend your tone."

"I apologize."

A stony silence fell between them. Kyril shifted, the toes of his imported Italian shoes striking the inside of the desk.

"The point remains," he said, "that you know Miss Murphy, that she is very much alive and she is obviously not averse to continuing your 'inconsequential' relationship—even if doing so involves potential risk to herself. What did you discuss after the fight?"

"She wanted to know how I had come to be involved in a gang battle."

"She was ignorant of your former profession and your connection to Raoul?"

"Yes. It wasn't difficult to provide a convincing story to explain my presence in the wrong place at the wrong time."

"Which she believed without question."

"She is human, and female. It is possible that she has become infatuated with me."

"You took her blood."

"For the purpose of survival only."

"You were never tempted to Convert her?"

"No."

"Did she remain with you while you healed?"

So Kyril's informer hadn't managed to follow him and Gwen to her hotel. If they had…

"I sent her away," Dorian said, "and retreated to complete my recovery."

"Without contacting your superiors."

Dorian lowered his head. "I was less fully competent. I allowed my physical weakness to interfere with my duty."

"Even experienced enforcers make mistakes." Kyril's amiability had returned. "You let Miss Murphy go. Did you feel no concern for her continued survival?"

Kyril kept coming back to that subject again and again. Dorian knew that one slip on his part would put an instant end to his plan.

"I had no desire to interfere in either her life or her death."

"You would have stopped her if you'd known she suspected that the waterfront deaths were not the work of humans?"

"Did she?" Dorian cocked his head. "Clever of her."

Kyril's eyes narrowed. "Admiration, Dorian?"

"Even humans can show vestiges of intelligence."

"Which someone clearly recognized as an imminent threat, even if you did not."

Someone. Kyril was speaking as if he hadn't ordered the hit on Gwen himself. "If, after I came to you," he said, "I had been directly informed of the danger she represented, I would have done whatever was necessary."

"Excellent. Then your next task will be that much simpler."

Dorian knew what Kyril would command the moment the faction leader finished his sentence. The chill of the grave closed around his heart.

"If, as you say," Kyril said, "this girl means nothing to you, you will have no objection to finishing the work that the previous assassins bungled."

He left the statement hanging as if it were a challenge. Dorian didn't rise to the bait. "You want me to silence her."

"By any means you choose, as long as it is discreet."

"And Hewitt? Is he also to be eliminated?"

"He will be dealt with in time. He is still far away from any significant discovery. Miss Murphy is mere inches away."

Dorian made as if to rise. "A pity I was not in your employ the first time."

"The first time was not our error, yet the problem that remains belongs to every *strigoi*. Christof failed to mend the consequences of his mistakes. We will not."

The room gave a sudden twist, nearly forcing Dorian down

again. *We had nothing to do with it,* Romana had told him, referring to the waterfront massacre. He'd been understandably skeptical of her denial. And after Gwen's apparent death, the evidence had so thoroughly pointed to Kyril that Dorian had ceased considering any viable alternative.

So who…?

Kyril interpreted his silence as acquiescence. He rose, compelling Dorian to follow suit.

"You are free of any other responsibilities until this task is completed," Kyril said. "But do it quickly. The proximity of death has obviously not discouraged Miss Murphy from pursuing the line of questioning to which she seems so devoted." He waved his hand. "You may go. Report to me when it's done."

Dorian circled the chair and walked toward the door, placing each foot with care until he was out of the room and well past the guards. Once he was alone, he leaned against the corridor wall and caught his breath.

He had gone to see Kyril with the intention of killing him and as many of his men as he could reach. Now he had every reason to doubt that Kyril had been responsible for the attempt on Gwen's life. That left Christof…and yet Dorian found that possibility even more difficult to believe.

If he couldn't determine the real threat and stop it once and for all, there would never be any safety for Gwen in New York. There would be no safety even if he *did,* since Kyril had found reason to take up where the original assassin had left off.

Should Dorian neglect to carry out Kyril's orders, he would lose all standing in the faction. The master would simply send another assassin in his place. But Gwen would never leave Manhattan. Not even if she knew that all the hounds of hell were sniffing at her heels.

There had to be another way. And there was. Dorian had run out of choices. There was always the risk that Kyril would consider his method of neutralizing Gwen a form of defiance, but that risk was more acceptable than the prospect of her death.

Dorian pushed away from the wall and continued to the stairs,

Grim resolve crossed the old man's face. "I saw the handiwork of these creatures when I was little more than a c[hild] in a village where folklore was often accepted as fact. Bu[t it's] not necessary for them to kill in order to feed. They have h[ad to] adapt to the growing human population and the world's inc[reas]ing sophistication. To kill indiscriminately in a city such as [New] York would surely bring about their downfall."

"At the hands of their prey."

"Can you imagine how the average man or woman w[ould] respond to the knowledge that they might, at any tim[e, be] accosted by a beast in human form who regards the[m as] nothing more than cattle? The vampires would surely be h[unted] to extinction."

"And that's what you hope will happen."

"I do not deny it." The professor's eyes narrowed. "Is [your] interest only a matter of obtaining a 'scoop,' as you call it, [or is] it personal?"

"I'm a reporter," Mitch said. "I want the scoop. But I [don't] want what you want."

"In that case, you must be fully prepared for any situation [you] may encounter in your search. Do you know in what [way] vampires are vulnerable, how they may be destroyed?"

"Didn't Bram Stoker write about that?"

[Professor] Perkowski made a rude noise. "Stoker. That charlatan." [He tap]ped the cover of his book, which now sat on the worn ca[rpet bet]ween him and Mitch. "This will tell you what you nee[d to know]. Vampires can reliably be killed in only two ways. The [first, wit]h a fatal blow to the heart or brain. Severing of the hea[d is e]ffective, but generally impractical."

"[Th]en a bullet can kill them?"

"[On]ly if precisely placed. Few have the skill to strike exa[ctly the righ]t spot."

"[And] the second method?"

"[Prolo]nged exposure to sunlight. Such light burns through [and] eats away the tissues beneath until the vampire g[oes into a state] of shock, from which he seldom recovers."

foreboding and anticipation warring for dominance in his mind. There was no time to lose. No possibility of making Gwen understand why she must surrender the freedom she so cherished.

And you're glad of it. She'll be yours, completely yours. Nothing will be able to come between you.

With a bitter laugh, he left the hotel. Dawn was very near; he would not go to her until sunset. If she attempted to escape, he would have to be prepared to follow.

When it was done, she would never be able to run again.

MITCH KNOCKED ON THE door of the dingy walk-up, wondering if he'd heard the address correctly. The man had certainly sounded well-educated, if elderly and a bit eccentric; this was a neighborhood better known for poor immigrants and working stiffs who could barely feed their families.

But his second knock brought the professor to the door. He was pretty much what Mitch had expected: his white hair was slightly wild, and he wore thick-lensed round spectacles, along with a tattered cardigan sweater missing several buttons.

"Mr. Hogan?" The old man extended his hand, papery and roped with blue veins. "I am so pleased that you contacted me. Come in, come in. We shall have tea."

Mitch entered the cluttered apartment, noting the aged furniture and books heaped on every available surface. Doctor Perkowski swept a pile of papers from a chair and offered it to Mitch. Then the elderly gentleman puttered off to the kitchen, leaving Mitch to examine some of the titles strewn across the floor.

Lure of the Blood. Romanian Myth and Legend. The shelves lining nearly every wall were crowded with similar titles, including volumes on linguistics and medicine. But one slender book held pride of place, sandwiched between two dusty bookends on a narrow table by the window.

"*Chronicles of the Vampires,*" Mitch read aloud, rising to examine the tome. He flipped the pages, skimming dry, scholarly text punctuated at rare intervals by awkward sketches. There was no publisher's imprint on the spine.

"When I was young," Perkowski said, coming up behind Mitch with a tea tray in his hands, "I had ambitions of having my research recognized as a legitimate contribution to science. I toiled for years on that book…traveled to every country where legends of vampires were common, interviewed hundreds of people. I thought my evidence would prove overwhelming. But they laughed when I submitted my manuscript. Would you mind making a space on that chair, young man?"

Mitch obliged. He tucked the book under his arm and helped the professor with the tray. Perkowski sat cross-legged on the floor, surprisingly nimble for one of his age, and poured out the steaming liquid. Mitch sat across from him.

"You were intriguingly vague on the telephone," Perkowski said, offering a sugar cube. "It is not often that I am consulted in my avocational capacity. Have you encountered a vampire, Mr. Hogan?"

His question startled Mitch. It hadn't been easy finding a supposed vampire "expert," and only the most persistent digging had led him from university archives to this moth-eaten old man who spoke so casually of monsters. It seemed he'd definitely come to the right place.

"I have reason to believe," Mitch said slowly, "that something inhuman exists in the city."

"Ah." Perkowski took a sip of his tea with an air of satisfaction. "I knew it was only a matter of time. Not all men are blind." He squinted at Mitch. "You are a reporter, are you not?"

"I write for the *Sentinel*."

"And you came across this knowledge in the course of an investigation?"

"Something like that."

The old man carefully set his cup on the tray. "Is it your intention to expose the existence of the vampire race?"

Mitch swirled the tea in his cup. "You assume I have proof."

"If you are as good a reporter as I have heard, you will find it." Perkowski leaned forward, his wrinkled face screwed up with emotion. "You must do what I could not, Mr. Hogan."

"Maybe no one will listen to me, either."

"Perhaps. But perhaps a young voice will catch the people's attention. Perhaps, in this modern world, the creatures will not find it so easy to hide." The professor settled back again. "But we get ahead of ourselves. Tell me how you came upon the knowledge that we humans are not alone in the world."

After a moment's consideration, Mitch said that he had taken an interest in the waterfront murders and had followed several leads, one of which had resulted in the encounter with Dorian in the alley. He left out all mention of Gwen.

Perkowski's eyes were bright with appreciation. "They are generally very careful," he said. "This one was not. But you are very fortunate to have survived, Mr. Hogan."

"I gathered as much." Mitch ardently wished for something stronger to put in his tea. "Why didn't he attack?"

"That I cannot say." Perkowski hesitated. "At any time did you feel as if you were losing conscious control of your body or your mind?"

"No. Are you saying he could have…hypnotized me?"

"Vampires are very capable of overcoming the will of a human. It is the way they subdue their prey and make certain one from whom they have fed will have no memory of the…"

Mitch felt ill. "He didn't try any of that with me."

"As I said, you are fortunate." Perkowski rubbed b[…] the other hand, there may have been an excellen[t] your vampire let you go without incident."

"Which would be…?"

"I think it very likely that these waterfro[nt] indeed carried out by vampires, and they m[…] commit any further acts that might attract But you must not underestimate the dan[ger] shaking as he poured Mitch another c[up] very bold. Very bold indeed."

Mitch joined the professor on the f[loor] dangerous, but this one didn't kill h[…] he'd…finished with her. Is that typi[cal]

tap
bet
kno
is wi
also
"T
"On
the righ
"And
"Prol
flesh and
into a form

"I can't see these creatures allowing themselves to be pinned down in sunlight."

"It would not be easy, I grant you that." The professor pushed his spectacles higher up on his nose. "I confess that I have had no personal experience of such activities. Only my thorough research has convinced me of their efficacy."

"Can you really hold them off with a cross?"

"The legends specify a crucifix…but I do not believe vampires have any particular aversion to religious symbols." He peered at Mitch. "Keep in mind that killing a vampire might very well attract the attention of any others who may live in the city."

Mitch picked up the book. "Do you mind if I borrow this?"

"By all means. And I would much appreciate regular reports, Mr. Hogan." The old man sighed. "I would give a great deal to accompany you in your hunt, but I haven't a young man's energy."

"Don't give it another thought, professor. This is something I have to do alone."

"Then I can only urge you once again to take the greatest care."

Mitch got up, helped the old man to his feet and offered his hand. "I appreciate your help, Mr. Perkowski."

"It was given with the greatest of pleasure." Perkowski followed Mitch to the door. "There is one other thing you should know now, in case you encounter your vampire before you read the book. Any man—or woman—bitten by a vampire may be turned into one himself, if the creature so chooses, and the bond between them is strong."

Mitch stopped, his hand tightening on the doorknob. "What?"

"How did you imagine that vampires reproduce their own kind? They cannot sire or bear offspring. Their breed, long-lived as they are, would eventually die out if not for Conversion. Here, this may prove useful in breaking the tie." He noted Mitch's expression as he handed him a vial and lifted a conciliatory hand. "It is merely another danger to be aware of, Mr. Hogan."

With a terse goodbye, Mitch left Perkowski among his books

and hurried down the stairs. He began skimming the professor's book while the taxi took him back to the paper, searching out the chapters on Conversions and vampire-killing.

When he entered the city room, Randolph Hewitt approached, his belly leading the way.

"Hogan," he said with his usual false joviality. "Nice to see you again. I was under the impression that you'd left us for a job at *Vanity Fair.*"

In no mood for Hewitt's spite, Mitch dropped the book onto his desk and glared at his colleague. "You know where the hell I've been. Gwen—"

"Touchy, touchy." Hewitt lifted a brow. "Has our Miss Murphy been mistreating you?"

"Don't you say a word about her."

"*You* might say a word *to* her, Hogan. She has brought her troubles on herself. I think Spellman is thinking of permanently dispensing with her services."

"And you had nothing to do with it."

"It isn't as if she hasn't been warned." Hewitt's smile vanished. "Better for the paper if she takes up some more feminine occupation, like knitting."

Mitch choked on his reply. Hewitt spoke only out of contempt, but what he'd said wasn't much different from what Mitch himself had planned for Gwen when she became his wife.

Do you want her now? Now that Black has been in her apartment, in her hotel room, doing God knows what?

"I see you've had second thoughts," Hewitt said. "There may be hope for you yet."

The fat man walked away. Mitch sat down, rigid with anger.

It isn't her fault. Perkowski said that vampires can make people do whatever they want. Black has her dancing like a puppet on a string.

That string would have to be snapped if he were to set Gwen free.

Mitch left his latest story unfinished and went to buy the most powerful gun he could find.

CHAPTER TWELVE

GWEN KNEW WHO it was even before she answered the knock.

She opened the door, her heart performing somersaults somewhere between her stomach and throat. Dorian stepped into the room, graceful and imposing, looking no different than he had when he'd left the hotel last night.

But nothing was really the same. Now she *knew.* And he was about to tell her everything.

"Are you all right?" he asked, looking her over intently.

"Sure. Why shouldn't I be?"

He didn't reply but made a circuit of the room, just as Mitch had the day before. "Gwen," he said, "there's something I must tell—"

"Something you have to tell me," Gwen said, finishing at the same time. They stared at each other. Dorian folded his hands behind his back and studied the far wall. Gwen forced herself to sit in a chair in the corner, defying her unease.

He wouldn't hurt her. No matter what he was, she was certain of that. And her feelings hadn't changed. Not in the least.

"I *know,*" she said softly.

His head came up. "I beg your pardon?"

"Mitch…came here after you left."

The pupils of Dorian's eyes shrank to pinpoints. He lifted his upper lip, and Gwen saw the glint of pointed teeth she'd somehow managed to ignore for months.

Because you weren't looking. You didn't even begin to suspect.

Dorian recovered quickly. "I should have known he'd come straight to you," he said. "He warned you against me."

"What did you expect?" She carefully folded her hands in her lap. "He was shocked and afraid. Who wouldn't be, after what he witnessed?" She smiled. "Funny. *I* should be afraid, shouldn't I?"

"Not you. Never you."

"I'll take that as a compliment as well as a promise."

Dorian's body was taut as a bowstring. "What did he tell you?"

"Everything he saw." She subdued her vivid imagination. "That the woman you…fed from walked away as if nothing had happened."

"I'm surprised he didn't claim otherwise."

"He's never been less than honest with me."

A sound very much like a growl rumbled from Dorian's throat. "You can't trust him."

"That's a funny thing to say, coming from someone who's been deceiving me ever since we met."

"If I had simply explained what I was, what would you have done?"

"I don't know. I hope I would have tried to understand. Are you part of a cult, Dorian?"

He ran his hand sharply through his hair. "Hardly. My kind have been living on this earth nearly as long as man."

"And you've managed to keep it a secret all this time."

"Not always." He looked at her in a way that made her keenly aware of the bed they'd occupied less than twenty-four hours ago. "Will Hogan go to the paper?"

"I told him no one would believe him."

"You believed."

"A lot of things made more sense to me when I considered the possibility that you were a…what was the name?"

"*Strigoi.*"

"Yes. *Strigoi.*" She got up and approached him cautiously. "Do you mind if I look a little more closely?"

"What do you expect to see that you didn't before?"

She knew he was referring to their lovemaking, but she didn't let self-consciousness stop her. "I don't know," she said. "I don't suppose you have scales or spines or anything like that?"

"No."

Gwen placed her palm on the center of his chest. His heart beat full and strong. "Don't the books say you're supposed to be dead?"

"I believe the word is *undead*."

"You seem very much alive to me."

"Because I am."

"Then you don't have to sleep in a coffin at night."

He covered her hand with his. "We prefer beds, just like humans."

Gwen felt a little weak. "Your eyes look pretty normal to me. Do you mind if I look at your teeth?"

The expression on his face wasn't encouraging. "If you insist."

She looked, wondering again how she'd managed to miss something that should have been so obvious to any newswoman worth her salt. "They don't look terribly sharp."

"They work well enough."

"Do you really bite people and drink their blood?"

"Isn't that what Hogan told you?"

"Yes, but…it's still a little hard to imagine."

"What else do you imagine, Gwen?"

"Is it true you can live forever?"

"No. Even we die eventually."

The thought of Dorian dead was far worse than the idea that he wasn't human. "How old are you?" she asked.

"Older than you."

"That's not what I meant, and you know it." She held his gaze. "A hundred years? A thousand?"

Grim amusement lit his eyes. "Sixty-three."

"That's all?"

"You sound disappointed."

"If I'm going to have strange and exotic men in my life, I might as well have them as strange and exotic as possible."

"There are others of my kind you might find more suitable. Some have been alive since the Crusades."

"You're kidding." She licked her lips. "Is that…regular 'bad mood' of yours part of being a vampire?"

Dorian's face closed like a fist. "We are no more all alike than humans are."

"But…" *Easy, Gwen. One thing at a time.* "You're not the only *strigoi* in New York."

"No."

"How many?"

She could see that he was reluctant to tell her, but she couldn't let him off the hook now. "It's *strigoi* who've wanted to kill me all along, isn't it?"

Abruptly he took her face between his hands. "Gwen, Gwen…"

She tried not to give way to his touch. "You worked for Raoul's gang," she said. "Did he know what you are?"

"Yes. He was one himself."

"And…and Kyril?"

"Yes."

It felt to Gwen as though someone had dropped a huge boulder directly in front of her and she'd stumbled right into it. "My God," she whispered. "Was the whole gang…?"

"Most of them." He dropped his hands and walked away, his movements tense and uncharacteristically awkward. "We call it the clan. But the clan was torn apart when Raoul died."

The world turned upside down. "They controlled nearly a quarter of the city," she said.

He faced her again. "That is not likely to change." His eyes glittered in just the way Mitch had described, and Gwen felt the full force of his power.

A vampire enforcer. She couldn't think of anything more fearsome. "The factions fighting for control of Raoul's territory…" she said, her voice not quite under perfect control. "All vampires?"

"Yes." He dropped his gaze. "I did not deceive you when I said that I believed the waterfront murders were the work of Kyril's faction."

"Why did he kill those men? Are humans involved with the vampire factions?"

"The victims were also *strigoi*."

Gwen remembered the coroner's reports she'd read when she'd begun her investigation. There had been no mention of unusual features, thought the flesh had been badly burned, presumably with the use of some kind of accelerant. Now she knew that the cause of the burns was far more disturbing.

"Were they members of Christof's faction?"

"I don't know. I was not serving either pretender at the time."

"Is…what was done to them a typical form of vampire retaliation?"

"It is a barbaric practice, and dangerous for obvious reasons."

"Isn't it barbaric for vampires to eliminate anyone who might expose them?"

She knew from Dorian's expression that Mitch's warnings had been right on the money. His suspicions crowded her thoughts like a mob of angry villagers armed with torches and pitchforks.

"Dad's notes said that there were a couple of similar murders years ago," she said. "Someone must have investigated them… cops, reporters, maybe others. I wonder who died to protect the killers' secrets then?" She moistened her lips. "Mitch said that maybe you were sent to watch me. To report on what I'd learned."

His reaction was almost too swift for her to follow up. He seized her shoulders, half lifting her from the ground, and stared into her eyes.

"No one sent me," he said harshly. "I left the clan when Raoul died. I was ready to die when you found me. Because of you…" His voice broke. He released her and backed away, as if he truly feared what he might do to her.

No longer certain of her balance, Gwen felt for the chair and sat down again. "I—I didn't mean it. I never really suspected— Oh, damn."

Dorian continued to retreat until he was as far away from her as he could get. Gwen closed her eyes, remembering all their conversations since the day he'd saved her from the river. It was so obvious now. So painfully obvious.

"Vampires live by taking blood from humans," she said slowly. "But they don't have to kill for it."

He shook his head, jaw set.

"You wanted to…do that to me when I came to see you at the warehouse, didn't you? That was another reason why you tried to send me away. But it's not as if I would have been hurt. Would I?"

"You wouldn't even have known."

The love she felt then was so overwhelming that tears came to her eyes. "You didn't do it. Why?"

"Because…"

"Because biting me would turn me into someone like you," she said.

Dorian didn't move. He even seemed to stop breathing. Then his body relaxed, and he stepped away from the wall.

"It's nothing like the legends say," he said. "It takes an act of will to create a *strigoi*."

The need to know eclipsed all other questions in Gwen's mind. "How did it happen? How did you become what you are?"

He began to speak, his voice flat and deliberate. He told her of his childhood in the slums, his time spent among the gangs, how Raoul had rescued him from death.

"Now I know why you were loyal to Raoul," she said. "It must have seemed that you owed him everything."

"Yes."

She got up and went to him, her arms aching to hold him. "Was it terrible? Was it hard to accept what you'd become?"

"No." At last he met her gaze. "It was like going to sleep and waking up to a new world."

A new world. A world of being confined to the darkness, forced to subsist on a single bitter liquid for the rest of your long life. Living apart from the rest of humanity, watching those human beings you came to know dying while you continued on.

A world in which you were stronger and faster than everyone else. Where you could heal from wounds that would kill a human instantly. Where you could experience the march of history as no mortal man or woman had ever done before.

Think what you could see. What you could learn, all the incredible stories you could record for posterity.

Temptation held her mute, dazzling her with uncounted possibilities. Her imagination conjured up a future with Dorian by her side, never ending.

And then she remembered that vampires had sucked the life from three men and left them to rot on the boardwalk. She remembered the legends and stories, none of which had ever presented vampires as anything but evil. Raoul's gang had been one of the worst in Manhattan. Maybe whatever changed people to *strigoi* also took away the best of their humanity.

Dorian isn't like that. But he'd threatened to kill Mitch if the reporter told anyone what he'd seen. He'd been an enforcer for a ruthless mob boss. He prowled the streets looking for humans to feed his hunger. Even now, he could be hiding essential secrets from her, secrets that might hang in the balance between *strigoi* and human, life and death.

Maybe she was being dangerously foolish for not fearing the man who stood before her.

"You can bite someone," she said, "without changing her."

He looked toward the window, and Gwen imagined him yearning for the darkness beyond. "Yes," he said.

"I want you to bite me."

His gaze remained fixed on the curtains. "Are you certain?"

"I want to know what it feels like." She gave him a lopsided smile. "No reporter worth her salt would turn down such an opportunity."

DORIAN TRIED TO IGNORE the urge to turn and run for the door like the abject coward he knew himself to be. But there were no other options, not anymore. Gwen couldn't leave this room except as a Convert. And she wouldn't know until it was done.

She'd asked him to bite her as if it would be the first time. For her, it would seem to be. Though she'd maintained a certain degree of consciousness after he'd bitten her, her memory of the bite had been safely erased.

That deception was nothing compared to what he was about to do.

"Dorian?"

He looked at her, memorized the guileless candor and simple decency of her features. He would never see that beloved face the same way again.

"As you wish," he said.

She shuffled her stockinged feet on the carpet. "Is there something I should be doing?"

"Just relax." He closed the distance between them in two steps. She flinched, squared her shoulders and blew out a long breath.

"I'm ready."

So was he. His cock strained against his trousers, and his mouth flooded with anticipation. For him it would be another taste of heaven. For Gwen...

For Gwen it would be the end of everything she had known.

He placed his hands on her shoulders and kissed her lightly on the lips. She began to respond, but he lowered his head to the juncture of her neck and shoulder, opening the collar of her blouse to expose the pale, veined skin. Her heartbeat quickened. He could not have withdrawn now even if he'd wanted to.

"Don't be afraid," he said. And bit her, quickly, his tongue laving the skin as blood began to seep from the wounds.

Her body went loose in his grip. He adjusted his hold to support her under her arms and sank to his knees, carrying her with him. She smiled and murmured endearments, half-aware, as she'd been the night before.

It was a matter of a single thought to alter the chemicals in his saliva just enough to pass on the substance that would alter Gwen's very nature. He sensed the change beginning even before he ended the feeding. Tremors moved through her body, irregular and small at first, but gradually growing more forceful. She sagged, her head lolling onto her shoulder.

Dorian scooped his arm under her knees and carried her to

the bed, freshly made up with clean sheets and blankets. He laid her down, flung back the covers and adjusted the pillows under her head. Her teeth had begun to chatter. Her eyes, though open, could no longer see. In a few moments she would lapse into a deep sleep that might last anywhere from a few hours to several days, a healing sleep that would allow her body to make the profound transformation.

Gently he cocooned her among the sheets and blankets, adjusting and readjusting until he was certain of her comfort. She had stopped moving, her lips slightly parted, her chest rising and falling more and more slowly. Soon it would seem as if she weren't breathing at all.

Dorian pulled a chair up beside the bed and sat as close as he could. There were instances in which humans suffered distress or even death during Conversion. He had never prayed in sixty-three years of existence, but now he cast his thoughts outward to whatever might exist beyond the world, promising his own life in exchange for hers.

She must live. Even if she were to hate him when she emerged from her trance, she must survive.

He barely altered his position as the hours of the night gave way to dawn. Near noon, he rose to stretch cramped muscles and splash water on his face. When he returned to the bed, he discovered that Gwen had changed position, her arms flung over her head and the sheets tangled around her feet.

For the next several hours she tossed in a fever, her skin blazing hot and her red hair soaked with sweat. Dorian brought cloths dipped in cold water to bathe her forehead, but her temperature remained high.

A strange, broken sound caught in Dorian's throat. His eyes remained dry, yet they burned with the tears he couldn't shed. He gathered her into his arms and willed the coolness of his own body into hers.

At last, just as the day was waning again, she threw off the fever and settled into a deeper sleep. The first crisis was past. Dorian rose from the bed and circled the room a dozen times,

ready to scrape the cheap wallpaper from the walls with his fingernails. A few minutes later he found Gwen's skin frigid to the
touch. He ran out into the corridor, seized a passing maid and
demanded more blankets. She stared at him in terror and scurried
off to obey.

A male employee returned in her place, eyeing Dorian with
nervous disapproval. Dorian grabbed the blankets and raced
back into the room. He piled the blankets over Gwen and slid
underneath them to lie beside her.

"Dorian?"

Her voice was slurred with sleep, as bewildered as a child's.
Dorian's muscles unlocked one by one. He held her close and
kissed her cheek, her eyelids, the curve of her neck.

She smiled lazily and traced her fingertip over his nose.
"Don't tell me I slept through the good part."

For a moment Dorian wondered if she actually had some con-
ception of what she'd just endured. But she yawned and
stretched and showed not the slightest sign of comprehension.

"If that's what a vampire's bite does to you," she said, "I
should get one every night. Better than bromides." She rolled
over to look at the window. "How long have I been sleeping? It
can't still be dark."

Dorian said nothing. He felt her contentment, and he couldn't
bear to destroy it. Best to let her talk. Best to let her discover the
changes gradually, naturally.

Because you're a coward.

Gwen sat up, fluffed her hair and sniffed. "Is that coffee I
smell?" She grinned at Dorian. "You're a sweetheart to think of
it." She swung her legs over the side of the bed and glanced
around the room. "I don't see it."

Nor would she. She was smelling someone else's early
breakfast in some other room. "What would you like?" Dorian
asked. "I'll send for it."

"Don't bother." She rubbed her stomach. "I feel hungry, but
it's a funny kind of feeling. I think I'll wait a bit." She began to
rise and plopped back down on the bed almost immediately.

"I feel a little dizzy," she said. "Another aftereffect?"

Dorian took her arm gently. "You should lie still for a while."

"But I don't want to." She cocked her head, her gaze turning inward. "Come to think of it, I don't think I've ever felt so alive. It's as if the air itself has substance it never had before." She smiled again. "Even colors look brighter. And my shoulder doesn't hurt anymore. Have you thought about patenting your bite as a cure-all? People would be lined up around the block." She peered into Dorian's face. "That's a joke."

She attempted to stand again, and this time succeeded. She did an odd little dance, spinning around with her arms outspread, then stopped abruptly.

"I guess I really am hungry after all," she said. "Oh." She doubled over, arms wrapped around her waist. Dorian leaped up and carried her back to the bed.

"You must rest a little while longer," he said.

She squeezed her eyes shut. "My…stomach hurts. Is something…going wrong?"

"No." He laid his hand on her forehead. Her temperature was slightly cool, not atypical for *strigoi*. She was simply beginning to feel the first hunger pangs, the driving need for blood that always afflicted the newly Converted.

He would have to tell her soon. He would need to take her out in search of safe prey before the sun rose.

"I think…you're right," she said. "I'll just lie down for a few minutes."

Dorian covered Gwen with a sheet and sat on the edge of the bed to wait. He was so deeply lost in thought that he almost didn't hear the door open.

Mitch stepped into the room, one hand clenched and the other hidden inside his jacket.

"You," he said, his voice filled with loathing. "Where's…?"

He looked past Dorian toward the bed and froze. "What have you done?" He pulled a gun from under his coat and aimed at Dorian. "You've killed her."

"I assure you," Dorian said softly, "she is quite alive."

Mitch moved to rush past Dorian, who barred his way with an extended arm. The human turned and pushed the muzzle of the gun into Dorian's temple.

"I know what you are," Hogan said with abnormal calm. "I know how to kill you. A bullet to the brain will do nicely."

Dorian lifted his lip. "Assuming you succeeded," he said, "you would then be guilty of murder."

"Murder? Of a thing like you?" He pushed harder. "I'd be doing the world a favor."

"Mitch?"

Gwen's voice distracted the other reporter for less than a second. Dorian kept still. He wouldn't allow Gwen to witness Mitch's death.

"It's all right, Gwen," Hogan said, keeping his gaze locked on Dorian. "You're safe now."

"Of course I am." Gwen got up with a smooth, graceful motion and started toward Mitch. "I told you that I'd talk to Dorian. He's been completely honest with me about who and what he is. We have nothing to be afraid of."

Mitch laughed. "Is that really what you think?" He stared into Dorian's face. "Ask him what he really wants to do to you."

"What are you talking about?"

"He's bitten you, hasn't he?"

"Do I look as though I've been hurt?"

"Would she know it?" Mitch asked Dorian, grinding flesh with the muzzle of the gun. "Would she know how you've changed her?"

"Leave the room, Gwen," Dorian said quietly.

"No." She stood very straight, and there was a reddish glint in her eyes. "Put the gun down, Mitch."

"I can't." A pleading tone entered Mitch's voice. "You don't even realize what he's capable of. He—"

Dorian spun, bringing the side of his hand down hard on the human's arm. But Hogan was not entirely unprepared. He let himself fall, rolled across the carpet and came up again with his gun aimed at Dorian's heart.

The gun's report boomed like cannon fire. Dorian felt the bullet strike his chest and penetrate flesh that had barely healed. He staggered. A pale blur flashed by him, hurling itself at Mitch with a banshee's cry. Mitch scrambled away, striking the wall as he tried to fight off the madwoman intent on his destruction.

It was over in less than a dozen seconds. Mitch lay in the corner, slumped and motionless. Gwen crouched in the center of the room, her breath sawing in and out of her throat. There was blood on her fingertips. Slowly she lifted her hands.

"My God," she whispered. "I've killed him."

CHAPTER THIRTEEN

DORIAN CAUGHT HIS BALANCE and ran to Gwen, pulling her to her feet. He gave her a rough hug, herded her to the bed and sat her down.

"Stay here," he ordered, and returned to Mitch. The human's face was covered with scratches, and there was evidence that he'd hit his head during the struggle. But Dorian could see that he was still breathing, and there were no other visible wounds.

"He'll be all right," Dorian said, returning to the bed. "You didn't kill him, Gwen."

She stared blankly across the room, bloodied hands palm-up on her lap. "What did I do?" she whispered. "What…what's happened to me?"

Dorian knew exactly what had happened. When he'd attacked Mitch, Gwen had felt his anger. And when he'd been shot, Gwen had shared at least some part of the pain. The bond was growing stronger by the minute.

Dorian glanced toward the window. They had perhaps an hour of darkness left. "We must leave," he said. "The gunshot will have attracted attention. Someone has surely called the police."

"Oh, God." Gwen looked up at Dorian. "He shot you. He… are you…?"

"It's no worse than the other wounds," he said. "I'll recover." He searched the room for her suitcases and found them tucked under the bed. "Do you have an evening gown with you?"

"What?"

"If you have one, pack it. What about a coat? Have you a long one? Gloves and a hat?"

An Important Message from the Editors

Dear Reader,

Because you've chosen to read one of our fine novels, we'd like to say "thank you!" And, as a **special** way to thank you, we're offering to send you a choice of <u>two more</u> of the books you love so well **plus** two exciting Mystery Gifts — absolutely <u>FREE</u>!

Please enjoy them with our compliments...

Pam Powers

Peel off seal and place inside...

The Editor's "Thank You" Free Gifts Include:

- *2 Romance OR 2 Suspense books!*
- *2 exciting mystery gifts!*

Yes! I have placed my
Editor's "Thank You" seal in the
space provided at right. Please
send me 2 free books, which
I have selected, and 2 fabulous
mystery gifts. I understand I am
under no obligation to purchase
any books, as explained on the
back of this card.

PLACE
FREE GIFT
SEAL
HERE

▼ DETACH AND MAIL CARD TODAY! ▼

| ☐ **ROMANCE** |
| 193 MDL ERQS 393 MDL ERRG |

| ☐ **SUSPENSE** |
| 192 MDL ERYS 392 MDL ERQ4 |

FIRST NAME

LAST NAME

ADDRESS

APT.#

CITY

STATE/PROV.

ZIP/POSTAL CODE

Thank You!

(EE2-H0N-08) © 2007 HARLEQUIN ENTERPRISES LIMITED

The Reader Service — Here's How It Works:

Accepting your 2 free books and 2 free gifts places you under no obligation to buy anything. You may keep the books and gifts and return the shipping statement marked "cancel." If you do not cancel, about a month later we'll send you 3 additional books and bill you just $5.49 each in the U.S. or $5.99 each in Canada, plus 25¢ shipping & handling per book and applicable taxes if any.* That's the complete price and — compared to cover prices starting from $6.99 each in the U.S. and $8.50 each in Canada — it's quite a bargain! You may cancel at any time, but if you choose to continue, every month we'll send you 3 more books, which you may either purchase at the discount price or return to us and cancel your subscription.

*Terms and prices subject to change without notice. Sales tax applicable in N.Y. Canadian residents will be charged applicable provincial taxes and GST. All orders subject to approval. Books received may vary. Credit or debit balances in a customer's account(s) may be offset by any other outstanding balance owed by or to the customer. Please allow 4 to 6 weeks for delivery. Offer available while quantities last.

BUSINESS REPLY MAIL

FIRST-CLASS MAIL   PERMIT NO. 717   BUFFALO, NY

POSTAGE WILL BE PAID BY ADDRESSEE

THE READER SERVICE
3010 WALDEN AVE
PO BOX 1341
BUFFALO NY 14240-8571

NO POSTAGE
NECESSARY
IF MAILED
IN THE
UNITED STATES

"Yes, of course."

"Put them on."

With visible effort, Gwen got to her feet. "The police... shouldn't we explain—"

"Would you have them see how little I've been affected by an injury that would kill most humans?"

She met his gaze, bewilderment in her eyes. "But Mitch—"

"Someone will find him soon enough."

'I can't just...leave him like this."

"You must," Dorian said. "Are you registered under your real name?" Gwen shook her head. "Then it may take some time for the authorities to discover that you were here when the gun was fired."

"Mitch may think...now that he's seen..." She swallowed. "He may think he has nothing to lose if he talks."

"You'll be well hidden before he does."

To her credit, Gwen recovered her wits and began to sort through the clothing folded in her suitcases. Dorian made up a quick bandage for his chest, threw on his overcoat and stayed by the door, listening. Apparently no hotel guest or employee dared to come near the source of the commotion—a wise decision in light of the mob violence so common in the city.

"I'm ready," Gwen said, her voice still shaky. "Where are we going?"

"To a safer place." He took the suitcase and hustled her out of the room. He found a service corridor that led to a door opening onto an alley. Gwen hesitated as they stepped outside.

"It's so bright," she said, lifting her hand to her eyes. "Has the sun come up?"

"Not yet." He took Gwen's arm and urged her out to the street. She gave a racking cough.

"I think I'm going to be sick," she moaned.

Dorian supported her weight. "Hold on just a little longer," he said. Lifting his head, he began to search for likely prey. The area was not fashionable for night life or blessed with prosperous residents, so the only pedestrians at this hour were those conducting shady business, deliverymen, or men and women with nowhere else to go. Gwen would need a great deal of blood for her first feeding, so the donor must be strong and healthy.

A few blocks farther on, he spotted a large, muscular man in a shabby coat and moth-eaten hat walking briskly up the street. Dorian pushed Gwen gently into the shelter of a doorway.

"Wait here," he said.

She sat on the steps, her head resting on her knees. "Where are you going?" she asked.

"Not far. I'll be back in a few minutes."

In fact it took less than two minutes to catch up to the big man, step in front of him and pacify him with the gentlest of bites. No one witnessed the incident or noticed Dorian as he led the human back to the doorway.

"Gwen," he said.

She raised her head. There were deep circles under her eyes, and the corners of her mouth were cracked and dry. "Help me, Dorian."

"You will help yourself." He lifted her to her feet. Slowly her attention was drawn to the man, who didn't even register her presence.

"Who is he?" she said faintly. "I don't—"

There was no subtlety in the change that came over her then. One moment she was weak and withdrawn, the next all fierce attention. She stepped toward the man, and her lips pulled back from her teeth.

"Drink," Dorian whispered. "Drink and be well."

Something inside her, some remnant of humanity, made her hesitate. But the demands of instinct were far too powerful to resist. She reached for the man, wrapping her hands around his upper arms, and bent over his neck. A trickle of blood marked the tiny wound Dorian had made. Her tongue darted out to taste the blood, and she closed her eyes in ecstasy.

The man's head fell back, exposing more of his throat. Gwen sank her teeth into his flesh. A shiver worked through the man's body as he began to experience the sensual pleasure that accompanied Gwen's bite. After five minutes his legs began to buckle, and Dorian knew he'd given all he could. He took Gwen's shoulders.

"Enough," he said.

She resisted, which surprised him a little. But she fell back with a whimper of protest, her lips painted red. Dorian kissed her, tasting her sweetness along with the blood. Then he eased the man down onto the steps and propped him against the door.

It was clear that Gwen was still not aware of what she had done. Dorian picked up her suitcase and continued to guide her in the direction of a busier street, where they could summon a taxi. Only when they were ensconced in the backseat did Gwen return to herself.

She raised her hand to her face and touched her lips, then the ridges of her white teeth. Confusion gave way to memory, wringing a cry of horror from her chest.

"You all right back there, lady?" the cabbie asked.

"She is fine," Dorian said in a tone that discouraged further inquiries.

The cabbie shrugged and turned his attention back to the road. Gwen stared down at her hands.

"What did I do?" she whispered. "What have I become?"

Desperate as he was to touch her, Dorian maintained as much distance as he could in the confined space. "It was necessary," he said. "It was the only way I could save you."

"What?" She looked at him, her eyes all pupil.

But she wasn't really asking a question. The knowledge was already within her. She saw and heard many times more keenly than any human ever born. She felt the new strength surging in her muscles, the quickening in her blood and nerves that would stave off aging for centuries. She knew instinctively that she could throw a man twice her size across a room in the same way she might throw a pencil.

She was still silent when the cab pulled up at the curb in front of Kyril's hotel. Dorian kept a proprietary hand on Gwen's arm as they passed the guards outside the hotel and inside the lobby.

Gwen walked like an automaton. She didn't acknowledge the

stares of Kyril's hatchet men, or the wary glances of the human staff. The boy in the lift gazed steadily at the mirrored walls as if he found his own reflection of the greatest interest. The elevator reached the third floor, and Dorian led her to the door of his private rooms.

Gwen stopped short. She leaned against the wall, breathing in quick bursts like sobs.

"You changed me," she said.

Dorian set down the suitcase. "Yes," he said.

"Why?" Her eyes were lucid now, hard with accusation and fear.

"I was ordered to eliminate you."

They were entering dangerous territory. Dorian scanned the corridor in both directions, listening. "We should go inside."

"Where are we?"

"I'll explain everything." He took her arm. "Come."

They entered the suite. Gwen ignored the expensive furnishings and stood in the center of the sitting room as if she had lost the will to move.

"Why did you change me?" she repeated.

Dorian braced himself. "I was ordered to kill you."

The blunt words made her flinch as if he'd struck her. "Then you were after me all along."

"No. I told you the truth, Gwen. I joined Kyril only after I believed you were dead. He ordered the hit when he learned that you were still alive."

She stared dazedly at the carpet. "You went back to see him."

"Yes. I was on my way to his headquarters when Hogan confronted me."

"You were going to kill Kyril. Because of me."

"I didn't have the chance. Gwen…"

"I knew whoever wanted me dead would probably keep trying," she said. "But he ordered you—" She shivered. "Did he know about us?"

"Not until someone reported to him that you'd helped me after the ambush by Christof's enforcers."

"And now you've brought me…" She glanced around the

room as if she were seeing it for the first time. "Those men outside. They looked like enforcers." As pale as she was, she lost even more color. "Are we at Kyril's headquarters?"

"It isn't what you think." Dorian found it difficult to speak. "I convinced Kyril that though you and I were acquainted, I felt nothing for you. If I fail in my assigned mission, he will only send another assassin in my place."

"Like he's sent you to mop up after the first try."

"I'm no longer certain that he was behind the first attempt."

Her throat produced a strange little giggle. "I must be very important to have so many enemies."

"Your current enemy is all that matters now." He tried to marshal his thoughts, knowing that the worst was yet to come. "I could have killed Kyril, but others would have succeeded him immediately, and you would be alone. I had to find a more permanent solution."

She pressed her hands to her forehead. "How in hell is making me like you supposed to save me?"

Suddenly he felt very weary. "Kyril wanted you neutralized," he said. "The most obvious way would be by killing you. But if you were to cease to be a threat…if you could no longer pursue your investigation of your father's theories…that would serve the same purpose."

Gwen laughed again, the sound trailing off to a croak. "You mean I wouldn't be able to do my job anymore once I changed."

"Even that likelihood might not convince Kyril."

She turned on him, fists clenched. "Why not? How easy do you suppose it would be for me to turn up at the paper and tell Spellman that I can only work nights from now on? How much use would I be to anyone?"

"You are a resourceful woman. You might find a way."

She made a warding gesture with her hands and walked halfway to the window. Dawn light was beginning to creep around the edges of the dark, heavy drapes. She went no closer.

"So let me get this straight," she said bitterly. "Kyril may not be satisfied with what you've done to 'neutralize' me. If there was a chance that my becoming a vampire wouldn't stop my investigation, what good did it do? Why...?" She seemed to lose her voice. Dorian closed his eyes.

"There is a very practical reason," he said. "When a *strigoi* Converts a human, a symbiotic relationship is created. A bond, if you will."

"Is that...is that what I feel?" she whispered.

"Yes," Dorian said, nearly unmanned by the powerful new emotions crowding his heart. "The bond can almost never be broken except by the death of the patron."

"What does that mean? We're stuck with each other forever?" Her question was exactly the one he had been dreading.

"Prolonged separation is...difficult."

"But that isn't all, is it?"

Dorian knew that explaining would never make her understand completely. He focused his will.

"Turn around, Gwen," he said. "Look at me."

She turned...not smoothly or naturally, but as if he had pulled a marionette's strings. Her face was caught in an expression of surprise. She hadn't completely realized what had happened.

"Go to the bed," Dorian said. "Sit down."

"I don't want—" Her eyes widened, and the muscles in her shoulders grew taut as she fought the command. She never had a chance. She walked to the bed, step by unwilling step, and sat on the edge.

"Now you see," Dorian said.

He winced as he felt her bewilderment and fury. "You... forced me."

"Yes."

"You mean you can make me do whatever you want?"

"With very few exceptions."

She tried to stand. Her legs quivered with the effort. She gave up only when she was out of breath and trembling with exhaustion.

"I never thought," she said, panting, "I never thought I could think of you as evil, no matter who you were or what you'd done.

But now…" She stared at him with loathing. "How do you justify slavery, Dorian?"

"It isn't—"

"Is this the future I have to look forward to? Centuries of being your plaything?"

Her accusation was a worse punishment than anything Dorian had endured since Raoul's death. "There is a purpose in this, as unlikely as it might appear now."

"I'll bet." She rubbed her hand across her mouth. "You'd better tell me to shut up, Dorian, or I'm likely to tell you what I really think of you."

Dorian looked away. She didn't have to tell him. He knew well enough. And he couldn't even promise that he would never restrict her speech, not when they had yet to face Kyril.

"I don't expect you to forgive me," he said. "I do expect you to obey until you're out of danger."

"Yes, master."

He went to the window, half tempted to raise the blinds and let the sun do what it would.

You're a fool and a coward. This is no time for regret. He gripped the drapes in his fist, nearly tearing them from their heavy rod.

"Soon we'll go to meet Kyril," he said, stripping his voice of emotion. "You will speak only when I command, or if Kyril asks you a direct question. You will do and say nothing to jeopardize your life."

"What life? You've left me no—"

"Once this is over, you will have as much freedom as I can grant you. You'll have nothing if I fail to convince Kyril. I—"

He broke off at the sound of a brisk knock on the door. One of Kyril's personal bodyguards stood in the corridor.

"Dorian," the bodyguard said, peering over his shoulder. "Kyril wants to speak with you."

Just as he'd expected. "I'll be there in a few minutes," he said.

The bodyguard continued to stare at Gwen. "Your first one, isn't she?" he asked. "Not bad. She must be even better without the clothes."

Dorian came within a hairsbreadth of breaking the boy's neck. He shut the door instead.

"Did you bring a gown, as I requested?" he asked Gwen without turning.

She didn't speak. Silence was her only means of defiance, but he couldn't allow her to continue.

"Answer me, Gwen."

"Yes," she said, squeezing the word between clenched teeth.

"Put it on. Comb your hair. Make yourself as attractive as possible."

"For Kyril? Are you going to give me to him?"

The question was as ignorant as it was appalling. "No. But he'll better understand why I Converted you if he sees your beauty." He jerked his head toward the lavatory. "Go. Be quick."

She rose, picked up her suitcase and went into the bathroom, slamming the door behind her. Dorian released his breath and waited. A good ten minutes had passed before she emerged, clad in a deep blue fishtail gown with a plunging back. She'd pulled her hair up in a way that complemented the delicate bones of her face, and her lips were stained a burgundy red.

She was utterly stunning.

With a mocking flourish she pivoted to display herself. "Well, master? Am I ready for auction?"

Dorian held out his arm. "Come quietly. Try to remember that your life is in Kyril's hands."

She looped her arm through the crook of his elbow, every muscle and tendon resisting his will. Her face was icy and pale as he led her out of the suite and down the corridor toward Kyril's apartments.

"He had Converted her," Taharial said.

Sammael stiffened, unable to believe what he'd just heard. "How is this possible?" he said, looming over the younger man. "How could you have bungled so badly?"

Taharial bent his head. Clearly he had no explanation for his failure. Sammael would certainly demote him in the Guard, but that would hardly affect the current disaster.

"Report," Sammael ordered tersely.

Shaken, Taharial began to relate how one of Pax's agents, who had recently been promoted to lieutenant in Kyril's organization, had overheard a conversation between Dorian Black and the faction leader…how he'd learned that Gwen was alive and in Manhattan.

"Our man reported that Kyril denied having had anything to do with the first attempt on Murphy's life."

"And what was Dorian's reaction to this information?" Sammael asked.

"His feelings were not apparent."

"Go on."

"Kyril asked Dorian if he cared for the girl. Black denied it. Then—" Taharial lifted his head. "Kyril ordered Dorian to eliminate her."

Immediately Sammael forgot his anger. "Yet Dorian did not carry out Kyril's orders."

"No. As soon as I received the report from our agent, I sent two of our best men to trail Black. At sunset he entered a hotel and went to a room on the third floor. Murphy answered the door."

Sammael took his chair again. "That was where he Converted her."

"Our agents had ample evidence of this after Black and Murphy left the hotel."

"And why didn't your men intervene?"

"They claimed there was too much human activity at the hotel to risk open conflict should Dorian refuse to cooperate."

Sammael's anger flared again. "Fools and cowards," he muttered. "What did these incompetents do?"

"They were not able to overhear the conversation between Dorian and the human, but after a full day had passed, another human approached the room."

"Who?"

"Mitch Hogan."

Mitch Hogan, one of Gwen Murphy's colleagues at the *Sentinel,* a man Sammael had regarded as of little importance. "What was the human's purpose there?"

Taharial explained how his men had heard a gunshot, after which Black and Murphy had quickly left the hotel. "It was evident that Black had been wounded," Taharial said. "My men were able to enter the room immediately afterward. There had been a fight. My men believed that Hogan had attempted to shoot Black and had been overcome. Hogan was still alive."

Sammael frowned. Perhaps he'd made his own mistake in assuming that Hogan was unimportant. Possibly the human had attacked Black out of purely human jealousy—or possibly because he'd known of Dorian's true nature.

"Continue," he said.

"Our men observed Black teaching the girl to feed, and then he took her to Kyril."

"What possible reason could he have for such a reckless action?"

"Our agent will do his best to learn, my liege."

"Get word to him immediately. He must under no circumstances allow Kyril to harm the girl. She must be brought to Pax."

"Yes, sir."

"And set two more men on Hogan. He may be of use to us later."

"I understand."

"Go."

Taharial left the room. Sammael picked up a letter opener and brought it down on the desk so hard that it snapped in two.

GWEN FELT AS IF she were living in a dream. There was no discomfort when she found herself compelled to obey Dorian's commands, no physical symptoms to match the horror in her mind. As long as she didn't resist, it was easy. So terribly easy.

And she was constantly aware of Dorian—his presence, his charisma, his power. He'd said they had an unbreakable bond. She believed it. She was eternally tied to the man she'd thought she loved. The man who had become a monster.

Somehow she made it down the corridor to the double doors that marked Kyril's apartments. Two thuggish-looking men— vampires, she could only presume—ushered her and Dorian into the reception room. A lovely, dark-haired woman greeted them and quickly vanished. Dorian continued through the doorway directly ahead, holding Gwen in a viselike grip.

Kyril was waiting in a wing chair in the sitting room, his legs stretched out on a velvet ottoman. Though the *Sentinel* had done several stories on the factions warring over leadership of Raoul's gang, no one, to Gwen's knowledge, had ever actually spoken with him. Kyril was notoriously elusive.

Now that she was in his presence, Gwen could understand why he ruled one of the factions, and why Dorian considered him so dangerous. Malevolent power radiated from him like the very embodiment of evil. He was as slender and handsome as an exotic aristocrat right out of a moving picture, and his blue eyes promised depths of both passion and iniquity.

"Dorian," he said, knocking ashes from his cigarette into a crystal ashtray. "It appears that you didn't take my orders as seriously as I would have wished."

Dorian led Gwen to face Kyril. "You commanded me to neutralize Miss Murphy. I have done so."

Kyril smashed his cigarette into the ashtray. "This is what you call elimination?"

"You ordered her silenced," Dorian said. "She will never trouble us again."

Kyril stared at Gwen with a strange mingling of contempt and appreciation. "Is this so, Miss Murphy?"

Gwen's fear dissolved into rage. "I guess you were pretty disappointed when I failed to expire on command."

Dorian jerked her arm. "Gwen," he said. "Keep a civil tongue in your head. Answer our liege."

Her throat closed up, shutting off the angry words. "No," she said hoarsely. "I'll never…trouble you again."

"Ah," Kyril said. He glanced at Dorian. "You interpreted my instructions rather liberally, Dorian."

"If you will pardon me, my liege, you did say some time ago that I had earned the right to create my own protégée."

Kyril showed the edges of his teeth. "You claimed to have no interest in making Miss Murphy your protégée."

There hadn't been too many times when Gwen had seen Dorian less than confident, but now he hesitated as if he had no ready answer for Kyril's accusation. "When I attempted to kill her," he said slowly, "I found that…a link had already been created between us."

"I see. You cannot be trusted."

Dorian bowed his head. "I ask forgiveness for my weakness."

The submissiveness of his tone made Gwen bristle. Seeing Dorian behave as a servant was like watching a timber wolf willingly put his head into a collar.

You hate him, remember?

The expression in Kyril's eyes seemed to suggest that he was weighing Dorian's fate as well as hers. "I'm unaccustomed to having my will flouted," he said in an almost mild tone. "Nevertheless, you are one of my most able enforcers. And I'm feeling inclined to be merciful." He rose and approached Gwen, taking her chin in his hand. "She is much lovelier than I had been led to believe. Perhaps I'll invoke my *droit de seigneur.*"

Dorian stiffened. Gwen tried to ignore the reptilian feel of Kyril's skin and searched her memory for the meaning of the phrase he had used. Something medieval, wasn't it?

"My liege," Dorian said, "while I am honored by your interest, such an act would…disturb the bond between me and the girl."

"I am well aware of the consequences. You would both suffer, would you not?"

Without warning Kyril seized Gwen and kissed her, scraping her lower lip with his teeth. He licked her blood from his mouth while Dorian pulled her away, flinging her behind him.

"Kyril," he said, his voice carefully controlled, "you will not have her."

A kind of ripple went through the faction leader. All traces of humor left his face.

"Will you challenge me, Dorian?" he asked softly.

"I have no wish to lead the clan," Dorian said. "But she is my protégée. Custom and law are clear on the matter."

"Law," Kyril spat. "There was a time when no one would question a master's wishes."

"A time of chaos," Dorian said. "If the clan is to be reborn, it must have order."

The two vampires stared at each other. Every hair on Gwen's neck stood erect. She was a rabbit in the presence of wolves, and if it came to a fight, she had a feeling the results would be very unpleasant.

Don't do it, she begged Dorian silently. *It's not worth your life.*

But she needn't have worried. Dorian inclined his head again, his shoulders drawn and his stance one of surrender. "I will keep her close," he said. "She'll cause no difficulty."

Kyril continued to stare at Dorian. "We shall see," he said. He smiled at Gwen. "Now you're one of us, little vixen. I wish you joy of your new life."

He dismissed Dorian with a wave of his hand. Dorian hustled Gwen out and dragged her back to his suite. Once they were inside, he began to pace furiously, paying no attention whatsoever to her. His agitation was like a high-pitched buzzing behind Gwen's ears. A knock on the door practically made him jump out of his skin; he spoke to someone in the corridor and abruptly left.

All the emotions Gwen had been holding in check poured through her body like molten flame. She ran to the window. It was only just midmorning, but she knew she had to escape.

She pulled off her gown, heedless of torn seams, and rummaged in her suitcase for a pair of loose-fitting slacks and a plain cotton blouse. She put on her gloves and coat, tucking her pocketbook into one of the coat pockets. The cloche hat she'd been wearing didn't seem adequate protection against the sun; she found a felt homburg on a shelf in the closet and pushed it down over her hair.

No one was watching the door. She rushed along the corridor in the opposite direction from Kyril's suite, all but tumbled down the stairs and crossed the hotel lobby as fast as her feet would carry her. No one stopped her. She continued to run until she'd gone several blocks from the hotel and then stopped to catch her breath.

Even through the wool of her coat she could feel the heat of the sun, its rays like a spider's web waiting to ensnare her. She pulled the homburg's brim as low as she could, tucking her chin into the raised collar of the coat. For a moment she didn't know where she was or what she should do.

Then she caught sight of a church steeple and everything became clear. She flagged down a taxi and whispered directions to the cabbie, half afraid her voice alone would reveal what she had become.

The cabbie let her off at the steps of St. Albert's. She hesitated as she looked up at the great oak doors, fear a living thing clawing at her insides. She clutched the silver cross around her neck and froze.

Nothing happened. She was wearing a holy symbol, and it wasn't bothering her in the least. It had been constantly touching her bare skin after the Conversion, and she hadn't felt anything at all.

God help me, she thought as she started up the steps.

Welcome darkness closed around her. She gazed at the great cross over the altar. It didn't frighten her. She walked up the nave between the pews. There was no change. She edged into a pew and knelt, bowing her head. She couldn't think of a single prayer. St. Albert's had let her in, but there was a barrier inside her. One of her own making.

And something else was happening, something that had nothing to do with old stories of vampires and churches. An ache throbbed under her ribs as if she'd been running for miles, a painful sort of emptiness impossible to ignore.

I didn't disobey him, she thought. *He didn't order me to stay in the room.*

But the ache persisted, and she remembered what he'd told her: *Prolonged separation is difficult.* Now she knew exactly what he'd meant. Not only couldn't she directly disobey him, but she couldn't leave him. Not even for an hour.

"Are you all right, my child?"

She jerked up her head, her new, alien senses taking in the warmth of the slender priest's body and the unique fragrance of his blood. She'd seen the young man before; he was homely, earnest and devoted to serving St. Albert's parishioners.

He should have known what she was. He should have felt how badly she wanted to take his blood.

I don't belong here, she cried silently. *I'm not human. I can never be human again.*

The priest leaned closer. "Is there something I can do for you?"

Gwen clasped her hands and closed her eyes. "I'm…I'm fine, thank you."

"You're Gwen Murphy, aren't you? Would you like to speak to Father Sullivan?"

"No!" She shot up, barely stopping herself from shoving him out of the way. "Please…just let me go."

He stepped aside. She plunged toward the door, the coat flapping around her. Only a lifetime of habit and the glare of a stern-faced nun slowed her to a more decorous walk.

Dorian met her at the door. He glanced past her into the nave, his expression half hidden beneath the brim of his hat.

"You've been very foolish, Gwen," he said. "We must go."

She didn't have to ask how he'd found her. The ache in her chest had already begun to fade. "Does this place frighten you, Dorian?" she asked.

"No. Why should it?"

"I guess that's a myth, too," Gwen said coldly. "Did it hurt?"

"I beg your pardon?"

"When we were apart. Did it hurt you?"

"It was not pleasant."

And now you're angry, Gwen thought. *That's just too bad.*

She looked through the doors at the brilliant noon light, a territory she could never enter unscathed again. "What now? Back to being Kyril's obedient servant?"

"We cannot go back."

"Did Kyril decide to punish you after all?"

Dorian took her arm and spun her out the door. "I've been told that he intends to kill us both."

CHAPTER FOURTEEN

GWEN STOPPED, STARTLED out of her self-pity. "*Who* told you?"

"That's unimportant. I was mistaken in taking you to Kyril. It was a calculated risk, but it did not serve us as I'd hoped."

"You mean…" She felt the powerful need to retch. "You mean what you did to me was all for nothing."

Pedestrians streamed past, oblivious to the undercurrents of emotion coiling between them. Dorian buried his hands in his coat pockets. Gwen fought an overwhelming urge to hit him. She wanted to kick him in the shins and pummel his chest until he begged for mercy.

"I'm not going to forgive you this time," she said calmly.

"I do not expect it." He got her moving again, his grip too strong for her to fight, even if their new bond hadn't prevented it.

"Is it true what you said about only death severing the bond?" she asked. "Or was that a lie, too?"

He never broke his stride. "I cannot let you go."

"But you could if you wanted to, couldn't you? No one has to die."

Abruptly he pulled her into a shadowed doorway, crowding a pair of matronly shoppers onto the sidewalk. "As long as you are a target," he said, "I fear we must both make the best of the situation."

"Damn you!" She shook him off. "What if I'd rather choose death than a life in bondage?"

"You will not have that choice." He seized her hands. "I will not allow you to take your own life. Do you understand?"

A harsh, inhuman cry stuck in her throat. Suicide was a mortal sin. And even if the rules didn't apply to someone like her, she could feel the instinct to survive as a tangible force inside her, as real as her need for blood.

"There is something else you must know," Dorian said, his voice slicing into her thoughts. "Your former colleague Randolph Hewitt is dead."

"What?"

He urged her into motion again. "The papers say it was an accident. He was struck by an automobile near the *Sentinel* offices."

An accident, Gwen thought numbly. "Kyril?"

"If so, he is a fool. The police will not ignore this."

And neither will Mitch. "If anyone at the *Sentinel* so much as suspects it was a hit, they'll never rest until they've exposed the killers."

"As they exposed yours?"

"They knew *I* was still alive." She grabbed Dorian's sleeve. "I've got to call Mitch, make sure he's all right."

"You will not."

"You bastard…" She took firm hold of her fury. "Mitch is my friend. I don't abandon my friends, even when I've nearly killed one of them. I have to warn him."

"He will continue to pursue you if he is given the least encouragement."

"After what I did?" She laughed. "Even a man in love has his limits."

"Do not underestimate human idiocy." He picked up the pace, almost dragging her along the sidewalk. "Listen carefully, Gwen. We are going to a place where I hope we will find sanctuary. It will be best if you hold your tongue and observe quietly until we are settled."

"Settled where?"

"While I've been serving Kyril, I've also been working for a *strigoi* organization dedicated to imposing peace on the factions. I was to remain with Kyril until the organization called on me, and others working undercover, to take action against the faction leaders."

Gwen forgot her anger, helplessly caught up in the scent of a new story. "Take action? What does that mean? What is this organization?"

"They call themselves Pax."

"Peace? Didn't you say they were vampires, too?"

Without slowing his headlong flight, Dorian outlined his dealings with the secret organization and how they hoped to achieve their ultimate goal of an enforced truce between the factions.

"They want to save lives and end the bloodshed," Dorian finished. "After I presumed you dead, there seemed no better course to take than to help them stop the men I believed to be responsible for your murder."

"By becoming Kyril's enforcer."

"Yes."

"Why didn't you tell me this before? Why did you let me believe you joined Kyril just to take revenge?"

"You already had enough to absorb at the time."

Gwen nearly laughed at the understatement. "You said Kyril is after us."

"I find that very probable."

"Won't these Pax people be upset that you may be leading Kyril right to them?"

"I will take adequate precautions."

At that he turned all his concentration to their movements, taking a circuitous route in the direction of the East River. Gwen followed, considering what Dorian had told her. *A secret vampire organization that wants to save humans and end the faction wars.* It seemed bizarre, to say the least, but Dorian obviously believed they were sincere.

And so, it seemed, was he.

Gwen had just begun to recognize the implications of what she'd learned when Dorian turned onto South Street and came to a stop before a large, ornate four-story building. Delivery trucks were unloading what appeared to be carved wooden statues at the adjoining warehouse doors, while men with manifests were checking off lists and arguing with the drivers. Women and men came and went through the glass-paned doors.

"Pax headquarters," Dorian said. He assumed a casual air and tucked Gwen's arm through the crook of his elbow. She watched with interest as he approached the building, came under the scrutiny of a pair of flannel-shirted men loitering about the doorway, and preceded Gwen into the lobby. He spoke briefly to a security guard seated behind a large desk near a bank of elevators and continued on through a door at the rear of the lobby. A corridor led to a smaller waiting room, where a pretty, darkhaired young woman glanced up at him with surprise.

"Dorian," she said, casting a sideways look at Gwen.

"I must see Sammael," Dorian said without preamble.

"Of course," the receptionist said. "Please come with me."

Yet another corridor deposited them at one of several plain doors, which opened to a small room furnished with a pair of chairs and a table. "Please wait here," the young woman said.

She closed the door. Dorian offered a seat to Gwen. She declined to take it.

"Very clever," she said, sweeping the homburg from her head. "Apparently vampires hide in plain sight all the time, but it seems that Pax has made a real art of it. No one would suspect this is anything but a regular import business."

Dorian nodded, but he was obviously preoccupied. He stared at the closed door, jaw set.

"Don't they trust you?" Gwen asked. "Or is this some kind of—"

The door opened. An extremely attractive blond woman entered with a smile.

"Dorian," she said. "We didn't expect you back so soon." She glanced at Gwen. "Who is this?"

"Angela," Dorian said with odd formality, "may I present Gwen Murphy. Gwen, this is Angela."

Angela's cool gaze swept over Gwen. "You know the protocols, Dorian. Why did you—"

"I must speak to Sammael immediately," Dorian interrupted.

The blonde pressed her lips together. "What's wrong?"

Dorian held her gaze. She looked again at Gwen, this time with open hostility, and turned back to Dorian. "What have you done?"

"Take me to Sammael."

"He can't be disturbed now. I will debrief you."

"I was not aware that Sammael had assigned such tasks to you."

"I've been promoted." She returned to the door. "Come with me. The girl will wait here."

"She can be trusted."

"Dorian—"

"I will not leave her alone."

Angela hesitated. "I'll be back in a few minutes." She left the room. Gwen listened for the click of a lock.

"Is it just me," she said, "or did the temperature in this room just dip below freezing?"

Dorian grunted.

"You're in real trouble, aren't you?" Gwen planted herself in front of him, arms folded across her chest. "Not just with Kyril, but with this bunch, too."

Dorian removed his hat and curled the brim between his fingers. "Pax's philosophy is one of preserving life. They will not object to my having saved yours."

"Why would they? Who *are* these people, Dorian?"

He didn't get the chance to answer. Angela reappeared with the dark-haired secretary and beckoned to Dorian. "Sammael will see you both," she said.

Dorian took the lead with Angela, while the secretary fell into step beside Gwen.

"You're Gwen Murphy," she said with a pleasant smile. "I'm Vida."

"How do you do," Gwen said. "Do you happen to know where we're going?"

"Why, to see Sammael, of course. May I take your coat?"

Gwen shrugged out of the coat and handed Vida the homburg. "They didn't have a hat in my size," she said.

Vida studied Gwen with far more friendliness than Angela had shown. "You're very pretty."

"Um…thanks."

"We didn't know Dorian intended to create a protégée. It's against the rules, you see."

So that's what this is all about, Gwen thought. But before she could start asking questions, Angela and Dorian walked through an open door and into a spacious office dominated by floor-to-ceiling bookshelves and a marble-topped desk.

The man standing behind the desk could have been any prosperous human businessman except for the faint air of menace that seemed to hang over just about every vampire Gwen had met. His hair was gray-frosted black, and his eyes were a piercing blue. He smiled at Gwen with an intensity that put her immediately on her guard.

"Welcome, Miss Murphy," he said. "My name is Sammael."

Reluctantly Gwen took his offered hand. "Sammael," she said, meeting his gaze.

"Please be seated."

Gwen edged into the armchair in front of the desk. She noted that Sammael didn't offer a seat to Dorian, who stood at a sort of parade rest with his hands clasped behind his back. Angela and Vida flanked him on either side.

"You may be surprised to learn that we have known of you for some time, Miss Murphy," Sammael said, settling into his own chair. "We became aware of your friendship with Dorian when we began watching him with an eye toward recruiting him for our cause. It is not often that our kind form platonic relationships with humans."

Platonic. That was an odd way of putting it. "You have the advantage of me," she said. "I only found out about you today."

"So I understand." He gave Dorian a stern look. "I regret we find ourselves meeting under such unfortunate circumstances."

Dorian's emotions were under strict control. "What I did was necessary to save Miss Murphy's life."

"After she was resurrected from her apparent first death,"

Sammael said. He continued to focus on Gwen, his hands folded on the desk. "Dorian chose to join us because he believed you had been killed by the factions due to your investigative work for the *Sentinel*. But you were in hiding, were you not?"

"Yes," Gwen said, growing more uneasy by the minute.

"It is unfortunate that you returned to place yourself in danger again."

Gwen put on her best interviewer's face. "Why should you concern yourself with my safety, Mr. Sammael? I realize that your organization is dedicated to peace, but I'm…" She paused. "I was only one insignificant human."

"No life is insignificant to us, Miss Murphy, least of all a human life." He raised his head. "Dorian."

"Yes, Sammael."

"You know that what you've done has contravened one of our most sacred laws."

"It was necessary."

"So you claim. Miss Murphy, I must ask a few questions of you in order to clarify the situation."

She held herself very still. "Of course."

"How long have you known that vampires exist?"

"For about three days."

"Dorian made you aware of this?"

"I would have discovered it myself if he hadn't told me."

"Because of your investigation into the waterfront murders?"

Gwen hesitated, playing for time to think. How much did these people know about her? They were obviously keen to protect their secrecy; could they have seen her as a threat just as Kyril had?

"I assure you," Sammael said, "we would not have interfered with your life in any way had the matter not been taken out of our hands."

"I understand."

"Do you?" He spread his hands and sighed. "I must make this very clear. Because we believe that unwilling Conversion itself is an unlawful act of violence, we forbid any of our *strigoi* members to Convert protégés without obtaining permission. Did you understand what would happen to you?"

"I…had a pretty good idea."

"And you agreed to this? You understood the full consequence of the act?"

A heaviness settled in Gwen's limbs, and she knew it wasn't merely her own dread at the prospect of answering such a question. It was Dorian's dread, as well. All she had to do was tell the truth, and he would become some kind of criminal in the eyes of his colleagues.

He stole my life, she thought. But every instinct told her that it would be crazy to give this Sammael what he so obviously wanted at Dorian's expense.

You don't know a damned thing about these people. And until you do…

"Neither one of us had any choice," she said. "Kyril was about to kill me. We thought my becoming Dorian's protégée would make Kyril believe that I couldn't cause any more trouble."

A palpable wave of relief rolled through Gwen as Dorian realized what she had chosen to do. Sammael frowned.

"If you are here now," he said to Dorian, "your ploy cannot have succeeded."

"It did not," Dorian said. "It would seem that Kyril intends to kill us both."

"And so you come to us."

"I took care to see that I was not followed."

"The consequences of your foolish act extend well beyond the danger of discovery."

"I am well aware that I have failed in my mission, and that my failure may impede our action against Kyril."

"Without question. Your absence from the faction will most likely delay our plans."

Gwen rose. "This would never have happened if it weren't for me," she said. "If I'd stayed away from New York, Kyril would have gone on believing I was dead."

"All blame rests with me," Dorian said sharply. "If there is anything I can do to atone for my mistakes, I will gladly do it. But Gwen must be kept safe."

Sammael shook his head. "The synod shall determine what is to be done. Vida, see that Dorian and Miss Murphy have all that they require for the night, and call the synod for a meeting at three." He turned back to Dorian. "Perhaps the synod will determine that your unorthodox actions were justifiable under the circumstances. Miss Murphy, I regret what you have suffered. You have been a true innocent in this." He gestured to Angela. "Though we have few recent Converts among us at this time, anyone here would be more than happy to aid you in your transition to *strigoi* life."

"Thank you."

"We have not forgotten that we, too, once were human." He rose to indicate that the interview was over. "If you require anything at all, please inform Angela."

"Gwen must feed soon," Dorian said.

"That can be arranged." He nodded to Vida, who took Gwen's arm and led her out of the room.

"Don't worry," Vida said. "You're safe here, among friends. What happened to you has happened to all of us."

Gwen glanced back at the door. "You sound as if you don't like being a vampire."

"Does that surprise you?" She gazed earnestly into Gwen's eyes as they walked along the corridor. "Are you happy that you must feed on human blood? Are you glad to know that you would be considered a monster by all humanity?"

"That doesn't seem to trouble Kyril or his gang."

"They have given up any pretense of morality. For too long *strigoi* have assumed a mantle of superiority they do not possess. We have committed ourselves to restoring virtue to our kind."

She stopped, taking Gwen's shoulders in her hands. "I know you told Sammael that you were a willing Convert, but I can see that isn't true."

"I—"

"Micah, the founder of Pax, taught that forgiveness is one of the greatest virtues. But he saw that the vampire race could not be permitted to go on as it had been, ignoring the fundamental right of humans to rule themselves and their world. We are not the superior ones. We are—"

"Vida."

Sammael walked up behind them, smiling benevolently. "Please get Miss Murphy settled and arrange for a volunteer to join her."

Vida was subdued and silent as she led Gwen up a staircase to the second floor. "We have several vacant guest rooms," she said as they reached the landing. "Will you want separate quarters?"

Gwen realized that Vida was asking if she would prefer to be apart from Dorian. The thought was like a needle plunging into Gwen's chest.

"You'll still be near each other," Vida said. "The separation only hurts when you're farther apart."

All at once Gwen realized that she wanted nothing more than to be away from Dorian, even if only for a few hours. "Thanks," she said stiffly.

"Just remember that you aren't alone anymore. I'll be happy to talk to you anytime you like." She opened the door to a small bedroom and ushered Gwen inside. "One of our humans will come soon," she said. "If there's anything else you need before then, press the buzzer near the bed."

She left, and Gwen gave the room a once-over. It was furnished with a bed, a table with a lamp, a bookshelf and a plain wooden chair. Another door led to a private bathroom. On the wall hung several floral paintings and a drawing of the outline of a triangle overlapping a flame. The window was covered over with dark paint, leaving Gwen with a frightening sense of isolation. She tugged off her gloves and stood in the center of the room, numb down to her bones.

Here I am, she thought. *A vampire among vampires.*

Pressure built in her throat and burst free in hysterical

laughter. She flung herself down on the bed, arms spread wide, and laughed until her throat was raw.

I am a monster.

The knowledge she'd pushed aside had finally begun to penetrate in a way it hadn't done when she'd first been driven to feed, when she'd met Kyril, or even when she'd gone to St. Albert's and realized her presence there was nothing but a lie.

Anger had kept her going until now…anger and the need to deal with a dangerous new set of rules. You couldn't be a good newsman if you didn't keep a clear head, even in the most dire of circumstances.

But the anger was no longer enough. Every defense was crumbling away. It was as if she'd been a motorcar running on fumes, and now the last of those fumes were gone. All the physical changes she'd tried to ignore—the sharper sight and hearing, the keener sensitivity to every stimulus, even the bond between her and Dorian—became devastatingly real.

I'm afraid.

She pressed her fists against her mouth to muffle her cry. The cotton of her blouse was suddenly harsh against her back, as if she were lying on a bed of nails. Her silver cross was icy cold on her neck, and the sounds of humans and *strigoi* moving about the building were hammer blows inside her skull. Her own pulse was deafening. Hunger sucked at the space under her ribs.

God help me.

But He couldn't. No one could. She'd already tried once to escape. That had been the worst kind of self-delusion. Even if she'd been able to get away from Dorian, she couldn't get away from what she'd become. Life would never be the same again. She would never be satisfied with a salad nicoise or a juicy steak; every few days she would have to go out and look for some poor, oblivious man or woman to "donate" blood to keep her alive.

Are you happy that you must feed on human blood? Vida had asked. *Are you glad to know that you would be considered a monster by all humanity?*

Gwen rolled over, burying her face in the hard pillow. She felt herself growing weaker by the moment.

Weak, like any nineteenth-century female. Weak enough to wonder where Dorian was, why he didn't come, why he didn't feel her pain.

And why should he come, after you cursed him for helping you? When you said you'd rather die than be stuck with him?

The pillow ticking tore between her teeth. She flung the pillow aside and pounded the mattress until the bed frame creaked.

You did this to me, Dorian Black. You can't leave me like this.

But Dorian didn't answer. Gwen jumped up from the bed, wild with grief and horror, and scraped at the paint covering the window with her fingernails. The stuff was layers deep. She picked up the chair in the corner of the room and held it over her head, imagining the window shattering into a million pieces. Imagining herself falling, falling…

I will not allow you to take your own life.

She froze. Dorian was right. She couldn't do it, and not only because he'd told her not to. It was that damned survival instinct, stronger than it had ever been when she was merely human.

The chair clattered to the floor. Gwen sank to her knees, unable to squeeze a single tear from her eyes.

Someone knocked at the door. Gwen drew a shuddering breath, smoothed her hair and clothes, and sat on the bed.

She could already smell the human's blood.

"Come in," she said.

The door opened and a sandy-haired, pleasant-faced young man walked in, smiling as if the world still spun on its axis. "Hello, Miss Murphy," he said. "I'm Jim."

Gwen rose, locked in the grip of a hunger so fierce that she could barely keep herself from attacking the boy. She cleared her throat. "How…how do you do, Jim?"

He seemed to sense her confusion. "Don't worry," he said. "I know you're a new Convert…just a few days, right? This must still be strange to you." He glanced at the window; Gwen didn't doubt that he saw the scrapes in the paint. He closed the door.

"I don't really know exactly what you're going through," he said, "but I hope to make it easier. It won't be necessary for you to hunt, not as long as you're with us."

"You…" Gwen pressed her hand to her stomach. "You mean you…"

"That's right. It's nothing, really. I've sworn myself to the cause, and the best way we humans can do that is by keeping our *strigoi* alive." He pursed his lips. "I know you haven't had time to learn much about Pax, but if you're here for a while, the mediants and master guides will begin to acquaint you with Micah's teachings."

"Micah," Gwen said faintly. "The man who founded Pax."

"*Strigoi,* actually. He was a great teacher, a missionary who came to realize that vampires and humans could live together in peace. That was why he created Pax, to work for that peace and preserve vampire and human lives." He ducked his head. "I'm still a novice, so there's a lot about the teachings I don't know yet. When I become a mediant I'll know a lot more. Until then…" He met Gwen's gaze with the warmth of offered friendship. "Until then it's enough to know that a new and better world is coming."

A new and better world. A world where Gwen wouldn't have to feel disgust for herself and the way she had to live. A world in which she could forgive Dorian with all her heart…

Jim touched her arm. "We can sit or do it standing, whatever's more comfortable for you."

"Oh, God." Gwen felt her skin flush the same way it had always done since she was a child. "This is crazy."

"What's crazy is the way the outsiders do it, treating people like animals. But let's not dwell on that." He offered his hand. "Come on. It won't be nearly as bad as you suppose."

Unable to think, Gwen allowed him to lead her back to the bed. He sat down beside her.

"Most *strigoi* prefer the neck," he said, "but some like the wrist. It's up to you."

"What if I…if I change you, too?"

"Not much chance of that. It's a skill, you know. Takes a while to learn." He bent back his head. "It's all right, Gwen. All…"

The siren call of blood reduced Gwen's intellect to mush. She seized Jim's arms, pulled him toward her and bit into the flesh of his neck. He sighed and closed his eyes.

Gwen lost all track of time. Jim felt wonderful in her arms, his blood like some angelic elixir that aroused her as only one other had ever done before. She unbuttoned Jim's shirt to midchest and licked up the trickle of blood that had escaped her attention, drawing a soft moan from his throat. He wrapped his arms around her, murmuring endearments.

That was when Dorian walked into the room.

He stopped in midstride, staring at Gwen and her donor as if he'd never witnessed such a spectacle before. Gwen sat up and pushed Jim away.

"I see that you require no assistance," Dorian said in a flat voice. He glanced at Jim, who rose and walked quickly toward the door.

"Don't go," Gwen called after him. He hesitated behind Dorian, who stood very still.

"Dorian," Gwen said, "this is Jim. Jim, Dorian."

"We've met," Jim said, shifting uneasily. "I've duties to attend to. Good afternoon, Miss Murphy."

He vanished. Gwen stood, concentrating on not letting Dorian realize how relieved she was to see him.

"I guess you've been busy yourself," she said.

Dorian glanced around the room. "I trust you are comfortable?"

"Very."

"I've been lodged in the next room."

"That's nice."

"I would prefer that you remain with me."

"Afraid of what might go on if I'm out of your sight?"

The exchange was like a dozen other conversations Gwen had had with Dorian. Familiar. Normal.

Too normal. Gwen couldn't feel a thing through the bond. It was as if Dorian had deliberately cut himself off from her.

"Could it be possible that you're jealous?" she asked.

She held her breath, stunned at her own question. It meant that she still cared what he thought. It meant that she might be able to keep feeling the emotions that she thought had died along with her humanity.

"I would advise you not to become too attached to anyone here," Dorian said, his face conceding nothing. "We are unlikely to remain for any length of time."

"How can I become attached when I'm bound to you?" she asked.

"I will try not to make our affiliation too onerous," he said. He turned to leave.

"Dorian…" Gwen walked halfway across the room, pausing before she reached him.

Give me a reason to stop hating you. Set me free. Let me choose to stay by your side.

But she wouldn't beg, and he had nothing to say. Without another word he left the room. Gwen stood where she was, unable to move or think. She felt desperately for some idea or image that could anchor her in a sea of despair. She found Eamon Murphy.

You never knew it would come to this, did you, Dad? If you'd had any idea, you would have burned those notes and buried the ashes in some forgotten graveyard.

Maybe he would have done just that. But if he'd known what she'd become, he wouldn't have turned his back in horror. He would have held her in his arms, let her cry it out, chucked her under the chin and told her that everything was going to be all right.

"Go after what you want, my beauty," he would say. "Use the strength you were born with. Don't let anything stop you, even if life's tossed you a few rotten potatoes."

Gwen covered her mouth. She couldn't weep. That ability seemed to have gone the way of walking in sunlight. But she could still dig down inside herself and find something to hang on to. Something she could fight for. Something that mattered.

She got up, straightened her clothing, splashed her face with water from the bathroom sink and ran a comb through her hair. There were no guards at her door, no one in the hall. She paused at the door of the room next to hers. It was open a crack, and she heard voices within—Dorian's and Angela's.

"I know that Sammael can find a new purpose for you here," Angela was saying. "There is no reason for you to leave us."

"There is every reason, and Sammael knows it," Dorian said. "Tegon himself told me that Kyril planned to kill us. Kyril can't afford to let anyone believe that he let one of his lieutenants defy him and get away with it. He'll be relentless in the hunt, and it's quite possible that he might discover Pax in the process."

"Neither faction has ever come close to suspecting our existence," Angela said. "You certainly didn't before I approached you."

"Yes, but—"

Silence. Gwen felt a sudden, incongruous flush of desire. She opened the door another fraction of an inch.

Angela was kissing Dorian. And he was letting her.

CHAPTER FIFTEEN

SHOCKED AND FLUSTERED, Gwen retreated to her room. In a strange sort of reversal she saw Angela through Dorian's eyes: her blond beauty, her competence, her obvious attraction to him. Angela, unlike Gwen, wasn't dependent on Dorian. She wasn't his responsibility or his slave; she was his equal, as experienced in vampire ways as he.

And Gwen had asked *him* if he were jealous of *Jim.*

She sank down on the edge of the bed and touched her lips, feeling them as if they were alien appendages. A flood of memory set them to tingling.

The first kiss had come after she'd taken Dorian back to her hotel to recover from the wounds he'd received during the faction fight. So much of that night had seemed like a dream, but she remembered that. He'd kissed her right after he'd said he was willing to kill Kyril to protect her. After he'd said he cared for her.

A wave of heat rolled through her. She lay back on the bed and closed her eyes. The kiss had been more wonderful than anything she could have imagined, as different from Mitch's as a lion's roar from a kitten's mew.

And there had been more beyond the kiss, much more, though the memories were blurred and as impossible to grasp as clouds. Dorian's hungry, burning eyes. Sighs and caresses, pleasure so overwhelming it had almost been like pain. Need as deep as the deepest abyss in the ocean. Heat and wetness stroking her most intimate places.

Make love to me. Had she really said those words? Had she

really lain down on the hotel bed, removed all her clothing and invited Dorian to relieve her of her virginity?

Gwen moaned and covered her face. The evidence of her participation was undeniable; when Mitch had knocked on the door, she'd found herself wearing nothing but her stockings and pumps, and Dorian had been standing half-dressed at the foot of the bed. Oh, she'd started something, all right. Something even she, a modern working woman, wouldn't have begun without knowing just what she was about.

Or so anyone would think if they knew Gwen Murphy. But it had all happened much too fast. She didn't remember suddenly deciding to toss away her virtue, no matter how she had begun to feel about Dorian, and even if she *had* been dizzy with shock and gratitude over his remarkable recovery.

Oh, she'd wanted to kiss him a long time before that night. She'd even allowed herself to think, more than once, about the virile body she'd caressed in the bedroom of her apartment, the hardness of his cock in her hand. She'd had a few disturbingly erotic dreams about him, and she'd imagined what it would be like to lie naked beside him.

But she hadn't been eager to make him think she was the kind of floozy who prowled the lower-class speakeasies, willing to pay any price for a drink. It wasn't that she was a prude like the old Victorians, but she didn't want a sexual relationship without any emotional glue to hold it together. And she hadn't had any proof that he'd wanted *her,* even after he'd come to work at the *Sentinel.* She hadn't been sure he ever *would* want her.

So she'd waited for him to make the first move. Wasn't that the way things were done, even in this modern world?

It's the way I would have done it—if I were in my right mind.

She rolled up again, hugging her knees against her chest. No matter how hard she concentrated, the details of that night were no clearer than the hours she'd lost after Dorian had Converted her. Dorian certainly hadn't given any sign that he had considered their…interlude of much importance when he'd returned to her hotel the next night to confirm Mitch's accusations about his true nature. But then, he'd been there to Convert her, not make love to her. When she'd woken up, he'd been most concerned about getting her to feed, presenting her to Kyril and escaping to Pax.

Was it any wonder, given all that had happened since, that Gwen had been able to put those unbearable, shameful, ecstatic images away in a little box where they wouldn't distract her with desires she was hardly in a position to express?

Well, that box was beginning to crack open. Jim had made the first dent when he'd given her his blood, reawakening the erotic sensations her body hadn't forgotten. Dorian had made the second when he walked into the room, glaring at Jim as if he wanted to kick the boy seven ways from Sunday, and she'd decided to go after what she wanted.

Only to find him kissing Angela.

Maybe you're reading too much into this, she thought. *Maybe Angela made the first move…*

Or maybe what Gwen thought had happened in the hotel room hadn't really happened at all. He *hadn't* said he cared for her. They *hadn't* almost made love.

Or maybe there were things going on in Dorian's life that she couldn't imagine, things that actually had nothing to do with her. The two of them had been apart for three months. A lot could happen in that time.

I care about you. Even if Dorian's words had been real, even though he had mourned her loss when he'd thought she was dead and risked his position with Kyril to save her life once again, made himself responsible for her in the most permanent way a vampire could…it didn't mean that he saw her as anything more than a burden.

A burden who'd done nothing but attack him for trying to protect her, never considering what *he* might have sacrificed.

Gwen closed her eyes. *You've been stupid, Gwen. Stupid and naive and selfish.*

Stupid to assume that she was the only female in Dorian's life. Naive to think their newfound bond would prevent either one of them from being with others. Selfish to believe that only her problems mattered.

No wonder he's been trying to keep me from knowing what he's feeling. Ever since we left St. Albert's, I've done nothing but call him a bastard and a liar. I told him I'd never forgive him.

But he has someone here who does *accept him. Someone he's worked with, who understands him the way I never could. And in spite of all that, he doesn't want to hurt me.*

Gwen got up, went into the bathroom and gave herself a good hard look. She was letting herself in for real trouble if she couldn't learn to keep her emotions under control instead of letting them drag her around by the hair. She couldn't alter what had happened to her. She couldn't undo it, and she couldn't keep blaming Dorian for doing what he'd thought was necessary to save her.

It was time to start thinking clearly again. And that meant taking responsibility for her own life, no matter how much it had changed.

The first thing she had to do was telephone Mitch, make sure he was all right and assure him that her attack on him had been an accident. Her chances of escaping this place to find a public telephone were virtually nil; Dorian wouldn't set her free to get herself in trouble again. Nor did it seem very likely that the people here, given the secrecy of their mission, would give her permission to call someone on the outside. Still, they had to have a telephone on the premises somewhere. She had to find it before someone found her—and make absolutely sure she didn't let Dorian feel her nervousness.

She went back out into the corridor and listened. No sound from Dorian's room, or from anywhere nearby. She crept down the hall, cautiously opening every door in hopes of finding what she needed. No one interrupted her. She'd nearly reached the landing when she found what appeared to be an empty office equipped with a telephone. With a glance over her shoulder

Gwen went into the office, shut the door and placed a call to the *Sentinel.*

"Mitch?"

She heard his sharp intake of breath, a beat of silence as he recognized her voice.

"Gwen?"

"Yes, it's me. Are you okay?"

"Where are you? Gwen, what—"

"I'm so sorry, Mitch. I wasn't myself. I—"

"Settle down. I'm all right." There was a long pause. "Are *you* all right?"

She wanted to laugh. "More or less."

"Is he with you?"

"Not now."

Mitch muttered a curse. "Do you know what he's done to you?"

"Yes. You tried to warn me—"

"It was already too late."

"I wanted to stay with you after…after I attacked you, but Dorian…"

"You don't have to explain, Gwen. I understand."

Gwen closed her eyes. Thank God. Thank God Mitch didn't condemn her. It was more than she'd dared to expect.

"I know I have no right to ask any favors," she said, "but I'd appreciate it if you could pass on my resignation to Spellman. Make up any excuse you like. I'll send a formal letter as soon as I'm able."

"Gwen, where are you? Are you in danger?"

"Dorian won't hurt me, Mitch. He's trying to protect me."

"So he claimed." Gwen thought she heard the rapping of pacing footsteps.

"You've got to get away from him, Gwen. If you'll just tell me where you are—"

"It won't work." She wondered how much she could explain about the bond and decided it wasn't the right time. "I don't know when it will be possible for me to leave."

"You mean Black's destroyed your life."

The urge to defend Dorian almost overcame Gwen's common sense. "I'm still alive, aren't I?"

"That's not good enough. I'm going to help you get away from Black, whatever it takes."

"You already tried, Mitch. You've done enough."

"Damn it, Gwen. Is that resignation I hear in your voice? Are you giving up?"

"I don't think there's any way to reverse this condition."

"Maybe not. But I know a man who's spent his life researching vampires. Black obviously has some kind of physical hold over you, but there must be a way of breaking it. If such a way exists, I'll find it. I'll stop him."

A chill raised the gooseflesh on Gwen's arms. "It's too dangerous, Mitch."

"For me—or for him?" He sucked in his breath. "Look, it's not only what he's done to you, Gwen. Black has been a killer for years. He's an inhuman monster, like—"

"Like me," Gwen said quietly.

"That isn't what I—" Mitch sighed. "You didn't ask for this. It's as if someone gave you leprosy. Would you be to blame for that?"

"I got myself into this."

"I want to help you. I still love you."

Gwen dropped her face into her hands. *Oh, Mitch.*

A faint sound outside the room reminded Gwen of her vulnerable position. "We can't keep talking," she said. "I don't know when someone will find me."

"If you'd tell me where you are—"

"I don't know how long I'll be here."

"Then where can we meet?"

"I don't know. I'll try to keep in touch."

"That isn't good enough."

Gwen rubbed at her eyes. Same old Mitch, always trying to take control. But this time he was out of his depth. They both were.

"It'll have to be," she said.

"Do you even want to leave him, Gwen?" Mitch asked, bitterness in his voice. "Are you still in love with him?"

The door to the office clicked. Gwen set down the receiver as quietly as possible and pretended to examine a book that had been left on the desk.

"Miss Murphy."

Gwen looked up and smiled at Angela. "Sorry. Were you looking for me?"

"Actually, I was." The blonde glanced around the room, her gaze settling on the telephone. "Did you find your room too confining?"

Her voice was completely pleasant, but Gwen wasn't deceived. "I apologize. I shouldn't be wandering around uninvited, but I was curious to learn more about Pax."

"That's only natural." The blond woman beckoned Gwen toward the door. "Nevertheless, it would be best if you stayed in your room for the time being."

"I understand." Gwen rose and walked into the corridor, trying to keep her body relaxed. "Can you tell me if anything's been decided about Dorian and me?"

"The synod is meeting now. I expect we'll know very soon." She opened the door to Gwen's room and ushered her in. "I promise I'll tell you as soon as Sammael informs me of the synod's decision."

"Thanks. I appreciate it."

Angela nodded, hesitated, and walked into the room after Gwen. "I'd like to give you some advice, if I may."

Warily Gwen sat on the edge of the bed. "Oh?"

"I know that Dorian Converted you to save your life. There's no question of that."

The room was suddenly very cold. "Should there be a question?"

The blonde's pretty mouth tightened. "There's so much you don't understand about us yet. How could you? You've had no time to comprehend, let alone accept, your Conversion."

"But you're about to tell me something I ought to know."

"Yes." She looked at Gwen with something like pity. "Has Dorian explained why vampires Convert humans?"

A shock of realization stunned Gwen like a punch to the solar plexus. In the several conversations she'd had with Dorian since she'd learned what he was, he'd never once told her why vampires ordinarily Converted humans. He'd said that Raoul had Converted him to save his life, but that was all.

"Vampires…can't have children," Gwen guessed, pretending a confidence she was far from feeling. "Since they can be killed, they have to Convert humans to…keep their race alive."

"*Our* race," Angela corrected gently. "You're right, Gwen. If we didn't create new *strigoi*, we would lose any hope of survival. But Pax is dedicated to the ideal of willing Conversion, and only once peace and acceptance between vampires and humans is truly established. Unfortunately, not all *strigoi* subscribe to such a philosophy."

"What does this have to do with Dorian and me?"

"Did he make love to you?"

Gwen shot up. "I don't see how that's any of your business."

"But it is very much to the point. You must understand, Gwen, for your own sake. I would not want to see you suffer needless pain."

"Your concern is unnecessary. I—"

"You're in love with him."

The statement sounded terrifyingly blunt coming from Angela's lips, just as they had when Mitch had asked the same question. But Gwen wasn't about to deny them. She couldn't. No matter what she'd speculated about Dorian's motives and behavior toward her, past and present, those five words were just as true now as when she'd spoken them in her heart that night in St. Albert's, after she'd learned that Dorian had been an enforcer.

Every time she had doubts, every time some new revelation shook the foundations of her love, she came back to the one essential truth, the bedrock of emotion that somehow survived the onslaughts of shock, suspicion, jealousy, resentment—and yes, even hate. Nothing could destroy it now.

Gwen met Angela's gaze. "Yes," she said simply. "I am."

Angela's smile was almost wishful. "Do you believe he loves you?"

"I…don't know."

The blonde sat beside her, drawing close in a sisterly fashion. "This will be difficult for you to hear, Gwen, but you must." She seemed to gather herself. "It's a simple matter for any *strigoi* to make a human fall in love with him or her. It's in our blood."

Gwen caught up to the sense of Angela's statement very slowly. "What…what are you saying?"

"Let me begin again," Angela said in that particularly saccharine tone people use when they're about to say something unpleasant and trying to pretend they aren't enjoying it. "You see, *strigoi* aren't random in their choice of Converts. Most of us are driven by strong attractions, much like humans. But it's almost entirely physical…physical in a way ordinary men and women can't comprehend. One might call it an obsession that can be assuaged in only one way."

The knot beginning to form in Gwen's stomach loosened. "Sounds like any average male to me," she quipped.

"But it isn't. Dorian was compelled to save your life. You think it's because he'd come to care for you, but much of that compulsion was based on his desire to make you his own in the way only *strigoi* can."

"He had plenty of chances to Convert me before. He didn't touch me."

"He is a man of powerful will. Doubtless he fought against it. But no *strigoi* is truly complete without protégés of his own. It's not only a matter of sexual desire, but also of power, the need to dominate. Just as the most primitive impulse in humans is to reproduce themselves in the form of children, so *strigoi* are driven to pass their lineage to as many others as possible. That instinct is a part of our being as much as the need for blood."

"Then why haven't vampires overrun the earth?"

"Because masters like Kyril and his predecessor controlled their protégés and vassals by regulating when and how they might acquire Converts of their own."

"You're saying that Dorian's former master didn't let him do it?"

"Yes. He was denied his natural needs for too long. He was highly vulnerable when he met you, and the act of saving you from the river created a connection that opened the path for your Conversion. He never even considered any other way of protecting you from Kyril."

Gwen pushed her fingers deep into the bedspread. "You must have discussed this with him in great detail."

"No. It wasn't necessary." Angela paused as if carefully considering her next words. "Sometimes, when a patron and his protégé are violently separated by death, the survivor goes mad. But with some *strigoi,* the madness takes hold while both still live. For them, the tie that binds a patron to his protégé is a fever, almost a kind of insanity. I fear that Dorian is one of those *strigoi.*"

Gwen forgot to breathe. "Why?"

"There are certain…signs."

"Even if what you say is true, what do you suggest I do about it? I can't change places with you, as much as you might like me to." She smiled grimly at the expression on Angela's face. "Of course your telling me all this has nothing to do with the fact that you're in love with him yourself."

"I assure you, I mean this only for your benefit."

Gwen marched to the door and held it open. "Don't worry a minute longer, Angela. I'm perfectly safe."

"But you're not, Gwen. Not as long as you're bound to Dorian."

"He isn't going to let me go."

Angela pried Gwen's hand from the doorknob and closed the door again. "We in Pax have made a careful study of *strigoi* lore and traditions. There may be a way of severing the bond…if that's what you wish."

The bottom dropped out of Gwen's stomach. "What do you mean?"

"Knowledge of this has been suppressed because it could make it impossible for patrons to maintain control over their protégés. But Micah—" She gave a start as if she'd heard something in the corridor that Gwen had missed. "I must go."

Angela slipped out the door, glanced up and down the corridor, and walked away. Gwen shut the door and retreated into the darkest corner of the room, letting her heartbeat return to a normal clip. Angela's words continued to race through her mind like mice in a maze.

Angela's "advice." Advice that would have been invaluable a few months ago, before Gwen had gotten in so deep. Advice that might be entirely useless except for that hint of hope at the end: *There may be another way of severing the bond.*

And is that what you want? she asked herself. *To destroy the only thing that holds you and Dorian together?*

She laughed at herself. What had she been thinking only minutes ago? That had been selfish, considering only her needs and not Dorian's?

But that really wasn't the question, was it? Everything Angela had said boiled down to one central premise: that none of the feelings that had grown between Gwen and Dorian are real. Not Gwen's love for him, because he had *made* it happen. And certainly not any he might have developed for her.

According to Angela, Dorian was incapable of feeling the most basic and beautiful of human emotions. He'd chosen Gwen because of some purely physical, arcane vampire drive to dominate and procreate.

And what if that were true? Gwen had already resigned herself to the strong possibility that what had brought her and Dorian together—certainly what held them together now—was something less than love. Even before she'd seen him with Angela and considered what that implied, long before she'd known anything about *strigoi* or Conversion, she had recognized the risk in loving a man of so many contradictions and such a checkered past.

Or so she'd told herself.

And what about the part where Angela said Dorian made you fall in love with him?

Gwen emerged from her corner and sat on the bed, fighting her crippling doubts. *She would have said anything to make me back away.*

Because Angela was a woman, vampire or not.

How many tests? Gwen thought. *How many am I to be given?*

She touched her cross with her fingertips. It was warm, as if another hand had been holding it.

It's real, her heart whispered. *Oh, it's real.*

A new calm settled over her. She lay back on the bed. She found she couldn't sleep, but she didn't seem to need it. She let her mind wander, not bothering to count the minutes or hours that passed. A bland young woman brought a tray with a glass of water and a sandwich, which tasted surprisingly good to whatever was left of Gwen's human nature. Gwen found a tooth-brush and other toiletries in the bathroom; she bathed in the claw-foot bathtub, washed her hair, then brushed her teeth. Af-terward she returned to the bed and continued to lie quietly, letting her mind and body absorb all that had happened in the last twenty-four hours.

It must have been near five o'clock in the evening when Angela entered the room, her demeanor wary and alert.

"The synod has decided," she said. "I am to get you and Dorian out of the city as quickly as possible."

So Dorian had been right. Pax's leader considered her and Dorian a liability. "Where are you taking us?" Gwen asked.

"You'll know soon enough." Angela opened the door and made an impatient gesture. Gwen followed Angela out the door.

The corridor was dark and silent. Gwen's skin prickled.

"Come with me," Angela whispered. "Make as little noise as possible."

Gwen balked. "Where is Dorian?"

"Here."

Dorian joined them, so silent that Gwen had never heard him leave his room. Gwen met his gaze. His eyes revealed little emotion, but she felt that something was wrong. It was as if she were standing in the presence of two Dorians instead of one. Beads of sweat had gathered on his forehead, and there was a tension around his mouth. A tic jumped in his cheek.

"Are you all right?" she whispered.

"Yes."

He was lying, but Gwen had no chance to question him further. "We must hurry," Angela said.

Dorian gently pushed Gwen ahead of him. His touch provoked a powerful, almost erotic response in her flesh, wildly inappropriate under the circumstances. She increased her pace as Angela led them along the corridor, down the stairs and through a service passageway to a seemingly blank wall. Angela pressed two sections of the wall, and a panel slid open to reveal a tiny anteroom well stocked with long overcoats, hats, scarves and tinted glasses.

"Here are your coats and hats," Angela said, gesturing toward the coat racks.

"Each of you take a scarf and a pair of glasses. It's still a few minutes until dusk."

Dorian gave a long, peculiar shudder. "Where are we going?"

"To meet someone who can get you out of the city." She looked into Dorian's eyes. "You'll be safe, I promise."

"My thanks," Dorian said. Gwen suppressed a pang of jealousy.

You have more important things to think about now, my girl, she thought. She put on her coat and hat and the sunglasses, and wound a scarf around her neck. Another mysterious pass of Angela's hands opened a second panel, this one leading to open air. It was a chilly evening, growing colder as the sun began to set. Gwen felt an inexplicable frisson of fear.

"You're ill," Dorian said as Angela directed them through the alley behind the building. "Have you fed?"

"Yes. And *I'm* not the one who's ill."

He frowned, deep lines creasing the skin between his brows and bracketing his mouth. Once again Gwen caught the glimpse of the shadow Dorian who seemed to stand beside him. But Angela was already moving at a fast pace, leading them from alley to alley as they headed westward, avoiding open areas as the shadows deepened. Gwen had begun to think they were going in circles when Angela abruptly stopped, her body tense under her billowing coat.

"He should be here any moment," she whispered.

They waited. The narrow street passed into shadow. No one came.

"Stay here," Angela said. "I'll be right back."

"No," Dorian said, his voice strained and hoarse.

"I won't be in any danger."

She slipped away like a wraith. Dorian leaned against the wall, shivers racing through him as if he had contracted a fever.

"What is it, Dorian?" Gwen asked, touching his sleeve. "Have you…drunk anything?"

"Yes."

"Then what—"

"I'm fine."

"No, you're not."

"I said I'm fine!"

Gwen flinched at his vehemence. She could sense his struggle to keep her from feeling his emotions, but those emotions leaked out around the edges of his mental shield like water from a cracking dike. Gwen remembered his long-ago warning about his "regular intervals" of irrationality—what Walter had called "moods" and "nasty spells"—periods during which he was drawn back to "another time and place." Was this one of those times? Was he reliving the horrors he'd seen as both enforcer and *strigoi?*

She was about to risk a question when Dorian straightened, his body throwing off its lassitude like a snake shedding its skin.

"Something is wrong," he said.

It took less than a second for Gwen to realize he was correct. The fetid air in the alley was suddenly so thick that she could hardly breathe.

"I think we'd better get out of here," she whispered. "Angela—"

Muffled figures rushed into the alley on silent feet, machine guns raised to fire. Dorian's coat whipped around him as he sprang toward them. Gwen had only an instant to register the attack before Dorian had both *strigoi* on the ground, his fist pounding into one face and then the other. A third man sprang out of the darkness to tackle him, and Dorian spun around with unbelievable speed to seize the muzzle of the man's Tommy gun. Metal bent like rubber. Dorian struck his assailant's neck with the side of his hand. Bones snapped. The man's head hung loose on his shoulders, and he collapsed.

Dorian crouched above the three *strigoi,* a gun in each hand. "Gwen," he rasped. "Run."

For a moment she couldn't move, imprisoned by the violent rage that spewed from Dorian's mind. With a great effort she broke her paralysis, darted toward Dorian and yanked one of the guns from his grip.

"Angela betrayed us," she gasped.

Dorian roared, his face a monster's mask, and threw his gun against the wall. All at once Gwen understood that something was seriously wrong with him. He'd tossed the attackers around as if they were paper dolls. He was no longer even remotely sane.

And she could feel his madness reaching out for her.

"Dorian," she said. "Listen to me. We've got to leave."

He took half a step toward her, his fist raised. Gwen recoiled. Dorian convulsed and staggered backward, his eyes rolling up in his head. He didn't see the fourth man enter the alley and take aim at his heart.

Too slowly Gwen lifted her own weapon, fumbling with the trigger. Someone moved between Dorian and the hatchet man just as he loosed a deadly stream of bullets. Dorian roused from his stupor, leaped over the woman fallen at his feet and tore the gunman's arm from its socket. He slammed the man's head against the wall until it was unrecognizable as even remotely human. Then he fell to his knees beside Angela, making a sound Gwen had never heard from any throat. He lifted her head and shoulders in his arms. Blood pumped from the gaping wound in her chest.

"I didn't," Angela gasped. "Didn't…betray—"

"No," Dorian cried. "No, no, no."

Angela struggled to raise her hand, her fingers drifting across

Dorian's cheek. "Save yourself," she whispered. She coughed up a terrible quantity of blood. "Gwen."

Gwen scrambled to Angela's side and took her hand. "I'm here."

"I...didn't lie. The bond...there is a way." She fell into another spasm of coughing. "Find...the book."

She fell back with a rattling sigh and her eyes fell shut.

Dorian laid Angela on the ground with a deliberate gentleness more terrifying than his earlier rampage. He turned on Gwen with a madman's gaze. In seconds he had her airborne, dangling from his arms as if she were a bundle of rags.

And then he ran. To say his speed was remarkable would have been a gross understatement. Gwen was too dazed and nauseated to note more than a blur of buildings, automobiles and people as they flashed by. If there was any pursuit, Dorian left it far behind.

He was breathing almost normally when he set her down in a quiet place that smelled of rust and stagnant water. The sky was black above the waterfront, any threat of sunlight gone. Gwen half fell onto a lopsided seat of coiled rope, pressing her palms to her eyes until her head stopped spinning.

A few minutes later she thought she might be able to speak without vomiting. She lifted her head.

Dorian was gone.

She got up and walked aimlessly around the storage area where Dorian had left her, staring at the distant streetlights. She had no idea why he had left, and even less of what she should do. The things she'd seen in the alley rushed back into memory, vivid and overwhelming: smashed faces, torn limbs, blood spattered like paint on walls and ground. She couldn't get Dorian's terrible emotions out of her head—his utter ruthlessness, his mindless ferocity, hatred that went far beyond anything she could imagine.

Dorian hadn't merely killed those men. He'd destroyed them. Maybe all vampires were capable of such savagery. Even *she* had attacked Mitch. But Dorian had been far stronger and swifter than the *strigoi* he fought. He had gone far beyond the disciplined efficiency of a trained killer.

She'd seen hints of this darkness in him from the very beginning. Walter hadn't shown much concern about them, even thought he'd claimed that they occurred every few weeks, and he shared close quarters with Dorian.

I'm not rational at such times. Wasn't that what Dorian had told her after she'd "rescued" him from starvation in Hell's Kitchen? He'd said it wasn't wise for anyone with less than friendly intention to approach him during his "intervals."

And he'd warned her away, not once but many times. Warnings she'd always interpreted as springing from other sources, such as his desire to conceal his past as an enforcer or his inhuman nature. He'd openly shared his concern he might hurt innocent people during one of his spells, but she hadn't taken him seriously. How could she, when he'd never come close to hurting her since that one brief time in the waterfront warehouse?

He'd never touched Walter. He'd threatened Mitch and never acted on the threat. But *they* hadn't been trying to kill him or someone under his protection.

This was why he'd tried to kill himself, just as he'd tried to tell her. Not because there was a chance he might, somewhere or someday, commit another act of mayhem. Not because he simply "lost himself" for a few hours every month.

No. He didn't merely lose himself. He became someone, some*thing* else, incapable of compassion. And the fact that he seemed to recover after each spell, able once again to carry on a relatively normal life, must be unbearable torment for a man who had tried so hard to escape his old life of violence.

Had it always been this way for him, all throughout his career as an enforcer? Had it gradually ground him down to a despair and self-loathing so great that he could find no way to live with himself?

He knew this would keep happening, not without warning, like the imagined lunacy of some *strigoi* Jekyll and Hyde, but again and again, month after month, perhaps for the rest of his long, long life. A madness from which he could never be free.

How does he know that? Gwen thought. *How do I?*

There might be a way to stop it. A cure, or at least a way to mitigate the symptoms and their deadly aftereffects. There had to be a reason behind the madness, a cause waiting to be discovered, lanced like an infected wound, and healed with time and care.

Still dizzy with reaction, Gwen returned to the coil of rope and sat down again. No matter what Dorian had done, *she* didn't have a lot of choice about what to do next. She knew that he hadn't abandoned her; the bond wouldn't allow it. He would be back again, free of the horror that had overwhelmed him. ✦

She had to believe that. And she must be ready to help him in any way she could.

The night was bitterly cold, and a light snow had begun to fall. Though Gwen felt little of the chill, she wrapped her coat close about her for the comfort it brought and closed her eyes. Midnight came and went. Exhaustion mantled her shoulders like the falling snow, and she began to drift. Her body slumped. She finally surrendered and made a lumpy nest of the coil of rope, unable to sleep but more than willing to steal whatever rest she could.

Dawn emerged as a yellow smudge behind a veil of mist. A deep stillness had fallen over the waterfront, broken only by the scuffling of rats and the creaking of boats on the river.

"Gwen."

The voice was harsh and raw, but at least it held a semblance of reason.

And grief. Terrible grief.

Gwen got up slowly, realizing with a start that she couldn't sense anything through the bond. "Are you…?"

She couldn't find the words. Dorian fixed his gaze on a point slightly below her chin.

"It's over," he said.

Gwen knew at once that he was telling the truth. The haze was gone from his eyes. His face was composed, his muscles no longer fighting against his body. The bloody reign of violence had lost its hold on him, but his coat was still blotched with red.

"What happened?" he asked.

At first Gwen was too stunned to answer. "You don't remember?"

"Some. Not…everything."

Gwen breathed a prayer. It must mean something if Dorian couldn't recall what he'd done or how he'd done it.

"There were several men," she said carefully. "They attacked us."

"How many did I kill?"

The words were a cry of pain. Gwen didn't have to feel that bond to recognize the horror that haunted him.

"I don't know," she said, then hesitated. "They killed Angela."

Dorian shrank in on himself. "Did she speak?"

"Only to say she didn't betray us. But Kyril's men must have found us somehow."

"She saved my life."

"Yes." Gwen swallowed. "I'm sorry. I know that you cared for her a great deal."

Dorian swept his hat from his head and stared out at the river. "We…"

"I know." Dorian had lost a friend—or perhaps much more than a friend—in the most horrible away imaginable. And now he was trying to keep Gwen out of the bond his bite had forged, just as he'd done at Pax.

He doesn't know what to do, Gwen thought. *He's lost himself. I'll have to find the way for both of us.*

"We can't let Angela's sacrifice have been in vain," she said, breaking the painful silence. "Kyril's men may still be hunting us. We need to find a way out of the city."

He climbed out of his own private hell, half turning in her direction. "How?"

"I know of a pilot who freelances for the *Sentinel*. We can probably hire him to take us out of state."

Dorian looked through her as if she were made of glass. "I have some money, but—"

"I took most of my savings out of the bank when I returned to New York. We should have enough for…for as long as it takes."

"Where do you suggest we go?"

Gwen thought quickly. "Mexico," she said, with more confidence than she felt. "My dad had a place there years ago, a little cabin in the desert outside a small village about ten miles east of Chihuahua. No one would find us there. And you…"

You'll have a lot less chance of hurting somebody if the madness comes over you again.

As if he'd heard her thoughts, Dorian turned away, his body hunched like an old man's. "Where do we find this pilot?" he asked.

"He's based at a field in Queens. I need to get to a telephone."

"I must inform Sammael of Angela's death."

"Not now," Gwen said quickly, hardly aware of the reason for her protest. "If you contact Pax, they'll try to come and help us. We don't want anyone else to get hurt."

"The bodies…the sun will destroy them."

"There's nothing we can do about that now."

He nodded, gazing blindly across the snow-covered docks. Gwen dared to look into his face. Such a short while ago he'd set out to protect her from enemies she could hardly comprehend; now their positions were reversed, and she was the one who had to try to save him from a force beyond her understanding. Even if she'd had the choice, she couldn't have abandoned him to the monster that lurked under his skin.

With a shake of her shoulders she extended her hand to Dorian, knowing that neither of them would find easy answers in the days ahead.

"Let's go," she said.

ONE HUNDRED MEN AND women, human and *strigoi,* stood in the auditorium, waiting for Sammael to finish his sermon. All three points of the Triangle were present on this early morning: novices like the human boy Jim; the mediants, including Vida; and the master guides, who stood at the forefront of the room. The synod ranged in a semicircle behind Sammael on the dais, clad in the white-and-red hooded robes that kept their identities secret from the congregation.

Only the Guard recruits were absent, immersed in training for the attack—young men Converted for the sole purpose of fighting the war to come. It would not be wise to show them to the novices and mediants, who had so little idea of Pax's true goals.

All would be brought into the fold eventually. And once the original book was found, there would be no risk of dangerous questions.

Sammael opened his copy to a new page, though he had memorized the contents long ago.

"'There can be no greater goal than peace,'" he quoted, holding the book high. "Those were Micah's words. No greater goal. 'No price is too great if the ultimate goal will be attained.'"

He set the book down, his gaze sweeping over the assembly with pride and impatience. "What will we not sacrifice to achieve peace, my brothers and sisters? What will we not surrender? Our pride? Our reason? Our lives?"

The congregation stirred, murmuring agreement. A young male *strigoi* cried out. Rapt faces turned up to Sammael, sincere and unafraid.

"Any sacrifice," Sammael said, gentling his voice. "It is a great thing to ask. But it is what Micah has asked of us…what he recognized as the necessary price for freedom from the chains of blood and flesh that keep us from redemption."

His last word echoed in the silence that followed. He let it stand alone for a full minute to remind the children of what they had yet to achieve.

"We," he said, "we *strigoi* have strayed from the path of righteousness. Salvation must be earned. We—"

There was a slight commotion as a young man entered through the side door of the auditorium and strode toward the dais. One of the synod members stepped down to intercept him. Voices whispered urgently, and then the councillor ascended the dais again.

Sammael listened to his message with a cold and brittle fury. He finished the sermon, hardly remembering the words he spoke, and dismissed the assembly. A few minutes later he was with the synod and senior guards in the private meeting room.

"The Guard have failed," he said as the synod members took their seats. "Taharial, explain."

The young guard, only six months Converted, held his chin high. "There is no evidence that Black had any assistance," he said. "It appears as if he overcame our men alone. I have no explanation."

Sammael pressed his fingers to his temples. No explanation. No possible reason why Black should have been able to overcome the four men sent to follow Angela and bring Gwen Murphy back.

"So now they have escaped," he said heavily. "Angela?"

"She was found barely alive, but it is believed that she will heal."

"Then we will question her as soon as she is capable of answering. You will redouble the watch on Mitch Hogan." He addressed the synod. "We now believe that Hogan's relationship to Murphy was closer than we initially supposed. It is possible that the girl will contact him."

The councillors nodded gravely. Sammael dismissed the guard and bowed his head.

"The Lord will aid us," he said. "We will find her. We will find both of them, and then there will be a true sacrifice."

CHAPTER SIXTEEN

GWEN AND DORIAN encountered no obstacles on their journey to Queens and saw no suspicious characters or men in black overcoats. Gwen breathed a sigh of relief when they finally descended into the subway. Once in Queens, she summoned a taxi, which took them out to the airfield where Ray Fowler kept his office.

The field was carpeted with rapidly melting snow, dotted here and there with biplanes salvaged from the War. Men moved briskly about the hangar. Ray came to meet them with a grin, his face and shirt stained with oil.

"Gwennie," he said, kissing her cheek. "You don't know how glad I was to hear that you were still alive."

"Not as glad as I was." She returned his hug and stepped back, noting his bemusement as he took in her dark glasses and masculine hat.

"Attractive, isn't it?" she said, touching the brim of the homburg. "But very useful when you want to remain anonymous."

"If you say so." His smile subsided. "You sure you're all right, Gwennie?"

"Everything's fine, Ray. I'm not in any danger now."

He accepted the lie with a slight narrowing of his brown eyes. "You shouldn't be doing this alone. Why isn't anyone from the *Sentinel* helping you out? Where's Mitch?"

"I told you I'd explain everything when I could." She followed Ray's guarded glance to Dorian. "Ray, this is Dorian Black. Dorian, Ray Fowler."

Ray began to extend his hand and stopped, puzzlement and wariness deepening the sunburned lines of his face. He felt it, too. He knew that Dorian was dangerous, and not just because Gwen had told him that Dorian had once worked for a leading gang. Though the bloodstains on Dorian's coat weren't obvious, Ray might very well have noticed them.

After a moment Ray wiped his palm on the leg of his dungarees. "Okay," he said, expelling his breath. "I'll have Betty ready to go in about an hour. Did anyone follow you?"

"No," Gwen said. "If anyone had, I wouldn't have come here."

"Sure, I know that." He shifted from foot to foot, never looking in Dorian's direction. "You can wait in my office. It's not much, but I can offer you a hot cup of joe."

"You're already doing enough for us—me—already."

"Mexico should be pretty nice this time of year. Just what I need." He wiped a smear of oil from his face with a stained rag. "Come on. I'll get you that coffee."

Gwen took a few steps after him, paused, and glanced back at Dorian. He stood very still, his breath forming curls of mist in the air.

"We can trust him," she said.

Muted light reflected from Dorian's sunglasses. "You're certain."

"Yes."

She started for the hangar, listening for Dorian's footsteps behind her. They dragged with reluctance, but they came.

Ray's office was cold, heated only by a small corner stove. The pilot already had two mugs of steaming coffee ready when Gwen and Dorian arrived. Gwen took one mug gratefully. Dorian ignored his. Ray set it down on a cluttered desk.

"Make yourselves comfortable," he said, addressing Gwen. "I'll keep you posted."

He walked out. Gwen considered the level of light in the office and lowered the Venetian blinds over the windows overlooking the airfield. She sat down in the desk chair, cradling the mug between her hands.

"I've been thinking," she said. "Shouldn't we let Walter know we're leaving town?"

Dorian removed his sunglasses and looked at her from under the brim of his hat, his eyes almost normal again. "Does he know you're alive?"

"No. Before I…" She swallowed. "Before, I didn't want whoever was after me to know about him."

"You haven't seen him since your return."

"I never had the chance. Did you keep in touch with him when you…joined the faction?"

Dorian studied the floor at his feet. "Only to make certain he had sufficient funds for his rent and food."

"I made sure of that while I was in New Jersey." She hesitated. "He never found out what you are, did he?"

"No."

"Do you think he's in danger?"

"Kyril is almost certainly aware of my past association with Walter," Dorian said slowly. "But I doubt he will consider threatening an elderly human a sufficient inducement for me to surrender."

"Still, we need to tell him how to reach us if he does get into trouble."

"Yes." Dorian reached inside his coat and pulled out a wallet bulging with bills. "If you have sufficient trust in your Mr. Fowler, I will leave Walter money and a brief letter outlining our situation. Once we've reached Mexico, we will supply him with the means to contact us."

"I agree," Gwen said. She scuffed her feet on the concrete floor, grateful that Dorian seemed to have completely recovered his reason. He was thinking clearly again, taking the lead as he had in the past.

She had to keep thinking clearly, too. Walter wasn't the only loose end that needed tying up before she and Dorian flew out of New York. She'd left Mitch hanging when she'd telephoned him from Pax headquarters; he had the right to know she was still well and whole.

And if you tell him, what then? If he knew where to find her, nothing would stop him from following. And that would mean trouble in more ways than one.

Once she knew she and Dorian were safe—once she better understood Dorian's madness and found a way to help him recover—then she could risk the call.

I'm sorry, Mitch. You don't deserve this. None of us do.

Dorian was gazing at her when she emerged from her thoughts. "What is it, Gwen?" he asked.

She guessed that he'd felt her inner turmoil, even though he continued to hide his own feelings from her. "I'll go check on Ray," she said, edging toward the door. "I didn't get a chance to ask—"

"I know how difficult this has been for you," he said, his voice little more than a whisper.

She didn't know what to say, but he didn't wait for a reply. "What you saw last night…" he said. "It has happened before."

"I…" Gwen's mouth went dry. "I guessed as much."

"Then you must understand." He came up behind her, fists clenched at his sides. "You must be prepared."

Prepared for the next time, he meant. As if anyone could ever be prepared for that. She braced herself.

"Tell me."

"It comes once a month," he said. "At the dark of the moon."

The dark of the moon. That had been last night. Gwen had noticed the lack of moonlight, never guessing that the lunar condition might have a connection to Dorian's madness.

The roots of the word "lunacy" had to do with the moon, but every legend she'd ever heard referred to a full moon, not the absence of one.

"How?" she asked hoarsely. "Why?"

Dorian faltered, withdrawing into some remote inner landscape she couldn't reach. "You will not see it happen again," he said.

"You mean you can control it?" She took a step toward him, hope beating hard in her chest.

Dorian retreated until his hip bumped the desk. "No," he said.

"When it comes again, I will stay away." He looked out the window at the airfield, glittering with water from the melting snow.

"Kyril will have double the reason to hunt us now," he said, abruptly changing the subject. "We may have to remain in Mexico for months."

"Kyril can't hunt us forever."

Whatever answer Dorian might have given was interrupted when Ray walked into the office. He glanced from Gwen to Dorian.

"Betty's ready to go," he said. "Are you sure you don't want to pick up some essentials before we head out?"

Gwen recovered her composure and shook her head. "We can't risk it. We'll have to stop along the way, won't we?"

"Yes." He pursed his lips. "You won't need those sunglasses and the hat once we're airborne."

Gwen cleared her throat. "Mr. Black has a sort of allergy to sunlight," she said.

"Yeah?" He gave Dorian another dubious glance. "There are blinds you can pull down over the rear windows. You can even sleep back there if you like."

"Thanks, Ray." She followed the pilot to the door. "Dorian?"

He came, his steps heavy enough to make almost as much noise as a human. Ray led them to the airfield and a well-seasoned De Havilland biplane, with an open cockpit and a covered cabin. The plane had obviously seen better days, but Ray patted it fondly and kissed the chipped painting of a long-legged beauty that graced the plane's battered nose behind the propeller. He opened the hinged top flap that provided access to the cabin and let down the ladder, helping Gwen up and leaving Dorian to climb in himself. One of Ray's fellow pilots spun the propeller while Ray started the engine.

Gwen had been in a plane only a few times in her career, but she took little pleasure in the novelty now. Dorian sat unmoving in his seat, showing no interest in raising the blinds for a view of the passing landscape far below.

Ray made several stops to gas up, usually on airfields that

were little more than meadows or flat strips of dirt. The weather grew progressively warmer as they traveled south and west. They spent the first night in a small hotel in Little Rock, the three of them in separate rooms. Gwen stopped by several modest shops to buy clothing and other necessities. She also found more casual apparel for Dorian, which he accepted without comment.

Near the middle of the second afternoon they set down on a primitive airfield just outside the city of Chihuahua. Ray exchanged a few stilted sentences with the ancient caretaker who watched over the largely abandoned antique planes, and the old gentleman sent a boy into town. Within an hour a young man arrived in a flivver to take Gwen, Dorian and Ray into Chihuahua. The weather was just warm enough to make wearing their wool overcoats a little uncomfortable, and Gwen felt many curious stares as she and Ray purchased food and additional supplies at the open-air market and surrounding shops.

By early evening, Ray had engaged the young man and his flivver to transport the three of them to the small village of San Luis. Ray was clearly worried about Gwen, and his wary glances at Dorian became more frequent. Dorian hadn't said more than a handful of words during the entire trip. And Gwen was beginning to imagine what life would be like, sharing a small *casa* with a man she loved…a man who could become a killer at the change of the moon.

The ride to San Luis was bumpy and uncomfortable, the road a dirt track overgrown with scrubby grass. Flat areas of trackless desert were broken by rocky hills and studded with cacti and mesquite, seeming otherwise lifeless. Gwen knew the lifelessness was an illusion, but the area was desolate nonetheless.

By the time they reached the village she was more concerned with her increasing hunger than her surroundings. She became intensely aware of the young man driving the automobile, and her thoughts turned to the practical aspects of feeding, a necessity she was still learning to consider. With a small human population nearby and a larger one within ten miles, she guessed that she and Dorian would be able to meet their needs for blood without depleting their resources.

Resources, she thought grimly as the jalopy rattled onto the village's narrow central street. *Is that how you think of humans already? Have you sunk so far?*

She was desperate to fully understand the changes within herself, understand and learn to accept them, but the only one who could help her was the same man who most needed her to be strong. Strong enough for both of them.

It was growing dark when they stopped in the village. The town consisted of about two dozen dwellings ranging from primitive shacks to plain adobe houses with tiny vegetable gardens. Several men of various ages dressed in light-colored shirts and trousers emerged from a house that obviously served as the local watering hole. An old woman with a shawl draped over her shoulders paused in her slow progress up the dusty center street. They watched the outsiders with curiosity that changed quickly to suspicion.

They might have known my father, but they don't know me, Gwen thought. And she didn't dare get too familiar with any of the villagers. How could she turn to them for blood if she regarded them as friends?

"I've been to places like this a few times," Ray said, interpreting the look on her face. "Village people are usually hospitable to strangers. I've seldom seen them act this way." He cast a glance at Dorian, his expression speaking volumes.

Gwen couldn't argue with his implication. Like Ray, the villagers didn't have to know Dorian was a vampire to suspect that he was dangerous. At least Gwen hoped that was all there was to it.

"I've only been to the *casa* once," she said, "when my father brought me here as a child. I hope we can find a guide to lead us there."

Indicating that Gwen and Dorian should wait with the jalopy and the crates of supplies, Ray jumped out of the car and approached the men standing in front of the saloon. He spoke in his halting Spanish. The men regarded him in silence. Finally one of them disappeared into the bar, which had begun to glow with candlelight.

An elderly man emerged and peered into Ray's face. He asked a question in Spanish. Ray responded by dropping a handful of coins into the old man's outstretched hand.

Apparently satisfied, the man spoke with the flivver's owner, who unloaded the crates, shifted the car into Reverse and drove out of the village.

"If I'm understanding him right," Ray said, "this old guy has been the caretaker for the cabin. Your father must have left some kind of payment for him to keep it up."

"That would be just like Dad," Gwen said. "He and my mother used to come here before I was born. Dad said it was one of the happiest times of his life."

As soon as she'd finished speaking, she realized what an irony it was that a place once filled with love would become tainted with tension and uncertainty.

Unless, she thought. *Unless…*

The old man made an impatient sound in his throat, gestured that Ray and Dorian should pick up the crates, and began marching up the road at a surprisingly fast pace. He led the Americans to a rickety stable and herded a pair of burros out of a malodorous stall.

"One is for the lady," Ray translated slowly. "Juan says the *casa* isn't too far…only about a mile from here."

"I can walk," Gwen protested.

"It's time to make a good impression," Ray whispered, and Gwen clambered reluctantly up onto the burro's back. Juan lashed the crates onto the second burro's hindquarters, pressed a lantern into Ray's hand and clucked his tongue. The burros broke into a jarring trot along a nearly invisible trail winding between wicked-looking cacti and unidentifiable shrubs. Snakes and lizards scurried out of the burros' path. Gwen quickly learned not to be startled by the sudden movements.

The *casa* came into view after a good twenty minutes. It

butted up against a ramshackle corral; the overgrown remains of a cobbled path meandered to its narrow front door. As they got closer, Gwen recognized the solid adobe walls she remembered touching as a child.

The villager spoke to Ray again and pointed toward the door. Dorian took the lead and opened it. The hinges squealed, and something small and very fast scurried back into the shadows.

The interior was different than Gwen remembered it, but she'd been considerably younger on her last visit. What had seemed spacious then was much smaller now. There was a central room with a fireplace, a tiny kitchen with a stove and water pump, and two other rooms connected by a short hallway. The walls were decorated with faded photographs of the local people and scenery; a colorful woven blanket covered the sprung sofa. The floor had been recently swept, and the plain furniture was all in one piece.

"It ain't so bad," Ray remarked, setting down his crate. While Dorian disappeared into the hallway, Ray pulled Gwen outside.

"Are you sure you want to stay with this guy?" he asked.

"I'm…responsible for him," Gwen said. "At least for a little while."

"You're going to be in pretty close quarters."

"Dorian helped me when the assassins came after me again. I owe him something for that."

"But it's more than that, isn't it?"

"If it is, that's my problem." She softened her tone, trying to ignore the sound and smell of the blood beating beneath Ray's skin. "You know I can take care of myself. Anyway, who's going to worry about my reputation? The villagers?" She squeezed his arm. "Don't worry, Ray. You've done enough already."

Ray shrugged, clearly unsatisfied, but said nothing more. Dorian came out of the house. He glanced narrow-eyed from Ray to Gwen.

"It is acceptable," he said. "How much do we owe you, Mr. Fowler?"

"Nothing," Ray said with uncharacteristic coldness. "I did it for Gwen. But I'll tell you right now, if you harm her in any way…"

Dorian showed his teeth. They glinted, long and white, in the lantern light. Gwen stepped between the two men.

"Do you have a ride to your plane?" she asked Ray.

"The kid's coming back for me in the morning. I'll find somewhere in the village to stay for the night." The old man approached, and spoke up again. Ray nodded. "Juan says there are more lanterns inside, extra blankets and some cans of food in the cupboard. If you need anything else, contact him. If the village can't provide it, he'll get you to Chihuahua."

Gwen understood that Ray was telling her how to escape if she needed to. She would certainly have to get to a telephone to contact Walter…and possibly Mitch, if and when she could risk it.

"Well," Ray said, "I guess I'll be going."

Gwen gave him a sudden, fierce hug. "Thanks, Ray. I owe you."

"Just keep yourself safe." He backed away quickly, nodded to Juan and looked one last time at Dorian. What he saw made him shudder. For a few minutes his lantern bobbed like a beacon in the night, receding until it disappeared. The darkness that remained was absolute, but Gwen could see well enough. Well enough to catch the flicker of red in Dorian's eyes.

"Shall we go in?" she said, opening the door.

He followed her into the living room and knelt in front of the fireplace, gathered a few of the logs stacked beside it and arranged them neatly. He lit the fire with matches found on top of a brightly painted table in the corner of the room and drew a chair before the fire.

"Sit," he said. "Rest."

It was the first real command he'd given since the fight in the alley. She felt an incongruous flash of hope.

Dorian wasn't completely lost. Part of him was still with her, still reachable. He might be wading through a personal limbo of shame, self-contempt and God knew what else. He might be crushed by the weight of his mourning for Angela, unable to speak of his pain. Hi might even be thinking that he should have jumped out of the De Havilland somewhere over the border.

She sat and glanced at her watch. Back in New York it would be eight o'clock. Past time for dinner. She cleared her throat.

"How long can we go without feeding?" she asked, hating the question and the necessity of asking it.

He met her gaze, still barricaded behind the wall he had raised between them. "As long as a week," he said. "Though the consequences of delaying are not pleasant."

"Then we can wait."

"For a day or two, no longer."

"I'd prefer—"

"No longer."

She opened her mouth to argue further, but it was pointless. Dorian had already pulled away from her.

He wouldn't be able to maintain that kind of distance forever. But she would have to chip away at it a little at a time, with all the courage and persistence she could muster.

"I think I'll go to bed," she said.

"You know you cannot sleep," Dorian said, his face turned away.

"I've already figured that out." She rose and walked to the hallway door. "I'll…see you in the morning."

He looked up, and Gwen saw something smoldering in his eyes, something she'd been finally begun to recognize in herself. Irrational, undeniable lust. He wanted her, though he refused to come near her. Maybe his hunger was only because of the monster curled up inside him, waiting to escape again at the dark of the moon. Or maybe his desire was as real and true as the Dorian she knew still existed, the one who had stolen her heart. The one who aroused needs to which she didn't dare surrender.

She might not be able to feel Dorian's emotions through the bond, but she was willing to bet that he could feel hers. She had to keep her emotions under rigid control, and that meant she couldn't let him know how much she wanted him…how much she loved him. Because she knew—deep in her heart she knew— that if she lost mastery of her feelings, he was in ever greater danger of losing control of his.

Someday. Someday, when he's well…

"Good night," she said.

He didn't follow as she looked into the two bedrooms and selected the smaller for herself. The furniture was all handmade, with rough carving on the bedstead and backs of the chairs. The single window was hung with muslin curtains, and there were hand-woven baskets hanging on the walls.

The bed was lumpy but welcome after the long day. The sheets were clean. Gwen changed into the pajamas she'd purchased in Little Rock and burrowed under the blankets. She could hear the crackling of the fire, the whisper of Dorian's feet as he entered the hall.

He passed by, and she didn't hear him again.

CHAPTER SEVENTEEN

LATE WINTER WAS peculiar in the desert; some days were warm and sunny, others chilled by wind and clouds racing across the plain. The nights remained cool as the weeks passed, but the hours of sunlight gradually began to lengthen, promising longer confinements within the small space of the cabin. Space that Dorian and Gwen shared in uneasy truce.

To Dorian, the days were much the same. He spent most of each night in the desert and returned to the *casa* before dawn. Sometimes he found Gwen preparing a pot of coffee on the primitive stove. Other times she was sitting alone in her room, writing in the journal she kept under her pillow. He never tried to learn what it contained.

During the first weeks Dorian showed Gwen how to stalk donors in San Luis. She learned to hunt—always by his side at the beginning, while he taught her how to let her body release the chemicals that enabled her to feed and then erase the donor's memory of the event. Once she'd learned how to take blood from the villagers, careful never to feed from the same donor twice in a week, Dorian allowed her to go alone. On such nights he paced the floor of the *casa* and around the house in ever-widening circles, counting the minutes, terrified that she would make some crucial mistake.

But her instincts were excellent, as was her sense of self-preservation. Still, she flinched from taking all the nourishment she needed. She waited the longest possible time between feedings, letting herself grow weak before Dorian was compelled to make her do what was necessary.

Such times were difficult. Dorian had sworn to himself that

he wouldn't interfere beyond what was necessary to keep her safe and alive. He tried to maintain his distance within the bond that held them together, tried not to let her feel the desire that consumed him every time he touched her.

But she, too, had become an expert at hiding. If she hated him for forcing her to obey him, if she felt loathing for him, for the things he'd done and would do again, she concealed it perfectly. She greeted him quietly every morning, shared the common room with him through the long days while they read the books her father had left, as companionable as a human couple in their waning years. She seldom smiled and never laughed, and Dorian knew that something had died inside her…died or become buried so deep that the old fire he'd admired in her would not easily be reignited. It was a strange and terrible kind of peace.

Except on the days when she tried to get him to talk. There was no peace then. She asked him about his past, probing beneath the dry facts he'd given her before. She pushed here and pulled there, like a Freudian psychiatrist, cool and ruthless, intent on making him speak of his madness and when it had first claimed him.

He couldn't talk about it, even when she urged him, in words stripped of emotion, to heal himself with confession. Each one-sided conversation always ended the same way. Gwen put on her hat and overcoat and left the cabin. He wouldn't see her again until evening. And she would ask no more questions. Until the next time.

During the fourth week the dark of the moon came again. Dorian went out into the desert, far from any human habitation. Far from Gwen. He raged without purpose, his crippled rationality fighting the monster as it drove him to return to the village and its helpless human inhabitants. Hunger tore at his belly. Three hours before dawn he found himself on the outskirts of San Luis, the last of his inhibitions riven asunder.

Only one thing stopped him. *She* stood blocking his path, a female his body recognized even when his mind did not. She didn't move when he approached her, trembling with the need to kill. Sharp and cool she waited, speaking words he didn't understand, until his fury turned to a different awareness. He smelled her ripeness, felt the desire that flowed hot in her blood.

He met no resistance when he carried her from the human place to another where he could take her without interference. But then her mouth moved, and he began to hear the sounds she made, to make sense of them in a distant part of his mind.

"This isn't you, Dorian," she said. "It's nearly dawn. Fight it. Hold fast just a little longer."

The monster roared denial. He bit her neck until blood flowed and licked the wound closed. He ground his mouth into hers to silence the flow of words. And still she spoke.

"Think," she said. "Use your mind, your intelligence. Fight!"

He pulled back, his will tugged in two directions at once. His muscles twitched and spasmed. His eyes grew blind. Then the first light skimmed the horizon, and he ran, leaving the female where she lay.

He woke to memory in the *casa,* every bone and muscle aching. Gwen sat in the rocking chair facing the cold fireplace, her face serene.

"You're all right now," she said. "The night is over."

The sofa creaked as he sat up. Distorted images flashed in his mind: Gwen lying beneath him, unafraid, speaking words of encouragement. The bright flow of her blood, her bruised lips. And her eyes, revealing nothing but pity.

"I…hurt you," he said.

"No." She planted her feet, halting the rocker's steady motion. "You stopped, Dorian. You stopped yourself."

But he didn't believe it. The monster was back in its cage, but he knew what it had done, how close it had come to using her without mercy. Only the coming dawn had stopped him, the end of the dark that also meant the end of his madness.

Once before he'd come very near to hurting or even killing her. The odds were against her escaping a third time.

He got up and walked to the window, deliberating opening the curtains. A wide beam of sunlight crawled over his hand and arm. He welcomed the pain. He thought, as he had so many times before, of going outside unprotected. Death would end this eternal limbo, this purgatory of fear and loathing. And Gwen would be safe.

Because she was lost to him, just as he was lost to himself. Her stoic acceptance of her captivity shamed him. Her compassion had become unendurable. The beauty of her eyes and body, the strength of her will, her stubborn courage, her quick intelligence—everything that made Gwen the person she was—they could never belong to him again.

He turned from the window, letting the shadows cool his burns. He remembered that Gwen had suspected that he'd lied when he'd told her that only a patron's death would free his protégé from the bond between them.

He hadn't lied. But he'd deceived himself into believing that she would always need his protection. In that he'd been wrong. Gwen had proved her strength. She had adapted. She could lead her changed life without his help, stay away from Kyril and make a new future free of his interference.

He would have let her go. He would have walked out and let himself die, if not for one terrible thought.

What happened to you might happen to her. A traumatic death severing a bond with pain and violence. Sinister passions rising out of the emptiness that remained.

Madness.

The only thing left to do was destroy Gwen's commitment to saving him. Keep her from approaching him when he was at his most deadly. Wear away at the crusader's habits that made her so determined to cure his illness, as she'd once determined to rescue him from a life of isolation at the waterfront.

She would never believe him if he told her he had no use for her, that he would gladly let her go if he could. But there was another way. A way that might work if he convinced himself first. It was not so great a step from despising the evil in himself to giving up and embracing it. Making Gwen believe that she would eventually embrace it, as well. Cutting through her mask of competent dispassion to tap the vulnerability that must still exist beneath.

If she learned to hate and fear him…not only because of what he'd done to her in the past, but because of what he could still do…she might withdraw so far from him that his death would cause her only discomfort, not agony or madness.

He would have to break Gwen to save her. But the circumstances must be right. Gwen must be made ready.

The first opportunity came a week and a half later, when she returned from a solo hunt, distressed in a way he hadn't seen her since immediately after the fight and Angela's death. She entered the *casa* and began to pace, her agitation reaching Dorian through the bond.

"I've made a mistake," she said, coming to stand in front of the stone fireplace. "I think the young man…my donor…saw me. Saw what I really am."

Dorian stared at her coldly. "You little fool," he said. "Haven't you learned any better?"

She looked up at him, bewildered. "It was a mistake."

"'A mistake,'" he mimicked. "That explains everything." He walked around her, deliberately opening the bond he'd striven so hard to obstruct. "We have a place here, and you may have destroyed it."

Her eyes searched his, wide and kindling to anger. "You made me what I am."

He laughed. "And now the little girl whines. Did they actually let you hold a man's job?"

If she had an answer, she didn't give it. She left the cabin, nearly running, and when she returned she only stared at him in the way of someone who had met with a difficult and unexpected puzzle.

For a week things went back to normal. Gwen ignored the contretemps as if it had never happened, and once again she tried to speak of Dorian's madness. He bided his time, waiting for another opportunity to strike at her obstinate loyalty.

It came on a relatively cool afternoon, when he heard the

sound of a small airplane flying low over San Luis. Within two hours Ray Fowler was walking up the path to the cabin, several boxes tucked under his arm.

He stopped when he saw Dorian standing outside the *casa* in his hat and overcoat.

"I've come to see Gwen," Fowler said, squaring his shoulders.

"You've made a mistake," Dorian said. "She doesn't want to see you."

Gwen emerged from the cabin. "Ray!" she said. "What are you doing here?"

Dorian stepped between them. "It doesn't matter," he said. "He's leaving. Now."

"Like hell I am," Fowler snapped. He circled Dorian and started toward Gwen. "I had to see how you were. I dropped by the *Sentinel*…no one had heard from you in weeks, not even Mitch."

"Is he all right?" Gwen asked. "Did he—"

Dorian seized Fowler by the arm and spun him around. "Go," he said, "or I will kill you."

There was a beat of stunned silence. Fowler raised his fist. Gwen tried to pry Dorian's fingers from Fowler's sleeve.

"Let him go," she said, breathing fast. "He's no threat to either of us."

But Dorian only twisted harder. Fowler gasped and dropped to his knees. Gwen crouched beside him.

"I'm sorry, Ray. He doesn't know what he's doing."

"But I do," Dorian said. He stepped back. "Convince him to leave, if you value his life."

The amazement in Gwen's eyes was not as great as before; her bewilderment was more quickly gone. She helped Ray up and walked with him some distance away. Their conversation was heated, at least on Fowler's side. She was clearly struggling to maintain her composure. Ten minutes passed, then fifteen. In the end Fowler left, muttering imprecations, and Gwen returned to Dorian.

"Why?" she asked. "Why did you turn on him? What has he ever done to you?"

"He's human," Dorian said. "And he desires you."

"Ray?" She laughed. "He never—"

"You are mine, Gwen," he said. "Don't forget that."

She walked away, just as he had known she would. Closer to hating him than before. Keeping her distance afterward, and making no further attempts to quiz him about his past.

Dorian's third opportunity came a few days later, when the mob appeared. They arrived just after dawn, gathering outside the *casa:* men and women Dorian recognized, folk from the village where he and Gwen had bought their necessities and found the majority of their donors. The men held torches above their heads, shouting curses and threats, while the women told their rosaries and cradled images of the Virgin Mary. A rain of small stones pelted the front of the cabin, narrowly missing the door.

Gwen followed Dorian when he stepped out to meet them.

"What is it?" she asked. She caught sight of the mob, went back inside and reemerged in her overcoat, hat and dark glasses. She stood beside Dorian as if they had become partners instead of adversaries. "They've come for us, haven't they?"

"You said one of them saw what you are," Dorian said harshly. "Are you surprised that he told the others? Doubtless they've been working up their courage for days."

The humans redoubled their shouts, drowning Gwen's reply.

"Stay here," Dorian said, pushing her back into the *casa.*

"What are you going to do?"

"Look at them," he said, painting each word with disgust and contempt. "What do you think they'll do to us if we give them the chance?"

"You can't blame them for being afraid."

"I condemn their superstition and stupidity."

She pushed forward again and clasped his arm. "Condemn me, then. I brought this on us."

"And now I must solve your problem," Dorian shook off her hand. "They're poorly armed," he said. "All they have are a few antique rifles and guns. Their holy relics won't do them any good. But they do have torches. That is the greatest threat."

"We can scare them off," Gwen said. "No one needs to be hurt."

"They must be stopped."

"At any cost?"

"Yes. At any cost. They must be taught to leave us alone."

"Will we leave *them* alone?"

Gwen gazed up at Dorian with those last, stubborn remnants of hope in her eyes, still unwilling to consign him to Hell. He almost wished that he could summon the monster at will so that he could cast his own lingering reservations aside.

He stepped farther out into the yard. The glare of many small fires mingled with the soft dawn light.

"You!" he called, addressing the mob. "What do you want?"

A low, threatening murmur swept through the crowd, a shuffling of feet and the clink of firearms. A single well-dressed man, rotund and florid, emerged from the first row of villagers.

"Vampiro!" he shouted, shaking his fist. *"Ya sabemos lo que eres, engendro del Diablo!"*

Echoing shouts followed his. Torches lifted. The leader took another step toward the cabin, a crucifix held high in one hand. *"Satanás no ganara,"* he intoned. *"Nosotros lo echaremos afuera!"*

Dorian knew little Spanish. He didn't have to. "Go," he said, "and I may spare your lives."

The crowd shuffled forward, a single seething mass. Someone began to pray loudly. Others took up the chant. The leader yelled something about the *rurales,* the local police force.

"We have to get out of here," Gwen said, coming to join him. "Come with me, Dorian. Please."

"They have gone too far," Dorian said. "Only fear will stop them now."

"I don't believe it," Gwen said. "They—"

A rock sailed out of nowhere, striking her on the side of her jaw. She swayed into Dorian's arms. He eased her onto the doorstep, the blood beating fast in his throat and temples.

"I'm all right," she said, swiping at her chin.

But her voice had become a meaningless drone in Dorian's ears. He turned back to the crowd.

"You will learn," he said, his voice rising above theirs, "what it means to attack a *strigoi*."

For a moment they listened, voices falling silent and faces frozen in expressions of fear and rage. That moment was all Dorian required. He strode in among them, snatching a rifle from one villager, twisting it into a useless hunk of metal. He dropped it and seized the nearest torch, sweeping it in front of him like a sword. People retreated with cries of alarm. The leader screamed epithets, and one of the younger men tried to aim his half-rusted pistol. Dorian knocked it aside.

"Who will be first to die?" he asked softly. "You?" He pointed the torch at a middle-aged man with a scar across his nose. "You?" A woman clutching her crucifix shrieked as he took it from her hand. He lifted it high, letting the villagers see that it did him no harm.

"You wish to kill us," he said, looking from one face to the next. "But many of you will be in the ground tonight. Who goes first?"

A tall man in a plaid shirt stepped back. Others followed, until the retreat became a flood. Torches guttered in the dirt, and no one uttered so much as a whisper.

But Dorian was far from finished. He grabbed the shirttail of the young man with the rusty pistol and pulled him back, letting him dangle two feet off the ground.

"Shall I begin with this one?" he said.

The villagers stopped. A woman began to weep.

"It's easy to kill a human," Dorian said, speaking as if to children. "I might snap his neck. That would be most merciful. Or I could tear out his heart."

Someone moaned. The boy's teeth began to chatter.

"Of course," Dorian said, "I might please myself and drain the blood from his body." He yanked the boy closer. "Or will one of you sacrifice yourself instead?"

"Piedad!" a young woman cried.

Dorian laughed. "Mercy? As you would have shown us?"

"Yes," a voice said at his elbow. "It's the only thing that separates us from what we fear."

Gwen stood beside him, shoulders straight and chin lifted. "Put him down, Dorian."

"Go back, Gwen."

She trembled, fighting his command. "I can't let you kill him."

Startled by her strength of will, Dorian loosened his hold on the young man. The boy leaped away. The crowd swayed and murmured. A lone voice shrieked a threat. His cry was taken up by the villagers as their outrage refreshed their courage.

Dorian started toward them again, but Gwen was faster. She rushed past him and stopped a few feet from the leader and his supporters.

"You have nothing more to fear from us," she said. "We're leaving. Within the next few days we'll be gone."

Her bid for peace was unsuccessful. Another young man rushed forward, a shotgun in his hands. He thrust the muzzle toward Gwen and pulled the trigger.

Dorian charged. A spray of shot fanned Gwen's arm as she stepped aside. Dorian reached the young man before he could lower the gun, ripping it from his hands and striking the human across the face with the butt.

But Gwen was still on her feet. "Stop!" she shouted. "Not for me, Dorian. Never for me!"

The boy lay on the ground, whimpering in terror. Dorian backed away. The mob's leader made a brief, aborted attempt to rally his followers, but they had lost their passion for the fight. The crowd began to splinter like rotten wood under an axe, breaking into smaller and smaller clumps as the villagers began to run.

Dorian's hands were not quite steady as he took Gwen back to the cabin. The sleeve of her blouse was stained with red, but he had already determined that the wounds were minor and would heal within hours. That knowledge had no effect on his fury. He carried her into the *casa* and to her bed, the thunder of his heart silencing the first words he would have spoken.

"You could have been killed," he said, struggling to balance his fear for her against the game he was playing for her sake.

Gwen refused to meet his gaze. "Better me than any of them."

"Better a hundred of them than you."

She rolled onto her side, away from him, and pressed her face into the pillow. Dorian knew there was nothing more he could say that wouldn't rouse her suspicions. He left her, hating himself for what he was compelled to do. Dreading the moment when she would finally accept that he had fallen too far for her to save by any means.

When that moment came, when there was nothing left in Gwen's heart but contempt for what he'd become, then he would finally set her free.

GWEN FOUND THE *CASA* still and silent when she left her room. Most of the day had passed without her realizing it, but the sky was still light. The lowering sun shone on a world she could no longer comprehend.

She stood in the doorway at the edge of the shadows and looked across the yard. Traces of the mob's attack lay forgotten in the dirt: burned-out torches, broken firearms, a statuette of some unfamiliar saint. Gwen felt sickened by the sight of them, and by the memories she couldn't erase.

Dorian had not killed any of those poor people. But he had come very close. Too close. The next time...

There mustn't be a next time.

Unable to think clearly, she knew she had to get away from this prison, if only for the night. The bond between her and Dorian had opened again, but now it was poisoned by Dorian's simmering rage. That and a seething lust for her, a lust so powerful that she'd expected him to act on it days ago, ever since the last dark of the moon.

He'd been distant after the fight in the alley, but not beyond her reach. She'd believed then that a searing guilt kept him trapped within himself, unable to confront the horror of what he'd done. She'd tried so hard to make him recognize that he wasn't beyond hope, tried to make him speak of the pain he kept locked inside.

She hadn't succeeded. The moon had gone dark, and Dorian had changed. It was as if that darkness had never left him when the sun rose, as if he'd deliberately clung to the monster when he should gladly have let it go.

And the monster was growing stronger. In a few days it would have its way with him again, and this time it might not give him up.

What did I do wrong?

For that she'd found no answer. And she wouldn't, not here, where she was reminded of her failure every hour. She needed to talk to someone, anyone, who didn't know what she was. She needed to remind herself that there were other beings in the world who weren't driven by fear or the need to destroy.

There was only one place she might go.

By the time the sun began to set, Gwen was ready. She'd put on a bright tiered skirt and white cotton blouse, both purchased from an old woman in the village when she and Dorian had first arrived. Her shoes were a variant of the woven leather sandals most of the villagers wore, and she'd drawn her hair back into a brilliant green band.

The ten-mile walk to Chihuahua was easy for a *strigoi*. Though Gwen felt a mild twinge of discomfort at her physical separation from Dorian, it didn't slow her pace or alter her intentions. The landscape grew less dry as Gwen approached the city, dotted with orchards, fields and small farms. The Sierra Madre mountains rose to the west behind the city, imposing against the sky.

It wasn't the first time Gwen had been to the city; twice, early in their residence at the *casa,* Dorian had taken her to familiarize her with the hunting possibilities there. Each time, she had been grateful for the distraction. Chihuahua was as lively as San Luis was somnolent; the colors were bright on walls and clothing and in the stalls of the marketplace. Automobiles were few and far between, as were modern conveniences any New Yorker would have taken for granted. Nevertheless, it was in its own way cosmopolitan; the population of Indians, *mestizos,* European descendants and the occasional tourist made for a fascinating mix of people and customs.

Gwen discovered soon after she arrived that this was not an ordinary night in the city. Many of the people she passed were dressed in especially vibrant clothing. The streets were draped with paper streamers and garlands and tissue flowers, and music came from every open window. The air of festivity immediately lifted Gwen's spirits.

"Carnivale," a portly shop owner told her, and went on to explain in good English. "It is the celebration before Lent, when all the people sing and dance. You will enjoy it, *señorita."*

Pleasure should have been the last thing on Gwen's mind. But the cheerful playing of the bands, the friendly voices, the smiling faces, surrounded her with warmth and humanity. For a while she let herself forget that she was not and could never again be one of them. She let herself forget that nothing had really changed.

She wandered the brightly lit streets, pausing to admire the shabby but magnificent colonial mansions bordering plazas filled with cavorting couples and street musicians. No one troubled her, and soon she lost any sense of time. The celebration hardly slowed, even in the wee hours of the morning. Men staggered in and out of saloons, slapping each other on the back with great good humor. Impromptu parades formed on the major streets, acquiring new participants at every house they passed. The musicians grew more raucous, the dancing more furious.

Sometime in the middle of the night Gwen found herself in a small plaza where a mariachi band of trumpets, guitars and violins played song after song with tireless abandon, while men and women spun and whirled over the cobblestones. She was standing on the curb, watching with real enjoyment, when a handsome young man with Valentino eyes approached her.

"Señorita," he said, sweeping her a bow. "Will you dance?"

His voice was pleasant, and his grin flashed white in the light of the street lamps. Gwen considered for only a moment. She dropped a shallow curtsey, took his hand and let him lead her into the plaza. The band was playing a waltz.

"What is your name, *señorita?*" her partner asked as he began to move.

There was no reason in the world to conceal her name. "Gwen," she said. "And yours?"

"Ignacio." He attempted another bow as they danced, and she laughed. Her throat was hardly capable of making the sound after so many days without it. She gave herself to the waltz, savoring the whisper of her skirt around her legs and Ignacio's light, inconsequential chatter.

The dance ended all too quickly. Another started almost immediately, but Ignacio refused to let her go. Gwen was aware that he found her attractive. She didn't know if it was because of her *strigoi* nature, and she didn't care. She'd forgotten what it was like to have fun without any thought of the future.

Two dances later Ignacio took her hand and pulled her to the edge of the plaza. He kissed her quickly, before she was fully aware of what he intended.

"Ignacio," she said, pulling away. "I hardly know you."

He grinned. "We have known each other since time began."

And he kissed her again, with an urgency that awoke feelings she'd been struggling to ignore for weeks. The vampire recognized willing prey. The woman...

The woman remembered that she didn't have to be alone.

"Come with me," Ignacio whispered. "You will not regret it."

Gwen hesitated, on the verge of surrender. Ignacio wrapped his fingers around her arm and pulled, insistent.

It was enough to break the spell. She jerked free.

"Not tonight," she said. "But thank you for the dance."

Ignacio frowned. "No woman—"

He choked on his words as the man behind him grabbed him by the back of his shirt and tossed him into the plaza. Dancers scattered as Ignacio crashed among them.

Dorian. He had materialized out of nothing, his approach so silent that Gwen hadn't heard or even suspected his presence. The feelings she'd been too preoccupied to detect surged through the bond: familiar rage tinged with lust and the desire to kill.

He was already moving again before Gwen could shake herself free of his overwhelming emotions. He cut through the throng of dancers with the precision of a well-aimed bullet, Ignacio firmly in his sights. He had the young man dangling in the air within seconds.

"Dorian!"

Chest heaving like a bellows, Dorian threw the younger man to the cobblestones at his feet. Ignacio crawled away.

"You've made another mistake, Gwen," Dorian said clearly, as if he were still capable of rational thought.

"I'm sorry," she said, lowering her gaze. "Why don't we leave this place. I'll do whatever you say."

He stared at her, unmoving. A crowd began to gather, faces curious and hostile. The muzzle of a gun jammed between Dorian's shoulder blades.

"Cabrón," Ignacio snarled in Dorian's ear. "It is you who have made the mistake."

CHAPTER EIGHTEEN

ALL SOUND AND MOVEMENT in the plaza came to a stop. Dorian turned his head, a terrible smile on his face.

"Shoot me," he said softly. "Go ahead. I won't die."

Ignacio began to laugh, but something in Dorian's eyes held him mute. The crowd had gotten larger, and men were beginning to make quiet bets, while the women pressed closer to watch the drama unfold.

Gwen worked her way closer to Ignacio, desperately watching Dorian out of the corner of her eye. "Please," she said. "It isn't worth a fight." She decided to take a gamble. "I'll go with you."

Ignacio sneered, prodding at Dorian's back. "You see, *pajero?*" he said thickly. "She prefers me. Maybe your rifle shoots blanks, eh? Or maybe you are *mayate* and don't know where to put your *miembrillo?*"

A choking blackness filled Gwen's mind. It was more than merely anger. It sucked up every other emotion as the desert sun soaks up a short spring rain. There was no fighting it, no way to escape.

The gun barrel ground deeper as Ignacio gained confidence. The safety clicked. Dorian thrust back with his elbows, moving so fast that Ignacio never had the chance to fire. Dorian spun and struck the young man in the chest with a stiffened palm. Gasping for air, eyes bulging, Ignacio fell onto his back.

Voices rose as money began to change hands. A woman in a dark décolleté blouse dropped to her knees beside Ignacio as he bucked and wheezed. She shouted imprecations at Dorian, while others among the crowd murmured with increasing agitation. A tomato sailed into the small open space surrounding Dorian and Gwen, landing with an audible splat.

The woman in the black blouse seized the gun Ignacio had dropped and aimed it wildly at Dorian. Gwen didn't think. She let the blackness take her and seized the woman's wrist, twisting until the woman shrieked in pain and dropped the gun. She pointed the weapon at Ignacio's chest.

"No!" wailed the woman in black. She clutched at Gwen's skirts. Gwen kicked her away and continued to stare at Ignacio, hating him as she'd never hated anything before.

Until Dorian ripped the gun from her hand and slammed the muzzle into Ignacio's temple.

The world snapped back into focus. Gwen's vision cleared. She closed her eyes, took a deep breath and fixed all her attention on Dorian.

"Come," she said.

Dorian's arm began to shake. The crowd hushed.

"Come," Gwen repeated. She swayed toward Dorian, moving her hips, giving way to feelings she didn't dare deny. "I want you, Dorian. Now."

He looked at her, his eyes like those of a predator reassessing its prey. He licked his lips. Ignacio groaned, and the smell of urine permeated the air.

Gwen laid her hand on Dorian's arm and carefully pulled. She spoke no more words, but words were unnecessary. Dorian understood her perfectly. He pushed the gun into the waistband of his trousers.

"Where?" he asked hoarsely.

Gwen led him out of the plaza, intent only on getting him away. A few men drifted after them, and Ignacio's woman shook her fist, but no one followed them beyond the edge of the square.

Caught in the grip of lust she had no way to control, Gwen dragged Dorian into a blind alley between two narrow buildings. Revelers danced and walked and staggered past the alley, oblivious. Someone moaned from the open window above them.

Dorian took her by the arms and turned her around so that her back was to the wall. His eyes were hot as molten metal. He cupped his hand behind her neck and kissed her, grinding his lips into hers.

Gwen knew that if she didn't get through to him quickly, he would take her right there in the alley. The horrible thing was that part of her wanted him to—the same part that couldn't separate her hunger from his.

"Not here," she gasped as he broke the kiss. "We'll…find a hotel. Then you can have me, Dorian."

He stared at her face as if searching for signs of a trick. Gwen let go of the control that kept her desire in check. Dorian recoiled, his eyes widening.

He felt it. He knew she wasn't deceiving him. She couldn't even deceive herself.

"Gwen," he said harshly. He lowered his head and ran his tongue along the upper curve of her breast. Gwen pushed as hard as she could. He retreated just enough for her to get away from the wall.

She ran. He followed. The streets were a noisy maze; Gwen could hardly breathe for wanting Dorian. The first two small hotels she found had posted signs indicating no vacancy. At the third hotel Dorian went inside ahead of her and had a brief conversation with the innkeeper, who hastily presented him with a key. Dorian took Gwen by the wrist and pulled her up the narrow staircase to the second floor.

Their room was modest but clean, with a sagging bed and a few sticks of furniture. The bedcovers had already been turned back. Dorian swept Gwen up in his arms. Springs creaked as he laid her down.

I can't be doing this, Gwen thought. *It's wrong. It's all wrong.*

Dorian answered her unspoken thoughts by kissing her again, thrusting his tongue inside while her arms encircled his shoulders. Her tongue met his in a silent duel, clashing and caressing and withdrawing.

They broke apart, breathing quickly. Gwen tore at Dorian's shirt. Buttons flew. He knelt between her thighs and pulled her blouse up over her shoulders and breasts. She wore no brassiere or bandeau; her nipples were hard and aching. He lowered his head and began to suckle. Gwen thrust her fingers into his hair and arched against him.

From somewhere outside herself another Gwen watched—the civilized Gwen, the human Gwen, the one who knew how far she had fallen. But that Gwen had no power. She could only stand by as the female *strigoi* spread her thighs, moaning encouragement as Dorian pushed her skirts up to her waist.

Dorian undid the buttons of his trousers and began to work them off. The gun he had put in his waistband tumbled onto Gwen's hip.

The two Gwens came together like colliding trains. She scooted up on the pillows and stared at the weapon, biting her lip so hard that it bled.

She remembered the moment when she'd pointed the gun at Ignacio's chest. She'd been ready to kill him. She would have done it without hesitation, without regret. One more step into the blackness… One more step and she would have become the same as Dorian.

She kicked him away as she scrambled out of the bed. "I can't," she said. "I can't do this."

Dorian came after her. She knew then that he wasn't going to stop, even if she had all the rational arguments in the world on her side.

Don't you see? We're no good for each other. All this time I've been fooling myself, thinking I could help you overcome the monster inside you. I was wrong.

Hadn't Angela told her that with some *strigoi* the bond between patron and protégée became a kind of insanity? Maybe Dorian had always been a little crazy, but not like this. He'd never come back from what happened that night in the alley. He'd already killed for Gwen's sake. Twice in as many days he'd nearly killed, and again it had been for her sake. She made his sickness a thousand times worse.

And he creates mine.

To speak such words now would only enrage him, if he understood them at all. He came on, half-naked, crouched and ready to spring. Desperate, Gwen worked her way in a circle back toward the bed where the gun still lay.

Perhaps Dorian was too far gone to guess what she intended. Perhaps he didn't care. She dived across the bed and grabbed the gun, rolling to point it at his chest.

"Don't come any closer," she said.

Dorian showed his teeth in an expression somewhere between a snarl and a grin. "Shoot me," he said in the same mocking voice he'd used with Ignacio.

Gwen took a firmer grip on the gun and held it steady. There was only one way to make him stop, and that was to make him believe. Believe that she would kill him without hesitation.

She drove the horror from her mind and filled it with hatred, all the anger and resentment she'd felt after he'd first converted her.

"Do you think I won't shoot?" she jeered. "You've destroyed my life. You've taken everything I've valued—my job, my friends, even the sunlight. I've watched you threaten to murder people who haven't half your strength. You've always been a killer, Dorian, but now you've gone so far that it would be a favor to the whole world if someone got rid of you."

Stunned by her own speech, Gwen fell silent. Dorian had gone still, every muscle frozen, his face stark and pale. She crept toward the door. He didn't get in her way.

Sick to her stomach, she ran out the door and paused on the landing, fear-thick fingers fumbling at her blouse and skirt. The small beaded pouch she'd hung at her waist was still in place. She needed only a little money for what she had to do next.

She engaged the safety, pushed the gun into the waistband of her skirt and went down the stairs. The innkeeper at the desk in the lobby regarded her with muted amazement. Gwen knew exactly what she looked like, and she didn't care.

"Telephone," she said, dialing in the air. "*Telefono.*"

"Ah, *sí!*" the man said, glancing nervously toward the stairs. He beckoned to Gwen and led her behind the counter into a musty back office, where an old-fashioned potbelly telephone sat on a weathered desk.

"How much?" Gwen asked.

The innkeeper gave her a long, assessing look and shook his head. *"Nada,"* he said. *"Nada para usted."*

That much Gwen understood. *"Gracias,"* she said. She turned away, opened her pouch and pulled out a handful of pesos. She placed them on the desk.

"Please don't let anyone find me here," she said. *"Comprende?"*

"Sí." The man nodded and hurried out into the lobby, shutting the door behind him.

Gwen knew she couldn't count on Dorian staying up in the room like a chastened child. If he meant to find her, she couldn't stop him. Time was of the essence.

Somehow she managed to get the local operator to understand what she wanted. After many delays and strange noises from the receiver, she heard someone pick up on the other end of the line.

Please be there, Mitch.

"Hogan," the voice said.

"Mitch? It's Gwen."

"Gwen!" There was a spate of crackling on the line. "I can barely hear you. Where are you?"

"Mexico."

"Good God, Gwen. What the hell…?"

"Listen, Mitch. I don't have much time. Do you remember when you mentioned the man who knows all about vampires?"

"Yes! If only you'd called me earlier…" Static hissed. "…found what we were looking for."

"What? Mitch, I can't—"

He raised his voice. "Professor Perkowski gave me some stuff that's supposed to break the bond between vampires and their victims."

"Thank God. That's exactly why I was calling you. I have to get out of this, Mitch. As soon as possible."

"You mean you've come to your senses?"

Yes, I finally have. "It's become necessary that I leave Dorian."

"And it wasn't before?" Another wave of static. "…has he done? Gwen, has he hurt you?"

"No. I'm all right."

Mitch's breathing quickened. "Tell me where you are, Gwen. I'll leave immediately."

"You can't come here, Mitch. It would only make things worse."

There was a long pause. "Are you afraid of what he'll do to me?"

"I'm afraid of what you two could do to each other."

"That's a chance I'm willing to take."

"It's out of the question." She struggled for calm. "This stuff you've found…what is it?"

"It's some kind of herbal powder. Perkowski didn't go into a lot of detail."

"What do I have to do?"

"It's pretty simple. You mix the stuff with water and drink it."

"Then you can send it to me if I give you an address?"

"You can't do this alone. Black's hold over you is too strong."

"Please, Mitch. Trust me."

"After you left me hanging for weeks, not knowing what the hell had happened to you?"

"I'm sorry. It was necessary."

"And now I'm of some use to you again."

His bitterness cut her to the quick. "Listen, Mitch. I'm calling from a hotel in Chihuahua, Mexico. I'm going to ask the innkeeper if he can accept a package from the States." She looked around the desk and found an envelope printed with the address of the hotel. "Here's the place to send the powder."

"Is that where you're staying, Gwen? In Chihuahua?"

"You mustn't try to find me. I'll come to you when this is finished."

"So that we can start all over as if nothing has happened? Do you think that Dorian will ever let you be?"

She squeezed the receiver until her hand ached. "It's the only way I know, Mitch. Please help me."

The line chose that moment to go dead. Gwen stared into the mouthpiece of the receiver, wondering if she'd made Mitch understand. Hoping that he was right about the powder.

Praying that she would have the chance to use it.

She set the receiver down on the desk and cautiously approached the door to the lobby. The innkeeper stood behind the counter, but the lobby was otherwise empty.

"Has anyone come down?" Gwen asked, miming a person walking down the steps.

"No, *señorita,*" the innkeeper said. *"Nadie ha venido."*

Which was in itself a miracle. Either she'd finally reached Dorian in some unexpected way, or he was planning something she couldn't guess. She'd been fortunate…so far.

Now all she had to do was hold Dorian at bay and survive the next few days until Mitch could send the potion. There wasn't any question of remaining in Chihuahua. She would have to go back to the cabin and hope that Dorian found no further excuses to kill for her sake.

MITCH SAT AT HIS DESK in the city room, tapping his pencil furiously against the scored wood. Gwen's voice still echoed in his mind, assuring him that she really wanted to leave Dorian. Almost making him believe that she'd regained her sanity.

Almost.

Pushing his chair back with a thrust of his legs, Mitch rose, threw on his overcoat and strode out to the second-floor lobby. The elevator couldn't carry him to the ground floor fast enough. He began a brisk walk around the block, hoping that the chill morning air would clear his head.

Nearly two months, and she hadn't bothered to telephone him. She'd let him stew, wondering what Dorian was doing to her, knowing how deeply she'd already fallen under the vampire's spell. Remembering that she'd never denied that she still loved the man who'd turned her into a monster.

Now it seemed she'd changed her mind. She wanted Mitch's help. But she didn't want him coming to find her…oh, no. *I'm*

afraid of what you two could do to each other, she'd said. Not
I'm afraid Dorian will kill you.

Mitch pulled a cigarette case from his coat pocket. Gwen was
sick. She'd been sick ever since Black had gotten his claws into
her. There was only one cure for that kind of disease, and it
wasn't some mysterious potion that might or might not work.

Pausing on the corner, Mitch pushed an unlit cigarette into
his mouth and stared blindly at the traffic rushing by. For nearly
six weeks he'd been biding his time like a lovesick fool, assuming that Gwen might be put in a difficult or even dangerous
position if he attempted to find her too soon. He had made only
sporadic efforts to learn where she'd gone. Even so, he'd already
considered every possible method by which she might have left
town, including air and sea. He'd made his list of contacts, any
and all individuals who might know more than he did.

The list was short. Mitch had already spoken to Lavinia and
everyone else in the newsroom. Gwen didn't have a lot of friends
outside the *Sentinel;* she'd always been devoted to her career. Even
the people who shared her apartment building didn't know her well.

Now it was time to dig deeper. Mitch knew that Gwen had
to be somewhere near Chihuahua, Mexico. That made things
considerably easier. He could simply charter a plane to fly him
over the border and start questioning the locals about the red-
haired American girl, even though there were no guarantees that
he would ever find Gwen's hiding place.

Or he could check off the last name on his list. A name he'd
never heard before he'd sent Pete to watch Gwen on his behalf.

Walter Brenner. An old man Gwen had gone several times to
visit in the hospital. Months ago Mitch had assumed he was just
some guy down on his luck, maybe Gwen's neighbor or one of
those pet "projects" she picked up the way other people would
pick up a penny dropped on the sidewalk.

Maybe that was all this Walter Brenner was. Maybe the odds
were a million to one that he knew anything about where Gwen
had gone. But Mitch had gambled on a crazy hunch more than
once in his life, and won.

He returned to the office, still chewing on the unlit cigarette, and telephoned the hospital. The nurse who answered was able to confirm that a Miss Murphy had indeed made a number of calls on one Walter Brenner, and that she'd been there to sign the old fellow out when he was well enough to leave. After a little judicious persuasion on Mitch's part, the nurse gave him Brenner's current address.

Mitch took a taxi to a boardinghouse on the edge of Greenwich Village. The middle-aged landlady was glad enough to show him to Brenner's room. She knocked on Mitch's behalf, and after a few moments an old man answered. He was grizzled and walked with a limp, but his eyes were sharp.

"Good morning," Mitch said, touching the brim of his hat. "My name is Mitch Hogan. I'm a colleague of Gwen Murphy. May I come in?"

The old man hesitated. "What's this about, young fella?"

Mitch flipped open his wallet and offered the old man a card. Brenner studied it with curious eyes. "I've heard of you," he said. "Come on in."

Mitch accepted a seat on the single armchair in the corner of the room. "I won't take up much of your time, Mr. Brenner," he said. "I'm aware that you're a friend of Miss Murphy's, and I've become very concerned about her."

"Oh?" Brenner sat down on the edge of his bed. "Gwennie's in trouble, is she?"

"Yes." Mitch met Brenner's eyes with all the earnestness he could muster. "Are you aware that Miss Murphy has been threatened by certain gangsters in the city…men who have already tried to claim her life?"

Brenner frowned. "No. I never heard that."

Old Brenner might be essentially harmless, but Mitch recognized disingenuousness when he saw it. "I have evidence that Miss Murphy has been forced to leave New York by a man I have every reason to believe is dangerous, even crazy," he said.

Immediately Brenner's pleasant face closed. "Sorry. Don't know anything about it."

"I think you're lying, Mr. Brenner."

Brenner got up stiffly and went to the door. "I think you'd better go."

"You care about Miss Murphy, don't you? You'd want to help her if she were in trouble."

"Gwen can take care of herself."

"Can she?" Mitch opened his hands. "The man Gwen has gone with is a former gangster. He has viciously murdered innocent people."

"I know Dorian. He'd never—" The old man stopped, his weathered skin going red.

"You know Dorian Black?" Mitch rose and stood in front of the door. "You know what he is?"

Brenner looked momentarily puzzled. "I don't get what you're talking about."

Maybe he didn't. Maybe this time he was telling the truth.

"Dorian Black is a monster," Mitch said, "in the most literal sense. He has already come very near to destroying Gwen. If you want to save her, you must tell me where they've gone."

"If this guy is such a monster, why would he tell an old man anything?"

Mitch drowned his scruples in a lake of anger. "If you know anything, you'd better say it now."

Brenner pushed past Mitch and opened the door. "Get outta here."

With a sharp movement Mitch seized Brenner and twisted his arm. The geezer gasped, his legs buckling.

"I don't have time for this," Mitch snapped. "Where are they?"

Tears leaked from Brenner's eyes. "Don't…"

"I'll break your arm if I have to. Gwen's life is more important than your comfort, old man."

Brenner began to wheeze. "They…they said—"

"Spill it."

"They flew. Out of the country. Mexico."

"Who took them?"

"Don't know."

Mitch twisted harder. *"Who?"*

"Got a note…from someone named Ray."

Memory clicked. "Ray Fowler?"

But the old man was on the floor, his free hand over his heart. Mitch released him. Brenner floundered like a fish out of water, unable to rise.

"I'll find her," Mitch said, half to himself. "I'll find her."

He left the old man where he lay and strode from the boardinghouse without returning the landlady's goodbye. *Ray Fowler.* He should have suspected as much. Gwen had always gotten along well with the pilot; naturally she would think of him if she wanted to get out of town.

Once he was some distance away from the boardinghouse, Mitch paused to get his bearings. He could telephone Fowler from the office, but what he was about to do next wouldn't be done for the paper. Better to complete the investigation from home.

He flagged a taxi at the next street corner and directed the cabbie to his apartment. Halfway there, the driver caught Mitch's attention.

"Someone's following us," the cabbie said.

Mitch turned to look out the rear window. The coupe behind them, dark and featureless, matched the taxi turn for turn.

"You got any enemies?" the cabbie asked nervously.

"No more than the average Joe."

"I don't want no trouble. I got to let you off, mister."

Mitch considered his options. Someone obviously wanted to talk to him rather badly—at least he hoped talking was all they had in mind. Whoever they were, they would surely catch up to him sooner or later. Mitch preferred that it be sooner.

"Okay," he said. "Pull over."

The taxi screeched to a halt at the curb. The neighborhood was quiet and residential. Most people were at work or in school; a few truants who had braved the cold to play ball stopped to look as Mitch got out of the cab. They watched curiously until the second car pulled up, disgorging a figure swathed in a black coat, sunglasses and a wide-brimmed hat.

"Mr. Hogan?" the man said.

Mitch planted his feet on the sidewalk. "That's me."

The man nodded. "We mean you no harm, Mr. Hogan. We merely wish to speak with you."

"Who are you?"

"Have you ever heard the axiom 'The enemy of my enemy is my friend'?"

"What does that mean? What do you want?"

"To clarify certain matters with regard to Miss Gwen Murphy and the man who has abducted her."

Mitch thought about pleading ignorance and decided against it. "What's your interest in Miss Murphy?"

"Come with us, Mr. Hogan, and all will become clear."

"What if I don't feel like talking a ride?"

"That would be unfortunate."

Mitch looked up and down the street. There were no witnesses. The kids had vanished. Even the houses seemed to hold their breath.

Sooner or later, Mitch thought.

"Okay," he said.

The man gestured toward the car and held the back door open for Mitch. He got in. The interior of the car was upholstered in the same forbidding black. Another man sat in the back seat. He made room for Mitch and his colleague. The coupe rolled into motion.

"We are sorry for this inconvenience," the second man said. He removed his hat to reveal a handsome face, hair graying at the temples and striking blue eyes. "My name is Sammael. It is absolutely necessary that we locate Dorian Black."

CHAPTER NINETEEN

MITCH HAD ALREADY guessed what Sammael was before he began to speak. There was the shadow of red in his eyes, the pointed teeth, the air of invincibility.

"I see you recognize what I am, Mr. Hogan," the vampire said with a gentle smile. "Not that I'm at all surprised. Did you attack Dorian in the hotel because he is a vampire, or was it simply jealousy?"

All the fine hairs on Mitch's body stood at attention. "I don't know what you're talking about."

"Come, Mr. Hogan. There is no need to be coy. You have been a close colleague of Miss Murphy's since before her Conversion. And we have been watching you since her second disappearance." He clasped his hands in his lap. "Now we learn that she has contacted you, and we are most anxious to hear more of the conversation."

My God, Mitch thought. Whoever this guy was, he must have someone working inside the *Sentinel,* something not even the biggest mobs in Manhattan had been able to pull off.

"I don't know what you're talking about," Mitch repeated. "What's your connection to Dorian Black?"

"Aside from the fact that we are both vampires?" Sammael chuckled. "How difficult it must have been for you to sit on such a story, Mr. Hogan. The temptation to publish an *exposé* on the presence of nonhumans in the city must have been overwhelming."

Mitch knew a trap when he saw it. "With what proof? And anyway, I wouldn't do anything that might hurt Gwen."

"I believe you. That is why we are here." The vampire continued to smile like a saint. Or maybe a madman. "Perhaps I should start from the beginning," he said.

What he told Mitch then was stunning. He spoke of a secret vampire organization known as Pax, devoted to ending the vampire wars that had taken innocent human lives.

"Then there *are* vampire gangs," Mitch said, trying to keep things straight in his mind.

"Most assuredly," Sammael said. "They believe that humans are little more than cattle and will stop at nothing to prove it. But not all of us desire *strigoi* dominion. We in Pax believe that such dominion was given to mankind and must not be subverted by those who deem themselves superior because of a blasphemous transformation." He paused. "It was one of those gangs who attempted to kill your Miss Murphy."

Of course. Now it all fit together perfectly. "Black was working for one of those gangs, wasn't he?" Mitch asked. "He set Gwen up."

"Not to our knowledge," Sammael said. "You see, Black worked for us. It was his task to infiltrate one of the *strigoi* gang's organizations. He not only failed but broke the covenant we have sworn to uphold. He Converted Miss Murphy."

"And that's against your rules?"

"It is in contradiction to everything we believe. He surrendered to his lust and the evil nature against which we all must fight. His act severely jeopardized our operations. Worse, he prevented Miss Murphy from finding sanctuary with Pax because of his obsession with her."

Mitch ground his teeth. "In other words," he said, "Black ruined things for everybody."

"Indeed. That is why we wish to locate him, Mr. Hogan. To make certain that he is incapable of creating any further mischief."

The tone of Sammael's voice had suddenly become much less pleasant. Mitch sat straighter. "What do you plan to do?"

"First, with your help, we must find him. Our most pressing responsibility is to the human Dorian has subverted. We must secure Miss Murphy's release."

The bottle of powder Mitch had received from Professor

Perkowski seemed to burn his skin through the cotton of his shirt. "You know a way to do that?" he asked.

"The death of the patron is generally sufficient."

"You plan to kill Black."

"I assure you that no harm will come to you or Miss Murphy. You are a man of obvious conviction and intelligence. We hope you will remain our ally, even after this work is complete."

"But I'm human."

"Our organization contains many humans. They are invaluable to us, and remind us of the righteousness of our mission."

Righteousness. Blasphemy. Sammael spoke like one of those preachers who perched on corner soapboxes and screamed about the end of the world.

"All you need do now," Sammael said, "is to take us to Dorian."

Mitch felt perspiration break out on his forehead. "You say you won't hurt Gwen."

"Far from it, Mr. Hogan. We want only to return as much of her life to her as is possible. She will be more than welcome among us, to join our cause and help prevent such perversions from ever happening again." He stared into Mitch's eyes. "Where are they?"

Perhaps Mitch could have lied to Sammael. Maybe he could have refused the *strigoi* request and still stayed alive…if these people at Pax really believed in the noble ideas they were spewing.

But he wasn't about to wager his life on that likelihood, especially when they wanted the same thing he did: to get rid of Black and set Gwen free. He couldn't think of any reason why they would want to hurt Gwen when they so obviously regarded her as a victim.

Provided, of course, that Sammael was really what he claimed to be. "How can I be sure you aren't really with one of those gangs?" he asked bluntly.

"I fear you will have to take my word, Mr. Hogan. The alternative…" The vampire shrugged. "If our primary purpose were to silence humans who know of the vampire presence in the city, we would hardly allow you to leave our sight even for a moment. Surely you see that."

"I can have a few hours to think it over?"

"A few hours, Mr. Hogan. No more. Here is my card. Call this number when you've made your decision." Sammael signaled his driver, who hit the accelerator. Soon they stopped in front of Mitch's apartment building.

"I hope you will see the advantages of helping us," Sammael said as his henchman saw Mitch out the door. "You will be aiding not only Gwen, but all of your race."

Mitch stood back as the car pulled away. He'd hardly noticed how fast his heart was pounding, or the way his shirt was glued to his chest and armpits.

Damn. If any of this is true…

He stumbled toward the building and climbed the stairs to his flat, trying to think. Whatever their affiliation and beliefs, it was clear that Sammael and Pax were as ruthless as any gangster. If they'd followed him this far, they would follow him when he went to find Gwen. If he did as they asked, there was a chance that he would be able to control some part of what would happen afterward. And the risk was well worth it if it meant the end of Dorian Black.

He walked into his apartment, turned on the radio, and waited two hours while he flipped Sammael's card over and over between his fingers. His telephone call was brief and to the point. When it was finished, Mitch returned to the office to set his affairs in order. Then he went out to see Ray Fowler and got him to admit that he had personally flown Gwen and her "friend," Mr. Black, to Mexico.

That night, when Mitch went to bed, he slept the sleep of the angels.

SAMMAEL CAME OUT OF the vision, his muscles rigid with pain and his heart beating with such force that any *strigoi* in the room would have heard it.

But he was alone. Alone with the images from the dream… images of the dark angel wielding the fiery sword.

He rose from the cot and paced the length of his cell, remembering the delirium that had come over him after last night's scourging. It was not uncommon for the discomfort of his wounds to overwhelm him for a time, but seldom had he been granted visions. He knew this one was real. And he knew what it must portend.

The dark angel had held the book in his hand, the original book for which Sammael had searched so long. That meant the book would be found in Mexico. And once it was found, the dark angel would ensure the ultimate victory.

With a prayer of thanks, Sammael removed his rough woolen shirt and prepared to prove his devotion once again.

GWEN RETURNED TO THE *casa* just before dawn. She'd wandered the desert for hours, knowing she had nowhere else to go.

The cabin was empty when she walked in the door. She sat in the rocking chair and listened for a long while, expecting the faint whisper of Dorian's footsteps, but they never came.

Maybe he isn't coming back, she thought. But she knew that wasn't possible. Neither one of them could long bear the separation; now she felt only a mild ache, but she knew instinctively that it would become far worse.

Yes, Dorian would be back. And then there would be no peace until she received the cure.

A day passed, then two. Dorian stayed away. Gwen began to believe that he would keep his distance until after the approaching dark of the moon. Sometimes she thought she felt a twinge in her heart, as if she were catching the echoes of his emotions. But she couldn't untangle one feeling from another. And she didn't dare let him suspect, even from some unguessable distance, what she was planning.

Unable to settle, Gwen browsed restlessly through the books Dad had left on the shelves at the *casa.* She'd already read a dozen of them on subjects ranging from ornithology to the history of China, but now she needed something different. Now she needed a source of comfort.

There was none to be found. Eamon Murphy had never been one for philosophy or the spiritual. On the third night of Dorian's absence Gwen began to take the books down one by one, paging through them with growing frustration. She had almost given up when she found a wooden panel behind two volumes of Gibbon's *The Decline and Fall of the Roman Empire*.

Curious, Gwen removed the books and ran her fingers over the panel. There was a kind of knob on one side. She pulled on it, and the panel opened onto a small compartment set into the *casa*'s adobe wall.

Inside the compartment was another book. Gwen pulled it out. It was smaller than the average book in Dad's library, and she sensed it was considerably older. The volume had obviously been handmade, with a much-worn leather binding. In the center of the cover an image had been etched in gold, an image she was certain she had seen before.

A triangle and a flame. The same picture that had hung in the room she'd been given during her brief stay at Pax.

A dozen thoughts raced simultaneously through Gwen's mind. What would a book somehow related to Pax be doing in Dad's collection? She thumbed the book open, fingers clumsy in her eagerness. The first page was dated March the third, eighteen-twenty-eight.

"My name is Micah," the coarse printing began.

Micah. *Of course.* Hadn't Vida told her that he was the founder of Pax, the man who'd taught forgiveness and brotherhood between humans and vampires?

She continued to read:

It is not the name with which I was born; that name is no longer of importance, for I left it behind with my humanity.

I will hold nothing back from you who reads this, the story of my damnation and quest for redemption. My faith tells me that the day may come when all the world will know of my kind, and there will be brotherhood between vampire and human. That time is not yet. But this book will find its way into the hands of one more capable than I, and these words will inspire that man to finish what I have merely begun.

Gwen walked slowly back to the rocker and sat, powerfully drawn to this memoir written nearly a hundred years ago. She continued to read of a gentle, sensitive boy who had grown up in a loving family; of an itinerant preacher whose deep faith had sustained him as he'd traveled from place to place and village to village, bringing the Word of God to people struggling to make new lives on the Kentucky frontier. Micah described in chilling detail the night of his Conversion by a wayfarer he met one lonely evening on the road.

> When I came to my senses, all the world was changed. My eyes were like unto those of a wolf by night, my hearing like a panther's, my strength that of Samson. And within me raged a terrible thirst.
> There was no one to teach me, but I learned. Even as I cursed the flesh that had betrayed me, I obeyed it. And thus I began my descent.

Gwen settled deeper in her chair. It was as if Micah spoke for her, recounting his bitter and shameful emotions as he was compelled to stalk humans for sustenance. In his agony he had come to believe he was damned forever, and he had abandoned the profession that had been his whole life. He had gone into the wilderness for days on end, wandering without purpose, starving himself until need compelled him to find new prey.

After five years of torment, Micah had come very near death by starvation. In his delirium, he had experienced an epiphany, a revelation that drew him out of the darkness and gave him his first real hope since his Conversion. For the next quarter of a century he had continued to meditate and pray, seeking the answers that would enable him to find redemption.

> The Lord had not abandoned me. He had only given me a great challenge: to overcome the beast within myself with the power of love. To find others like myself and minister unto them, carrying His Word to those who had been lost.

To form the first chapter of Pax, a group dedicated to peace and the promotion of loving cooperation with the humans upon whom his kind depended. It had not been easy to bring the scattered American *strigoi* together; they were by nature as wild as the frontier. But Micah had persevered. Thirty years after his revelation, Pax had fifty members, both vampire and human. And Micah began to record his philosophy in a simple book.

The world had been made for man, and *strigoi* must be humble in the face of that single truth. No human was to be Converted against his or her will. Blood was to be taken from conscious, willing donors whenever possible. A vampire must be prepared to die to preserve human life, and to work toward the ultimate goal of peace and brotherhood between *strigoi* and humans. In such would he find true redemption, fighting for the good of all men.

Forgiveness, both of self and of others. Discipline, to overcome the temptations inherent in vampire nature. And above all, love.

When Gwen finished reading it was just after dawn. She stood abruptly, half afraid that Dorian had returned without her noticing.

He hadn't. There was nothing to fear.

Nothing to fear. That, too, was one of Micah's teachings.

A calmness came over Gwen. Her mind was clearer than it had been in weeks; the self-disgust and revulsion with which she'd struggled since her Conversion had faded to a distant murmur. She remembered Dad's note about the book he'd acquired from a man named Aadon…a man who'd promised him information on certain gangland murders and then had turned up dead in the East River.

Dad knew, she thought. He'd known there were vampires in New York, yet he hadn't attempted to publish another article or share the evidence with anyone. Instead, he'd hidden the book here, where no one was ever likely to find it.

No one but herself, of course.

When you died you knew there really was a kind of blood cult after all, Gwen thought. *You knew you weren't crazy.*

And he'd known there had to be at least a few decent

vampires in the world. If he'd lived…if he'd known what Gwen had become…

Oh, Dad. You would have stood by me, no matter what. You would have helped me to accept what I—

The sound of footsteps outside the *casa* brought Gwen to full alert. Dorian made far less noise when he moved, and she knew she would have sensed it if he were anywhere nearby. Without thinking, she returned the book to its secret compartment, put all the other books back in place and went to the door.

Someone knocked. Gwen hesitated only for a moment and opened it.

"Gwen," the man said. "Thank God I've found you."

"Mitch!" She stepped back, her instincts shouting a warning. "What are you doing here? How did you—"

He stepped over the threshold and embraced her. The feeling of his arms around her was foreign and unwelcome, as if he had become a complete and total stranger.

After a moment Mitch seemed to feel her stiffness. He released her and stared into her face, brows drawn and mouth tight.

"Are you all right?" he asked. "Gwen, look at me."

She met his gaze. What he read in her eyes didn't seem to please him.

"I've been watching this place for hours," he said, his voice sharp. "I didn't see Black. You *are* alone?"

"Yes. Mitch, why did you come here? I asked you—"

"I know what you asked me." He loomed in the doorway until Gwen moved out of his way. He removed his hat and unbuttoned his light trench coat, laying it over the back of the rocker. "This is where you've been living for the past two months?"

Gwen ignored the question. "How did you find me?"

"It wasn't that difficult, once I knew who to ask." He watched her, his expression growing increasingly bleak. "Don't blame Fowler. He was convinced you were in trouble." He went into the tiny kitchen, found a glass and filled it with water from the pump. "Where is Black?"

"He could be back any moment." She took a step toward him. "You shouldn't have come. It was too big a risk."

"Do you really think I can't handle myself?"

"I don't want to see anyone hurt."

"No one will be, as long as Black stays away." Mitch smiled unpleasantly. "The good citizens of San Luis told me he hasn't been here in a couple of days. Seems the villagers like to keep an eye on this place. They didn't sound very friendly when I mentioned your name." He sipped his water, pulling a face at the taste. "What did you do to them?"

"Nothing."

"Nothing except drink their blood."

"You should go, Mitch. Now."

He set down the glass. "Not without you.'

Gwen went to the window, standing clear of the light that entered between the curtains. "Did Ray bring you here?"

"No. He was tied up."

"But you have a plane waiting for you."

"For us."

"You…have the powder?"

Mitch reached inside his jacket and withdrew a small glass bottle filled with a greenish-gray powder. He unscrewed the lid. The smell of dried herbs rose from the open container, acrid and pungent.

"My friend collected this stuff years ago, in the Balkans," Mitch said. He tapped the powder into his palm. "It can work as a general vampire repellent, but it has certain other qualities, as well."

Gwen stared at the powder, hardly able to believe that it could all be so simple. When Angela had hinted that there was a way to break the bond between patron and protégée, she'd said that the knowledge had been suppressed. Yet Mitch had found the answer. He held Gwen's future in his hand.

It's what you wanted. It's what has to be done. With her gone, Dorian would have one less source of provocation when the dark of the moon overcame him, one less reason to kill.

And he would be left to face his demons alone.

"Well?" Mitch said.

Gwen swallowed and lifted her head. "What do I have to do?"

Mitch fetched his glass, refilled it with water and poured the powder into it. He swirled the powder in the glass until the water was a uniform gray. "Drink."

Gwen took the glass from him, suddenly queasy. She lifted the concoction to her lips. The first taste was every bit as bad as she'd expected. She downed the rest of it before she could change her mind.

Nothing. No sudden awareness of change, no sense that she had lost all connection to Dorian. Perhaps the effects took a while to show. Or perhaps the bond had grown so tenuous that she wouldn't know the powder had worked until she was on the plane headed back to the States.

"It's done," Mitch said, his voice high with triumph. "Now we get out of here."

"If the potion doesn't work, I won't be able to leave."

"That's what we're about to find out." He took her elbow and herded her toward the door. Gwen dug in her heels.

"No," she said. "I can't…I can't just leave like this."

Mitch stared at her in disbelief. "Why the hell not? You're not still in love with the bastard?"

"No. I—"

He grabbed her arm again. She took a few steps and stopped again.

"I can't, Mitch," she said. "I have to speak to Dorian."

His laugh was incredulous. "What do you think he'll do? Just let you go?"

"I'm willing to take that chance. Go back to the plane, Mitch. I'll join you as soon as I can."

Mitch's expression was almost cruel. "Like hell," he said. "I won't let him claim you again."

He strode to the door and opened it, raising his hand to signal someone out of sight. Five men appeared from behind a low hill.

"Who are they?" she demanded, getting ready to fight.

"You should know them, Gwen. They're members of Pax. The people Dorian betrayed."

Gwen backed into the cabin. "He didn't betray anyone."

She didn't have time for further argument, because the five Pax members were almost on the doorstep. The first among them stepped into the shadow of the cabin and lowered his sunglasses.

"Miss Murphy," he said. "Praise the Lord that we've found you."

"Sammael?" She glanced from him to Mitch. "What are you doing here?"

He smiled benignly. "We also have been looking for you, my dear. You cannot imagine how worried we've been." He walked into the cabin, his dark-coated men behind him. "Where is Dorian?" he asked.

Immediately Gwen went on her guard. There was no reason to feel suspicious of Sammael, but Mitch had said something about Dorian betraying Pax. If Mitch knew enough to have become Pax's ally, he must have heard that accusation somewhere.

"Dorian is out," Gwen said. 'I don't know when he'll be back."

"I see." Sammael glanced about the room and finally settled his gaze on Gwen. "Why didn't you contact us, Miss Murphy?"

She leaned against the fireplace, letting her hands rest casually at her sides. "Angela took us to meet someone who was supposed to get us out of the city," she said. "We were attacked. Dorian and I thought it would be better if we—"

"Angela betrayed us," Sammael said, all the gentle concern gone from his voice. "She did not consult with the synod before she took action."

"Who is Angela?" Mitch interjected.

Gwen ignored him. "Was she working for Kyril?" she asked Sammael.

"We have yet to determine the reason for her actions," Sammael said. His four men scattered around the living room, taking up positions like soldiers expecting attack. Gwen began to feel more than a little uneasy.

"What other motive would Angela have had for leading us into an ambush?" she asked, choosing her words with care.

"We may never know. But that is past now." Sammael looked at the bookshelf with a peculiar intensity. "It was a mistake for you to leave New York. We are far better able to protect you from Kyril if you remain with us."

"We thought we'd cause more trouble if we stayed."

"Quite the opposite. If Kyril were to find you and compel you to talk, our entire organization could be exposed."

"Dorian would never talk."

"And you, Miss Murphy? Can you guarantee the same of yourself?" He shook his head. "Surely you must see that we can't take the chance that our careful work should be destroyed. Too many innocent lives hang in the balance." He drifted toward the bookshelf. "Even when you were shot, blameless humans were involved. The young woman and child who were standing near you when the shooting occurred could just as easily have fallen victim to the same bullets. Only when the wars end can we prevent such things from happening again."

Sammael's final sentence had hardly passed through Gwen's mind when she realized exactly what he had just said. *The young woman and her child.* Innocent bystanders who just happened to be in the wrong place at the wrong time—and the only direct witnesses to the crime. They'd fled the scene immediately after the shooting.

No one but Gwen knew that the mother and child had been on that street corner. She hadn't even told the police, for fear that she'd put someone else in harm's way. No one except someone who knew more than either Gwen or the police.

But there *was* someone who would know even more than Gwen did. The assassins themselves.

Gwen hid her thoughts behind an expression of sympathetic

agreement. "Of course I understand," she said. "I'm sure Dorian will agree."

"Then we shall wait for him." He signaled to his men. Two of them slipped through the door to the hallway. Sammael bent to examine the books, running his fingers along their spines. Mitch made an aborted movement, as if about to speak, then subsided.

Gwen glanced at him out of the corner of her eye. How had he learned about Pax, and how much did he really know about them? Why had he agreed to lead them to her and Dorian? Why had he lied to her about their presence here?

And what about Micah's book? Who was Aadon, and in what way, if any, was he related to Pax? Sammael obviously didn't know that Eamon Murphy had been aware of the existence of *strigoi,* or he surely would have mentioned it when Gwen had come to Pax with Dorian.

Or would he? If they tried to kill me…

No. Dad died of a heart attack. There was nothing fishy about it.

Chilled to the marrow, Gwen smiled at Sammael. "Would you like to sit down? I can offer you something to drink. Coffee, perhaps?"

Sammael straightened from his examination of the bookshelf. "We would be delighted," he said.

He took a seat on the sofa, while his two remaining men continued to keep their silent vigil. Mitch stood near the door, his gaze moving from Gwen to Sammael and back again. Gwen knew him well enough to guess that he also sensed that something was amiss.

Gwen put the water on the stove to boil and took out several mugs from one of the cupboards, thinking furiously. Why had Pax tried to kill her? If it was for the same reason Dorian had attributed to Kyril's gang—because she'd gotten a little too close to exposing the presence of vampires in Manhattan—then Mitch must be in danger, too. There certainly didn't seem to be much chance that she could escape, with or without Mitch, and she had no way to warn Dorian.

If they only wanted me, they wouldn't wait for him. But they didn't dare let Dorian live if they hoped to get rid of her.

If the blood bond was really broken, it might actually be to Dorian's advantage. He wouldn't feel her agitation. And if he had the sense to stay away, Pax couldn't use her to lure him in.

Stay away, Dorian. For God's sake, stay away.

THE SUN HAD REACHED its zenith when Sammael called Mitch outside.

The Pax leader made no attempt to maintain the peaceable act he'd used with Gwen. He stared across the desert, his eyes concealed beneath his dark glasses and his mouth tense in the shadow of his wide-brimmed hat.

"My men have not reported back," he said. "Dorian cannot be very far away, or he would find the separation from Miss Murphy too painful. Nevertheless, we must locate him soon."

"I understand."

"I wonder if you do, Mr. Hogan." Sammael tugged at the fingers of his gloves as if he found them too tight. "I shall take three of my men and go after him myself. You will stay here with Miss Murphy and my remaining man."

"What if Dorian comes back while you're gone?"

"I believe he'll sense the trap and stay away, at least until nightfall. However, I will leave two of my men to assist you. Dorian must be taken alive, but serious wounds will slow him. Shoot anywhere but in the heart or head." Sammael turned his hidden gaze back to Mitch. "You are not to let Miss Murphy leave the house under any circumstances."

"I thought you wanted Black dead."

"In time, Mr. Hogan. In time. Remember that Miss Murphy will be safe only as long as Dorian is unable to reach her."

He went back into the house and gathered up his men, leaving two to stand watch outside. *The bastard doesn't trust me,* Mitch thought. *And now he says he wants Black alive.*

Sammael didn't know about the potion, of course; Mitch hadn't seen any reason to tell him about it. But Black's death would end any doubt that the bond was broken.

Something was wrong here, something Mitch couldn't put his finger on. Gwen obviously didn't entirely trust Sammael. *What don't I know about him? What is he hiding?* And why was he afraid that Gwen was going to run off when Mitch had assured him how much she wanted to be free of Dorian?

Well aware that he wasn't likely to find any answers by talking to himself, Mitch nodded to the two guards and went inside. Gwen was still standing beside the fireplace, her hands behind her back.

"Is he gone?" she asked.

"Yes, but he's left a couple of men outside." Gwen shifted, and Mitch glimpsed the poker she was trying to conceal. "You don't plan to use that on me, do you?"

Her lips drew back from her teeth. "Give me one reason why I shouldn't."

He moved closer to her. "What's wrong, Gwen? What are you afraid of?"

"Are you really that naive, Mitch?"

"They said they wanted to help you."

"They're lying." She banged the poker against the fireplace, cracking the stone facade. "How did they get to you?"

"They were watching me. They knew I'd talked to you on the telephone, and since they said they only wanted to make sure you were safe…"

"They know details about how I was shot that no one else does. Things only the shooters would know."

"What?" His eyes widened. "What are you saying, Gwen?"

"I think they tried to kill me."

Mitch sank into the rocking chair. "Why would they want to kill you?"

"To keep me from revealing the presence of vampires in the city."

The blood drained from his face. "They…they assured me—"

"They're fanatically devoted to their cause," she said. "Every bit as much as Kyril and his followers are devoted to obtaining wealth and power. I don't think they'd stop at anything to protect it."

Mitch burrowed deeper into the chair, his thoughts spinning. "You're sure, Gwen?"

"I have to assume they're the enemy. The question is, are you?"

"I swear I didn't know. They gave me every reason to believe they wanted to protect you."

"And Dorian?"

It was impossible for Mitch to hide his own reaction to her question. Gwen cursed in a way she could only have learned from the veterans in the newsroom.

"They told you they wanted Dorian dead, didn't they?" she demanded. "They said he betrayed them. Is that how they got you to help them?"

"Look what he's done to you, Guinevere. He's nearly destroyed you."

Her face and voice became utterly calm. "Well, now you'll get more than you bargained for. I have a feeling all three of us will be under the ground if we don't get out of here fast."

Mitch shivered. She was right. If Pax wanted both Gwen and Dorian dead, they weren't likely to leave an inconvenient human witness alive to report on it.

My God. What have I done?

"What do you want me to do?" he asked.

"We have to get rid of the guards first, and then try to find Dorian. Where are the planes that brought you and the others?"

"Just on the far side of those hills to the north."

"And there might be guards there, as well, or at least the pilots. Well, we'll deal with that when we get to it." She blew out her breath. "All right. This is what we're going to do."

CHAPTER TWENTY

"IT'S REALLY VERY SIMPLE," Gwen told Mitch. "I'm going to go crazy, and you're going to alert the guards."

Mitch gave her a look as if she'd already become a lunatic. "What?"

Gwen struggled for patience. "Did you know that vampires who are bound by blood—patrons and their protégés—can't be separated for long?"

"Perkowski didn't mention it."

"It causes discomfort, even pain, for both of them. And I've been told..." She paused, half-afraid to speak the words aloud. "Sometimes, when the patron dies, the protégé goes insane."

"But you are no longer bound to Black."

"The guards don't know that, do they?"

"So you propose to act as if Black is dead?"

Gwen's urge to plant her fist in Mitch's face was almost overwhelming. "Yes," she said coldly. "If I put on a good enough show, the guards will believe he really *is* dead."

"What if it doesn't work?"

"Are you afraid of the risk to yourself? Maybe the guards will let you go back to the plane if you ask nicely."

Mitch bristled. "I'm not going to abandon you."

"Then do just as I tell you."

A few minutes later Gwen retired to her bedroom and lay on the bed, preparing herself for the performance of her life. She tore at her hair, scratched at her face and arms, ripped her blouse and generally put on the airs of a madwoman. By the time Mitch returned with the first guard, the sky was dark and she was screaming.

"What's wrong with her?" Mitch asked, his face pinched with anxiety.

The guard leaned over Gwen, who launched herself at him in a frenzy. He pushed her back down.

"When did this occur?" the guard asked.

"Less than an hour ago. It just came on her suddenly."

The guard seized Gwen's arm. "Listen to me," he said. "What has happened?"

Gwen tossed her head from side to side, keening like a banshee. The guard struck her across the face. Mitch lunged, only to be flung against the wall by the vampire's casual backhand.

"No!" Gwen wailed.

Pinning her to the bed, the guard leaned over her again and pried open her eyes. Gwen subsided for a few seconds and then began to thrash wildly.

"Dead," she moaned. "Dead."

The guard jerked up, clearly startled. "Dorian?" he said.

"What about Black?" Mitch said, rubbing at his jaw.

"Is Dorian dead?" the guard demanded, gripping Gwen's shoulders so hard that she thought her bones would snap.

Gwen screamed again, and at last the guard seemed satisfied. He backed away, brushing his palms over his trousers.

"Black is dead," he said without turning. "It's the only explanation."

"I don't get it," Mitch said. But the guard didn't look at him. He didn't notice when Mitch pulled the gun from his jacket. The bullet caught the vampire in the shoulder. The wound was far from fatal, but Gwen was ready. She leaped from the bed and reached the guard just as he seized Mitch by the neck.

The fight was almost equal, the Pax member's strength countered by his injury, but Mitch tipped the balance. He shot the guard twice more through the chest. The vampire staggered against the wall and slid down, leaving streaks of blood on the whitewashed surface.

There was no time to see how badly the man was injured. The second guard charged into the house, his own weapon at the ready, and Gwen was barely able to intercept him before he reached the bedroom.

"The human," she cried. "He—" She spun sideways as the second guard plowed past her. Mitch stood in the center of the bedroom, his arms braced to fire. He flinched for one crucial instant. The vampire glanced at his downed associate and took aim.

He never completed the motion. Another figure charged through the bedroom door, grabbed the second guard's gun arm and twisted it until bones grated and the man yelled in agony. Dorian slammed the guard against the wall until he slumped, unconscious, beside his partner.

"We must leave immediately," Dorian said, taking Gwen's hand as she came up behind him. "Kyril has—"

He broke off. Mitch was still aiming his gun, this time at Dorian's chest.

"You can't control her anymore," he said, his voice shaking.

"Mitch!" Gwen said, stepping in front of Dorian. "He just saved your life!"

"Move away, Gwen," Dorian said.

"No." She stared into Mitch's eyes. "If you kill him, be sure to save a couple of bullets for me."

The gun wavered. "How did it go so wrong, Guinevere?" Mitch asked, his eyes filled with tears. "We could have been happy."

"But we can't go back," Gwen said. She took Dorian's hand again. "Decide, Mitch. Kill us, or come with us now."

A hoarse sound broke from Mitch's throat. "It's true, then." He lowered the gun and slowly tucked it into his jacket. "There's nothing else I can do."

"Come with us," Gwen urged.

Mitch nodded, though his gaze was fixed on something no one else could see. Dorian took a step toward him.

"You brought Kyril here," he accused.

"It isn't Kyril, Dorian," Gwen said, ready to step between them. "It's Pax."

Dorian narrowed his eyes. "What did you tell them, human?" he demanded of Mitch. "Why are they armed and watching this house?"

Mitch was silent. Dorian took another step, muscles tensed to strike. Gwen prepared herself to hold Dorian back with all the strength she possessed.

But a peculiar thing happened then. Dorian didn't attack. He simply stood and stared at Mitch as if he had forgotten how easy it would be to kill a human.

"You're a fool, Hogan," he said. He turned and began to pull Gwen toward the front door.

"Wait," Gwen said. She grabbed Dorian's arm and forced him to stop, staring into his face. Perspiration stood out on his temples and upper lip, and a tic jumped in his cheek; it was obvious that he was feeling the effects of the coming moonless night. But his face was composed, his eyes rational and clear. He didn't seem to recognize that the bond was broken.

What's changed, Dorian? Why did you leave Mitch alone? Where is the monster?

Was it possible that simply breaking the bond had been enough to restore his sanity?

"How did you know what was happening here?" she asked aloud.

"This afternoon I found a message from Walter waiting for us in Chihuahua. Someone vigorously questioned him about where we had gone." He gave Mitch a hard look. "Fortunately, Walter was not badly hurt. But what he said warned me that we might no longer be safe."

"Oh, God. Walter…" Gwen rubbed at her eyes. "He was right. If you'd come back any earlier…"

"I saw the men from a distance. It seemed sensible to wait until most of them had left."

Gwen listened to the even rhythm of his voice with profound gratitude. She was grateful that he didn't ask what Pax wanted of them; she wasn't prepared to tell him what she'd come to believe about their attempt to kill her. Not while there was still a chance the knowledge would set Dorian off again.

If she was going to be offered a miracle, she would gladly accept it.

"Mitch says there are planes waiting on the other side of the hills," she said. "We've got to reach them before Sammael realizes we're gone."

Dorian glanced toward the door. "Yes. We have no more time to waste."

Gwen rushed ahead of him into the living room and stopped at the bookshelf. She pushed the Gibbon volumes aside and opened the hidden panel. She couldn't have said why the book was so important, but everything in her gut told her it was, and that she should by no means let anyone else see it. She put the book in the colorful woven shopping bag she'd left in the kitchen, hooked it over her shoulder, and accompanied Mitch and Dorian to the front door.

Dorian paused on the threshold, scanning the horizon. Mitch joined them, perspiration soaking his collar and the front of his shirt.

"They intend to kill you," he said to Dorian. "They told me that you betrayed them by Converting Gwen and running away."

"They lied," Gwen said. She followed Dorian's gaze. "Do you see them?"

"Not yet." He looked at Mitch, expressionless. "Can you make your way in the dark?"

"I have a flashlight in my coat."

"Good. Escort Gwen to the planes, and do whatever you must to get her in the air."

"No, Dorian," Gwen said. "We're all in this together now."

"Gwen." He seemed to grow taller, his shoulders more massive. "I will brook no disobedience, not this time."

"I'm afraid you'll have to." She felt a paralyzing wave of overwhelming sadness. "The bond is broken."

Startled disbelief passed over Dorian's face. His eyes lost their focus and slowly cleared with comprehension.

"It's true," she said, filled with self-contempt. "I'm sorry."

Dorian stared at her, his hands clenched at his sides. "I felt the emptiness," he whispered. "But I didn't believe it was possible."

She faced him squarely. "I thought it was necessary. I thought you were getting worse with me here, that I only made you... Ever since the dark of the moon..."

He glanced away. "Perhaps you were right," he said, as if to himself. "Perhaps I was only deceiving myself." He turned to Mitch. "Take her and go."

"I won't leave without you," Gwen said.

Dorian remained very still for another half a minute and then took himself in hand. "If I don't stay behind," he said, "Pax may reach us too soon."

"That's a chance I'm willing to take."

Mitch hissed a warning. Gwen looked where he pointed and saw the flicker of reflected light on a hill less than a quarter mile away.

"That's it," Mitch said, looking steadily at Dorian. "You won't be able to hold them off now."

Dorian didn't answer. "The planes," he said.

Shoulders hunched as if he'd just suffered a nasty beating, Mitch took the lead. They didn't dare use the flashlight, so the three of them stuck close together. Gwen helped Mitch when he stumbled in the darkness, while Dorian watched for pursuit. Fifteen minutes later they scrambled up the last low hill overlooking the flat expanse of desert that served as a makeshift landing strip. Dorian pulled Gwen flat beside him.

"Two planes," he said. "We can only take one of them."

"We have a shot at both," Mitch said. "The pilots are human, not vampires." His voice had grown stronger, as if he'd begun to regain his confidence. "Black, you and Gwen go for the left. I'll handle the other one."

Dorian shot Mitch an incredulous glance. Mitch laughed.

"I know. Why should you trust me? Except I want to live, too. And I don't think Pax will be too keen on letting me go when this is over." He touched Gwen's arm. "The pilots probably have no idea what's been going on. Chances are good that they'll trust me. As soon as I have control of my plane, I'll flash twice with the lights."

"You can't fly it," Gwen protested.

"Don't worry about that just yet." He held Gwen's gaze. "Let me do this, Guinevere."

"All right. But if you get into trouble, flash your lights three times and we'll come running."

"You bet." He gave her arm a squeeze and gathered himself for a dash down the hill. Dorian watched him go.

"We may fail," he said, his words emotionless. "If I fall, get to Hogan. I believe he will do his best to care for you."

"No one's going to fail."

She began running down the hill, holding her body low. Dorian kept pace, and soon they were skimming across the airfield. For the first time since her Conversion, Gwen allowed herself to really feel the glorious strength of her altered body…the power of her muscles, the perfect night vision, the easy swiftness that ate up the yards as if they were inches.

The human pilots didn't see them coming. Dorian indicated that Gwen should wait out of sight while he crept to the wing of the four-passenger De Havilland and climbed up behind the open cockpit. She heard nothing for several minutes; then there was a muffled cry. She clambered up the wing to find Dorian standing over the pilot, who she recognized with a start.

"Jim!" she said.

The young man looked from her to Dorian and back again. "You're making a mistake," he said. "You may still have a chance, if only you'll—"

Dorian caught him by the back of his collar. "Quiet."

Jim continued to stare at Gwen with an urgent expression in his eyes. He was trying to tell her something, of that she was certain. But he wouldn't speak in front of Dorian.

"Dorian," she said, "I think I should hear what Jim has to say. Will you go down while I question him?"

It was another test of Dorian's newfound control, and he

passed it. With a terse nod, he jumped down to the wing and took up a position where he could watch for intruders.

"I'm sorry I can't offer you a seat," Jim said, "but these cockpits are pretty cramped. Would you rather go into the cabin?"

"No. We don't have time." Gwen settled herself on the rim of the cockpit. "What do you want to tell me?"

Jim mopped at his face with a damp handkerchief. "I was praying you'd turn up. I volunteered for this trip hoping I'd get a chance to warn you, but I wasn't given permission to leave the plane."

"Warn me about what?" Gwen asked. "That Sammael wants to kill us?"

"Angela told me before she took you from Pax headquarters," he said, "but I didn't believe it until I overheard…" His Adam's apple bobbed nervously. "Angela said she was taking you away without Sammael's permission because she knew they intended to murder Dorian and interrogate you about the book. But Sammael found out and sent men after her." His eyes welled with tears. "*They* killed her."

"I guessed as much when I realized they tried to kill me before," Gwen said. She touched Jim's arm. "She died to save us."

Jim's gaze hardened. "I trusted Pax. I gave my life to it. Now…" He shifted in his seat. "You don't have the book, do you?"

The book. Gwen almost reached for the bag slung over her shoulder. "What book?"

"Micah's book. One of the few originals left to us. A vampire named Aadon stole it from Pax. Sammael believes he gave it to your father."

Gwen's heart climbed into her throat. "Why would he give it to my father?"

"Because of what he'd written in the *Sentinel*. Aadon believed that members of Pax had killed people in the city, even though Micah taught only peace. He believed that Sammael was distorting Micah's words for his own purposes. Angela saw the original book before Aadon stole it. Just before that she'd been promoted from novice to mediant. She said what Sammael was teaching the mediants wasn't the same as what was in the book, what they teach the novices."

Wild speculation stole Gwen's breath. It was almost too much to take in. "Aadon wanted my father to expose Pax for murder?"

"I don't know. Aadon may also have learned what Angela discovered shortly before she decided to help you. Sammael is building a secret army that only a few people in Pax know about." He turned his head, gazing out toward the desert. "There's no more time to talk. If you have the book, keep it hidden. You mustn't let Sammael take it."

Dorian climbed on the wing. "We must go."

"You'll fly us out, Jim?" she asked.

"Yes. I'm not going back to Pax, in any case." He looked sideways at Dorian. "Can you start the prop when I tell you?"

Dorian nodded. Jim jumped to the ground, opened the cloth cover of the cabin and let down the ladder. He set the engine throttle and magnetos, then motioned for Dorian to start the propeller. The engine roared to life.

Gwen hesitated at the foot of the ladder. "Mitch's plane is still dark," she said. "He may be in trouble. We'd better—"

Before she could finish speaking, the plane's headlights flashed once and again.

"He's got it!" Gwen said. Her sharp vision caught movement across the plain. "They're coming."

Without a word Dorian lifted Gwen into the cabin and climbed up behind her. Human shapes were emerging from the blackness. One of them was Sammael.

"Close the cover and hold on tight!" Jim shouted from the cockpit. Dorian pulled down the top frame of the passenger compartment and secured it. Gwen continued to watch through the windows as Jim began to taxi. The De Havilland rolled along the bumpy ground, jolting Gwen from side to side. She heard shouts over the engine's rumble and knew Pax had nearly caught them.

But Mitch's plane wasn't moving. There was a flurry of activity beside it as several figures clashed and struggled.

"Wait!" Gwen cried. "I think they've got Mitch!"

Dorian came to crouch beside her at the window. "I see him," he said. "He's left the plane."

"What?"

"He's shooting at Sammael's men."

Gwen made her way to the front of the compartment and pounded on the wall that partitioned the cabin from the cockpit. "Stop the plane!" she shouted.

She wasn't sure that Jim had heard her until the De Havilland began to slow. She returned to the window and grabbed Dorian's arm.

"They'll kill him," she said. "Why did he do it?"

Then she remembered one of the last things Mitch had said in the *casa: There's nothing I can do.* Nothing he could do to win her back. Nothing he could do to make her love him again.

Nothing but give up his life.

"It's my fault," she whispered as the plane shuddered to a halt. "He's sacrificed himself for me."

The rattle and boom of gunfire shattered her paralysis. She grabbed her bag, shouldered Dorian aside and opened the cabin flap. Before he could stop her, she'd jumped to the ground and scrambled back up the wing to the cockpit.

"Keep this for me," she said, dumping the bag into Jim's lap.

He cast her a startled look, which swiftly changed to one of comprehension. Gwen leaped to the ground and started for Mitch's plane.

Dorian stepped in front of her. "You can't save him now," he said.

"I have to try."

She'd barely drawn another breath when Dorian pushed her aside and began to run. He was twice as fast as she was. By the time she was halfway to Mitch's plane, Dorian had reached the battle. There was a spate of gunfire, muffled cries, and then a sudden lull far more terrible.

Gwen came upon a scene of carnage. Two *strigoi* sprawled on the ground, one with his head half blown away and the other with fatal wounds to the chest. Mitch lay near the wheel of the plane, gasping as his life's blood poured out of holes in his gut and shoulder.

During the handful of seconds while Gwen took in the scene, Dorian had already launched his attack. Sammael and four of his lieutenants met him with equal fury. Knowing she would only get in Dorian's way, Gwen rushed to Mitch and knelt at his side.

"Mitch!" she said. She lifted him against her and held him in the circle of her arms. "I'm sorry. So sorry."

He opened his eyes. Blood ran from the corner of his mouth, but his eyes were clear. "It's all right, Guinevere."

"Why? Why did you do it?"

A racking cough shook his body. "The only way…to make up for my mistakes."

"Oh, God." She pressed her cheek to his. "I never hated you, Mitch. Never."

"I know." He clutched at the front of her blouse. "Tell Walter… I'm sorry." His back arched in a spasm of pain. "Get…out of here. Take him with—" A gasp swallowed his words.

Gwen's eyes burned, but no tears would come. She stroked Mitch's face until the light went out of his eyes. She passed her hand gently over his face, and then the world crashed into focus around her.

"Don't try to get up," Sammael's voice said. "I would not wish to do you an injury."

She looked up. Sammael was standing over her, his Tommy gun pointed at her head. The pair of *strigoi* behind him sported obviously broken limbs, and one of the guards she and Mitch had dispatched in the *casa* stood nearby, his glare promising a painful reckoning. Dorian sagged between two other *strigoi*, his arms wrenched behind his back.

"You have caused a great deal of trouble for us," Sammael said, looking from Gwen to Dorian. "But your behavior has only strengthened our resolve."

"Your resolve to do what?" Gwen asked. "Murder Dorian? Make up for your failure to kill me?"

Sammael raised a brow. "Kill you? My dear, I assure you that I have no desire to harm you in any way."

"You're a liar. You slipped up, Sammael." She eased Mitch's body to the ground. "All this time I thought it was Kyril who wanted me dead. Did you murder Hewitt, too?"

Anger broke Sammael's composure. "Hewitt's death was necessary to preserve our great purpose."

"As mine is. You probably would have killed Mitch, too, even if he hadn't turned against you."

"A pity he was so foolish. But you are quite wrong, Miss Murphy. We never intended to kill you nor have we any intention of killing Dorian."

"Then why have you done this?"

Sammael didn't answer. He gestured to the men holding Dorian. "Take him into the plane and secure him well. The rest of you go with them. We will leave the bodies. Miss Murphy and I will ride in the other plane."

Dorian struggled briefly as his captors dragged him toward the plane, but he hadn't yet reached the pinnacle of strength that would come with his madness. One of the *strigoi* jammed a revolver into his back and forced him up the ladder into the cabin.

"Stand up, if you please," Sammael said to Gwen.

"I won't leave Mitch here like this."

Sammael took Gwen's arm. "You will come with me, willingly or otherwise."

Gwen jerked out of his hold and rose. She stared down into Mitch's face, her eyes stinging with grief.

At least he was at peace. There was nothing more they could do to him now.

She walked ahead of Sammael, praying that Dorian was all right. She couldn't reach him now, not even to let him know that she was well and whole.

Four nights until the dark of the moon. Four nights until Dorian lost control. And she could do nothing to help him.

Jim stood waiting at the foot of the plane. He had managed

to make himself look as though he'd been soundly beaten; his shirt was torn, he had a small cut on his right cheek and an impressive shiner was beginning to appear around his left eye. He began to speak when Sammael was still several yards away.

"I'm sorry, Sammael," he said, rubbing the back of his neck and averting his gaze. "I didn't hear them coming until they were already on top of me. I've failed you."

Sammael bestowed his false, benevolent smile on the human. "We did not expect you to fight *strigoi* and win, Jim," he said. "All is well. Dorian will not harm you again."

Jim gave him a pitifully grateful look. Sammael continued past him to the De Havilland.

"We leave immediately," he said.

"Of course, Sammael," Jim said, slinking up behind him, "but it would be better if we don't fly all night."

Sammael grunted. "Get us over the border and we'll stop in San Antonio."

Jim nodded and repeated the procedure for starting the plane. Sammael herded Gwen into the cabin and secured the top flap. He pushed her into a seat and took the one opposite. The De Havilland began to taxi, and in a few minutes it was airborne.

Gwen stared out the window, looking for the second plane. "Where are you taking us?" she asked.

"Back to Pax, of course."

"Dorian—"

"Have no fear. Your separation will be brief and should not be unduly painful."

His words reminded Gwen that he didn't know she'd broken her bond with Dorian. "That's very generous of you," she said coldly. "But you still haven't told me what you really want."

Sammael leaned forward in his seat, a frightening sort of earnestness brimming behind his eyes. "There is so much you don't understand, Miss Murphy," he said. "So much that will only be made clear if you truly comprehend us."

"You think I'll approve of what you've done if I 'comprehend' you?"

"Our sole purpose is to work for the greater good."

"*Your* greater good."

"The good of humanity, Miss Murphy. Of the entire world."

"You actually think that killing people will save the world?"

"Yes. From us."

"From Pax?"

"From *us,* Miss Murphy," he said quietly. "From *strigoi* lust and corruption."

He reached within his coat and pulled out a small, leather-bound book, its covers buffed and worn by many years of handling. There was a symbol engraved on the front—an upward-pointing triangle surrounding a stylized flame.

"Have you seen this before?" he asked intently.

It took all of Gwen's effort to conceal her recognition. She pretended to study the book. "I recognize the symbol. It was in my room at Pax."

"But you have not seen another book exactly like this one?"

"No. Why should I have?"

Sammael's eyes sharpened. "Are you lying to me, Miss Murphy?"

"No." She held his gaze. "Why is this book so important?"

Sammael held his copy in his lap, rubbing his thumb over the worn symbol again and again. "What were your thoughts when you were first Converted, Miss Murphy?"

"Why does that matter?"

"Indulge me."

"I wasn't prepared for it. No one could be."

"And you hated Dorian for what he had done."

She was careful not to look away. "He was trying to save my life."

"At the cost of your soul." He shook his head. "You would become human again if you had the choice, would you not?"

And that, Gwen thought, was a question she couldn't answer. Micah's writings had inspired her to accept what she couldn't change. But if she had a choice…

"Unless you know of a cure," she said, "I can't go back."

"And you are bound to Dorian as his chattel," Sammael said. "Do you not see the perversion of such a relationship, how deeply it offends Heaven?"

Gwen began to see how badly Sammael wanted and needed an audience, even if that audience was a single female prisoner. *The more you can learn about him and his weaknesses, the better chance you'll have at fighting him when the opportunity arises.*

"What does Heaven have to do with it?" she asked, taking his bait.

Sammael smiled, his face upturned. "I shall tell you, my child," he said. "When man was created, the Lord offered him dominion over the earth so long as he did not eat from the Tree of Knowledge or seek to learn the secret of eternal life."

"I know the story."

"You know *nothing,*" Sammael snapped. "No human upon this earth knows the truth as it was vouchsafed to…" He stopped and took a long breath. "When Adam and Eve were cast out of Eden, they were given two sons."

"Cain and Abel," Gwen said, watching Sammael's face.

"But the Serpent went unto Cain." Sammael closed his eyes, and the words took on the singsong rhythm of a sermon. "And Cain took from the Evil One the secret of eternal life. When Abel, his brother, discovered his transgression, Cain slew him."

He's crazy, Gwen thought. "I never heard that Cain—"

"Be silent." He began again. "Cain drained the blood from Abel's body and drank it until he had taken his fill. In shame he fled and wandered the earth, undying. He took unto him disciples, bestowing upon them the secret he had stolen. And his cursed breed walked the land like a plague, feeding upon the Children of God."

Gwen went cold. "You're talking about vampires."

"Yes. We are the Children of Cain." He laid his palm on the book. "We bear the mark of bloodlust, forever separated from the promise of Heaven."

And that's why you want to save the rest of humanity from

us, Gwen thought, beginning to feel a premonition of something more terrible than she could have imagined.

"If you believe that," she said cautiously, "I can understand why you want to stop people like Kyril."

"Yes." Sammael's eyes were as cool as blue crystal, faceted with zealotry and single-minded devotion. "But that is only the beginning. We are a plague upon the earth. The plague must be eliminated." He traced the figure on the front of his book in a hypnotic rhythm. "Only then will man be restored to his rightful dominion, as the Lord ordained. This is the great task we have been given. And when we have carried it out, we shall be redeemed."

CHAPTER TWENTY-ONE

THE PLAGUE MUST BE eliminated.

Sammael's words were so startling that Gwen had to run them through her mind several times before she fully understood. With an effort she reclaimed her old reporter's coolheadedness and met Sammael's gaze.

"You want all vampires to die," she said.

The Pax leader opened his book to a page marked with a silk ribbon, his demeanor untroubled. "That is an unfortunate way of putting it, Miss Murphy."

"But that's exactly what it means, isn't it? You think you can earn some kind of salvation by destroying your own kind."

"Destroying only to save, Miss Murphy. As the Lord requires." He began to read aloud. "'I saw those who drank the blood of innocents cast down,'" he said, "'and those who suffered raised above them.'"

"Who wrote that?" Gwen asked, leaning forward.

"Our greatest teacher, Micah, the author of our salvation." Sammael continued to read, running his fingertip over the lines.

"'Only the greatest sacrifice shall set them free. They shall die to be reborn, and thus shall they enter the Kingdom of Heaven.'" He looked up. "It cannot be more clear, Miss Murphy."

Gwen knew that she walked a very fine line between gathering essential information and feeding Sammael's madness. "May I see the book?"

Sammael closed the volume and tucked it inside his jacket. "It is not for the unconsecrated," he said.

Which meant he didn't want her to read it. Gwen remembered

clearly what Jim had told her: *Aadon believed that Sammael was distorting Micah's words for his own purposes.*

The words he'd quoted had not been in the book Gwen had read in the cabin. She'd seen nothing even remotely like them. It was as if a different person had written them. A person whose agenda and beliefs were the very opposite of Micah's.

"What does it take to be consecrated?" she asked. "Does everyone in Pax believe what's in that book?"

"Yes."

Gwen was certain he was lying. Jim had suggested that what Sammael was teaching the mediants at Pax—whoever they were—wasn't the same as what was in Micah's original book. *And you obviously didn't tell Dorian your real plan. He believed you really wanted peace. How many others have been deceived?*

"I'm curious," she said. "How do you plan to kill all vampires? Even in New York, there must be—"

"Many hundreds, yes. And there are thousands more in the United States alone, thousands upon thousands throughout the world."

"And how many in Pax?"

"Ah." He smiled as if pleased by her questions. "There are more than you have seen, my dear. Many more, young men trained and hardened for battle. And we have used our resources carefully. Our agents within the factions have already laid the groundwork. Soon it will be over."

"Then you plan to go after them soon?"

He relaxed in his seat. "It is not necessary for you to know the details of our plans. Suffice it to say that Kyril, Christof and their followers may reckon the remainder of their lives in days."

Gwen felt the wild urge to laugh. "You really think you can kill all of them in one attack?"

"Perhaps not. But once both factions are in disarray, how much easier it will be to remove those who remain. The city will be rid of this disease."

"And then you'll start on the rest of the world?"

"If our faith remains strong."

"Strong enough to let you take your own lives? Is that the next step, after you've killed everyone else?"

The plane hit an air pocket, jolting Gwen half out of her seat. Sammael recovered quickly, gave Gwen a vicious look and made his way to the cockpit.

That's a question he doesn't want to answer, Gwen thought. *I'll bet there's nothing about suicide in that little book of his.*

But it was the book she'd given Jim that worried her now, the book about peace and love and brotherhood, written by a man who couldn't possibly believe the things Sammael claimed.

A light seemed to switch on in Gwen's brain. *Vida, Jim...they all revere Micah's words as truth. They trust Sammael with their lives, but he's fooled them all. He has to find Dad's copy so he can destroy it, because it refutes everything he wants Pax to believe.*

And the Pax members who didn't know any better would follow him blindly into blood and fire, all in the name of Sammael's obsession.

But maybe if those naive people got a chance to see Dad's book, with its talk of hope and real redemption, they would begin to question whatever lies Sammael had told them.

Keep the book safe, Jim. For all our sakes, keep it safe.

THEY FLEW FOR A little over three hours, then landed in San Antonio, where Jim refueled the plane and they took rooms for the night in a cheap hotel. They left at dawn the next morning and flew another thousand miles, with appropriate stops for fuel, before landing again in Nashville, Tennessee. The following afternoon found them at a landing field in Jersey City.

Gwen looked for Dorian's plane as soon as she jumped to the ground. It was already on the field, apparently deserted.

"Where is he?" Gwen demanded as Sammael took hold of her arm.

"You will see him soon, I assure you," Sammael said. He waited with her while Jim checked in at the office and went to fetch a dark and very plain coupe with tinged windows. Within two hours they were in Manhattan.

As soon as the coupe drew up in front of Pax headquarters, Sammael spoke briefly with Jim, who walked through the door without a single glance in Gwen's direction. He was inside the building for perhaps ten minutes before returning with a pair of hard-faced *strigoi,* who took Gwen into custody.

There was an edgy silence in Pax headquarters, a sense of anticipation mingled with fear. Sammael had hinted that the time for the attack on the rival factions was very near. She asked again to see Dorian, but was taken instead to the room where she'd stayed on the previous visit. She tested the door, knowing it would be firmly locked. The window proved to be bolted in place.

No one came for the next several hours. Gwen sat on the edge of the bed, senses straining for Dorian's voice. *Tomorrow,* she thought. *Tomorrow night is the dark of the moon.* If she and Dorian were still here when it happened, Sammael would witness just how powerful and ruthless Dorian could become. And perhaps Sammael would see in him not an enemy but a tool to be used in his violent quest for redemption.

I can't let that happen. One more time like the last...

She was beginning to climb the walls when the door opened and a pair of male *strigoi* she didn't recognize came to collect her. They were far from gentle as they chivvied her along the hall, down a narrow staircase and into a small, cold room furnished only with a single chair.

They ordered her to sit. She sat. And then they began the interrogation. Their first question was about the book. But Sammael's earlier questions had prepared her; she gave not the slightest sign that she knew what they were talking about.

The questioning rapidly proceeded from harsh voices to shouts and then to physical persuasion. They started with her face, slapping and then progressing to punches. She discovered that vampires were perfectly capable of feeling and enduring considerable pain. Blood streamed from her nose, soaking her soiled trousers and blouse. Soon she could barely see her interrogators through the swelling around her eyes.

Still they screamed about the book until her ears rang and her body slumped, no longer able to support itself. She could only offer thanks that the bond was broken. If Dorian had been able to feel what was happening, he would have done everything possible to come to her, monster or no. And he would probably have gotten himself killed in the attempt.

You did the right thing by breaking the bond. The right...

One of the *strigoi* grabbed her arm and began to pull. Gwen could feel her shoulder begin to slip out of its socket. Her vision went red and then black with agony.

"The book! Where is it?"

"Don't...know," she mumbled through thickened lips. "Don't—"

"Stop."

The new voice was clear and cold, its authority unquestionable. The torment ended. Sammael walked into the room, his lip curled in disgust.

"That is enough," he said sharply to his men. "You have overstepped your authority, Camarion." He knelt beside Gwen's chair and peered up into her face. "Poor child," he said. "I never intended it to go this far. You will be cared for immediately."

Gwen wished she had enough spit left in her mouth to show him what she thought of his promises. "Where is Dorian?" she asked.

"He is quite comfortable."

"You haven't...tortured him, too?"

"My dear, this has been a terrible mistake." He gestured to the interrogators, who quickly left the room. A moment later two others, the young *strigoi* named Vida and a male he called Nathaniel, arrived to help Gwen to her feet. Together with Sammael, they half carried her back to her room on the floor above.

Once she was in her bed, Sammael sent Nathaniel to fetch warm cloths and a glass of cool water. Gwen would gladly have fought off their attempts to ease her discomfort if she'd had the strength. As it was, she endured it just as she had the torture, and within a half hour the pain had begun to recede, and the swelling around her eyes and mouth had subsided.

Vida remained with Gwen when Sammael and Nathaniel left. Over the dark-haired woman's protests, Gwen propped herself up and drained the water glass. She wiped the last traces of blood from her mouth.

"You must be very proud today," she said to Vida.

The young woman moved her shoulders uncomfortably. "I don't understand."

"Proud of Pax, I mean. I wonder how many other people Sammael has tortured to further your cause?"

Vida stood up, her eyes darting from side to side. "It was a mistake."

Gwen touched the fading cut on her cheek. "I didn't know you could do this to people by mistake."

Vida moved toward the door, but Gwen wasn't finished. "Have you ever read Micah's book, Vida? The one they thought I had?"

The young woman hesitated a long while in her answer. "Only Sammael has read the book. He teaches us according to Micah's words."

"Does he? That must mean that Micah condoned beating people up and trying to kill them, right?"

Vida swung around, her skin very white. "Micah taught…that some will suffer so that more may be saved."

She's bought the whole line, Gwen thought. *The line Sammael's been feeding them, while only he knows the real truth.*

"Is that what you were told when you joined Pax, Vida?"

A disconcerted look froze the young woman's face, and she backed away. Just as she reached the door, Sammael opened it. He glanced at Vida without seeming to notice her agitation.

"You may go," he told her, and took her place at Gwen's bedside. "You seem much improved," he said. "I am pleased."

Gwen sat straighter in the bed. "If I'd still been human, it wouldn't have come out quite so well."

Sammael showed not the slightest regret. "I do admire your pluck, Miss Murphy, though your defiance is misplaced."

"I told you I didn't have your damned book."

"It seems I have no choice but to believe you."

"Did you kill my father?"

He looked genuinely shocked. "No. We were not even aware that he had been given the book until…" He shook his head. "That is no longer important, Miss Murphy. However, there is a service you can perform for us."

Gwen laughed aloud. "You want me to *help* you?"

"It is not so difficult a task. I only request that you convince Dorian to work with us."

"You've got to be kidding." Gwen swung her legs over the bed, found that they would support her, and went to stand as far from Sammael as she could. "Why should I do that? Why should he have any desire to help you, when you set out to kill him?"

Sammael rose to face her. "I thought I made it clear that we had no intention of killing either one of you."

"Why should we believe you?"

Sammael smiled. "My dear, you have no choice in the matter. You are here, and you will not be leaving until I am certain that you have provided Pax with what we require."

"And what can you possibly require from Dorian? He lost his position with Kyril. He—"

"He is more than we ever believed," Sammael interrupted.

The back of Gwen's neck began to prickle. *He knows. He knows what Dorian can become.*

"In what way?" she asked, with a calm she didn't feel.

"I have been told that he is the key to our victory."

"Told by whom?"

"By the Lord."

Gwen kept her expression a careful blank, but Sammael guessed what she didn't say. "You are skeptical," he said. "It is always so with unbelievers. But in my vision I have *seen* Dorian fighting among us. He is essential to our preservation and the fulfillment of Micah's vision."

Micah's vision? Gwen thought. *You've twisted it out of all recognition.*

"You still haven't given me a reason to convince him," she

said. "Once he finds out what you really intend to do, he'll never agree."

"You will not tell him."

"Don't you think he'll figure it out once you start killing everyone in sight?"

Sammael sighed. "I see I must be blunt, Miss Murphy. Though I have no desire to harm you further, I will do so if it becomes necessary to win Dorian's cooperation. The life of one recent Convert is of no importance."

"You mean I can either die right away or die later."

"If you help us, you will remain with us as we carry on the fight. We will not sacrifice ourselves until our work is complete."

In other words, you'll try to kill every other vampire and ignore your own evil.

"And Dorian? Will you keep him, too?"

"Naturally, Miss Murphy. Unless he proves intransigent."

Gwen pretended to consider the matter. "You'll let me speak with him?"

"I will insist on it. Everything is ready. We will carry out our attack on Kyril's and Christof's forces tomorrow night."

"No!" Gwen said before she could stop herself. Sammael looked at her sharply.

"Why do you protest, Miss Murphy?"

She fought for composure. "I…I was under the impression that you weren't ready."

"Please don't concern yourself. The Lord has us in the palm of His hand." He turned for the door. "I will send Dorian to you. You will be permitted to speak freely and privately." He paused in the doorway. "Persuade him, Miss Murphy, and you will both live."

The door closed. Gwen sat down on the bed, dizzy with fear. An endless hour passed before Dorian walked in. He was pale, his lips almost bloodless, his eyes deeply shadowed. All signs of the beating he'd endured were gone. The waning moon pulled at him with a demon's claws.

He rushed in and knelt before Gwen, seizing her hands.

"What have they done to you?" he demanded hoarsely. "Gwen, are you all right?"

She knew that lying wouldn't work very well when her skin still showed visible evidence of the guards' handiwork. "They pushed me around a little," she said. "But I'll live."

Her attempt at humor fell flat. Death stared out of Dorian's eyes. "They will suffer," he whispered. "Every blow, every indignity they inflicted on you."

She didn't embrace him, though holding back was one of the hardest things she'd ever done in her life. "They went a lot easier on me than they did on you," she said. "And anyway, I think we have more to worry about right now than revenge."

She held her breath, waiting to see if her calm tone would settle him. After a long, searching stare, Dorian's rage seemed to subside. "They have made a mistake in letting us see each other," he said.

"Then I'm grateful for their mistake. Can you check the door?"

Dorian got up again and pressed his ear to the wood. "I hear no movement outside," he said.

"Maybe Sammael was telling the truth this time."

Dorian returned to her, his movements almost awkward. "I regret the death of your friend," he said.

"Mitch…made his choice, but I'll never—" For a moment Gwen found it difficult to speak.

"He proved his courage," Dorian said. "He redeemed—" He stopped as if he'd thought better of what he was about to say. "He will not be forgotten," he finished. He sat in the chair facing her. "Gwen, there is something I must tell you."

"Dorian, Sammael—"

"Listen to me." He stared into her eyes so that she couldn't look away. "I have been deceiving you, Gwen. Since the last dark of the moon, I…I have felt it best to keep you away." He raised his hand and let it fall again, clenching his fist on his thigh. "I feigned madness even after I was free of it. I have come to regret doing so."

Gwen flushed. "You mean all this month, ever since… You've been faking it?"

"I believed it necessary, for your sake." He smiled with self-mockery. "I did not realize our bond could be broken, and I feared for your sanity. I thought that by driving you away—"

"You'd protect me."

He bowed his head. "Yes."

"Even though you knew that we couldn't be permanently separated even if you managed to make me mad enough to leave you?"

"There have been cases where a patron and protégé's separation only caused mild…" He trailed off. "It was a foolish attempt. Clearly I have *not* been able to protect you."

The need to touch him was almost unbearable. "I didn't ask that, Dorian. I never asked that."

"I know. It seems my judgment has been poor from the beginning."

"Regrets aren't much use to us now."

"No." He looked at her from underneath his dark brows. "How did you do it, Gwen?"

She knew what he meant without his having to say another word. "Mitch brought me herbs that he'd collected from some man in the city. He wasn't sure they'd work." She leaned toward Dorian, her whole body begging her to surrender. "I thought it was the only way to help you. Nothing I did seemed to make any difference. I couldn't get you to talk, and anytime I was in trouble…" She shivered. "I made it worse."

He got up and walked across the room, his hands knotted at his back. "You could not make it worse. I earned my punishment."

"How, Dorian? When did it begin?"

"It first came upon me after I killed my master."

Gwen started. "Boucher?"

"Yes."

"Protégés can kill their patrons?"

"Not easily. Not often. But it can be done."

While Gwen listened with horror and pity, Dorian told her everything that had happened in the weeks before Raoul's death and the dissolution of the clan. He spoke in flat, emotionless tones of a girl named Allegra Chase, of her rebellion against Boucher, and how Dorian had come to see that the Master's death was necessary.

"Others have gone insane when their first bond was broken," he said. "I feared the same for you. But my fears were groundless."

Like all my assumptions, Gwen thought. *First I condemned him for being an enforcer, then for Converting me against my will. And then I assumed he'd given in to the monster.*

"I'm sorry, Dorian," she whispered.

He turned to face her. "Do not apologize to me," he said. "I'm hardly worth the effort."

She got up and moved toward him slowly. He backed away. They stood facing each other like adversaries, neither one daring to cross the chasm between them.

"Whatever you did in the past," Gwen said, "you tried to make a difference. Maybe you still can." She took a deep breath and let it out again. "Sammael wants to use you, Dorian. He had some kind of vision that showed you fighting with Pax against the factions. He thinks you're essential to their victory."

The hardened enforcer woke in Dorian's eyes. "I will never fight for them."

Gwen closed her eyes, relieved and terrified. "There's more. Sammael is insane. He believes that all vampires have to die for the good of the world and the salvation of their souls."

Dorian absorbed her words quietly. "All vampires?" he asked.

"Except for themselves. They have to stay alive to fight the good fight."

"The good fight." Dorian laughed in his throat. "How well he deceived me."

"He's deceived everyone. He claims his Lord has commanded this purge."

"And who is to say he is wrong?"

"Dorian, you can't—"

He met her gaze. "I will not let Sammael use me," he said.

"Then you have to understand. He intends to attack Kyril tomorrow night. The dark of the moon, Dorian. If he takes you with him…"

"I'm to slaughter whoever escapes Pax."

"You mustn't do it, Dorian. Not for any reason."

Dorian searched her face. "What else did Sammael tell you? Did he say you would die if I failed to cooperate?"

"No."

"You have always lied poorly, Gwen."

"I'm not lying when I say that life won't be worth living if you go through with this. Not for either one of us."

"Even if I kill Sammael?"

Her heart stopped, then slammed into motion again. "No. It won't make any difference."

But he wasn't listening. She could see the veil falling over his eyes as he started for the door.

Unable to restrain herself, Gwen grabbed his hands. They were tense and corded with muscle and tendon, their bones like steel rods.

"If you kill anyone in my name," she said, "even Sammael, you will destroy all the good you've tried to do." She squeezed his hands with all her strength. "If we have to die, let it be for something that has meaning. The real Micah taught peace, Dorian. I believe peace is still possible, if we don't give in."

Dorian freed one hand to lift it toward her cheek. "Are you not afraid to die?"

"Of course I am. But there are things bigger than we are. I have faith. Faith that there are good people in Pax who will recognize what he's doing and stop him." She set her jaw. "Pax is only a threat as long as its members blindly follow Sammael and his perverted teachings. If they can be shown the truth…"

"How?" he asked, his voice hollow with weariness. "Sammael will never allow it."

Of course he wouldn't. But Jim had Micah's book…the book that proved how heinously Sammael had distorted Micah's dreams of peace and redemption into words of violence and hate.

I have to get to Jim.

"There is hope, Dorian. There's always hope. It took a

while for me to realize that after my Conversion. Now I'm certain of it."

His expression softened as he looked at her, a sad and gentle resignation. "You must hope for both of us," he said. "If we do not meet again…"

"You listen to me, Dorian Black. This isn't over. You still owe me. Don't give up. Don't give up without a fight."

The tenderness in his eyes took her breath away. But he didn't caress her cheek or take her in his arms. He only backed away, easing from her grasp, and slipped out the door.

Jim came to her a few hours later.

"I've been sent to provide blood," he said, standing with his back to the door. He refused to look at Gwen, and she knew at once that something was very wrong.

She jumped off the bed and went to meet him. "Is anyone outside?" she asked in a whisper.

He shook his head, his gaze darting about the room. A block of ice settled in the pit of Gwen's stomach.

"Where is the book, Jim?" she asked.

He licked his lips. "I…I had to—"

The ice expanded until Gwen's body was rigid with dread. "What did you do with it?"

At last he met her stare. "I had to," he said desperately. "Angela is alive, but he planned to kill her. I thought if I gave him the book he'd…he'd spare her life."

Gwen felt her way to the chair, shocked by the news that Angela was alive, and sat down. "Sammael has the book."

"I *had* to," Jim repeated. "Don't you see?"

Oh yes, she saw. She'd trusted Jim because she had no choice, but she hadn't let herself think about what might lead him to betray her.

Love. A power so great that it could overcome every obstacle… or cause a man to surrender everything he held dear.

"Do you know what you've done?" she asked quietly. "Sammael is planning to attack Kyril tonight. He intends to kill every vampire in his path. That is his goal, not peace. And now there's nothing to stop him."

Jim covered his eyes. "Nothing can stop him. Not the book, not anything."

"If you'd shown the book to others, let them see what Micah really taught—"

"It would have made no difference. I told you about Sammael's secret army. He's been Converting men for a year, training them to obey without question."

Converting them against the very rules he espoused. Gwen clasped her stomach, seized by the growing blood-hunger and the deep, frightening anger that urged her to punish the one who had failed her.

"You've made a terrible mistake, Jim," she said. "Sammael will never keep his word. And now…"

Now there wasn't a chance in hell that the members of Pax would turn against Sammael. Unless she could get out of here, find the book, make them listen…

"You've got to help me escape, Jim."

He looked up, eyes wild. "I can't. It isn't possible."

"It must be." She rose and advanced on him, calling on the *strigoi* power she had disregarded for so long. "Do you think Angela will thank you for letting Sammael murder people—not just Kyril and his enforcers, but protégés who've been Converted against their will? I have to get that book back, Jim."

And I have to be with Dorian when the madness comes.

Jim stared at her, shaking. And then, like Dorian, he fled without another word, taking her hope with him.

CHAPTER TWENTY-TWO

THE GUARDSMEN STOOD in soldiers' ranks, wearing simple uniforms of plain white shirts, khaki trousers and low workman's boots. Fifty men ready to hang on Sammael's every word, fifty valiant warriors trained to eliminate the abominations they might once have called brothers. And at the foot of the dais, bound between the two strongest guards, was Dorian Black.

Sammael might have felt pity. For a time, Dorian had served him well. The fact that he had been kept in ignorance of Pax's true mission had not lessened his value; in that way he was no different than the novices and new mediants, who had not yet earned the right to know all that Sammael's visions had shown him.

But Dorian had failed in his service…failed in a way that defied Sammael's law. Had it not been for the new vision, Black would be dead. Had it not been for Dorian's bond to Gwen Murphy, he would not be standing in this room, his head bowed to Sammael's rule, a willing tool to be wielded by the righteous until he was of no further use to the great cause.

"You will let Gwen live," he'd said, facing Sammael with a wan face and dead eyes. "If I do your will, no harm must come to her."

Naturally Sammael had agreed. It was easy to bargain with a desperate man, easy to convince him that the agreement would be kept.

Because Dorian dared not believe otherwise. He could see no other way out for himself or his protégée, nothing but the blackness of death. Already he suffered. His black hair was soaked with perspiration, his exposed skin jumped and twitched with numerous tics, and his eyes…his eyes were haunted not with fear but a profound and terrible sadness.

Yet no sorrow, no reluctance, would keep the dark angel from fulfilling his purpose. Sammael knew that victory was at hand.

He straightened, casting his gaze over his holy army. "You are the chosen ones," he said, his voice carrying like a trumpet. "You are the avenging angels, sent by Heaven to destroy the wickedness Cain brought into the world. Tonight you shall act without hesitation, without doubt, for you know your mission is blessed by Micah himself." Sammael raised the leather-bound book above his head. "'Go forth and destroy all that which is evil, for then shalt thou enter the Kingdom of Heaven.'"

The Guardsmen were quiet, but their eyes shone with unquestioning belief. Sammael smiled, letting their energy flow into him like sacramental wine.

"Our brothers within the factions have already done their part," he continued. "Tonight they have drawn our enemies together with promises of pleasure and beauty. There shall be no expectation of attack. Evidence has been planted that will lay suspicion for the raids upon the human gangs. The police have been bribed and will not interfere." He lifted his eyes heavenward. "Tonight you, my warriors, will enter the lion's den and pull the fangs of the Lord's enemies."

A subtle movement rippled among the men, a wave like the unfurling of mighty wings.

Once again Sammael raised the book of Micah, turning slowly so that everyone in the room could see the symbol of the cleansing flame. "Tonight," he said, "is only the beginning. Our brothers from across the oceans will carry word of our victory to the ends of the earth. And Micah shall at last see his dreams fulfilled."

The flutter of invisible wings became a storm of sound. One of Sammael's own men raised his voice in a shout, and the others followed, until the room echoed with their acclamations.

"Sammael!" they cried. "Sammael!"

Only Dorian was silent. He lifted his head with great effort, as if the yoke of Heaven lay on his shoulders.

Sammael climbed down from the dais and faced his servant. "Remember," he said gently. "Tonight you earn the life of your protégée. Fight well, and even if you fall, she will survive."

He gave Dorian no further opportunity for speech but gestured for the guards to take him away. Now they all must wait. But the waiting would be brief, and when the battle was over, it was not Micah whose triumph would be remembered.

Your words will be erased and forgotten, Sammael thought, *though it takes the extermination of every* strigoi *on the earth.*

THE DOOR WAS UNLOCKED when Gwen tested it for the hundredth time. The knob gave under her fingers, and she stepped carefully into the empty corridor, expecting a trap.

There was none. No one came to stop her; she heard no sound, saw no movement, nothing to slow her progress as she made her way along the corridor to the staircase.

She paused, reaching out with all her senses. The air itself carried a message of emptiness, as if almost everyone had left the building.

It's begun, Gwen thought.

Moving quickly, she descended the stairs. The first floor was a maze of corridors and offices; one of them was Sammael's. And somewhere in this building she would find Micah's book, the key to stopping Sammael once and for all.

But the night had already come. Sammael was on his way to attack Kyril. And if her worst fears were true, Dorian was with him.

She ran lightly toward the back of the building, mentally re-constructing her first visit to Pax. She reached the door she thought was Sammael's and opened it slowly. The room was dark, its high bookshelves looming like guardians over the paper-strewn desk.

Let it be here, Gwen prayed.

She began with the desk, testing the locked drawers. It was a simple matter to break the locks; Sammael clearly hadn't expected that any of his loyal followers would attempt to look at whatever he kept in the desk.

But the book wasn't there. Nor did Gwen find it among the books on the shelves, or anywhere else she could think of.

Maybe it was somewhere else in the building, in any one of the dozens of other rooms she had never seen.

Or maybe he's destroyed it.

A jolt of fear almost stopped her. If the book was lost...

You can't let yourself think of that now. Just keep looking. It's the best chance you've got.

She left Sammael's office and retraced her steps down the corridor to the reception area. She had only the slightest hope of finding the person she sought, but Vida was still behind the desk, typing a letter on her Remington.

"Vida," Gwen said.

The young woman looked up, startled and wary.

"Gwen! What are you doing out of your room?"

"Someone left the door unlocked," Gwen said. She walked toward Vida, getting ready for a scuffle. "Where is the book?"

Vida rose, her hands rubbing at the front of her skirt. "I don't know what you're talking about."

"Micah's book. The one Jim gave to Sammael."

Genuine puzzlement crossed Vida's face. "I don't know about any book," she said. "Gwen—"

"Where is Sammael?"

Vida looked over her shoulder, as if she expected reinforcements. "He's...not here."

"I know he's going to attack Kyril," Gwen said, moving closer. "Did he take Dorian with him?"

With a quiet sob, Vida sank back into her chair. "They've gone," she said. "They're going to kill everyone."

"Tell me where they are, Vida. Quickly."

Divided loyalties warred behind Vida's eyes. "They've... gone to Kyril's hotel."

Gwen released her breath sharply. "Swear to me you won't tell anyone that I've escaped."

The young woman shivered. "Were we wrong? Were we really so wrong?"

"It wasn't you, Vida. It was always Sammael." Gwen strode for the door, leaving Vida staring after her. There was no more time to search for a book she might never find. Only one thing was important now. And if she failed, at least she could say that she'd gone down fighting.

DORIAN SHIVERED, the fever of oncoming night sending violent chills through his body. The sun had already vanished beneath the unseen horizon. The sky still held a trace of deep blue light, but soon that, too, would be gone.

He swung his head from left to right and back again, looking for Sammael. The Pax leader had remained with the group of two dozen men who were to attack Kyril's hotel; he had been moving among them, touching a shoulder here, speaking a few quiet words there. His followers hardly needed the encouragement. Their eyes mirrored Sammael's zealotry, and they could not be turned from their purpose.

Once Dorian had been a soldier, like them. Day by day, year after year, he had permitted himself the luxury of unquestioning obedience, slowly destroying himself a little more with every act of violence. He had begun the final descent into madness on the day he had chosen to betray his master.

Then he had met Gwen Murphy. He had sensed without any real understanding that she alone might become his antidote to the monster within. He had used her, afraid of what he might do and yet unable to let her go.

When it had seemed that she was gone—when he'd believed her truly lost—once again he'd sought salvation from something outside himself. He'd been blind to Pax's true nature, too ready to hope that he could yet serve some higher purpose in memory of the one he'd failed so badly.

Now there was no escape. Soon, very soon, he would no longer be able to resist the call of the night. Sammael believed he would fight alongside Pax's soldiers as one of them, driven by his desire to protect Gwen. But Sammael didn't know what he was about to become. Sammael didn't realize that his own life was about to end.

Pax's fervent soldiers—Abdiel and Balthial, Cassiel and Camarion, Mihr and Nisroc and the others—had readied their arsenal and now awaited Sammael's command. Dorian's escort fell in around him. They left headquarters silently through a back door, attracting no attention from the oblivious humans or female *strigoi* who administered Pax's daily business. A light snow was falling, lending an air of peace to an evening soon to be stained with blood.

Dorian's guards moved closer to him, watching him narrowly from the corners of their eyes. Like Sammael, they had no idea what awaited them.

The snow was falling more heavily when they reached Broadway. Sammael's men scattered. Some—anonymous in their ordinary street clothes—set about clearing the street of human bystanders, while others flowed like shadows closer to the hotel. The world was a muffling curtain of white. Sammael stared up at the hotel's second-story windows, watching for a signal.

It came suddenly, a windowpane sliding open to the chill wind and then closing again. Sammael nodded to the men beside him, who ran across the street. Dorian's guards followed, half dragging him between them.

He could have cast them aside without a thought, torn out their throats and split them open from chest to belly. The monstrous thing clawing at his insides howled for blood. He fought it step by step, promising it that soon it would have its fill.

I couldn't let you die, Gwen, the last rags of his rational mind insisted. *Forgive me.*

The hotel doorman was absent when Sammael and the others passed through. The gilded lobby was almost deserted, without a single clerk behind the desk to welcome new arrivals. The men Sammael had sent ahead emerged from doorways and corridors, disguised as ordinary human guests in their plain overcoats and hats. One of them joined Sammael and spoke in a brief whisper.

"They are in the grand ballroom," Sammael said to the others with him. "Take your positions."

The soldiers faded away. A bellhop who happened to be crossing the lobby froze, his eyes wide with understanding, and dived behind the bell desk. Dorian's escorts herded him toward a wide corridor. He shook them off, staring at first one and then the other until they retreated.

The corridor opened onto a half-dozen rooms, all with doors firmly closed. Sammael led them to the end of the hallway, marked by a pair of ornate double doors, and stood with his ear pressed to the wood.

Dorian could no longer detect the muted colors of the corridor's wallpaper or thick pile carpet. Everything was veiled in red. A deep pain had started in his belly and was working its way through his chest and into his shoulders as if his bones would burst through his skin. His fingers had become claws, his teeth a tiger's fangs. His blood ran hot and then cold. He stared at Sammael, remembering limbs snapping in his hands and blood painting alley walls.

This isn't over, a half-familiar voice whispered. *You still owe me. Don't give up. Don't give up without a fight.*

He rid himself of the distant memory and shoved past the guards, until he stood directly behind Sammael, muscles coiled for attack.

The booming roar of gunfire echoed through the door, freezing Dorian in midstrike. Sammael turned to meet his stare. There was no surprise in his eyes, no horror at the creature that crouched before him.

"It's begun," he said. "Come, my angel, and kill."

He flung open the doors and ran into the room beyond. Dorian raced after him, the inside of his skull reverberating with the screams of dying *strigoi.*

Kyril and his vassals, their tuxedos spattered with blood, crouched barricaded behind a flimsy wall of overturned tables and chairs. Terrified women in expensive gowns cowered in the corners. A dead human bartender sprawled over his counter, and a half-dozen male vampires lay shot through head or heart on the elaborately figured carpet.

A fresh spray of bullets laced the air as Dorian sprang across the no-man's-land between the door and Kyril's flimsy refuge. Dorian felt the sting as the bullets struck him in the arms and legs, but the pain was no more to him than the bites of fleas. He leaped over the table, knocking vassals and lieutenants aside like bowling pins.

Then he was facing Kyril, and all the hatred burning in his belly broke like a festering wound. He lashed out, striking Kyril to the ground with one blow. Kyril's enforcers tackled him. He twitched his shoulders and they fell away, eyes wide with shock.

Kill, the master's voice demanded. *Kill.*

This one was not the true enemy. This one did not hold *her* life in his hands. But he was here, and helpless, and the other was gone. Dorian caught Kyril by the throat and lifted him off his feet.

"Dorian!" Kyril choked, his breath coming in short gasps. "I'll give you…anything…anything you want…."

Dorian tightened his grip and shook Kyril like a rat. The vertebrae in Kyril's neck began to grate under Dorian's fingers.

"Dorian!"

The woman's voice, sharp as a switchblade, penetrated Dorian's frenzy. He turned his head slowly. A woman stood exposed in the center of the room, her red hair tangled above a pale, freckled face, green eyes wide and desperate.

"Dorian," the woman said. "Don't—"

A single Tommy gun stuttered its message of death. The girl dived for the floor. Dorian released Kyril and leaped the barricade. Bullets hummed past his ears. He swept the girl up in his arms, raced across the room to the bar and set her down behind it.

"Dorian," the girl said, rising to her knees. "We've got to get away from here."

He listened, hearing the words but not understanding. The smell of blood was in his nose, drowning every other scent. When the gunfire began again, he pushed the girl down and rose to his feet, searching for his prey.

Kyril still cowered behind his barricade. The other stood at the end of the room, shielded by a quartet of *strigoi* in pale shirts and trousers.

"Kill them!" the dark one shouted.

Small hands tugged at his leg. "Fight it, Dorian!"

"Kill!"

The voices crashed together inside his skull, burning a searing red labyrinth through his brain. The monster roared and screamed. The girl's grip was like a chain holding it back, denying its need for blood.

He turned on her, snarling. He lifted his hand. She stared at him, unafraid.

Gwen.

His muscles locked in midswing. His body went rigid, paralyzed by the chaos of memories. Pain cascaded through his nerves. The monster clawed at his eyes, blinding him. It grew larger and larger, crushing his organs, forcing the air out of his lungs. It began to punch through his skin, each blow more powerful than the last.

Gwen.

He carried the name with him into the blackness.

THEY BROUGHT GWEN BACK to Pax headquarters, bound and gagged and suspended like a slab of meat between two of the less badly injured guards. She could see very little beyond the terrible image burned into her mind: Dorian sprawled at her feet, his eyes turned up in his head, jerking in a seizure like a dog gone rabid.

He's alive, she told herself. *He must be.*

But she had no evidence of it. She'd had the sense that Sammael's soldiers had left the hotel soon after Dorian had fallen, and that they had been victorious over Kyril's unprepared followers. Surely they wouldn't have left Dorian behind.

Unless they killed him.

Gwen stumbled as her escorts reached the rear of the import building and pushed her through ahead of them. She caught a whiff of chaos, men and women moving quickly through the halls, anxious faces and cries of shock. Before she could gain any sense of what was happening, the guards forced her down the stairs and into the interrogation room they had used before. They threw her to the cold cement floor and left her in darkness.

She'd lost all track of time when they came for her again. The guards were new; they removed her gag and dragged her into the corridor, pulling her off her feet whenever she began to find her footing.

He's not dead. I would know.

Would she? Hadn't she deliberately severed the bond between them?

He needed me, and I couldn't reach him. He needed me.

Sick with helpless anger, she struggled to find a single thread of hope. Her guards increased their pace as they led her down another set of stairs that ended at a heavy steel door. It opened under the taller man's push to reveal a short hallway and a second wooden door carved with the triangle and flame.

The room behind the door was no ordinary basement. It covered a space equivalent to a dozen large rooms on the floor above. Heavy pylons supported the ceiling, and the walls were painted with scenes of sword-wielding angels battling demons depicted with jagged fangs and claws sprouting from their fingertips.

At the head of the room was a dais, and upon that was a podium draped with red-and-white cloth marked with Pax's symbol. Golden goblets stood on a side table. Ranged behind the podium were six figures in white robes, their faces obscured by red-trimmed hoods. Each held a blazing torch in his hand. To either side of the room, Sammael's soldiers stood at attention.

Gwen's guards stopped just inside the door and waited stiffly as if anticipating a command to proceed. Gwen searched every corner of the room for Dorian. She couldn't find him. But she knew something was about to happen, something she dreaded with all her heart.

She'd barely finished the thought when a man stepped onto

the dais and took a position behind the lectern. He, too, wore white robes, but his head was uncovered, and a single beam of electric light spilled over his face and shoulders, outlining his features in sharp relief. He removed the book he had shown her on the plane from his robes and placed it on the lectern.

"My children," he said. "Tonight the Lord has turned His face away from us. Tonight we have failed."

A low, collective groan sighed through the room, seeming to come from nowhere and everywhere at once.

"Tonight," Sammael said, his voice hoarse with anger, "the demon Christof and his creatures have escaped us. Many of our brothers have been lost. Our holy work is incomplete."

There was another ripple of sound as men shifted and shoes scuffed the concrete floor. Sammael stared down at his audience as if he would gladly have condemned each of them to a slow and painful death.

"It is true," he said, "that Kyril and most of his acolytes have been neutralized. But that is not enough. Not nearly enough." He slammed his hands on the podium. "Ask yourselves now why your resolve has failed you, why the Lord denied you victory. Ask where you have failed to follow Micah's plan. Fall on your knees and beg forgiveness."

The condemnation in Sammael's words descended like the crack of a whip. The figures on the dais remained still and silent. Flames crackled, and somewhere above, floorboards creaked.

One of the soldiers standing between the pylons dropped to his knees. The others followed in a ragged rhythm until every one of them was crouched in an attitude of humility and repentance.

Sammael lifted his hands, palms down, and his lips moved in a soundless chant. "All is not lost, my children," he said. "The time has come for renewal according to Micah's law." He opened the book lying on the podium. "Micah said, 'He shall be sinless who gives his life in the pursuit of good. The sons of angels shall slaughter the unbelievers and bathe in their blood.'" He raised his head and smiled. "We shall be cleansed. The Lord will look upon us with favor again. He—"

"You're a liar, Sammael," Gwen said.

Fifty pairs of eyes turned toward her in astonishment. The white-robed figures stirred. Sammael lowered his head and met her gaze, his mouth twitching loose from its smile.

"Micah never said any of those things," she said, addressing the audience. "He—"

The blow came from the side, striking her temple and knocking her to the floor. Streaks of light bounced around inside her skull.

"Get her up," Sammael said. Fingers dug into the muscles of her arms, jerking her back to her feet.

"Behold the fruit of evil," Sammael said. "Behold one who has been robbed of all hope of salvation by the monster that dwells within each of us." He beckoned to Gwen's guards, who dragged her to the foot of the dais.

Sammael descended, his robes flowing about him. With the gentlest of touches, he laid his hand on Gwen's hair.

"Poor child," he said. "The madness of your corrupter had blackened your soul." He raised his voice again. "Such is the price the Lord exacts from all of us," he said. "Madness, damnation…or the righteous power of the sword."

Gwen twisted her head away. "I'm not the one who's crazy," she said. "Where is Dorian?"

Slowly Sammael's smile returned, as evil an expression as Gwen had ever seen. "You will see him very soon," he said. He gestured to the men holding her. "Keep her quiet."

They carried her away from the dais. She opened her mouth to speak, and one of them pushed a wad of cloth into her mouth, nearly choking her.

Dorian is alive, she thought, hardly feeling the brutal touch of her keepers. *He's alive.*

A renewed hush fell over the room. Sammael stepped onto the dais and faced the white-robed men. Each of them bowed to him solemnly and filed off the stage, taking their smoking torches with them. A contingent of Sammael's soldiers followed them. They disappeared through the dark rectangle of a doorway behind the stage.

Every face was turned toward the dais. Gwen's pulse hammered in her throat. A terrible premonition leached the feeling from her arms and legs. Five minutes passed before the first of the robed men returned, followed by four soldiers herding several slumped figures between them.

One of them was Angela. The second was Kyril. And the third was Dorian, weighted with chains and dressed in rags, his face not even remotely human. His gaze swept over the room, and his lips peeled back from his teeth.

It's still the dark of the moon, Gwen thought. *God help us.*

The soldiers marched their prisoners to the area just below the podium. The white-robes took the goblets from the table and formed a loose circle around the guards and captives. Sammael watched from above, his expression gone from rage to rapture.

The silence became a live thing, eager to escape its confinement. A low, thrumming chant began among the robed men, a swaying, hypnotic cadence that penetrated to the center of Gwen's body. The soldiers on the sidelines rose as one. Sammael descended from the dais, and for the first time Gwen saw what he held in his hand: a knife, its blade curved and shining by firelight.

Gwen surged against the arms that held her. Her guards forced her down. Sammael circled the robed men three times counterclockwise, each step measured and precise. He stopped in front of the podium again, the knife's blade pointed toward the ceiling.

"Micah," he said "look down upon us. Intercede for us. Accept this sacrifice and renew our purpose."

He turned the knife around and walked between the white-robes, coming to stand before Angela. The young woman was half-unconscious between the soldiers who held her, oblivious to the glittering knife. In one smooth motion Sammael sliced down, stabbing between Angela's neck and shoulder, nearly severing her head.

Gwen bit hard into the cloth between her teeth. Angela's body fell, spraying an arc of blood over the watchers and the other captives. Kyril cursed, real horror on his face. Almost immediately a white-robe knelt in the blood and dipped his goblet into the spray. He carried it to Sammael, who drank the offered libation. When he was finished, his lips were as red as the drops spattered across his face.

Unable to breathe, Gwen fixed her gaze on Dorian. She thought at first that he hadn't moved, but then she saw the direction of his stare. He was looking down at Angela, his expression as blank as a featureless mask.

Sammael didn't so much as glance at him. He stood over Angela's body as the other five white-robes dipped their own goblets and drank, letting blood spill onto their robes.

"Bring the girl," Sammael said.

Gwen had just a moment to prepare before she was jerked up again and the gag was ripped from her mouth. Her guards marched her to the center of the room. Her battered pumps squelched in congealing blood.

Sammael grabbed her by the hair and pulled her against him, pressing the edge of the stained knife to her throat.

"You may still have an easier death, Miss Murphy," he said, "if your lover finishes his work."

Gwen spat threads of cloth from her mouth. "What did you do to him?"

"Nothing. He is lost in his madness. That is why I require you to make him understand what he must do."

"You made him kill, you bastard."

The blade nicked her skin. "That is precisely the problem. He declined to fulfill his purpose."

"Declined?" She closed her eyes. "Thank God."

"I doubt He can hear you." Hot liquid flowed over her skin. "You should pray that Dorian will."

She gasped involuntarily as the knife sawed deeper. Movement flashed at the corner of her vision: Dorian shifting among his chains, swinging his head blindly from side to side. He wasn't looking at her. He hardly seemed to notice she was there.

"One last chance," Sammael said, licking his lips. "Tell him to kill Kyril."

It took all the discipline Gwen could find to keep from calling Dorian's name. She wanted to know he was still alive in there, somehow…still capable of resisting the horror that would destroy him.

"I won't help you," she said, no longer caring if the knife cut her to the bone. "Listen to me, all of you!" she shouted. "Sammael has made a mockery of Micah's words. Micah believed in peace, not war! He—"

Sammael hissed in fury. He cut deep, slicing through muscle and tendon. Gwen choked and began to fall. Dorian snapped the shackles that bound his feet and arms, flinging the loose chains in deadly arcs.

The chaos was immediate. Sammael retreated and was instantly surrounded by a half-dozen soldiers. Kyril leaped out of the way as a flying chain caught a white-robe full across the face and sent him spinning to the ground. The men who had watched from the sidelines sprang to their feet and charged the dais.

Then Gwen was in the crook of Dorian's arm as he continued to attack—still blind, still lost in madness. Her throat was already beginning to heal, and she could finally breathe again. With the healing came clarity. She focused her attention on the podium and the book that lay there, forgotten.

"Dorian!" she shouted above the screams and pounding feet. "Free Kyril!"

She prayed that Dorian would hear him. He did. He swung out with his chains, clearing the space around them, and made for Kyril. The faction leader shrank away in terror.

"Kyril!" Gwen said sharply, knowing they had only a matter of seconds. "Take that book on the podium and get out of here. It's the only way to stop Sammael. Whatever you do, don't let him get it back!"

Kyril stared at her with incomprehension, but when Dorian tore free the ropes that bound the faction leader, Kyril jumped onto the dais and seized the book. He sprinted across the room toward the stairs and the wooden door.

Let it be unlocked, Gwen thought. *Let him do what I told him….*

With an impressive burst of speed, Kyril managed to stay ahead of the soldiers who'd turned to follow him. He opened the door and raced through.

What he did on the other side of that door was beyond Gwen's control. Ten of Sammael's soldiers continued to pursue Kyril, while the rest surrounded her and Dorian in a double circle bristling with weapons. The *strigoi* Dorian had injured lay unconscious or moaning in pain; Sammael stood apart and untouched, wearing the look of a man who's been trapped in a nightmare of his own creation.

"Take him!" he cried, his voice shaking with rage. "Shoot him if you must, but do not kill him!" He addressed two of his bodyguards. "Return the book to me. Fail and die." At last he turned to Gwen. "You have made a fatal mistake. Your death will be far from painless."

A pair of *strigoi* grabbed Gwen and held her, while the others closed in around Dorian. He roared and spun about like a wounded panther. Three men shot him at once, in both legs and one shoulder.

Gwen screamed. Dorian's legs buckled. He tried to rise again, but the damage was too great. The men swooped in on him, battering him with their feet and fists. Gwen was hauled behind the dais, through the rear door and into an unlit corridor. Her guards nearly pushed her down the narrow steps at the end, and she barely caught herself from falling.

There was another steel door at the base of the stairs. The guards opened it and threw her into the room beyond. She was plunged into a darkness so profound that it took several minutes for her eyes to pick out the details of the room.

But there were none. Four walls, an icy concrete floor ten feet square…no cot, no chair, no color save for long-dried streaks and splashes of blood.

Gwen put her back to one of the walls and folded her arms across her chest. Her skin was hot, blazing like a brand at her neck. No sound penetrated the chamber, no hint of whatever might be happening in that grotesque parody of a place of worship. She sagged to the floor, praying that Dorian might somehow escape, regain his sanity, do what she could not.

The steel door swung open with a groan. Dorian was hurled into the room. The door clanged shut again as he landed hard against the wall.

"Dorian!" Gwen scrambled to her feet and dropped to her knees beside him. His shirt and trousers were gone; his back and chest were scored with deep, ragged welts and cuts that had laid open his skin to the raw muscle beneath. His hair was not black, but red; the bullet wounds in his legs and shoulder oozed as if someone had repeatedly jabbed at them with something wide and sharp.

Gwen hovered over him, afraid to touch him lest she cause more pain. "Dorian. Look at me!"

He moved, his bones pulling his skin taut as if his flesh would burst. He raised his head. His face was like a skull, gaunt and staring and striped with terrible cuts. His teeth were washed in scarlet. His eyes held no recognition, their gray irises absorbed in unrelieved black.

"Dorian," Gwen whispered.

He flung out his arm, catching her across the shoulders. The blow sent her skidding to the far wall. Her head struck concrete, and she saw and heard nothing for a lost span of time.

When she opened her eyes again, she knew Dorian was going to kill her.

CHAPTER TWENTY-THREE

THERE WAS NO FORM, no shape, no substance, to the cage that held him. The world was agony and violence, flickering in piercing light and absolute darkness.

One other shared this place of suffering with him. He could not see it well; the bringers of pain had slashed at his face so many times that blood seeped continuously into his eyes.

You must be punished, the voices commanded.

You are unclean.

There is only one way to redeem yourself.

The one responsible is waiting. Kill it, and you will be free.

The one responsible. The one who crouched in the corner, faceless and nameless and so easily destroyed.

He started toward it, each movement crippled with pain. The thing before him pressed against the wall and struggled to its feet.

"Dorian!"

He paused, startled by a sound that had once had meaning.

"Dorian, I know you're badly hurt. I know you can't really see me. But you have to try. You have to listen to me."

He clawed at the side of his face, scraping skin from his cheek.

The thing will try to deceive you. Do not let it.

Another step, then another. The thing's breath rasped in and out, in and out.

"They want you to kill me," it said softly, forcing him to stop and listen. "They've tortured you, Dorian. They think they've driven you so far into the madness that it won't matter who you kill."

He lowered his head, tracking the sounds until they began to form a pattern he could almost understand.

Female. It is female.

"You can fight this," the female said. "You must, Dorian."

Dorian. A name. An identity he had almost forgotten.

"I made a terrible mistake," she said. "I was so determined to break our bond that I didn't realize how important it was to both of us." Her body trembled. "I was wrong, Dorian. A bond like ours can't just be broken with some concoction of water and herbs."

He took another step toward her. His hands ached to curl around her neck, his teeth to tear into the soft flesh at her throat.

"We have to save the bond, Dorian," she said. "We have to rebuild what I've destroyed. We have to find the heart of the monster and heal it."

He stopped for a moment, bewildered. But the other voice was stronger. *She will deceive you. Close your ears. Do what must be done.*

Dorian reached out to seize her. She didn't shrink away.

"I understand now," she said. "You can't escape the monster, because you can't escape yourself. It's made of all the things you've done, Dorian…all the things you hate yourself for, all the regret, all the guilt. They won't let you go."

Dorian's fingers curled around her fragile arm. One jerk would shatter it. But her face shone in the darkness, pure and beautiful and bright with revelation.

"I didn't know how I could help you before," she said. "I was blind. Now I can see."

A shooting pain filled Dorian's skull. He battered at his temples, trying to drive it out.

She caught his hands and held them. "Forgive yourself," she whispered. "End the punishment. There is good in you. So much good. You would have given your life for Mitch, for me. You were ready to work for peace, even though Pax deceived you." She brought her face closer to his. "There is still hope, Dorian. For you, for me, for the world."

All sensation went out of Dorian's legs. He fell. The female fell with him. She put her arms around him.

"There's only one thing in the world stronger than pain, stronger than guilt, even stronger than death. I'll stay with you as long as you need me, as long as we live." She pressed her lips to his ear. "I love you, Dorian Black."

GWEN WAITED, PRAYING THAT she'd reached him with the words she'd waited so long to say. At first she thought she'd failed once again. But then something changed. Dorian raised his head, and in his eyes she saw the war taking place in his brain, man against monster.

"Yes," she whispered. "Come back to me, Dorian."

He got to his knees and stared into her face as if he were trying to memorize her features. He lifted his hand, and his fingers grazed her cheek.

"Gwen," he said hoarsely.

"Yes." She covered her hand with his. "Gwen."

A tremor ran through his body. He leaned closer until his face was only an inch from hers. His hot breath touched her lips. Then his mouth came down on hers, hard at first, then slowly gentling.

She returned the kiss with the same gentleness, willing him to feel her love and desire. She felt a sudden shift in her mind, as if a key had been turned in a lock.

And then he was there with her in that place where the bond had lain broken and empty. His struggle was hers; she fought her instinctive fear and welcomed both monster and man, accepting without judgment.

I forgive you, Dorian, she thought. *Now it's time to forgive yourself.*

He pulled back. Bewildered astonishment flickered behind his gaze. She heard his unspoken question.

Yes. You can, she answered.

Dorian turned to face the wall. He placed both palms on the filthy concrete and stood, the muscles of his arms and back flexing under the healing skin. Then he went to the door, pressing his weight against it and feeling along the seams.

"Get out?" he asked.

"Yes," Gwen said, going to stand beside him. "But it's steel, Dorian. Even you—"

He pounded the metal with his fists. The door shook. He leaned into it. The door groaned and swung open.

A young male *strigoi* in soldier's garb stood just outside, a heavy key in one hand and a Tommy gun in the other. He quickly scrambled out of reach, body tensed to run.

Gwen stepped in front of Dorian, but the soldier made no attempt to raise his gun. "Who are you?" she demanded.

The young man watched Dorian as if he expected an attack at any second. "My name is Taharial," he said. "I'm here to let you go."

Keeping a tight grip on Dorian's arm, Gwen looked beyond him into the dark corridor. "Who sent you?"

"No one."

"Why do you want to help us?"

"Because Sammael…" He wet his lips. "I saw what Sammael did. It was evil."

A trap, Gwen thought. But why would Sammael make such a move if he thought Dorian was going to kill her anyway?

"Where is he?" she asked.

"They've left the great hall. I didn't go with them."

"And Kyril?"

"I don't know."

"You haven't seen the book? The book Kyril took?"

He shook his head. Gwen glanced up at Dorian. "We have to find Kyril," she said.

Dorian met her gaze. He inclined his head in the slightest of nods. The monster was under control.

"You don't have to be afraid of Dorian," she told Taharial. "He's all right now. Can you lead us out of this place?"

Taharial nodded, though he never quite took his eyes off Dorian. Instead of returning to the room he'd called the great hall, he turned in the other direction and led Gwen and Dorian up a narrow staircase to the floor above. He paused at the top of the stairs, listening.

"Something's wrong," he said. "Strangers are in the building."

Strangers. The survivors of Kyril's gang, come for revenge?

"Where?" she asked.

"Near the back entrance, I think."

"Then that's where we have to go. Taharial, Kyril has Sammael's copy of Micah's book. We have to find it, so that we can prove that Sammael's been misleading everyone in Pax."

Taharial clearly didn't understand, but he didn't question. "I'll help you," he said. "Come this way."

Taking a series of narrow service corridors, they worked their way through the building. Soon Gwen could hear distant sounds of fighting, muffled shouts and gunfire. Dorian pushed ahead of her, dogging Taharial like a half-tame wolf.

When it was clear that they were approaching the area of conflict, Taharial checked his gun and slowed his pace to a crawl. They had just turned another corner when a man in a dark suit careened into view. He raised his gun. Taharial raised his in response. Dorian snarled.

"Stop!" Gwen cried. She took a chance. "We're not with Pax. They've been holding us prisoner."

The man lowered his gun. "Black?"

"Pietro," Dorian said, his voice a rough whisper. "Where is Christof?"

Christof. The leader of the opposing vampire faction, and Kyril's deadly enemy. The one Sammael's soldiers had failed to destroy.

"We aren't your enemies," Gwen said, raising her hands. "We know what Sammael tried to do tonight. We're trying to stop him from ever doing it again."

Pietro's eyes narrowed. "You're Gwen Murphy," he said.

"Yes."

"Christof told us to find you. The human warned us about the attack, and—"

"What human?"

"A man called Jim." Pietro glared at Dorian. "You're both to come with me."

Taharial hesitated. Dorian lowered his head bristling. Gwen knew the situation might explode at any moment.

"We'll come," she said. "If you'll guarantee that you won't harm Dorian or Taharial."

Pietro grunted. "We were ordered not to hurt you. Hurry up."

With a calming glance at Dorian, Gwen started forward. Dorian hovered at her shoulder, his unformed thoughts filled with suspicion.

It must be near dawn, Gwen thought. "What time is it?" she asked Taharial.

But he was no longer behind them. Pietro followed her gaze and cursed.

"Come on," he said.

They continued into a wide corridor, where they passed a pair of Sammael's soldiers lying dead on the floor. Gwen noticed that the sounds of gunfire had ceased. Dorian continued to radiate hostility, but he made no attempt to act on his feelings. The slight stiffening of his body warned her just before they turned another corner and found themselves facing a dozen armed men in black enforcers' coats.

Pietro stopped, his gun pointed toward the floor. "Tell Christof I've got them," he said.

One of the men turned and disappeared. The others stared at Dorian with less than friendly intent. Gwen planted herself in front of him.

"We aren't your enemies," she repeated. "Whatever quarrels you may have had with Dorian in the past, he's on your side now. We—"

There was a commotion among the enforcers, and Jim emerged from the crowd.

"Gwen!"

"Jim! Are you all right?"

He approached her slowly. "Thank God," he said. "Thank God you're both still alive." He stopped several feet away. "I told them you had to be protected because you knew what Pax really was. I was afraid—"

"We're all right," Gwen said. She searched the young man's ashen face. "Pietro said it was you who warned Christof of the attack."

Jim rubbed his hand over his deeply shadowed eyes. "I realized…I was wrong about the book," he said. "I had to do something. Sammael never suspected that I would…betray him after…"

He trailed off, but Gwen completed his thought. *After you'd given him the book to save Angela's life.*

"She's dead, isn't she?" he asked.

"I'm sorry, Jim. I wish we could have saved her."

Jim turned away. "You were right," he whispered. "Sammael never would have kept his word." Tears welled in his eyes. "Did she…die quickly?"

The truth would be too much for the poor kid to bear. "Yes," she said. "She didn't suffer."

Jim whispered a prayer. "I wanted to be there, with her," he said. "But I left to warn Christof's people as soon as I knew how Sammael planned to attack his headquarters."

Gwen wondered why he'd chosen Christof over Kyril, but there was no time for such unimportant questions. "You led them back here," she said.

Jim nodded, though he still wouldn't meet her gaze. "I tried to explain that not everyone in Pax wanted to kill them. I asked them not to hurt anyone here unless they were attacked."

Gwen remembered the two dead soldiers they had passed in the corridor. None of Pax's misguided civilian *strigoi* and humans deserved that fate. "Sammael didn't suspect what was happening. He had most of his surviving soldiers with him." She tried to focus her thoughts on the facts. "They'd taken Kyril prisoner during the raid and intended for Dorian to kill him, but Dorian fought them, and Kyril got away. Have you seen him?"

"I heard that Christof captured him."

Gwen reached behind herself, feeling for Dorian's hand. His fingers closed over hers. "Is Kyril still alive?" she asked.

"I…I think so."

"This is very important, Jim. Did he have a book with him? Micah's book?"

Jim lifted his head. "I don't understand."

Gwen's stomach clenched. *Please don't let the book be lost.* "He has Sammael's copy," she said. "It's still the only way to prove that Sammael's been lying about Micah all along."

With a look of sudden comprehension, Jim returned to the enforcers and spoke to them in low, urgent tones. There were several shrugs and head shakes, but one man raised his voice.

"Christof has a book," he said. "I think he took it from Kyril."

Gwen gave a silent prayer of thanks. "Where are the rest of the Pax members?" she asked.

"They are trapped," a new voice said. "Along with their leader."

A *strigoi* in a well-cut suit pushed through the mob of enforcers, his bearing proclaiming him their leader. He paused to glance at Jim and then looked pointedly at Dorian. "Black," he said, "you are fortunate in your friends. If not for this human's intercession…"

"I'm Gwen Murphy," Gwen said. "Dorian is ill. He can't speak for himself at the moment, but I assure you that we're on your side."

"So Jim insisted." Christof frowned at Gwen. "You're the reporter. How did you become Black's protégée?"

"It's a long story. Suffice it to say that he was trying to save me from Kyril." She held Christof's stare, unblinking. "I understand that you have Kyril in custody."

His frown deepened. "You asked about a book."

"Yes. It's the book written by Pax's original founder. Sammael's been distorting its message of peace so that he could force his followers to kill any *strigoi* he considered the enemy."

"Message of peace?" Christof laughed. "I have never even heard of this Micah."

"And you probably never heard of Pax before today. That doesn't mean it isn't real." She squeezed Dorian's hand, feeling his protective solidity like a shield at her back. "You said Sammael and the others are trapped. What do you intend to do with them?"

The enforcers behind Christof muttered. Christof raised his hand for silence.

"I have been led to believe that not all of them are our enemies," he said. "But we can't just allow them to go free."

"You can if you know Pax will never attack you again. Sammael has his soldiers who do his bidding without question. But there are plenty of civilian members—decent humans and *strigoi,* people like Jim—who had no idea what Sammael has been planning. They believed they'd been working toward peace among the factions. You have to give them a chance."

"What chance?"

"All I need is Micah's book and an opportunity to talk to them."

"And why should I believe you, Miss Murphy? You are my enemy's protégée."

"Dorian also thought he was working for peace by infiltrating Kyril's gang as an enforcer. He fought Sammael when he realized what Sammael intended to do. You have to believe—"

Dorian stirred behind her. "Mistake," he said, his voice rough but clear. "I'm...sorry."

Christof stared at him as if he'd grown a second head. "Dorian Black...sorry?" He began to laugh again and suddenly stopped. "I have no desire to see unnecessary bloodshed," he said. "Jim has already prevented many deaths among my people. If you can convince these civilians to give themselves up peacefully, I will reconsider the situation." His expression hardened. "Sammael, however, will not be allowed to escape."

To that Gwen had no objection. Sammael was both insane and undeniably evil. And he would drag his followers down with him into death rather than surrender.

"Get me the book," she said.

Christof stared at her for a moment longer, then rejoined his men. Two of them broke from the company and disappeared into the corridor.

"I will give you one chance," Christof said, facing Gwen again. "Black will remain with us."

"*No,*" Dorian said.

Gwen kept her composure. "I need him," she said. "And I'm pretty sure he won't be willing to stay behind."

Christof scowled. Dorian rested his hands on Gwen's shoulders.

"I will go first," he said, the words calm and rational.

Gwen's legs nearly buckled with relief. She knew that the monster was still there—she felt it banging inside the cage of Dorian's will—but Dorian was winning the battle.

"Please," she said to Christof. "Even if you don't trust us, there's not much we can do to hurt you with all your men here."

The faction leader stared at Dorian, his mouth set in a hard, grim line. "Very well," he said. "Come with me."

Gwen took Dorian's hand, and they followed Jim and Christof through the shifting wall of enforcers. Another contingent of hatchet men stood near a door at the end of the corridor, their Tommy guns aimed at the wall.

"They're inside that room," Christof said. "There are no other entrances."

"The auditorium," Dorian said. He bent his head to look into Gwen's eyes. "There are many. Sammael is with them."

Gwen nodded. She didn't doubt that Dorian's senses were still keener than hers. "Christof," she said. "The book."

The men Christof had sent ahead suddenly reappeared, one of them carrying the book in one hand. He gave it to Christof, who opened it to a random page. He turned the open book toward Gwen. The coarse printing of Micah's words was obscured by thick scrawls of handwriting above and below each line, trailing off into the margins as if the writer could not contain the violence of his thoughts.

Sammael.

Gwen took the book and held it to her chest. "Proof," she said softly. She glanced toward the door. "I assume it's locked?"

Dorian slipped past her before Christof could answer. He put his hand on the latch. "I can break it," he said.

Gwen met Christof's gaze. "Stay back from the door," she

said. "Once we're inside, you mustn't interfere. I've got to get through to them so that they don't throw their lives away fighting you."

"You are very clear, Miss Murphy," Christof said. "No interference."

"Even if you hear fighting," Gwen added. "You'll have plenty of time to act if we fail."

Christof looked far from pleased. "You'd be foolish to go in unarmed. At least take guns with you."

"That will only undermine what I'm trying to achieve. You'll lose nothing if something happens to us."

With a shake of his head, Christof waved to his men, who began to back away from the door. Gwen looked up at Dorian.

"Are you ready?" she asked.

His gray eyes were as intense as she'd ever seen them, but the madness was retreating. "Yes," he said.

"All I need you to do is keep Sammael's soldiers away while I speak to the people," she said. "Only keep them away, Dorian. Don't kill them."

"I understand."

She took his face between her hands. "We'll win this fight, Dorian. We'll do it together."

He turned his lips against her palm and kissed it, a gesture so incongruously tender that it took Gwen's breath away. It was all she could do to let him go.

Dorian put his ear to the door, closed his eyes and exerted his weight as he manipulated the door latch. The door gave a loud groan and a click. Metal grated as it swung open. Immediately Dorian was through the door, Gwen right behind him.

The reaction in the auditorium was immediate. The Pax soldiers waiting just inside the room opened fire, their bullets slamming into the door where Dorian had been standing an instant before. Gwen scrambled in among the rows of chairs that occupied the central area, catching brief glimpses of startled faces as she made her way toward the front of the room.

Sammael stood on a raised stage, backed by three of his

robed acolytes. He shouted something to his soldiers, and there was more gunfire, which stopped abruptly as Dorian went to work. Gwen didn't look behind to see what he'd done, trusting that he'd only incapacitated the shooters.

She straightened when she was a few yards from the stage, the book tucked under her arm. Sammael, his hair in disarray and his bloody robes torn, stared down at her with shock and rage; he'd clearly never expected to see her alive again, let alone capable of confronting him. But he hadn't yet noticed the book. He must still believe that he was in control.

"Take them!" Sammael cried.

No one moved. Dorian stood over the half-dozen soldiers he'd overpowered, most of them unconscious and the remainder in no condition to renew the fight. If there were other soldiers in the room, they didn't respond to Sammael's command.

"Listen to me!" Sammael shouted. "They are the children of Satan, and they will steal your souls!"

Gwen looked out at his audience. She recognized a few faces scattered among the subdued company: Vida, her face wan with fear and confusion; the young *strigoi* Nathaniel, his arms folded around his rigid body; three score men and women just like them, each one fearful and bewildered, unable to understand what had become of the world to which they'd given themselves with such devotion.

It took Gwen a moment to realize that each Pax member held in his or her hand a small glass filled with a dark, viscous liquid. A similar glass sat on a chair beside Sammael up on the stage. Gwen knew that there was no time to lose.

"Friends," she called, moving to the foot of the stage. "Some of you know me. My name is Gwen Murphy. I came to Pax with my patron, Dorian Black, requesting sanctuary from those who intended to kill us. What I found was treachery."

The audience made a low, collective sound of disbelief. Gwen stared up at Sammael, who seemed suddenly shrunken and paralyzed—not so powerful or charismatic now, but only an ordinary man lost for words.

A man who wasn't about to surrender so easily.

"Tonight," she continued, raising her voice so that all could hear, "Sammael ordered his soldiers to secretly attack Kyril's and Christof's factions with the intent of killing every vampire beyond Pax's walls. Tonight he sacrificed the life of Angela, who tried to save Dorian and me when Sammael would have killed us both. He—"

"Liar!" Sammael screamed. He leaped down from the stage, his blood-soaked robes flapping about him. "These creatures are enemies to Pax, traitors who have brought the demons down upon us!"

"Only because Sammael has claimed to speak for Micah, when he's substituted his own evil philosophy in place of Micah's words of peace." She raised the book, moving toward the men and women in the nearest chairs. "See for yourselves!"

The young human closest to the book leaned forward. "I don't understand," he whispered.

Gwen heard Sammael move behind her and turned just in time. She scrambled out of his reach as he tried to snatch the book out of her hands. The three robed acolytes scattered to help their leader. Then Dorian was there, moving like a dervish, spinning the acolytes one by one with practiced efficiency. He caught Sammael and held him in an unbreakable grip.

Gwen knew Dorian could kill Sammael with a twist of his hands. She knew he wanted to; the hatred was like acid eating through his heart. But he did not. He simply kept his grip as Sammael cursed and struggled and called for help.

The young man who'd spoken earlier rose from his seat. "Why are you doing this?" he asked Gwen. "Sammael is our leader. He is Micah's heir."

"Is he?" Gwen jumped up on the stage and opened the book to a random page. "These are Micah's words: 'There can be no peace without sacrifice. But the sacrifice the Lord demands is neither death nor suffering. It is the willingness to give of the self, to remember the human that still lives within us, to control our most selfish desires.'"

"We have heard these words before," the young man said.

"Sammael taught us!" a woman cried.

"Yes," Gwen said, "but have you heard this? 'The sacrifice the Lord demands is a terrible one, but only by making it will we achieve salvation. The vampire is an abomination against nature, and any who do not come to us must be cleansed from the face of the earth.'" She raised the book high. "Those were Sammael's words…words he wrote over Micah's to obscure the teachings of the man you all revere."

A ripple of voices worked through the audience, cries of protest and shock. Gwen stepped down from the stage and slowly crossed in front of the first row of chairs, letting the people in them look at the page from which she'd been reading.

"Sammael never intended to follow Micah's teachings," she said. "Why do you think only *he* was allowed to see the book? Why did he teach some of you one thing and some another? Micah spoke of brotherhood between humans and vampires, an end to fear and secrecy. He believed that vampires could be redeemed by overcoming their belief in human inferiority and becoming a force for good in the world. But Sammael…" She turned the pages to show more of Sammael's furious scribbles. "Sammael wanted to kill every vampire in New York and even beyond."

"Don't listen to the bitch!" Sammael cried. "She is the temptress, the bride of Cain! You will all be damned!"

Dorian pushed his hand over Sammael's mouth, but Gwen shook her head. "No," she said. "His words can't hurt anyone now. Your time is past, Sammael. Once your people know what you believe, what you've done, they'll never trust you again."

She looked over the crowd, praying that they'd begun to understand. Men and women murmured to each other, some moving forward in hopes of seeing the book. Even the recovering soldiers remained still, making no attempt to resume their attack.

"Choose for yourselves," Gwen said. "Choose between life or death, hope or oblivion. We all face that choice sometime in our lives." She looked at Dorian, knowing how apt her words must sound to him. "I was in despair after Dorian Converted me, full of anger and self-pity. I would have given anything to become human again. Now I know that I've been given this new life to make a difference in the world."

Silence fell. The young man at the foot of the stage held out his hands. Gwen gave him the book. He turned to show it to the woman beside him. Others crowded close, but most remained in their seats, clutching the cups of dark liquid in their hands.

"Listen to me," Gwen said. "Whatever Sammael told you tonight, you don't have to die. The men outside are here only because Sammael intended to kill them. Jim is out there with them. He warned them because he knew Sammael was wrong. Angela gave her life because she knew he was wrong."

"Angela betrayed us!" Sammael shouted. "Dorian Black betrayed us! They would have undone all our work…robbed us of the Lord's absolution!"

"He wants *you* to pay for his mistakes!" Gwen said. "What is that you hold in your hands? Is it poison? Is he some pagan god that he demands you prove your loyalty to him through suicide?"

Fifty heads bowed as the men and women, human and *strigoi,* looked down at the cups in their hands. The young man who held Micah's book turned to face the people behind him.

"She's right," he said. "I can see what Sammael has done. Micah never said—"

"They will kill you!" Sammael cried. "The demons will enter this room, and you will all die in torment!"

"No," Dorian said.

His voice was strong and sure, commanding the attention of everyone in the room. He dragged Sammael up to the stage and stood straight and tall, as different from Sammael as a prince from a beggar.

"Some of you have known me," he said, shaping each word as if the language had only just become familiar to him again.

"Once I worked for Pax, believing as you did. For Pax I did harm to others, believing that the end justified the means." He lowered his head. "I was wrong. I have heard Micah's words. He was a man of peace for whom no violence was justified." Abruptly he released Sammael. "I have done terrible things in my life. But I believe there is a chance." He looked directly at Gwen. "I believe that there is hope. For all of us."

"There is no hope!" Sammael screamed. "He is damned! All of you are damned!" He lunged to the side of the stage and rose with a revolver in his hand. He aimed it at Gwen and fired.

Gwen felt the bullet pass clearly through her upper arm, almost as painless as a bee sting. Dorian hesitated for half a second and then leaped down to her, throwing himself between her and Sammael.

There were no more bullets. The people closest to the stage swarmed onto it en masse, bearing down on Sammael and wrestling the gun away from him. Others surrounded the acolytes, who were just beginning to recover from Dorian's pummeling.

Gwen swayed, clamping her hand over her wound. Dorian caught her.

"I'm all right,' she said, her voice slightly blurred. "I'm all right, Dorian."

He cradled her head in his palm and pulled her face into his shoulder. She could hear the clamoring of his heart and the roughness of his breathing, feel his fear for her like a knot in her throat.

"Gwen," he murmured. "Gwen."

She pulled away. "It isn't finished yet," she said. She kissed his cheek and returned to the stage. Sammael stood between two of his captors, his face drained of color.

"You are all damned," he said, his voice breaking. "My children. My poor children."

Gwen supported her injured arm with her other hand and met Sammael's gaze. "You've lost them, Sammael," she said. "Soon everyone in Pax will know what Micah taught and how you changed his words. Even your soldiers will come to realize the truth."

Tears ran down Sammael's cheeks. "The world will fall," he whispered.

"Not yet," Gwen said. "Not as long as there are brave and decent humans and *strigoi* to work for the good of everyone." She looked directly at Dorian. "Not as long as people keep fighting the monsters within themselves."

The men holding Sammael exchanged glances, bewildered and uncertain. A woman climbed up on the stage: Vida, who had made it possible for Gwen to reach Dorian at Kyril's hotel.

"What do we do now?" the dark-haired girl asked. "Those men outside will kill us."

"No," Gwen said. "They'll have no reason to hurt anyone once they realize Pax has no desire to keep attacking them."

"How do we prove that?" one of the men said. "What do we do with Sammael?"

Gwen hesitated. She knew that Christof wouldn't be satisfied until he had Sammael in his hands. And Sammael wouldn't long survive his captivity.

If I turn Sammael over to Christof just to be killed, I'm no better than he is.

Dorian came up beside her, pressing against her so that his warmth seeped into her chilled body. "I will offer myself as hostage," he said. "Christof has no reason to love me. He will know that I would not give myself up unless I believed that Pax would abandon hostilities against him."

"And I'll go with Dorian," Gwen said. "It will be up to all of you to prove that Micah's real words are true."

Vida bit her lip. "You'd do this for us?"

"I believe in Micah's teachings. In a way, I've become one of you, too." She glanced back toward the door. "I have to speak to Christof. Whatever you do, don't trust Sammael. He'll—"

Sammael moved before she could finish her sentence. But instead of lunging forward to attack, he jerked backward, throwing his captors aside with unexpected strength. They went after him immediately, but not before he'd snatched up the cup from the chair behind him.

"The devils shall not have me," he said, and lifted the cup to his mouth. Heavy liquid spilled over his lips. He swallowed convulsively, showed his teeth in a grimace, and fell.

The acolytes gave a collective moan of grief. Vida dropped to her knees beside Sammael. Her fingers trembled as she laid them against his neck.

"He's dead," she said. "The poison…"

The poison he would have made all of them drink if Gwen and Dorian hadn't disrupted his plans. Gwen rubbed at her wounded arm, grateful to find that it was already healing, and took Dorian's hand. A stunned hush had fallen over the room. The men and women who had remained in their chairs dropped their glasses, painting the floor with splashes of crimson as they emptied the contents of their glasses.

But the peace was only temporary. Cries of terror broke out in the auditorium as Sammael's own protégés—a scattering of civilians and the soldiers he had Converted to create his personal army—felt the shock of the bond's dissolution. Some dropped to their knees, wailing. Others simply stood where they were, struck dumb with the realization that they were alone. And free.

"It's over," Gwen whispered.

Dorian put his arm around her shoulders. She allowed herself a moment to bask in his presence, in the profound new peace she sensed inside him. Dawn had broken, but it wasn't only the end of night that had saved him. He had saved himself.

"Vida," she said, when she felt ready to speak again, "gather everyone together. Keep them calm, and watch those men—" she pointed to the acolytes "—very carefully. Dorian and I will deal with Christof. No harm will come to any of you."

"But…but the Guard…"

"If what Jim told me is correct, most of them were personally Converted by Sammael. I suspect the fight's gone out of them."

Vida followed Gwen's gaze and nodded slowly. "I see," she said. "I'll do what I can."

"That's all I ask." Gwen took Dorian's hand, looked once more around the room and began walking toward the door.

EPILOGUE

THE APARTMENT WAS COLD when Gwen and Dorian entered, cold and musty from months of abandonment. A thick layer of dust covered every surface, and Gwen suspected that a mouse had taken up residence in the kitchen.

She sat down on the sofa, remembering how often she'd curled up there in her pajamas, listening to the radio or reading a good book. Those days seemed a million years away. Nothing about the apartment seemed to belong to her anymore; it hadn't changed, but she had. More than even she had realized.

"Gwen?" Dorian said, concern in his voice.

She smiled up at him, trying to set his mind at ease. He'd been restless ever since they'd struck their deal with Christof; Gwen knew he wasn't any more satisfied with it than she was, but at least the people of Pax were safe. They had been allowed to continue to live in the building on the waterfront, but Christof had insisted that they be kept under careful surveillance for as long as he deemed necessary. Jim and Vida had stepped with surprising ease into the roles of leaders, and there was every indication that they were anxious to restore Micah's original purpose of redemption through acceptance and love.

As for Gwen and Dorian's offer of themselves as hostages, Christof had declined. The faction leader had proved to be considerably more merciful than Kyril would have been in his place; though he was deeply skeptical of Micah's belief in peace and brotherhood, he had allowed Sammael's soldiers to live— provided they accepted Christof as patron and liege. Any deviation in their behavior would be a death sentence.

Kyril was another problem altogether. He had made it possible for Gwen to confront Sammael with his lies, but the faction leader—in spite of the decimation of his gang—remained a potential threat to Christof's group. Gwen had pointed out what he'd done to neutralize Pax, but she couldn't hope to dictate Kyril's fate. Nor could she quite bring herself to feel much pity for him. He would gladly have killed both her and Dorian, and he had a roster of other murders to his name.

The important thing was that the *strigoi* wars were essentially over. Gwen suspected that Christof would locate the survivors of Kyril's faction and offer them the same deal he'd given Sammael's soldiers: come into the fold, or face the consequences.

As for Pax, it had a chance to begin again, become what it was always meant to be…an organization devoted to peace and brotherhood.

"Everything is going to be all right," Gwen said, though she couldn't shake off the weight of sadness that had been with her since Sammael's death.

"You were always a poor liar," Dorian said gently. He sat down beside her. "What troubles you?"

She sighed and rubbed her temples. "I was just thinking of Mitch. He made sure my rent was paid all the time I was in New Jersey. It's hard to believe he's really gone."

Dorian gathered her hand in his. "I understand," he said.

And she knew he did. The bond they'd somehow reestablished in Sammael's dungeon was still there, woven more strongly than ever before.

Gwen got up and went to her desk. The lock to the drawer was still broken, never repaired after Dorian had smashed it. She took out Eamon Murphy's folders and laid them on the desk.

You were right, Dad, she thought. *Right about the murders, the blood cult, everything. You would have run into vampires eventually, if you hadn't…*

She swallowed and picked up the photo of Eamon holding his Pulitzer. He'd touched on a story that would have blown the whole city apart if he'd chosen to pursue it. But human civilization wasn't ready to face the existence of vampires, even if a few privileged men and women would continue to be part of the *strigoi* world.

Dorian rested his hands on her shoulders and brushed his lips across her neck. "Your father must have been an extraordinary man," he said.

"He was." She replaced the folders in the drawer and closed it gently. "I wish he could have seen the things I have."

Dorian turned her about to face him. "Do you regret it, Gwen? The things you've seen and done?"

The feel of his warm breath on her face was like a drug working through her veins. She knew the answer to his question, but she wasn't yet ready to follow where it might lead.

"I can't stop thinking about Sammael," she said, moving away. "Why did he do what he did? How did he become so twisted in his beliefs?"

Dorian lowered his head, averting his eyes from hers. "I was told that he was Micah's protégé."

"What?" Gwen ducked to catch his gaze. "You mean Sammael…he was Micah's direct heir?"

"So it would seem."

Gwen shook her head. "What could have happened to him to make him so crazy?"

Too late, Gwen realized what she'd said. But Dorian only looked at her with a faint, sad smile.

"Perhaps," he said, "he lost his patron in an act of violence."

Maybe he even killed Micah, Gwen thought, shuddering. The idea didn't seem so far-fetched when she thought of Sammael's extreme fanaticism. All he had to do was begin to believe that his way was the right one, and act on that conviction….

"Or maybe," she said aloud, "maybe he was just sick in the head. He wouldn't be the first man to believe it was his right and duty to destroy what he hated in himself. I don't suppose he'll be the last."

"No."

"I guess all we can do is keep our eyes open and make sure

the next fanatic doesn't get a chance to follow through with his plans."

"Yes." Dorian walked from one end of the room to the other and stopped abruptly, as if he'd just come to a decision. Gwen felt his agitation and waited, every other thought flying from her mind.

"You need not stay with me, Gwen," he said.

Her mouth went dry. "What…what are you talking about?"

He faced her, his gray gaze steady and unreadable. "Once I thought you in need of my protection. That time is long past. You have saved me on more than one occasion. You did more than anyone could be asked to do. You nearly died for my sake, and that is not acceptable." He breathed in and out slowly. "The bond was broken once. It can be broken again."

Gwen clenched her fists. "Oh, really?" she said. "That's damned generous of you."

"I understand why you did it," he said, deliberately ignoring her anger. "Your explanation made perfect sense. You had no ally but Mitch to help you. There was no other way for you."

"But that's not the way it is now. We have the bond back."

"Is it enough?"

She couldn't have been more shocked if he'd run her through the chest with a wooden stake. "Doesn't it mean anything to you that I…that I said…"

"Be reasonable, Gwen. You can make a new life again, without hindrance. Christof has assured me that you will be allowed your freedom in perpetuity."

"And is that the most important thing in life? Freedom?" She marched up to him and grabbed a handful of his shirt. "Did it ever occur to you that freedom's not what I want? Oh, no." She glared into his eyes.

She shook him. "Do you think I'm going to up and leave just when you're starting to get better? I'm going to be here at the next dark of the moon, and the one after that, and as long as it takes for you to be rid of the monster once and for all."

Dorian caught her wrists. "I…I'm better now, Gwen. I no longer need your assistance."

Gwen listened with her heart and found that she couldn't read his emotions. It was as if he'd tried to sever the bond himself.

He hadn't quite succeeded.

"So you 'no longer need my assistance,'" she said mockingly. "You'll just go on your merry way and let me go mine. What do you plan to do with your life, Dorian? Offer your services to Christof? Start working as a janitor again? Or maybe you'll go back to the waterfront and hide away for the next hundred years. Which is it?"

Dorian remained mute. Gwen paced back and forth, wishing she could put her fist through the wall. She'd thought her love had helped save Dorian from himself. But what if she were wrong? What if he really *didn't* need her after all?

"What do you want, Dorian?" she asked softly. "Do you want me to go?"

For a long, painful moment she waited for his answer. Then, without warning, he moved toward her and took her in his arms. A flood of desire overwhelmed her, so powerful that she couldn't tell if it was hers or Dorian's.

"I want you," he said, kissing her mouth and cheek and forehead. "I want you, Gwen."

Gwen tangled her hands in his black hair and pulled him down for more. The bedroom was too far away. They fell onto the couch, limbs entwined, breath coming hot and short. Dorian's fingers made quick work of Gwen's blouse; his cock was heavy and hard inside his trousers, pressing insistently against her inner thighs.

She worked urgently at the buttons of her own slacks, struggling to push them down as Dorian kissed and licked the upper curve of her breasts. Her bandeau was no impediment to a determined vampire; he made quick work of it and began to suckle her nipples while she reached blindly for the waistband of his trousers.

Dorian was there ahead of her. He shifted, and his cock slipped from its confinement. Gwen closed her fingers around it, awed and excited. It was warm and smooth, its head polished like marble.

She began to slide her hand up and down. Immediately she felt Dorian's pleasure, echoing and redoubling as it met her own. She kicked her trousers onto the floor and arched her back to remove her step-ins, the only barrier left between them.

The fragile bit of silk lasted another five seconds, and then Dorian was between her thighs. She tilted to grant him full access, and with a groan he eased inside her.

She expected discomfort. There was none. Instead, she felt as if she had become whole for the first time in her life. Dorian filled her up completely. And when he began to move, she understood at last why men and women had been hungry for sex since the first human beings—and *strigoi*—had walked the earth.

Bracing his weight above her, Dorian withdrew and began to thrust, slowly at first and then with increasing speed. Gwen dug her fingers into his shirt, tearing the cotton with her nails. She felt herself flying upward on invisible wings, rising through the clouds, higher and higher. Dorian's ecstasy was her own as hers was his. He shuddered, and suddenly Gwen was at the very center of the sun, burning with joy.

Dorian dropped his head, resting his cheek against hers. He didn't have to ask if he'd satisfied her. He could feel every part of her, inside and out.

And he wasn't nearly finished. He lifted Gwen in his arms, leaving the litter of her clothing behind, and carried her into the bedroom. He tossed back the bedspread, laid her down on her belly and stretched out beside her, running his hands over her shoulders and back, down to her waist and over the flare of her hips and buttocks.

Gwen gave a nervous laugh that quickly became a moan as Dorian kissed her bottom. He lifted her hips as he caressed her, uncovering the hidden pink folds of her vulva. He licked the delicate petals, shuddering as he shared her excitement through the bond. Then he circled her cleft with his tongue and pushed inside.

Gwen gasped. Dorian continued to tease her, eagerly tasting the wetness that flowed over his tongue. His cock hardened again.

"Oh," Gwen whispered. "You aren't…surely we can't…"

Dorian proved her wrong. He lifted her higher and knelt behind her, steadying her hips between his hands. He slid his cock over her slick, swollen flesh, forcing himself to hold back until her ragged breathing told him she was ready.

He thrust, drawing a cry from Gwen's throat. She bit hard on the sheets as he moved inside her, rocking her with each vigorous push of his hips. This time he drew it out as long as he could, savoring her little whimpers of pleasure and the glory of the bond. Only when she began to tighten around him did he allow himself to finish. Once again they rose together, reached the heights and tumbled back to earth in glorious unity.

Gwen collapsed on the sheets, panting and limp. "Oh," she said. "Oh, my." She rolled over to face him, heavy-lidded and flushed. "That was…"

Dorian looked down at her lovely body and licked his lips. Gwen's gaze fell to his thighs.

"Oh, my," she repeated. "I thought that men…I mean, doesn't it…go away?"

With a slow, catlike stretch Dorian lay beside her. "I'm not a man, remember?"

She grinned, her eyes bright with anticipation. And he showed her how much she still had to look forward to.

GWEN ROLLED ONTO HER back, throbbing pleasantly in every part of her body. Though she had not slept since their last session of lovemaking, she had found an equally pleasant alternative, a kind of dormancy that enabled her body to rest as well as any deep slumber.

But now she was alert again, and ready for more sexual adventures. She stretched, feeling for Dorian's hard, delectable body.

He wasn't there. She reached more urgently, sweeping the sheets with her hand. They were cool. She rolled over. There wasn't even so much as a dent in the mattress.

She sat up, staring around the cramped, familiar bedroom. If she hadn't known that Dorian had been there with her only a few hours ago, she would have thought all the events of the past few months had been a dream.

"Dorian?"

No answer. She swung her feet over the side of the bed, grabbed the robe draped over the chair near the bed and draped it around her shoulders.

Dorian wasn't in the living room, or in the tiny kitchen or bathroom. His coat, hat and scarf were gone. And Gwen couldn't feel even the most distant sense of his mind or emotions through the bond. Not even the ache that had once marked any kind of separation.

Gwen went to the window over her secretary and flipped the curtains aside. Still daylight. Why had Dorian gone out now, without telling her, without so much as leaving a note?

Because he didn't want you to know. Because he's left for good.

Gwen laughed at her own paranoia. She moved to the sofa, made herself comfortable with a copy of *Vanity Fair* and turned on the radio in search of music. Every so often she concentrated on the bond, trying to make it function again.

Midnight came and went. Gwen got up and began to pace. She crossed the small room several hundred times before she finally recognized the truth.

He's not coming back.

She remembered the last conversation they'd had. He'd talked a lot about letting her go, hadn't he? But she hadn't taken him seriously. Not after all they'd been through together.

"I want you," he'd told her. And he'd done everything to make her believe it.

But maybe his wanting her still wasn't enough. *The bond was broken once. It can be broken again.*

Gwen sat back down on the sofa. Her hands and feet were numb, and the numbness was quickly spreading to the rest of her. Was that what he'd done? Broken the bond? He didn't have any of the potion she'd used to do it in Mexico. He had to have managed it himself, with his own considerable will.

She couldn't feel him because there was no way to feel him.

The clock on the table across the room ticked on interminably. Gwen's eyes burned, but nothing would soothe them. She finally got up, went to her closet and selected a skirt, blouse and jacket. She combed her hair, got dressed and walked outside.

The early morning was cold. She really didn't feel it…one of the benefits of being a vampire.

Benefits. She would rather have been the lowliest human on the planet than the pathetic creature she was now.

Without thinking about her destination, she found herself standing at the foot of the stairs leading up to the door of Walter's boardinghouse. Dorian didn't live there anymore, of course. He'd given up his room when he'd joined Kyril's faction. And now that he and Gwen were facing a normal life again…

Gwen shook her head. No point in thinking about what might have been. She climbed the stairs. Though it was still dark, she knew the landlady kept the front door unlocked. She went into the lobby and down the hall to Walter's room.

He opened the door almost immediately after her knock, almost as if he'd been expecting her.

"Gwennie!" he exclaimed, a pleased smile creasing his face. "What'cha doing here this hour of the morning?"

She smiled. Maybe she would tell him the truth. Maybe she wouldn't. But she had to be around someone who could understand what she was feeling at this moment.

"I felt the need to talk," she said. "I don't sleep anymore, Walter. I'm sorry if I woke you."

"Woke me? Nah. Come on in."

He held open the door for her, and she entered the room. It smelled of old man and cheap cologne.

"Excuse the mess," Walter said as he finished buttoning his plaid flannel shirt. "Still not completely used to livin' in a nice place like this. Too much stuff, I guess." He gestured Gwen to one of the two chairs arranged at one side of the room. After she sat, he joined her, a bulldog pipe in his hand.

"Mind if I smoke?" he said. "Like to have a puff first thing after I get up."

Gwen waved her permission, her gaze on the somewhat worn carpet under her feet.

"Okay," Walter said, lighting the pipe and holding at the ready. "What's eatin' you, missy?"

"I just…" She shrugged. "It's a little lonely being a vampire."

"Yeah." He took a contemplative puff. "Always knew there was something a little peculiar about ol' Dory, but when he told me…" He screwed up his face. "Well, it took a little gettin' used to."

To put it mildly. Though Walter had taken it all in remarkably good stride.

She folded her hands in her lap. Walter waited while wreaths of aromatic smoke coiled around his head.

"Have you seen Dorian?" she asked.

He raised one wiry gray brow. "Why? Haven't you seen him?"

"Of course. I just…"

"Ain't things goin' well with you two?"

"It's nothing like that."

Walter nodded sagely. "It's always the same with newly-weds, no matter what they like to eat for supper."

She started at his choice of words. Newlyweds? Where had he gotten that idea?

"You just be patient, Gwennie. Give him time. He's been a bachelor for a long, long time, but he'll come around."

"We…" She spoke the rest of the words in a rush. "We aren't married."

The old man nodded. "I know. But you will be soon."

Gwen stared at him. "What do you mean?" She got up, ready to run out the door. "Don't you understand, Walter? He's gone."

She expected him to express shock or surprise, begin to question her, or at least stop smoking that damnable pipe. He didn't react at all.

"What are you worried about, Gwennie?" he said at last. "He'll be back."

"Not this time." She swallowed hard. "I can't feel him."

"You sure 'bout that?" He peered up at her, a deceptively innocuous cunning in his eyes.

"Of course I'm sure," she whispered. "I would know if he—"

Without any warning at all complete awareness enveloped her, surging through her veins and exploding in her mind like fireworks. Five seconds later the door opened and Dorian walked in, a leather satchel over one shoulder. He stopped dead when he saw Gwen.

"Gwen! What are you doing here?" He glanced at Walter, who beamed at him as if nothing had ever been wrong.

"She came to talk," he said. "You been makin' things hard on her, Dory?" He clucked disapproval. "That ain't the way to start, you know."

Dorian stood in the doorway, openmouthed. His teeth clicked together as he snapped his jaws shut.

"Gwen," he said, almost stammering. "I...I realize that you must have thought..."

Her glorious relief gave way to very different emotions. "Don't explain," she said coldly. "It wasn't as if I had anything better to do than wait up for you and wonder if you were ever coming back." She charged toward him, sidestepped at the last minute and plunged out into the hall.

Dorian stopped her. He caught her arm and spun her around, his eyes stricken.

"I was wrong," he said softly. "And..." He dropped his gaze. "I was afraid, Gwen."

"It ain't nothin', Gwennie," Walter said, observing them from his chair like an inscrutable Chinese patriarch. "It's just like I told you. He got cold feet. Happens to the best of 'em."

"Cold feet?" Gwen lifted her hand and drew back her arm. Dorian waited stoically for the blow. She found that her entire arm was trembling and let it fall.

"Cold feet?" she repeated. All the anger went out of her, leaving her limp as a deflated balloon. "This isn't going to work."

Dorian met her gaze. "I don't understand."

"You don't have to mince words with me, Dorian," she said. "Not anymore. There are a lot of things I know now that I didn't when you first Converted me. I know that when vampires Convert humans, it's a kind of instinct that drives them to do it."

"Who told you this, Gwen?"

"Angela. Just before she tried to rescue us from Sammael."

Dorian's expression froze. "What else did she tell you?"

"She said that it was only natural for you to want to protect me from Kyril, because you were already feeling driven to make me your protégée. We…we both wanted each other. By Converting me, you could keep me safe and obey your instincts at the same time."

She studied a point on his chin.

"I cannot deny it."

"After…after we went to Mexico, it was only the physical bond that really held us together. I know you were afraid for me…afraid that I'd get too close when the monster ran loose. I'm grateful for that. But you were right when you said we don't really need each other anymore. I didn't do you any good when I tried to fix you in Mexico."

"You saved me, Gwen."

"No, Dorian. I only gave you a little push. You saved yourself. And I…" She forced the last words through stiff, aching lips. "I know how to take care of myself now."

"Yes, but—"

"I've accepted what I am. You don't have to make any more apologies. You don't owe me anything." She tried to shake him off, but he was still stronger than she was. "You're forgiven, Dorian. You can let me go."

He raised his hand. She flinched. He ran the tips of his fingers down her cheek from temple to chin.

"I believe you've forgiven me," he said quietly. "But there is one other question I must ask."

With an effort, she held his gaze. "Go ahead."

"Did you mean it when you said you loved me?"

Gwen's body went numb all over again. *He remembers.* The monster had listened, and so had the man.

"I wasn't lying," she whispered.

"If we were human, would that be enough?"

"We aren't human, are we?"

"Did Angela tell you that vampires are incapable of love?"

"She…she implied…"

"Poor Angela," he said, deep regret in his voice. "I would have done anything to save her."

Gwen couldn't bear to read what might be in his eyes. "I know how much she meant to you."

"She saved our lives."

"She cared deeply for you."

"Why should you believe—"

"I saw her kissing you." She flushed. "I didn't mean to intrude."

"Ah." He nodded as if to himself. "And you believed that I cared deeply for *her.* Perhaps as much as any vampire can."

Her hands began to shake, and she clasped them behind her back. "She was a match for you when I couldn't be. You understood each other. It was only natural—"

"I could not love her, Gwen."

"Sure. I realize—"

"I could not love her because I love you."

The violently spinning world skidded to a stop. Gwen stared at him, hardly daring to believe what she'd just heard.

"Are you sure you've got that right?" she asked, not ready to believe. "You just walk out of the apartment, with no word to me, and then the bond goes dark…"

"I told you I was afraid." Dorian cupped his hand over her hair. "I've always had more than a little coward in me, Gwen."

"Sure. Anyone could see that."

"I had to think. Away from you, from the sight and sound and smell of you."

"I know. I'm intoxicating."

He chuckled, a warm sound as precious as it was rare, and

then grew serious again. "I knew you'd used a special concoction to break the bond, but I had to see if I could do it myself. I had to make certain that you could be free if you ever wanted to be."

Gwen hissed through her teeth, trying not to melt under Dorian's caresses. "Oh," she said, "I'm getting sick of that word." She didn't touch him, though her arms were aching to hold and be held. "You did a damned good job of cutting me off."

"I was more successful than I would have believed possible. And I couldn't bear it, Gwen." He took a deep breath and released it with painful slowness, as if it were his last. "I've felt what it's like to die. What it's like to have nothing left of yourself. But I could have born that far better than losing you."

Hope darted around inside Gwen's heart like a fluttering bird. "It wasn't exactly fun for me, either," she said. "I don't think I ever want to go through that again. So if you think you're going to get 'cold feet' some time in the future…"

Sliding his hands from her hair, Dorian dropped to his knees. He reached inside the satchel and pulled out a small black box.

"I think some traditions have remained the same since last I was human," he said. He opened the box. There was a ring inside.

"Gwen," he said, "will you marry me?"

Her knees were trembling so badly that she was sure she was about to join Dorian on the floor. "Would you mind repeating that?" she whispered.

He took her hand, turned it palm down and slid the ring onto her finger. He lifted her hand to his lips.

"I love you, Gwen Murphy," he said. "And I beg that you never leave me. Not until we have seen the last night fall on the world."

Across the room, still ensconced in his chair, Walter withdrew his pipe from his mouth and tapped out the ashes. "Lovers' quarrels," he said with satisfaction. "They haven't changed since Adam met Eve."

THERE WAS NO WEDDING. Though her faith remained strong, Gwen knew the time hadn't come when vampires could stand together in the church and exchange vows of lifelong devotion. It was enough that she and Dorian could join hands in Central Park with the full moon overhead, a beaming Walter looking on, while they pledged themselves to each other for all time.

Walter looked as proud as a mother cat with a new litter of kittens. He planted a broad kiss on Gwen's cheek and pumped Dorian's arm furiously. As the three of them strolled through the park afterward, he continued to pepper them with questions.

"Where you goin' to live now, you two?" he asked. "You gonna stay in Gwen's apartment?"

Dorian deferred to Gwen with a smile, and she shook her head. "That's part of my old life," she said. "We've been thinking of getting a new place a little closer to you, Walter, if you don't object."

"Object!" Walter chortled. "Whatta you take me for?" He sobered. "You ain't hurtin' for moola, are you?"

"Nope," Gwen said. "I've still got my savings, and Dad left me a modest inheritance when he passed. We think that Dorian can find some sort of job that will allow him to work at night. And as for me…" She tucked her arm through Dorian's. "I've been thinking that I might like to try writing a book about my father's life. Maybe freelance a little for the *Sentinel*, if they'll have me back."

"'Course they will. Be crazy not to, and they don't ever have to know…" He puffed out his chest. "It'll be our secret."

Gwen winked at Dorian. "That's right. Our secret."

She and Dorian escorted Walter back to his boardinghouse and continued their walk through the nighttime city. Somehow they ended up at the waterfront.

"This is where it all began," Gwen said, her voice hushed. "Funny. It seems so long since you pulled me out of the river."

So long, Dorian thought. Only a handful of months, a blink of an eye in the long life of a *strigoi*. Just enough time to be reborn.

The dark of the moon was two weeks away, but he wasn't afraid. The monster hadn't left him, not entirely, but it would never control him again. Gwen had healed him with her love and forgiveness; she'd taught him how to begin healing himself.

And if the guilt never entirely faded from his thoughts, he would find a way to use that guilt to do some good in the world. Gwen made that possible.

"Look!" she said, tugging on his arm.

He followed her gaze and recognized the warehouse where he had taken her to recover from her plunge in the East River. It was hardly recognizable. Someone had given it a fresh coat of paint, a new door and a sign that read Fortunata & Sons Shipping Company.

"It's a good sign, don't you think?" Gwen asked.

Dorian turned her about and kissed her gently on the lips. "A very good sign," he said.

And he knew his life was just beginning.

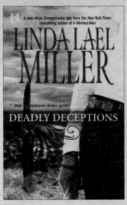

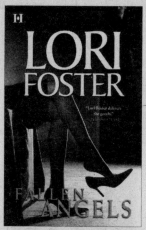

REQUEST YOUR FREE BOOKS!

2 FREE NOVELS FROM THE ROMANCE/SUSPENSE COLLECTION PLUS 2 FREE GIFTS!

YES! Please send me 2 FREE novels from the Romance/Suspense Collection and my 2 FREE gifts (gifts are worth about $10). After receiving them, if I don't wish to receive any more books, I can return the shipping statement marked "cancel." If I don't cancel, I will receive 4 brand-new novels every month and be billed just $5.49 per book in the U.S. or $5.99 per book in Canada, plus 25¢ shipping and handling per book plus applicable taxes, if any*. That's a savings of at least 20% off the cover price! I understand that accepting the 2 free books and gifts places me under no obligation to buy anything. I can always return a shipment and cancel at any time. Even if I never buy another book from the Reader Service, the two free books and gifts are mine to keep forever.

185 MDN EF5Y   385 MDN EF6C

Name _____ (PLEASE PRINT) _____

Address _____ Apt. # _____

City _____ State/Prov. _____ Zip/Postal Code _____

Signature (if under 18, a parent or guardian must sign)

Mail to **The Reader Service:**
IN U.S.A.: P.O. Box 1867, Buffalo, NY 14240-1867
IN CANADA: P.O. Box 609, Fort Erie, Ontario L2A 5X3

Not valid to current subscribers to the Romance Collection,
the Suspense Collection or the Romance/Suspense Collection.

Want to try two free books from another line?
Call 1-800-873-8635 or visit www.morefreebooks.com.

* Terms and prices subject to change without notice. N.Y. residents add applicable sales tax. Canadian residents will be charged applicable provinãal taxes and GST. This offer is limited to one order per household. All orders subject to approval. Credit or debit balances in a customer's account(s) may be offset by any other outstanding balance owed by or to the customer. Please allow 4 to 6 weeks for delivery. Offer available while quantities last.

Your Privacy: Harlequin is committed to protecting your privacy. Our Privacy Policy is available online at www.eHarlequin.com or upon request from the Reader Service. From time to time we make our lists of customers available to reputable third parties who may have a product or service of interest to you. If you would prefer we not share your name and address, please check here. ☐

BOB08

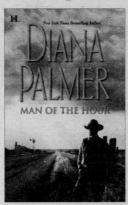

HARLEQUIN

More Than Words

"Jeanne proves that one woman can change the world, with vision, compassion and hard work."

—**Linda Lael Miller,** author

*Linda wrote "Queen of the Rodeo," inspired by Jeanne Greenberg, founder of **SARI Therapeutic Riding.** Since 1978 Jeanne has devoted her life to enriching the lives of disabled children and their families through innovative and exciting therapies on horseback.*

Look for "Queen of the Rodeo" in
More Than Words, Vol. 4,
available in April 2008 at eHarlequin.com
or wherever books are sold.

SUPPORTING CAUSES OF CONCERN TO WOMEN ‡ HARLEQUIN
WWW.HARLEQUINMORETHANWORDS.COM

MTW07JG2

SUSAN KRINARD

| 77139 | LORD OF THE BEASTS | ___ $5.99 U.S. ___ $6.99 CAN. |
| 77218 | CHASING MIDNIGHT | ___ $6.99 U.S. ___ $8.50 CAN. |

(limited quantities available)

TOTAL AMOUNT $ _____
POSTAGE & HANDLING $ _____
($1.00 FOR 1 BOOK, 50¢ for each additional)
APPLICABLE TAXES* $ _____
TOTAL PAYABLE $ _____

(check or money order—please do not send cash)

To order, complete this form and send it, along with a check or money
order for the total above, payable to HQN Books, to: **In the U.S.:**
3010 Walden Avenu_____77;
In Canada: P.O. Bo___

Name: _____
Address: _____
State/Prov.: _____
Account Number (if appl___

075 CSAS

*New York
*Canadian resider___

Santa Clara County
LIBRARY

Renewals:
(800) 471-0991
www.santaclaracountylib.org

We___

w___